ROWDY THING

Dark WILD NIGHT

"Full of expertly drawn characters who will grab your heart and never let go, humor that will have you howling, and off-the-charts, toe-curling chemistry, _Dark Wild Night_ is absolutely unforgettable. This is contemporary romance at its best!"

—Sarah J. Maas, _New York Times_ bestselling
author of _Throne of Glass_

"Comic book nerds can be sexy too. . . . _Dark Wild Night_ won't disappoint."

—_Hypable_

The Beautiful series

"Hot . . . if you like your hookups early and plentiful. . . ."
—_EW_ on _Beautiful Stranger_

"A devilishly depraved cross between a hardcore porn and a very special episode of _The Office_."
—_Perez Hilton_ on _Beautiful Bastard_

"A beautiful read, an astonishing love story, a couple whose journey I understood and felt from beginning to end—this is a book I would recommend with all my heart."
—_Natasha Is a Book Junkie_ on _Beautiful Secret_

"The perfect blend of sex, sass, and heart, _Beautiful Bastard_ is a steamy battle of wills that will get your blood pumping!"
—S. C. Stephens, #1 _New York Times_ bestselling
author of _Thoughtless_

Books By CHRISTINA LAUREN

WILD SEASONS

Sweet Filthy Boy

Dirty Rowdy Thing

Dark Wild Night

Wicked Sexy Liar

THE BEAUTIFUL SERIES

Beautiful Bastard

Beautiful Stranger

Beautiful Bitch

Beautiful Bombshell

Beautiful Player

Beautiful Beginning

Beautiful Beloved

Beautiful Secret

Beautiful Boss

SEXY LIAR

BOOK FOUR OF WILD SEASONS

CHRISTINA LAUREN

G
GALLERY BOOKS
NEW YORK   LONDON   TORONTO   SYDNEY   NEW DELHI

G

Gallery Books
An Imprint of Simon & Schuster, Inc.
1230 Avenue of the Americas
New York, NY 10020

Copyright © 2016 by Christina Hobbs and Lauren Billings

First Gallery Books trade paperback edition February 2016

GALLERY BOOKS and colophon are registered trademarks of Simon & Schuster, Inc.

For information about special discounts for bulk purchases, please contact Simon & Schuster Special Sales at 1-866-506-1949 or business@simonandschuster.com.

The Simon & Schuster Speakers Bureau can bring authors to your live event. For more information or to book an event contact the Simon & Schuster Speakers Bureau at 1-866-248-3049 or visit our website at www.simonspeakers.com.

Manufactured in the United States of America

10 9 8

Library of Congress Cataloging-in-Publication Data

Lauren, Christina.
  Wicked sexy liar / Christina Lauren.—First Gallery Books trade paperback edition.
     pages ; cm.—(Wild seasons ; 4)
1. Women college graduates—Fiction. I. Title.
  PS3612.A9442273W53 2016
  813'.6--dc23   2015032022

ISBN 978-1-4767-7798-6
ISBN 978-1-4767-7799-3 (ebook)

For our Captain Hookers, Alice & Nina.
There it is.

Chapter ONE

London

*T*HERE ARE A number of things that happen when you haven't had sex in a while: You inadvertently emit a sound during the kissing scenes in romantic movies—a noise that falls somewhere between a snort and an audible eye roll and which almost always elicits a pillow being lobbed at you from the other end of the couch. You can name at least three online adult toy stores from memory, accurately quoting their shipping rates, reliability, and speed. At least two of these stores auto-fill after only a single letter is typed into the URL bar, and you are *always* the roommate expected to replace the batteries on the remote control, hand vacuum, and flashlights.

Which is ridiculous when you think about it because everyone knows the best sex toys are corded or rechargeable. *Amateurs.*

You become good at masturbating, too. Like, *really* good, Olympic sport good. And by that point, having sex with yourself is the only option because how can any man possibly hope to compete with your own hand or a vibrator with 120 volts and seventeen variable speed settings?

The side effects of a less-than-social vagina are particularly noticeable when you're constantly surrounded by three of the most disgustingly happy couples around. My roommate, Lola, and her two best friends, Harlow and Mia, met their significant others in a totally insane, it-never-happens-in-real-life weekend of debauchery in Las Vegas. Mia and Ansel are married and barely come up for air. Harlow and Finn seem to have mastered sex via eye contact. And Lola and her boyfriend, Oliver, are at that stage in a new relationship where touching is constant and sex seems to happen almost spontaneously. Cooking turns into sex. Watching *The Walking Dead*? Obviously arousing. Time for sex. Sometimes they'll just walk in the door, chatting casually, and then stop, look at each other, and here we go again.

TMI alert? Oliver is loud, and I had no idea the c-word was used quite so readily in Australia. It's a good thing I love them both so much.

And Lord, I do. I met Lola in the art program at UCSD, and although we didn't really start hanging out regularly until she moved in as my roommate last summer, I feel like I've known her my entire life.

Hearing her feet dragging down the hall, I smile. She emerges, hair a mess and face still flushed.

"Oliver just left," I tell her around a spoonful of Raisin Bran. He'd stumbled out less than ten minutes ago, sporting a dazed grin and a similar level of dishevelment. "I gave him a high five and a bottle of Gatorade for the road because he *has* to be dehydrated after all that. Seriously, Lola, I'm impressed."

I wouldn't have thought it possible for Lola's cheeks to get any pinker. I would have lost that bet.

"Sorry," she says, offering me a sheepish smile from behind the cupboard door. "You've got to be sick to death of us, but I'm about to leave for L.A. and—"

"You are *not* apologizing because you've got a gorgeous, sweet Australian guy banging you senseless," I tell her, and stand to rinse out my bowl. "I'd give you more shit if you weren't hitting that daily."

"Sometimes it feels like driving all the way to his place takes forever." Lola closes the cupboard door and stares off, contemplating. "That is insane. We are *insane.*"

"I tried to convince him to stay," I tell her. "I'm leaving for the day and have work tonight. You two could have had the place to yourselves."

"You're working again tonight?" Lola fills her glass and props a hip against the counter. "You've closed every night this week."

I shrug. "Fred needed someone and the extra hours don't hurt." I dry my bowl and reach to put it away. "Don't you have panels to finish, anyway?"

"I do, but I'd love to hang out . . . You're always at the beach or working a—"

"And *you've* got a fuckhot boyfriend and a blazing career," I say. Lola is probably the busiest person I know. When she isn't editing her new graphic novel, *Junebug,* or visiting the set for the film adaptation of her first book, *Razor Fish,* she's jetting off to L.A. or New York or wherever the studio and her publisher want her. "I knew you were working today and would probably spend the night with Oliver." Squeezing her shoulder, I add, "Besides, what else is there to do on a beautiful day like this but surf?"

She grins at me over the rim of her cup. "I don't know . . . maybe go out on a date?"

I snort as I shut the cupboard door. "You're cute."

"*London*," she says, pinning me with a serious expression.

"*Lola*," I volley back.

"Oliver mentioned he has a friend coming in from home, maybe we could all get together." She looks down, feigning fascination with something on her fingernail. "See a movie or something?"

"No setups," I say. "My darling of darlings, we've had this conversation at least ten times."

Lola smiles sheepishly again and I laugh, turning to walk out of the kitchen. But she's there, hot on my heels.

"You can't fault me for worrying about you a little," she says. "You're alone all the time and—"

I wave a flippant hand. "Alone is not the same as lonely." Because as appealing as the idea of sex with an actual person is, the drama that inevitably comes along with it is not. I've got enough on my social plate trying to keep up with Lola and her tight-knit and ever-expanding group of friends and their significant others. I'm barely past the Learning Their Last Names stage. "Stop channeling Harlow."

Lola frowns as I lean forward to kiss her cheek.

"You don't have to worry about me," I tell her, then check the time. "Gotta go, mid-tide in twenty."

AFTER A LONG day on the water, I step behind the counter of Fred's—the place nearly everyone lovingly calls "the Regal Beagle" due to the name of its owner, Fred Furley—and tie an apron around my waist.

The tip jar is just over half-full, which means it's been pretty steady, but not so crazy that Fred will have to call in an extra hand. There's a couple talking quietly at one end of the bar, half-empty wineglasses in front of them. They're deep in conversation and barely look up when I step into view; they won't need much. Four older women sit at the other end. Nice clothes, I notice, even nicer handbags. They're laughing and possibly here to celebrate something, which means they'll probably be entertaining and great tippers. I make a mental note to check on them in a few minutes.

Raucous laughter and the sound of cheering draw my attention toward the back, and I spot Fred delivering beers to a group of guys circled around the pool table. Satisfied he's got them covered, I begin checking inventory.

I've only been at Fred's about a month, but it's a bar like any other and the routine has been easy enough to pick up. It has stained glass lights, warm wood, and round leather booths, and is a lot less seedy than the dance club where I worked my last two years of college. Still, it has its share of creeps, an inevitable drawback to this kind of job. It's not that I'm particularly attractive, or even the best-looking woman in the place, but there's something about seeing a female on this side of the counter that sometimes leads even the most well-intentioned men to forget their manners. With no barback here, I have to do a lot of the running and prep myself, but Fred is a great boss and fun to joke around with. He's also better at spotting the creeps than I am.

Which is why he's dealing with the guys in the back, and I am not.

I'm pretty particular when it comes to setup, and start my shift by arranging everything behind the bar exactly the way I like: ticket spike, knife, peeler, muddler, juice press, Y peeler, channel knife, julep strainer, bar spoons, mixing glass. *Mise en place*—everything in its place.

I'm about to start cutting fruit when a customer leans over the counter and asks for two White Russians, one with ice, one without. I nod, lifting two clean glasses from the rack, when Fred steps behind me.

"Let me know if those kids give you any trouble," he says, and nods to the pool table group, which is currently whooping about something boy-related in the back.

They seem pretty typical for the UCSD guys who come in here: tall, fit, tan. A few are wearing graphic tees and others wear collared shirts. I study them in tiny flickers of attention as I mix the drinks, taking an educated guess from their height, physique, and tans that they're water polo players.

One of them, with dark hair and a jaw you could probably have sex with, looks up just as I do, and our eyes snag. He's good-looking—though to be fair, they're all pretty good-looking—but there's something about this guy that makes me do a double take and hold his gaze for the space of a breath, not quite ready to let it go. Unfortunately, he's gorgeous in that unattainable, brooding douchebag sort of way.

With that reminder of the past, I immediately disengage.

I turn back to Fred and pull a second glass jar labeled CAR FUND from under the counter and place it in front of him. "I think we both know you don't have to worry about me," I say, and he smiles, shaking his head at the jar as he finishes his pours. "So is it just the two of us tonight?"

"Think so," he says, and slides the beers onto the bar. "There aren't any big games this weekend. Expect it'll be steady, but slow. Maybe we'll have a chance to get through some inventory."

I nod as I finish the drinks and ring them up before washing my hands and checking my station for anything else I'll need. A throat clears behind me and I turn, finding myself now only a foot away from the eyes that were all the way across the room only seconds before.

"What can I get you?" I ask, and it's polite enough, delivered with what I know to be a friendly-but-professional smile. His eyes narrow and even though I don't track them moving down my body in any perceptible way, I get the feeling he's already checked me out, made up his mind, and filed me away in the same way all men categorize women: fuckable, or not. From my experience, there isn't a whole lot of in-between.

"Can I get another round, please?" he says, and motions vaguely over his shoulder. His phone vibrates in his hand and he glances down at it, tapping out a quick message before returning his attention to me.

I pull out a tray. I don't know what they'd ordered since Fred brought them their first round, but I can easily guess.

"Heineken?" I ask.

His eyes narrow in playful insult, and it makes me laugh.

"Okay, *not* Heineken," I say, holding up my hands in apology. "What were you drinking?"

Now that I really look, he's even prettier up close: brown eyes framed with the kind of lashes mascara companies charge a fortune for and dark hair that looks so soft and thick I just know it would feel *amazing* to dig my fingers—

But I assume he knows this, and the confidence I noticed from across the room practically saturates the air. His phone buzzes again, but he gives it only the briefest glance down and silences it. "Why would you assume *Heineken?*" he asks.

I stack a handful of coasters on the tray and shrug again, trying to nip the conversation in the bud. "No reason."

He's not buying it. The corner of his mouth turns up a little and he says, "Come on, Dimples."

At almost the same time, I hear Fred's "God*dammit*" and hold out my hand, ready when he slaps a crisp dollar bill into it. I smugly tuck it into the jar.

The guy follows my movement and blinks back up at me. " 'Car Fund'?" he asks, reading the label. "What's that about?"

"It's nothing," I tell him, and then wave to the line of draft beers. "What were you guys drinking?"

"You just made a buck off of something I said and you're not even going to tell me what it was?"

I tuck a loose strand of hair behind my ear and give in when I realize he isn't going to order until I've answered him. "It's just something I hear a lot," I say. In fact, it's probably something I've heard more than my own name. Deep dimples dent each of my cheeks, and I'd be lying if I didn't say they're both my most and least favorite feature. Couple that with sun-streaked—often wind-blown—hair and a smattering of freckles, and I'm about as Girl Next Door as they come.

"Fred didn't believe it happens as often as I said," I continue, jerking my thumb over my shoulder. "So we made a little bet: a dollar every time someone calls me Dimples, or references said dimples. I'm going to buy a car."

"Next week at this rate," Fred complains from somewhere behind me.

Dudebro's phone chirps again, but this time he doesn't check it, doesn't even look down. Instead, he tucks it into the back pocket of his jeans, glances from Fred to me again, and grins.

And I might actually need a moment.

If I thought this guy was pretty before, it has nothing on the way his entire face changes when he smiles. A light has been switched on behind his eyes, and every trace of arrogance seems to just . . . evaporate. His skin is clear and tan—it practically glows with a warmth that seems to radiate out, coloring his cheeks. The sharpness of his features soften; his eyes crinkle a little at the corners. I know it's just a smile but it's like I can't decide which part I like more: the full lips; white, perfect teeth; or how one side of his mouth lifts just a fraction higher than the other. He makes me want to smile back.

He spins a coaster on the bar top in front of him and continues to grin up at me. "So you're calling me unoriginal," he says.

"I'm not calling you anything," I tell him, matching his grin. "But I appreciate that it seems to be true, because I am raking in the cash."

He considers my cheeks for a moment. "They are pretty great dimples. I can imagine a lot of worse things to be known for. Nobody's calling you Peg Leg or the Bearded Lady."

No way is this guy trying to be cute. "So back to your beer," I say. "Bottle or draft?"

"I want to know why you assumed I'd order Heineken. I think my wounded pride deserves at least that much."

I glance over his shoulder, to where his friends are ostensibly playing pool but currently attempting to hit each other in the balls with their cue sticks, and decide to be honest.

"Typically—and by 'typically,' I really mean 'always'— Heineken drinkers tend to be big with the self-esteem and suck with the modesty. They're also the first person to need the bathroom when the check comes and a third more likely to drive sports cars."

The guy nods, laughing. "I see. And this is a scientific study?"

His laugh is even sweet. It's goofy in the way his shoulders rise just a tiny bit as if he's a *giggler*.

"Rigorous," I tell him. "I performed the clinical trials myself."

I can see him biting back a broader laugh. "Then you'll be comforted to know that I was in fact *not* ordering Heineken, and was actually going to ask what you had on tap because we just had a round of Stella, and I wanted something more interesting."

Without looking down at the row of draft beers, I list, "Bud, Stone IPA, Pliny the Elder, Guinness, Allagash White, and Green Flash."

"We'll go with the Pliny," he says, and I try to hide how much this surprises me—an occupational necessity. He must know his beers because it's the best choice there. "Six of them, please. I'm Luke, by the way. Luke Sutter."

He holds out his hand and after only a moment of hesitation, I take it.

"Nice to meet you, Luke."

His hand is huge, not too soft . . . and really nice. With long fingers, clean nails, and a strong grip. I pull my own hand back almost immediately and begin pouring his beers.

"And your name is . . ." he asks, the last word stretching into a question.

"That'll be thirty dollars," I tell him instead.

Luke's smile twists a little, amused, and he looks down at his wallet, pulling two twenties out and placing them on top of the bar. He reaches for the first three glasses and nods to me before he turns. "I'll be back to get the rest," he says. And he's gone.

The door opens and a bachelorette party files in. Over the next three hours I make more pink drinks and sexually explicit cocktails than I can count, and whether it's Luke or one of the other guys who ends up grabbing the rest of their beers, I don't notice. Which is just as well, I remind myself, because if there's one rule I've made that I stick to hard and fast, it's that I don't date guys I meet at work. Ever.

And Luke is . . . well, he's a reflection of every reason rule number one exists in the first place.

————

WHEN THE LAST customer has left, I help Fred close up, drive home to an empty apartment, and tumble into bed.

My parents are less than thrilled with the life I've built in San Diego, and are careful to remind me of this at every visit. They don't understand why I took a roommate when Nana left me the loft, free and clear. Although I spent much of my childhood here, they also don't understand why I didn't just sell the loft after graduation and move right back home— which, come on. Freezing Colorado over sunny San Diego? I don't think so. And they definitely don't agree with my surfing all day and tending bar at night when the graphic arts degree I busted my ass for is sitting around, gathering dust.

And okay, I'll give them that last one.

But for now, I'm fine with my life. Lola worries that I'm alone too much—and I *am* alone a lot of the time, but I'm never unhappy. Bartending is a fun job, and surfing is bigger than that. It's a part of me. I love watching water slowly rising and curling, seeing the tips break into these foamy, glass cylinders. I love climbing inside waves so big they tunnel me in as they crest, roaring in my ear. I love the feel of salt-water-rich air filling my mouth, dusting my lungs. Every second the ocean builds a castle and breaks it down. I will never get tired of it.

And I like falling into bed, tired because I've surfed my ass off all day and been on my feet all night, and not because I've been sitting at a desk, staring at a computer.

For now, life is pretty good.

BUT AT THE start of my shift at Fred's Saturday night, I feel both wrecked and antsy: my ribs hurt and I still have the sensation of coughing up a lungful of salt water.

Some days the ocean cooperates and the waves come right to me. Today was not one of those days. The swells were decent at first, but I couldn't seem to hit a single one. I took off early or popped up late. I lost count of how many times I fell or was knocked flat on my ass. I spent every holiday of my life precollege at my grandmother's, and I've surfed Black's Beach and Windansea since I was old enough to carry my own board. But the longer I stayed out there today the more frustrated I got, and the last straw came when I was surprised by a big wave, and rolled . . . *hard*.

The guy with the hair and the smile is back. Luke, I remember, in some sort of breathy echo. He's at a booth tonight with more of his friends, but I spot him as soon as I walk in.

The place is packed and I feel a brief pulse of longing when I hear Harlow's laugh rise above the music. I'd rather be sitting with them than working tonight, and so I have a noticeable chip on my shoulder by the time I step behind the counter and slip my apron over my shirt.

"Someone's having a bad day," Fred says, putting the finishing touches on a tray of margaritas. "Weren't you the one who told me the worst day on the water still beats the best day anywhere else?"

Ugh. I did tell him that. Why do people always remind you of your best parts when you're having a bad day? "Just sore and cranky," I say, trying to smile. "I'll get over it."

"Well, you're in the right place. Loud drunk people are always the right thing for a bad mood."

This pulls my reluctant grin free, and Fred reaches forward, gently chucking my chin.

A row of tickets sit on the counter and I reach for one. Two martinis, dirty, extra olives. I place two glasses on a tray, fill a shaker with ice, pour in vermouth and four ounces of gin, a little olive juice. I fall into the rhythm of the work: measuring, shaking, pouring, serving . . . and the familiar movements relax me, they do.

But I still feel restless with the breathlessness, the few terrifying seconds I thought I might not be able to fight my way up from the tide. It's happened to me a handful of times, and even though logically I know I'll be okay, it's hard to shake the lingering sense of drowning.

Luke moves in my peripheral vision, and I glance up as he

walks around the back of the booth, typing on his phone. *So he's one of those,* I think, imagining how many girls he's texting right now. There's a brunette at their table who seems pretty interested in what he's doing, and I'm tempted to walk over to her under the guise of serving drinks and tell her to cut her losses: invest in one of the kind nerds in the far booth instead.

I shake and pour the cloudy liquid into the glasses, rereading the ticket again before adding two skewers packed with olives. The waitress smiles and leaves with the order, and I move to the next, reaching for a bottle of amaretto when I hear a barstool scrape across the floor behind me.

"So how's the car fund?"

I recognize his voice immediately. "Nothing today," I tell him without looking up, finishing the drink. "But I'm not really in a smiling mood, so I'm not holding out much hope."

"Want to talk about that?" he asks.

I turn to look at him: this time wearing a dark blue T-shirt, same perfect hair, and still entirely too good-looking not to be trouble. Unable to resist, I give him a tiny smile. "I think that's supposed to be *my* line."

Luke acknowledges this with a cute flick of one eyebrow skyward before glancing back at his group.

"Besides, it looks like you've got some people waiting for you," I say, noting the way the brunette's eyes track his every move. He reaches into his pocket, checks his phone, and looks back at me.

"They're not going anywhere," he says, and his eyes smile

a split second before his lips make that soft, crooked curve. "Figured I'd come up here and get myself a drink."

"What can I get you?" I ask. "Another beer?"

"Sure," he says. "And your name. Unless you want me to keep calling you Dimples for the rest of our lives."

Luke's eyes widen playfully as he whispers a deliberate *"Oops"* at this, and produces a dollar bill from his pocket, slipping it into the jar. "I came prepared tonight," he says, watching me pour an IPA into a pint glass. "Just in case you were working again."

I try not to linger on the thought that he specifically brought a pocketful of singles with him for me and this little game.

"It's Lon—" I start to say, just as the bar door opens and Mia walks in with Ansel behind her. Luke's head turns toward them just as I finish with a mumbled "—don."

After a beat, he looks back up at me, eyes oddly tight. He nods quickly. "Nice to officially meet you."

I'm pretty sure he didn't get my name, but if he's fine not knowing it, I'm fine not repeating it.

Another customer sits at the bar and waves to get my attention. I slide Luke's beer over to him and smile as he looks up, the coaster touching the edge of his hand. "That's five dollars."

Blinking at me slowly, he says, "Thanks," and pulls out his wallet.

I move to help the new customer, but out of the corner of my eye, I see Luke slap a bill down on the bar and return to his friends without waiting for change. Either he didn't leave a tip, or he left a big one.

Unfortunately for my determination to find him douchey, I'm pretty sure I can guess which.

Two whiskey sours, four Blue Moons, and a pitcher of margaritas later, I'm at the register. Mia, Ansel, and Harlow are standing nearby, waiting for Finn before they all head out to a movie. I watch them for the span of three deep breaths, struggling for what feels like an eternity over my relationship ambivalence. On the one hand, I see the people around me so happy—some of them even *married*—and I want that. On the other hand, I know I'm not ready.

It's been just over a year since Justin and I ended things, and I still remember what it's like to be paired off like that, where all plans have to be created with another person in mind, and then decided on again in a group of friends like this. I'm sure most people wouldn't believe me, but after busting my ass in school and dating the same boy throughout, it's nice not to *have* to do anything. I surf, I work, I go home. I make all my decisions based on what's good for me as a person, rather than one-half of a couple.

Still, there are times like tonight where I realize it *can* be lonely, actually, and it's not just about sex but about companionship and having someone who looks at me like he's waited all day for it. It's about having someone there to distract me with movies or conversation or a warm body to help me fall asleep.

The register clangs as I push the cash drawer closed and

hand a guy his change. I lift my head in the direction of Harlow's laughter, and am surprised to see Luke and Mia now standing near the bathrooms, talking.

We all attended UCSD, so even though there are several schools within the university, it doesn't surprise me that they might know each other. Still, it makes me laugh a little inside because I will constantly feel like there are so many details to be plugged into my working map of Lola's friends.

I knew Harlow had famous parents, but only recently put it together that her mother was *my* mom's favorite actress when I was little.

I knew Mia used to dance, but only recently learned that her trajectory was ruined when she was hit by a truck.

I knew Finn was close to his father and two brothers, but didn't know until I put my foot in it and asked him what he was doing for Mother's Day that his mom died when he was a kid.

My name is called from down the bar, and I blink back into focus. I run a tray of drinks out to a table and Harlow grabs me on my way back, pulling me into a fierce hug.

"Hey, stranger," she says, her eyes moving over my face before she reaches for a strand of my hair. "Feels like ages since I've seen you. Think you could put some sunblock on and leave some cute for the rest of us? Jesus, you look like an ad for the *Sports Illustrated* Swimsuit Edition, surfer girl. Fuck you *and* your adorable freckles."

I give her a wide smile. "I should take you with me everywhere, Ego Boost."

"Can you cut out and see a movie with us tonight?" she asks.

I shake my head and her lips turn down into a pout. "It's just me, Fred, and one waitress here, and that new band is coming in later," I explain.

"Maybe this weekend? All three Roberts boys are in town."

I nod, perking up at the idea of a fun night out with a big group. "I'll check my schedule." Her husband, Finn, formerly a commercial fisherman, is now about to become television's hottest reality star on *The Fisher Men,* a show featuring Finn, his father, and his two younger brothers out on the water.

Harlow's eyebrows slowly rise and I realize my mistake. I may have only known Harlow for about nine months, but her meddling skills are legendary.

"Maybe we can get you and Levi—"

I'm already looking for an exit. "Nope. *Nope*," I tell her, and glance up at the bar to see a few people waiting for service. "I need to get back, Miss Matchmaker, but I'll text you tomorrow and let you know if I can make it."

Harlow nods before turning toward her table. "All right, you stubborn shit!" she calls out as I head back.

When I get there, I see Fred pouring some beers, talking with some regulars. Just down the bar, sitting alone, is Luke.

He looks . . . well, he looks upset, with a serious expression I don't imagine he wears often. Granted, I know next to nothing about this guy except that he has girls constantly watching him, looks like a total douchebag, yet sort of isn't when you actually get him talking, and gets more texts in a single night than I do in a week. But what do I know.

I glance over to where Mia, Ansel, and Harlow are gathering their things and wave as they head toward Finn, standing near the exit.

"You okay there?" I say to Luke, pulling a shot glass from below the counter.

He nods, and as soon as he looks up at me, the serious face is gone, replaced again by the cute smile. On instinct, I look away, digging into the icebox with a small shovel.

"Just spacing out and thinking too much," he says. "A bar seems like a good place to do that."

I nod. And because he seems to be waiting for me to say something more, I do. "Best place to mull things over. Bad grades. Lost job. Money problems. First loves."

His eyes catch mine again. "Speaking from experience?" he asks.

"Yeah," I say, pouring him a shot of whiskey and sliding it across the counter. Even with the smile, he looks like he could use it. "*Bartender* experience. Maybe you just need a distraction." I look over his shoulder to where his group of friends is sitting, along with the brunette whose eyes still track him everywhere. He follows my gaze and then turns back with a little shake of his head.

Luke lifts the shot, tilting his head back and swallowing it in one go. He sets the glass on the bar top and exhales, coughing a little. "Thanks."

"No problem."

"What about you?" he asks.

I move to the sink to set the glass inside. "What about me what?"

"Are *you* in need of a distraction?"

Inside, something sharp recoils into my lungs, but I manage a friendly smile. "I'm good."

Luke dips his head, looking up at me through his lashes as he asks, "What does that mean, you're 'good'?"

I pick up a bar towel, looking down at it as I tell him, "It means I don't date guys I meet at work."

"I'm not asking you to go steady, Dimples." With a sneaky smile, he reaches into his pocket and pulls out another dollar, tucking it away inside the jar. His eyes meet mine and something tightens between my ribs and belly button. His look is *knowing*, as if he can see that I had a shitty day, and I see he's having a shitty night, and he likes that we both see these things.

I don't like having this chemistry with him, don't like the wordless connection.

Or maybe I don't like *how much* I like it. I still have that choking-breathless feel from this morning, but it loosens inexplicably the longer he's here, talking to me.

"Speaking of," he says quietly, "I haven't seen much of those dimples tonight."

Shrugging, I say, "Let's just say it's been a day."

He leans both elbows on the bar, studying me. "Sounds like you could blow off some steam, too."

I laugh at this, unable to resist admitting, "Probably true."

Reaching for a coaster, he spins it slowly in front of him. "Maybe someone could help you out with that."

I ignore him and start wiping down the bar. It isn't the first time I've been propositioned at work, not by a long shot. But it's the first time I'm tempted to accept, because inside, I'm thrumming as I imagine what he's offering.

"Do you have a boyfriend?" he asks, undeterred, and I shake my head.

"No," I tell him. If the way his arms look in that T-shirt is any indication, I bet he looks fantastic naked.

I bet he knows he does, too.

It's a sign that it's been way too long since I've had sex if I'm even having this conversation with myself. The last thing I need in my life is a guy like Luke. I take a sharp breath and get some physical distance, stepping away a little.

Following me with his eyes, he asks, "So is this no-dating-guys-you-meet-at-work thing, like, an actual rule?"

"Sort of." I fold the bar towel and tuck it into the back of my apron, meeting his eyes.

"What if I promised I was absolutely worth it?"

Why do I think he is *absolutely* telling the truth? He smiles shyly, but behind his honey-brown eyes, I can see he's still hunting.

"I'm sure you're amazing." I lean back against the sink, staring him down and shocked that I'm even still standing here. "But I don't even remember your name."

"Yes, you do." He leans forward, crossing his arms on the glossy wood.

I bite back a smile.

"What time do you get off tonight?" he asks.

I can't help but look at his mouth and imagine how it would feel moving, hot and open, down my neck, my breasts, over my ribs.

It occurs to me that if one wanted to break a losing streak, one would go with a sure thing, right? Who better to bust me out of my sex drought than someone who clearly knows what he's doing? And someone who wouldn't need it to mean anything?

A few beats of silence pass between us before I straighten, reaching for a ticket one of the waitresses sets down next to me. It's now or never.

"I get off at one."

Chapter TWO

Luke

I'M NOT SURE what it is about this girl that's so different from every other girl I've let into my house, but I find myself racing up the steps and getting to the door before her, doing a quick scan of the dark living room, a tiny peek toward the kitchen.

Not too bad.

No food left out on the coffee table and—more important—no boxers on the kitchen floor. I'm doing the mental trigger finger salute to the gods to make sure we're on the same page here: there'd better not be any condom wrappers visible in the bedroom. Or the bathroom, for that matter.

I open the door wider for her and grin. "Come on in."

Logan looks at my face and then into the darkness before taking a cautious step forward. I reach past her, flicking on the living room lights.

And there it is: the difference. Most girls enter my house walking backward, with their fists curled in my shirt. Some step inside with their eyes on my face, waiting for the tiny lift of my chin to the left, the silent *The bedroom is that way.* This one walks in looking at everything the way she looks at *me,* like she's not sure she wants to touch anything.

I can almost hear the words embedded in her deep inhale before she says them out loud: "I just realized I have no idea what I'm doing here."

I step back a little. Without hesitation, my answer is, "Nothing you don't want to do."

But inside I'm letting out a long-suffering groan; it's been a long day with a lot of drama. I'd really like to lose myself in some fast sex tonight, but don't want it to be a long, drawn-out seduction.

As if it's already given up on plan A, my stomach rumbles and I glance toward the kitchen. "Hungry?"

She shrugs. "A little?"

"I have some . . ." Walking over, I open the fridge and lean in, inspecting. "Beer. Tortillas. Sriracha. Celery, pepperoni, and . . ." Opening a drawer, I say, "String cheese."

I turn and look at her when I'm met with silence, and her wary expression is hilarious. I draw a circle in the air, asking, "What is that face?"

"I have no idea what face I'm making," she says, straightening and giving me a little smile instead.

I lean my arm on the open refrigerator door. "Then tell me what you're thinking."

Her brows lift as if to confirm that I really want to hear it. When I nod, she says, "You're almost too stereotypical to be real."

A laugh barks out of me. "Am I?"

The truth comes out in a torrent: "You're hot as sin, had to double-check to make sure the last girl didn't leave her underwear on the couch, and your fridge is bachelor-level empty."

So let's add *observant* to the list of things that intrigue me about this girl.

I shrug, flashing her a quick grin. "I eat out a lot."

She skirts past my innuendo with a tiny smirk. "But if these things are all as well correlated as I suspect, it means you're really good in bed and probably have an enormous penis."

A smile tugs at the side of my mouth, and I fight it as long as I can but end up bursting out laughing. Finally, she gives in to a real smile of her own and it snags me somewhere dusty and unexpected. Sexy smiles go straight to my cock, but her smile isn't just sexy, it's *happy*. And it isn't just the dimples. It's the twinkle in her eyes, something that seems to look deeper than the surface. I don't even know if it's possible for a true smile to be anything other than happy but hers is the best happy smile I've seen in . . .

I wipe my face with a palm and then move closer to her, fighting the ratcheting tension in my gut as I reach for a loose strand of her hair. I smooth it behind the curve of her ear, whispering, "Look, Logan."

Her eyes narrow skeptically for a moment, and then she's biting back a grin.

I consider asking her about it, but it's a little disarming to see her like this, away from the dim, colorful lighting at Fred's. There, she looked a little harder: guarded eyes behind her teasing smile. Here, I can see that her eyes aren't just blue but a ring of deep cobalt around the brightest turquoise, and her nose is dusted with the faintest freckles. She chews the corner of her lip as she surveys my living room again.

Holy shit, is she a virgin?

Should I ask?

No. She's wearing shit-kicking boots with a short plaid skirt, and there's no way I'm risking taking those steel toes to my shin, or worse.

"If you want to fool around, I'm down," I tell her. "You're beautiful, and sweet, and your mouth looks like candy." I'm looking at her lips when I say this, but I can't help sense that she's just rolled her eyes. She gives off the oddest duality: a tough exterior coupled with the impression that she still requires careful handling.

"Or," I say, taking a step back, "we can order pizza and play some Titanfall on the Xbox." I'm guessing she'll pass on that one—which we all know is fine by me, because I can't imagine a girl this hot even knows what Titanfall is.

I don't expect the way her eyes brighten and, before she can put the expression away, I see her glance at my living room. Clearly, I've pegged her all wrong.

Kicking off my shoes, I walk back into the kitchen, grab two beers, and nod to the living room. "Let's go."

With a smile and a little bounce in her step, she walks over and settles on the couch beside me. I watch her grab the controller with her right hand, her thumb expertly sliding across the small joystick. "Will it embarrass you if I kick your ass?" she asks.

I shake my head, smiling as I boot up the system. "Nope.

My Grams got this for me last week, and I'm sure she'd be tickled to know a lady friend beat me."

I feel her stare on the side of my face as I click through the start-up menu. When I turn to look at her, her dimples flash as she smiles. "That's cute."

"It's cute that my grandma got me a first-person-shooter game?" I'm tempted to tell her about the year Grams sent me to Vegas for my twenty-first birthday and told me tattoos were okay but made me promise I wouldn't hire any hookers. When I replied that I never needed to pay for sex, she smacked me on the back of the head.

"Yeah." Logan looks away, at the television. "Although you're what? Twenty-two?"

"Twenty-three. Twenty-four in October."

"*Aw*. Twenty-three and a half!" She pinches my cheek. "My eleven-and-a-half-year-old cousin does that, too."

"You're very funny."

Her answering laugh vibrates through me. "*Almost* twenty-four," she says. "So maybe it's time to give up the video games?"

I nod toward her hands. "You look pretty comfortable holding that controller, Pot."

She shrugs, and looks at me again. "Let's just say I've held one of these more recently than one of those." She nods to my lap in return and I cough, nearly choking on my sip of beer. When she looks back to the television, she barks out a laugh, pointing to the screen. "Please tell me you're not GiantD92."

With a wink, I tell her, "I think you know I am."

Logan shakes her head at me, but it doesn't read like exasperation. Her cheeks are clearly pink, visible even in the dim light from the television, and she's sitting only a few inches away from me.

She joins the game and we choose our pilot types. It's only once the game loads and we're dropped into the map when I realize I've never played video games with a girl, other than my sister Margot, who's terrible. I've got the basics of running up walls, vaulting and the like, but am still trying to easily transition into the Titan controls and some of the tactical tricks. Beside me, Logan has no problem with any of it; I'm beginning to think maybe she's a hustler.

She's not a small-talker. She's sweet, but not giggly, and is clearly not trying to impress me. Even so, she is already kicking my ass. Regardless, it's easy between us like this, with nothing but the sound of video game gunfire and our occasional string of curse words in victory or frustration.

"Use your sniper rifle!" she shouts, even though she's right next to me.

Our thumbs hammer on the controllers.

"No, I like the MK5."

"Dude, you're blasting everywhere, you're going to hit me, just be more precise for like two fucking seconds!"

Laughing, I switch my gun and in a few shots manage to take down an Ogre, clearing a path forward.

"Tell me I was right," she sings.

"You were—*fuck*!" I yell. In a rain of blood, my pilot is

killed by fire from a chain gun from the other team. "Where the hell did that one come from?"

She pauses the game. "Wow. You didn't last very long." Her eyes are bright with amusement, lips twisted in a sardonic grin.

She seems so comfortable cracking innuendo, joking about sex—about why we're here—but I sense the act itself is what she can't initiate.

"Can I ask you a question?" I say.

She reaches for her beer. "You mean another one?"

I stare at her, straight-faced.

Giving in with a teasing smile—those fucking dimples make something inside me melt then begin to boil—she says, "Yes, fine. As long as you won't be offended if I decline to answer."

"Why did you leave with me tonight? At the risk of sounding like a complete asshole, you said you don't go home with customers, but here you are."

"I don't," she says quickly, but quietly. "Ever."

I meant the question generally, but her answer surprises me. *"Never?"*

She shakes her head.

I wonder if that's all I'm going to get. She didn't answer my question, but when I look at her, it feels like she's still mulling it over. Finally, she pulls one leg up on the couch, facing me.

"Let me ask you a question, too," she says.

Lifting my chin in a small nod, I take a sip of my beer, waiting.

"Do *you* do this a lot?" she asks.

Although her gesture when she says this encompasses the whole room, I'm pretty sure she doesn't mean the video game.

I try to do a quick count in my head. Maybe ten in the past couple of months? That might sound like a lot to her. "I mean . . . not every night, but yeah, sometimes."

"Why?" she asks.

Why? The question sounds absurd. Why do I have sex? Is she for real?

I study her; those brilliant blue eyes are fixed on my face, waiting for an answer. How is it possible for someone to seem so innocent and so wary all at the same time?

Truthfully, I've been asked some variation of this before, maybe a handful of times. Usually the woman looks up at me in bed, before or after we fuck, and voices it as casually as possible.

You must have a lot of girls in your bed.

When was the last time you just brought someone home?

I hope you know I don't do this all the time. This is different, Luke.

But I never get this question on the couch, conversationally, while fully dressed, with clear eyes staring at me and mostly free of judgment. It just feels like Logan wants to understand.

"Right now I'd be terrible at anything more," I tell her. "I don't mean I'm scared of commitment or any shit like that. I mean, I've been in love before and am not sure I could do all that again."

She lets out a short, sharp laugh at this, nodding as she tilts her beer to her mouth.

"At least," I continue, "not right now when I'm working like crazy." This sounds ridiculous. I can hear it, can hear the absurdity. We're *all* working like crazy. We're all busy and young and chaotic. "But, regardless, I'm a guy. I like sex. I like women. Is that the level of honesty you're looking for?"

She nods.

"Your turn," I say. Something ancient seems to be creaking to life inside my chest. It's been forever since I've had a conversation like this—earnest, and open—with someone other than my family, and I forgot how nice it feels.

She drinks deeply from her beer again before answering. I watch her throat as she swallows. It's long, pale, and smooth. "I left with you because I was barreled by a wave this morning."

She surfs . . . that certainly explains her body.

"It's been so long since I was rolled like that," she says, staring down at the bottle in her hand. "I forgot how scary it is. For the first part of the morning, I couldn't catch a single good wave. And then one came along that just ground me to dust. All day, I've been tense and out of sorts. It's like it never occurs to me to work out tension with sex. Tonight I figured, Why not?"

"Why not?" I repeat quietly, feeling my pulse charge forward as it seems to become a possibility.

She nods but her eyes are on my lips now.

"Whatever you want, okay?" I tell her.

Slowly, so slowly I can see every emotion pass through her eyes—uncertainty, fear, desire, determination—she leans forward and brushes her mouth over mine. It feels like silk.

"We're only doing this tonight," she says, pulling back a few inches to meet my eyes. And when she says it, it sounds *nothing* like it has coming from other girls. She's not worried *she'll* fall into the trap of thinking it's more; she's worried I will. Her dimples dig into her cheeks as she smiles, saying, "So make sure to show me all your tricks."

I laugh into another kiss. "Yes, ma'am."

"And don't come back to the bar expecting to get head in the parking lot," she says against my mouth. "I'm not that girl."

See? I was right.

I pull back to look her in the eye and salute her with my fingers at my forehead. "Understood."

Without much ceremony, she reaches for the hem of my shirt and helps me out of it. Her hands come up, warm but tentative, fingertips before palms smoothing over my skin. Exploring, as if it's been forever since she did this and she's forgotten what skin feels like. Her hands are soft; her nails are only long enough to scratch lightly down my chest and over my stomach before she gets to work on the buttons of my jeans.

Whoa. Jesus.

I slide my hips just out of her reach, pulling a condom out of my pocket and placing it near her hip. "Do you want to go to my room?"

She shakes her head. "Here is good." She tugs me closer and works my pants and boxers down my hips before a thought seems to halt her movements. "Do you live alone?"

I kiss her, speaking against her lips, as I kick my pants to the floor. "You're getting me naked on my couch, so, God, I hope so."

I feel her giggle against my mouth when I bend to suck at her throat, and subtly shift away from her hands. I don't want her hands on my cock yet; neither of us is ready to fuck and what's the hurry? It's a complete one-eighty from only five minutes ago. She's not hesitant anymore, not even a little. I wonder if she's like that in everything: cautious, then almost recklessly committed. Even so, there's still a film of detachment there, as if she's checking things off a mental list without really giving over to anything.

It's weird.

Usually I sense a frantic need for connection—the inescapable snare of eye contact, a quiet string of questions, kisses that feel like secrets being offered—and it means I can choose how much of it I want. But Logan isn't looking for deep connection with me; she seems to want the paradox of getting it over with *and* being consumed.

I'm oddly reminded of driving through the Rockies with my parents during a snowstorm: Mom happily remarking on how lovely it was while Dad focused intently on the mechanics of getting us all there safely. My job is to navigate us both through this.

She guides my hands to her shirt and then closes her eyes

as I unbutton it down her front, kissing. She smells like oranges and the sweet scent of girl.

I pull her shirt from her shoulders, down her arms, and unclasp her bra. Fuck, her chest is nice, too. Breasts just bigger than my hands. Flat, toned stomach. She has the body of a girl who unself-consciously surfs in a bikini: curved, tanned, and defined. I want to lose myself in this, want to sense her own relief from it, or even feel some urgency overwhelm her ability to control. For once I want to linger on my bed, lights on, talking nonsense while I kiss all these perfect parts of her.

But I can feel the tension in her abdomen, the way she just wants to move forward, keep going, get there.

Is this how it feels to be with me when *I'm* distracted and simply need to fuck?

Bending, I kiss her chin, her lips, parting them with mine. Her tongue is small and soft in my mouth and beneath the tang of beer she *tastes* like oranges, too. I imagine her reaching for one at the bar, idly sucking on it between mixing drinks.

"Come on," I whisper, sucking at her lower lip. *Give me something.* "Touch me."

She licks my upper lip and a tight noise of want escapes her mouth.

"It's okay to want this. *I* want this. You're not doing anything wrong here."

A tentative hand slides around my neck, her legs spreading as she pulls me between them and come on

come on

there.

I feel it, when she softens under me, giving in. Her hand comes up to my face, the other reaching for me, curling around my dick. I harden from her touch, and inhale the sweet citrus smell of her, bending to suck a soft nipple into my mouth, groaning at the way it stiffens against my tongue.

I get to work on her skirt, easing it down her hips.

"Oh, shit," she says, and then stifles a laugh with her hand.

I freeze, looking up at her.

Goddamnit—of course this will be when she remembers she's on her period.

"What?" I ask, as calmly as I can.

Her blue eyes stare up at me, wide with playful apology. "I haven't shaved my legs in . . . a while."

I exhale, relief making my hands clumsy as I yank the skirt the rest of the way off.

"Don't worry. I haven't, either."

She giggles, and when I look down at her, she's fucking stunning. She stills under my attention, letting me look up and down the length of her naked body. Her legs may be un-shaven, but I'd never be able to tell. Suffice to say, Logan is a natural blonde, and every other bikini-conscious part of her makes my mouth water.

It's only when I'm over her like this, positioned between her thighs and registering how entirely relaxed she is being nude before me, that I appreciate it fully: Dimples isn't here for anyone but herself.

Most girls *don't* come home with me solely for their own pleasure. As much as they may insist that's the reason, they come because they want a relationship, want to be adored. They want me to keep them beyond a single night, to *like* them beyond what we do together in bed.

But Logan doesn't seem to really care what I think of her or whether we even see each other again. She's *using* me.

I feel the sting of rejection and the warmth of respect at the same time.

She worries that sweet bottom lip with her teeth. "Everything okay?"

I close my eyes, taking a deep inhale of her. "Just looking at you," I tell her. "You're . . ." *You're surprising.* "You're really fucking pretty."

She doesn't thank me. She barely reacts at all, only watches me with heavy eyes.

I run my hand down between her breasts—full swells, small pink tips—and across her ribs, lower down her toned stomach. Her hips mirror the movement of my palm, chasing my touch.

"Let me kiss you here?" I ask, drawing my fingers between her legs. She's soft, wet enough to tempt me but not enough that I'm sure she'll go off like a bomb the way I want.

She shakes her head a little, smiling that wide-open smile at me. "No way, sir. That's special."

Fuck. It *is* special and for the length of a sharp inhale, it thrills me that she feels that way. But then frustration inches in: the more time I spend with her, the more eager I am to ensure this night blows her goddamn mind. If she's come to a movie theater to be entertained, I'm going to show her the motherfucking *Godfather*.

She reaches down to the cushion by her hip and finds the condom, handing it to me.

"I thought you wanted me to pull out all my tricks?" I tease.

She laughs, a single burst of sound, but the smile stays. "Just come here."

Shaking my head I tell her, "If we're skipping the previews, you're at least putting that on me."

With a cute little eye roll, she pushes herself up on an elbow, tearing the condom wrapper with her teeth. Slowly, slowly, she rolls it down the length of me and I bite my lower lip, groaning.

Seeing her naked . . . tasting her tongue . . . the warm grip of her hand on my cock and I'm ready to fuck, but her hands don't immediately leave me. She touches my cock, my balls, my hips and stomach. *Now* she's deliberate, *now* she's relishing. Her fingertips explore me, soft and gently tickling up my chest until she curls a hand around the back of my neck, pulling me over her.

"Come here," she whispers again, kissing my chin, my jaw, my neck.

Maybe I should be in charge; she's got more innocence buried beneath her steel than she does true cynicism. But I don't want to lead right now. She reaches for me, slipping me around, playing with the tip of my cock on her clit, and I feel the way my arms shake, planted beside her head. She wants to lead it, wants me to stay still, wants to use this part of my body to feel good. Every muscle along my spine is bunched, every thought banished but the feel of her. The fucking *feel*. I watch her face and the million expressions I see tense and relax across it. I've never been so wrapped up in watching someone give in before.

Finally, she slides me lower. I sense the dip, the invitation, and ease my way inside.

She holds her breath but doesn't make a sound. *I* want to roar. She's warm—crazy warm—and wetter now. I have to ease in and out, an inch at a time because she's small, and I worry I'm hurting her but her hands find my ass and she pulls me forward, rocking with me to get me deeper, more, all the way.

I groan when I'm finally there, but she's quiet. She's so quiet even with the clench of her all around me; with the way I'm squeezed inside her, how can she not make a single sound? I'm all the way in, grinding to get the feel of her, mouth on her neck, her tits. I feel unleashed, ravenous.

I could lose myself. I could fuck hard.

But, God, when she rolls her hips under me I know I could also fuck slow.

Whatever the hell she wants, it's so good and her tits pressed to my chest make me rub against her, skin to skin.

"It's okay?" I ask, quietly checking in.

She nods, swallowing. "It's good."

I groan, pulling back and then moving back into her.

The slow drag out, long easing in.

So good.

She smells good, too.

Hands all over my back, up my neck.

Logan's quiet, but it feels good for her, I can tell. I sense it in the way her fingers tangle in my hair, the rolling of her hips and tightening of her nipples. She's had good sex before; she knows what her body wants. She wants deep, she wants me pressed right up against her and grinding. She's not getting shy now that we're getting down to it. No, she's taking and taking and taking.

Women sometimes talk. Either that or I do. But here we're just breathing; there's only the sound of inhales, forceful exhales, and the shifting of our bodies together. And then the involuntary gasps we both make when I start moving faster, and harder. Her breasts move beneath me, hips rise from the couch. She rides me from below, showing me the speed, the pattern she needs.

That she remains so quiet means her orgasm comes as a total shock to me; it comes like the crashing of a wave and when I hear the noise she makes—a tight, relieved cry—I am completely frantic: I need to hear it again, and longer.

I ride it out for her until she seems to deflate under me in relief, but then I'm rolling onto the floor, carrying her with me so that she straddles my hips.

"*Take,*" I whisper, hoping she understands. I want to give her every drop of relief tonight.

The way her eyes shine when she looks at me tells me she

needs this. She loves sex. I mean, holy hell, why a woman with this degree of experience and sensuality doesn't fuck whenever she wants is beyond me. She rolls her hips, starting to ride me, and then she's off on a new tear, working herself closer to that tipping point again. Her skin grows shiny with sweat, fingers press sharply into my chest, up my neck, gripping me. Almost threatening. *It's got to be better this second time,* her body says. *Bigger. Longer. Harder.*

"*Oh, shit,*" she says on an exhale and there—*fuck*—there it is. Wild and tight and wet, so fucking *wet* she's all around me pushing herself farther onto my cock. I groan, fighting the way my body wants to give in, wants to come so hard I'll see stars.

But I know we're not done here.

I find myself staring at the smooth arch of her throat, the grace of her straight collarbone as she rides me slower now, coming down. I study the quick rise and fall of her breasts as she gasps for air. She's completely given herself over to it. To *me*. For this perfect moment she trusts me.

She's beautiful, smart, and a little defensive, but even so, she's here, letting me feel her. I want to deserve this. And I worry I'm going to come hard and wild, and still be left unsatisfied because the tiny taste she's giving me isn't going to be enough.

"You're good?" I manage, running my hands up her waist and higher, cupping her breasts.

She lifts her head with effort, eyes hungry. "I want you behind me," she says.

Without a word, I lift her off me, help her onto her knees, and then slide back in, unable to keep from groaning, low and long.

I'm obsessed with the muscular lines in her back, the way her clit feels under the slide of my fingers. I'm obsessed with the way she moves no matter what position she's in, with the sound she makes when she comes.

I know when this is over I'll drive her home—because she won't want to stay. But right now, the sex is good—it's *so* good—and every time she turns her brain off long enough for her body to take over and collapse into orgasm, I feel some tiny shell chip away.

I want to see her tender pieces.

Fuck. It's been forever since I wanted tender.

———

"WHERE'D YOU DISAPPEAR to last night?" Dylan asks.

I close the car door and lock it behind us remotely. "Went home with someone. What did you guys do?"

"Went back to Dan's." Dylan pulls the door open to Fred's. "I don't know how to describe the weed he had other than to say it made Jenny bark like a dog."

I follow him in, not sure I heard his answer correctly over a hundred people yelling, and the loud, pounding music: "Did you say Jenny *barked like a dog*?"

He nods, his wild blond hair bobbing with the movement, and leads us to the bar. My chest tightens when I see Logan there, working. She looks hot: hair piled high and messy on her head, arms bare in a white tank top that shows off the shape of her perfect tits, a face free of makeup save for her shiny mouth. I feel like an odd mix of idiot and asshole for not anticipating that she might be here tonight.

I hope she doesn't think I've come because of her.

But, shit. I also don't want her to think I'd avoid her, either. I don't think I want her to avoid *me*.

I make a mental fist and imagine punching myself in the jaw.

"Hey, Freak," Dylan says to Logan with a grin.

They know each other?

She looks up, smiling easily. "Hey, Sideshow."

She doesn't react the way I expect her to after last night, so I assume she doesn't see me behind him . . . but then she tosses two coasters down on the bar top and I realize she's just greeting me like she would any other customer. It makes something in me grow tense at the same time something else unwinds. What did I expect? That she would suddenly go from a girl determined to have one wild night to a stage-five clinger?

She puts her palms on the bar and looks at us, waiting. "What can I get you guys?"

"A snack," he says. She laughs, reaching for a cherry and tossing it into the air. Dylan catches it in his mouth, chewing it while he eyes her playfully.

Holy fuck. Dylan not only knows Logan, but he *likes* her?

Swallowing, he says, "And now an amaretto sour."

"Amaretto sour?" Logan and I say in unison.

"They're delicious," he insists.

"Cultivating your feminine side?" I ask.

He shakes his head, dismissing me. "London makes the best amaretto sours. Seriously, try one."

I open my mouth to ask him who the hell London is when Logan leans forward, handing him another cherry. "Aww, thanks."

Every muscle in my body hits pause and my brain seems to trip over the sudden stillness.

She isn't watching my reaction. Without asking what I want, she pops open some obscure IPA for me, sets it on the bar, and gets to work on Dylan's drink. But I wouldn't be able to tear my eyes from her even if someone shot a gun on the other side of the room.

"London?" I say, leaning my elbows on the bar. I grab my beer, taking a sip as she lifts her face to me and pours his shaken drink into a tumbler.

"Hmm?" she answers, blinking quickly to Dylan and then back to me, eyes tight with warning.

I lean in, giving her a tiny shake of my head. I told him I went home with someone, but not who. Besides, he's distracted—as he usually is—nodding his head to the music and looking around the room as if it's his first day out of the cave and he can't believe everything that's happening all around us.

"Your name is *London?*" I ask quietly, heart hammering while I try to remember how many times I said the wrong name last night. Trying—and failing—to remember whether I grunted out the wrong name when I came. "I've been calling you Logan."

Her dimples appear a split second before a smile curls up the corners of her mouth. "You have."

"You let me call you by the wrong name?" My smile feels like a bare flash of teeth. Inside I'm a chaotic swarm of reactions: amused, irritated, embarrassed, confused.

"It wasn't a big deal," she explains. "You got all the important details right." With a wink, she takes the twenty I've put on the bar, rings up our drinks, and drops my change back in front of me. Without another lingering look, or even another word, she steps away and helps another customer.

Okay, what the fuck just happened?

I can be pretty casual about sex, but even I would correct someone if they were calling me Lucas or Jake. Especially if we were *fucking*. To think the entire time I was calling her by the wrong name and it mattered so little to her she didn't even bother to correct me . . .

Dylan turns back to me, grabbing his drink and taking a sip. His expression softens into euphoria.

"I think I just saw your O face," I say, squeezing my eyes closed. "That will never be unseen."

"Try this." He shoves it in front of me.

I take it from him, sliding the straws out of the way to sip directly from the glass. *Ugh.* "I'm not really an amaretto sour connoisseur," I tell him. "It tastes like amaretto and sour to me."

I look over his shoulder and my eyes snag on the sight of . . .

Shit, I am so bad with names.

"Dyl." I lift my chin, indicating he should subtly follow my attention to the overly made-up brunette and her pixie-cut friend making their way over to us.

But of course he whips around.

"What's her name?" I ask.

"Aubrey," he answers, waving to her. "I think her friend's name is Lou?" And then his brows pull together as he turns back to me. "Wait. Didn't you sleep with her last summer?"

I nod, giving him a guilty wince as he calls me an *absolute asshole* under his breath, and then Aubrey is there with her tits and hopeful smile aimed right at me.

"I haven't seen you in ages," she purrs into my ear.

"Hey, Aubrey." I hold my breath, hoping that I haven't messed up her name, too.

"You remembered my name!"

Dylan coughs out a single syllable: *"Dick."*

Aubrey doesn't hear him. Her wide brown eyes meet mine, and the invitation is there, so clear. I feel a tightening in my abdomen, the warm rush of adrenaline.

She was sweet, I remember now, looking at her. Unlike London, Aubrey seemed to want more than just one night. She reassured me she didn't take guys home often, made porn star noises in bed, and faked about seventeen orgasms, but it still managed to be fun. I didn't nearly pass out when I came the way I did last night with London, but I managed to get off just fine.

I glance over at London as the thought rolls through me, and for a stabbing, panicked second I worry about how this must look. I'm standing at the bar, not ten feet from the woman I had sex with last night, and there's a woman I've obviously slept with standing with her arm around my waist, her cheek resting flirtatiously against my shoulder.

It isn't the first time two women I've hooked up with have been in such close proximity, but it's the first time I feel like I'm tangled in Saran Wrap, mildly claustrophobic.

Though I don't know why I'm worried; London still hasn't looked back over at me. She doesn't even seem to want to remember it happened.

I lead our little group away from the bar and lean closer to Aubrey so we can hear each other over the shouting and cheers from the overhead TVs. Her lips are sticky with gloss, eyes lined heavily with dark mascara. I don't remember noticing this before.

"How's it going?" she asks, and then bites her bottom lip.

I give her my best smile. "Not bad at all."

Chapter THREE

London

*I*T'S NOT LIKE I've never done this before—had a one-night stand—but the number of guys I've slept with is still small enough that when I see Luke walk into Fred's the next night, the thought *I've had sex with him* is the first thing that flashes through my head.

Thankfully, it's there and gone, replaced just as quickly with *What the hell is he doing here?* Sex with a guy like Luke is supposed to mean multiple orgasms and a smile you have to explain to your friends the next day. It's also supposed to be a *one-time thing.* I'm fairly certain we were both clear on that point.

I never planned on seeing Luke again, which is exactly why I didn't bother correcting him when he kept calling me by the wrong name. It's also why it takes me a moment to get my bearings when he walks into Fred's with Not-Joe, Oliver's goofy employee and one of my favorite people.

They head straight toward me, but when I do nothing more than get them drinks and go about my business, I think Luke gets it. I can't quite make out his reaction, though, and I wonder briefly if he's disappointed that I'm not falling all over myself to see him or asking for a repeat performance. Which—let's be real for a second—wouldn't be the worst idea I've ever had, because when Luke claimed he knew what he was doing? He wasn't lying. Not even a little.

But I'm *not* looking for a repeat. I knew it last night— even when it was so good I kept thinking, *I don't want this to end, I don't ever want him to come and this to be over*—and my instinct is reaffirmed now as I watch yet another brunette sidle up next to him.

This is why hookups never work for me: I don't like having to mentally process it all after. I don't like questioning my behavior, questioning theirs. There are too many rules to such a game that are purported to have no strings attached.

The place gradually starts to fill. There's a game blasting from a few of the overhead TVs, and the periodic roar of the crowd tears through the bar. It's so busy I've almost forgotten Luke is even here when I turn to ring someone up and see him—and the brunette—making their way toward the exit. Together.

There's an uncomfortable, almost stinging sensation in my chest as I watch her hook her arm through his. She laughs at something he's said and they disappear through the door. This feeling is strange—it's not anger, and it's not hurt. But it *is* mild irritation, at best, and I'll definitely serve him Heineken if he ever comes back.

I don't realize I'm still watching the empty doorway until Fred moves into the space next to me.

"What's so interesting?" he says, following my gaze.

I snap out of it. "Nothing." I look up at Fred and grin. "Just someone proving I was right."

"Well, that *sounds* interesting," he says, and props a hip against the counter. "Guy? *Girl?*"

"Guy," I say, and reach across to poke him in the ribs. I'd give Fred more of a hard time for being so nosy, but watching him tease Harlow never fails to make my life. "Don't let anyone tell you subtlety isn't your strong point."

He chuckles as he steps out of my reach. "I try. And this night just went up about three hundred points on the interesting scale. Not sure I've heard you mention a guy since you've been here."

"That's because we're not sitting under a dryer at the hair salon."

Fred laughs at that and sets up a round of shots for one of the waitresses. "Not sure I have enough hair left to sit under a dryer these days, anyway," he says, and I catch his eyes flicker back toward the door. "Too bad he left, huh?"

My fingers pause on the cash register and I look over at him. "What are you talking about?"

"The guy you were giving shit to yesterday."

"I think we both know that doesn't really narrow it down for me, Fred," I say with a saccharine smile.

He snorts. "You know who I'm talking about. Cocky one with all the hair."

"Luke is really going to like that you complimented his hair."

"Oh, *Luke*. You learned his *name*," he says mockingly.

He continues, laughing only half to himself. "He looks like a Luke. Luke and London . . . Luke and London of San Diego and Port Charles. You could be living a soap opera, kiddo."

I brush by him on my way to the cooler.

Fred finishes ringing up a customer and turns back to me. "So tell me. What point did he prove to you?"

I consider this while I open a bottle of Zinfandel, thinking back on what exactly it was about Luke leaving with the brunette that bothered me most. "I think it reminded me I need to trust my instincts."

Fred's smile softens. "We could probably all stand to do a little more of that."

"Probably."

After he opens a couple of beers for two guys at the bar, Fred turns back to me. "Who was that dragging him out of here?"

I laugh. It definitely didn't look like Luke was being dragged anywhere. "I have no idea. Random Girl Number Whatever."

"You two know each other pretty well, then?"

Giving Fred a little warning glance, I duck down to shelve the wine bottle, saying, "Don't you have something else you should be doing?"

He looks exceedingly pleased with himself. "Something besides mixing drinks and hassling you?"

"Yeah."

"Unless Harlow's coming around, then not really." He pauses. "But I *am* a bartender and have been told I'm a pretty good listener if you need to talk when things slow down a little."

I lift my chin to him in thanks and move to the other end of the bar. The thing is, I don't need to talk. Does it sting that Luke had sex with me less than twenty-four hours ago and just walked out of the bar with another woman? A little. Not because I feel like my honor has been tarnished or I wanted more of Luke for myself, but because it makes me feel a little disposable, and, despite my better judgment, I liked him.

I'll get over it.

———

A COUPLE OF hours later, I walk out of the storage room carrying a case of hard liquor and see that Luke is back. Alone.

I slow my steps as I close the distance between us, trying to figure out how I'm going to get out of interacting with him, but he looks up at the sound of bottles clanking and his face lights up.

"If it isn't my favorite bartender," he says, flashing me his warm smile. "I thought you'd left, *London*."

I feel my own smile flicker across my mouth when he emphasizes using my correct name, and he watches me balance the box on the sink and open it, pulling out bottles and setting them on the counter. My fallback persona is *bubbly,* but in this job—and especially with guys like Luke—I've had to train myself to be a bit more reserved. So far with him I sort of suck at it.

But what sucks even more right now is I'm a captive audience behind the bar, and I just don't know what else we possibly have to talk about.

He's still smiling as if he's genuinely happy to see me, and damn if that same pull isn't still there between us, drawing the hesitation out of me.

"Here all night," I say, and I hope my smile is the appropriate balance of friendly yet distant. "I didn't see you come back in."

He's in the middle of taking a drink when I say this, and his eyes widen over the top of it.

" 'Come back in'?" Luke sets his beer down in front of him and spins the coaster so the logo is facing up.

My mom says when I was younger, she could always tell when I was lying or stalling for time: I'd frown and scrunch my brows together until I had this little line in the center of my forehead. Apparently I still do it; she says it's my tell. I wonder now if Luke has a tell, too, and if that's what I'm seeing in the subtle way he's fidgeting. He's been so calm and smooth all this time, seeing him like this is like watching a gazelle play cards with a lion.

"Yeah, I saw you leave with your friend. And yet, here you are."

"You mean Dylan?" He turns his cocktail napkin so that it's facing logo side up, too.

It takes me a second to realize *he* means Not-Joe. I smile, knowing I've inadvertently cracked an enormous mystery among my friends: *Who in the ever-loving hell* is *Not-Joe?*

"I think we both know I'm not talking about *Dylan*."

Luke laughs and I know the second he's pulled himself together because he smiles and it's a magic trick the way the cocky-jock-curtain parts across his face. I have zero doubt Luke Sutter could charm his way out of almost anything.

"You mean *Aubrey*," he says, nodding as if the pieces are finally coming together for him. "I just drove her home."

I snort. "I bet you did."

"I was making sure she didn't try to drive," he says. "Besides, you had your wicked way with me yesterday and then barely looked at me tonight. When could you possibly have noticed me leaving?"

Now it's my turn to laugh. "Luke, it's totally fine. There's zero weirdness on this end because you know where I stand. I'm just giving you shit."

"Come on now, Dimples." He immediately reaches into his pocket and pulls out a dollar bill, stuffing it in the jar. "I was just being a friend."

Unable to resist, I tease, "Is 'being a friend' code for getting your dick sucked in the backseat?"

A laugh bursts from his throat. "It wasn't like that," he says, and one side of his mouth ratchets up a tiny bit higher than the other. "I promise."

I pull a bottle from the group, open it, and replace the cap with a pour spout.

"Hang out with me for a bit," he says quietly. "Tell me a story."

I'm pulled up short for a breath by the sweetness of this request. As much as I want to, I just can't peg this guy.

"In case you didn't notice," I say, motioning to my white shirt, apron, and the bar around us, "I'm sort of working right now."

He looks around the bar. "Yeah, but it's slow. Only about half the tables are full and most of those are dudes eating potato skins and drinking beer. They'd only call you over to see your legs in that skirt." He stretches on his barstool to get a better look. "I know I would."

I swat at him with a bar towel. "Why aren't *you* hanging out with your friends?"

He shrugs. "My friends are all assholes, and none of them can beat me at Titanfall."

I bite the inside of my cheek to keep from smiling. "I'd think that'd be a selling point, given your sad performance. How's the manly pride today?"

He leans in and grins. "I think we both know my manly pride recovered just fine last night."

I roll my eyes, fighting a laugh, and move to step away, but he reaches for my arm.

"And totally serious for a minute," Luke says. "Tell me how you got so good at that game. I'm man enough to admit that I got spanked, but I need you to tell me all your secrets."

I shrug, working my arm away from his gentle grip. The feel of his hand makes me flush, and I remember how they felt curled around my hips, working my body over his. "Just a lot of practice."

"See, now I never would have guessed that. And not because you're a girl," he says, holding up a hand when he seems to anticipate what I guarantee would be a brilliant feminist rant, "but because you look like you spend all your time on a surfboard, not sitting on a couch."

"Well, I *should be* building my portfolio to start looking for a real job, but I'm a brilliant procrastinator," I tell him. "The video games call to me."

Luke considers this. "Portfolio? Where'd you go to school?"

"UCSD. Graduated last spring. Graphic design."

He looks confused, glancing to the colored bottles of liquor over my shoulder, to the rest of the bar, and then back to me. "And yet you're here."

"I am," I say, and he seems to let it drop for now.

Luke and I fucked and we aren't really even friends, so I have to give him credit for not asking why I'm tending bar at Fred's instead of using the degree I obviously paid a small fortune for. Points for the boy.

"What about you?" I ask. "There were some hefty stacks of books at your place."

"I graduated last spring, too. Studied poli-sci."

"Wow," I say, impressed. "What about sports?"

"Soccer for fun, water polo more seriously."

Water polo. I give myself a mental high five for having guessed this the first time I saw him, and then my heart dips a little. The UCSD men's water polo team won two national championships while we were there. Luke has to be an amazing athlete.

I swipe a bar towel across the prep space in front of me. "Wow," I say quietly. "Water polo. That's . . ." *Impressive.*

He waves this off. "So you spend all day surfing and work here at night, somehow perfecting your man-crushing gamer talents in your downtime."

"Pretty much," I tell him.

"Are you woman enough for a rematch?"

I'm about to remind him that no, last night was a one-time thing, when the outside door opens and a slice of the setting sun cuts across the floor. It's Mia, followed by towering, gangly Ansel.

I smile and she bounces on her feet, waving. It's only when I turn back to Luke that I see he's followed the shift in my attention, and he's looking right at my friend and her oversexed husband. Luke's sixty-watt smile dims and he blinks quickly down to his beer, continuing to spin the coaster beneath it.

When I turn, I see that Ansel has his arms wrapped around Mia's front, and is steering them both toward a booth in the far corner. Luke still hasn't said anything.

It doesn't take a genius to figure out there's some sort of connection between Luke and Mia, especially since I did see them in conversation the other day, I recall. So I guess it's up to me to decide if I care enough to ask.

I'm not sure I do.

"Well, as fun as this has been, I have a few more things to grab," I say, stepping out from behind the bar.

Luke still doesn't seem to have snapped out of whatever was bothering him, and quietly nods in my general direction.

I wave at Fred as I head back to the stockroom. Fred was recovering from a slipped disk when I started, and Harlow basically threatened to hang his balls from the dartboard if she caught him lifting anything heavier than a bottle of Bombay.

I'm still getting to know Harlow, but I've learned enough to know that she's 1) nosy, 2) *really* nosy when she cares about someone, and 3) in possession of one hell of a temper. I'll carry as many boxes from the storeroom as it takes to never experience that temper firsthand.

When I get back to the bar—arms full—Luke slides off his stool to greet me.

"Jesus, let me help you," he says, taking the cardboard box off my hands.

"Thanks," I say, and shake out my arms. "That one was heavier than it looked."

"How many more of those do you have?" he asks, looking back over my shoulder.

"Just a few," I tell him, cutting the tape open to check the contents inside.

"Show me where they are and I'll help you. I helped my sister move a few weeks ago, and according to her I missed my calling in manual labor."

"No, I can—" I start to say, but he's already shaking his head.

"I'm not offering because of some chivalrous bullshit reason or because you're a girl and I think you can't do it alone—I think we both know you can probably do whatever the hell you want," he says with a wink. "I'm offering because the sooner you're done, the sooner I can monopolize more of your time."

"Thanks," I say again, ignoring the way his words make my blood vibrate in unexpected pleasure, and motioning for him to follow me. "But there'll be no *hanging out* going on back there. No *being a friend*. Just to clarify."

"I know, I know," Luke says, rounding the bar and offering Fred the requisite Man Nod as we pass. I don't miss Fred's smug *I told you so* expression when his gaze flickers to me, and I give him a threatening look before ducking around the corner and down the hall.

It's so much quieter back here, away from the sharp crack of the pool table, the clink of glasses, or shouts aimed at the TVs.

Luke peeks inside Fred's office, and then stops just outside our tiny break room. It's more of a kitchen, really, with a refrigerator and a microwave, and sometimes after work I fall asleep in the worn leather chair in the corner.

"Glamour, right?" I say, and lean in to see what's caught his eye.

He looks around and shrugs. "I like it," he says. "The break room at my office has ergonomic chairs and three different espresso machines. Honestly, I feel like an asshole just sitting in there."

I laugh as I continue on into the storeroom. Luke follows me in, standing in the middle and looking around for a moment, before joining me where the boxes are stacked and reaching out for me to hand him something.

"Hey, can I ask you a question?" he says.

I check my list and then search the boxes for the right label. "Sure."

"This is really none of my business, but how do you know Mia?"

I look up at him, surprised. "Mia? She's best friends with my roommate, Lola. Why?"

Instead of answering, he asks, "You live with Lola?"

"Yeah, we were always in the art buildings at the same time," I tell him. "We didn't hang out much outside of school, but she moved in last summer and is quickly becoming my favorite human."

"Other than me, of course," he says with a grin, before helping me by grabbing a box high on the shelf.

I mumble out a thanks and go back to studying my list. Luke is sweet, definitely attentive, and a total fucking flirt.

Danger.

"No problem," he says. "So Mia is more Lola's friend than yours?"

That's an odd question. "I guess. I mean, we're friends, but I haven't known her that long. How do *you* know them?" I ask.

Luke shifts the box to one arm and runs a hand along the edge of a shelf. "We grew up together: Me, Mia, Lola, and Harlow. We all went to the same high school."

When I don't say anything in response, he looks up. He must notice the subtle lift of my brow implying *and?* because he adds, "We've sort of known each other forever."

It feels like there's more, but this is Luke and there probably always is.

Besides, I can certainly appreciate his desire to keep his cards close to the chest.

I turn away and go back to my boxes.

"So have you been in Fred's before?" I ask. "I don't think I've ever seen you."

"Once, a few months ago, but Dylan likes the vibe so we came back. Lucky for me you work here," he says with another grin.

I roll my eyes but it's surprisingly hard not to smile back. His smile is infectious.

And as if I need a reminder that his good mood is likely the direct result of a booty call, his phone goes off in his pocket. He pulls it out and glances down at the screen, and I watch the way it illuminates his face. I'd consider giving up every dollar in the car fund tonight to see what is making his eyes go wide right now.

"Good news?" I ask.

He knows he's been caught, but I'm not sure if it's that or whatever he's just read that has him more flustered.

"Just a friend," he says, pocketing his phone again.

"Uh-huh." I straighten and check the last thing off my list, and feel him just behind me. He reaches around to take a small box of cocktail straws out of my hands and I can smell his subtle cologne, feel the heat of his arm through the fabric of my shirt.

"Thanks for letting me help," he says, and I look over my shoulder, his face only inches from mine. This room suddenly feels way too dark and way too small for two people. Especially if those two people have had sex and aren't supposed to do it again.

"You're a lot of fun, Logan."

"Easy, tiger."

Luke laughs, sending little bursts of warm air across my skin. "I meant in more of a general sense but, yeah. That, too, obviously," he says, gently squeezing my hip before he steps back and toward the door. Goose bumps make their way across my body and I try to hide a shiver.

Luke Sutter is going to be trouble.

Chapter FOUR

Luke

"DO YOU NEED me to send them?"

For a beat, I think I haven't heard Margot correctly, but knowing my sister, odds are I have.

I pull into a parking spot, shut off the ignition, and put my phone to my ear when my car's Bluetooth disconnects. "Do I need you to mail my law school applications?"

"It's just that the bulk of them are due Tuesday," she continues, "and—"

"Margot—"

"—the post office is just down from here so it's easy for—"

"Margot." I cut her off as gently as possible. "Seriously. I can handle this. Everything is all taken care of. Listen, I just got off work and am starving. Can we talk later?"

"I'm just excited for you," she says, mildly sheepish now. "Your application is so strong. I know I'm being super-controlling, but it's such a big deal . . ."

I sigh, nodding. I'm lucky to have such an involved older sister, but there are days I want her to have just a few more things in her life to distract her from living mine as well. "I know, Gogo."

She quiets, sighing as the name I've used for as long as I can remember makes her stop and take a breath. "Do you feel ready for all of this?" she asks. "It's only a few months left here and then somewhere new."

"Unless I go to UCSD."

"But you won't. I know you. I can tell you want to move."

"Yeah," I agree. "I think I'm ready for a change." We've had this conversation a hundred times—maybe more—and I do want to prepare her for the chance that I'll be across the country this time next year. Margot gives me more shit than everyone else in my life combined, but she's still my best friend. Staying close to her is really the only argument for going to UCSD Law next year. "I mean, sometimes it's overwhelming. Like, yesterday—"

"Wait, let me conference in Mom."

I sit up in my seat, eyes wide. "For the love of God, *why?*" But she's already gone.

I stare around the parking lot—home of the most delicious Mexican food in my neighborhood, and where I hope is also the location of my dinner sometime in the near future—and watch a handful of seagulls fight over a few scraps of tortilla someone has thrown their way. My stomach growls.

Two seconds later I hear the line click, and Margot asks, "Everyone here?"

"Yeah," I mumble.

"Here," Mom says brightly. "What's going on, Bubbles?"

Mothers and nicknames. Honestly.

"Nothing," I say. "I honestly have no idea why I'm not eating dinner right now instead of having a conference call."

"Luke was nervous about applications," Margot says.

"Margot, I swear I'm not nervous!" I tell her. "They're all *done*."

"Oh, that's wonderful, honey! Did you mail them?" Mom asks, and I groan.

"They're due Tuesday," my mother and sister remind me in unison.

"Funny thing," I say. "I dressed myself this morning. Had breakfast. Managed to get to work without any help at—"

"It's easy for me or Daddy to take them down," Mom says over me.

"Or me," Margot adds.

"I even shaved without incident," I tell them, but I know they're not listening to me.

"Luker," Margot says, completely undeterred, "did you ever apologize to Mia?"

Oh, my evil bitch of a sister.

"Mia *Holland*?" Mom asks.

Margot confirms with a chirped, "Yep."

I close my eyes, pinching the bridge of my nose and muttering, *"Jesus Christ."*

"Why does he need to apologize to Mia?" Mom presses.

I shake my head. "I should never tell you anything, Margot."

My sister laughs. "As if you could keep a secret from me."

"Luke," Mom interjects, "what happened with Mia?"

"Tell her," Margot urges.

I let my head thump back against the headrest and try to quickly figure out how much I really want to talk about this right now. I know they're invested. They truly love Mia, and always will. But life moves on. *We've* moved on.

Mia was my best friend. We didn't just share our first kiss and first touch and lose our virginity to each other—we were fucking *in love*. She was calm and quiet; I was outgoing and sometimes wild. She knew me better than I knew myself and that's so fucking clichéd, but it's the reality. I told her every-thing, and if I didn't tell her something it was only because she already figured it out on her own. That kind of shorthand came from knowing each other as kids and growing up in synch. We shared history. Any other woman coming into my life would get the abbreviated version of me, but get held up to the same yardstick. And I know that, at least for now, any other woman would fail. It wouldn't be fair.

I close my eyes as the conversation at Fred's the other night comes back to me.

Mia, introducing me to her husband.

Husband.

She looks older, but not physically. It's in her eyes, the way they're steadier now, they don't blink away as readily. She didn't stutter or prolong a single word. She introduced him—I couldn't even hear his name over the sound of blood pounding in my ears—and I was . . .

I was horrible.

"Husband? You're . . . married?" I'd asked, dumb-founded. We don't run in the same circles anymore. I knew she was seeing someone, but married? The information floored me. Literally tossed my lungs onto the floor.

Her husband stepped closer to her side as she told me, "We got married in June."

Ignoring him, I asked her, "After knowing him how long?"

"Not that it's your business," she said with a tiny smile up at him, "but, yeah, we were in Vegas and—it just happened."

I felt my face tighten in disgust. No, not disgust. Hurt. "Seriously? A cliché Vegas wedding, Mia? There really is nothing left of the girl I knew, is there?"

The memory of her expression after I'd said it makes me feel like I've been kicked in the chest.

"Seriously, you guys," I say, shaking my head to clear it. "It was *nothing*. We ran into each other, I was rude."

"Rude?" Mom asks, and God love her for seeming unable to imagine such a thing.

"Mia is married," Margot says in a scandalized hiss. "To a *French guy*. A *law instructor* at *UCSD*."

"How wonderful!" Mom practically shouts. "I need to send them a gift."

"Yes, good idea," I agree dryly. "You guys, I'm starving. Can I go?"

"You should call Mia," Margot says.

"I'm not calling Mia, you brat."

"Are you eating out, Luke?" Mom asks. "Why don't you just come home for dinner? I made chicken and rice."

"Bye, Mom, I love you. Margot, you're dead."

I hang up.

I STEP INTO the restaurant, dodging other customers in my peripheral vision as I scroll through my texts. Just as I get in line to order, I hear a tiny snort and look up, catching the whip of blond hair as the snorter-in-question turns toward the counter.

So I'm left facing the back of a blond head that looks awfully familiar.

I pocket my phone. "Hello, Amsterdam."

I didn't expect to see London here, in line at my favorite Mexican joint only a few miles from work. But here she is, and my heart does something unfamiliar: it sort of jumps and then hammers, as if I'm particularly excited to see her.

She looks over her shoulder at me, and then tilts her head down as she does the lengthy inspection of my entire body. "Nice suit."

"Same," I tell her. Holy shit, I mean I've seen her naked, but catching her in a bikini top, little cutoff shorts, and flip-flops at sunset makes me feel moderately dizzy. "But who forgot to tell you it's cold outside?"

Tilting her head, she asks, "It's someone's job to tell me when it's cold?"

I open my mouth and close it, realizing I have nothing

witty to say. She turns back to the counter with a little smile, leaning forward to order. I can see the curve of her ass peeking out beneath her shorts. Honestly, I could wait in line all damn day with a view like this.

While she waits for her change, she turns a little to look back at me. "I don't think I know what you do during the day, because I would not have predicted the suit."

"What would you have predicted?"

"A Speedo?"

"Well," I say, "the one time I wore a Speedo to court I was fined."

She fights a smile, and studies me. "You're a *lawyer*?"

"Easy, high roller. I'm twenty-three and a half; still only a clerk. I'm *applying* to law school."

I watch her fight a groan. "Of course you are."

"I mean, it's not surfing all day and pouring drinks all night, but it's a start."

Fuck. That was sort of dickish.

I can tell how hard it is for Sunshine London to be outright dismissive of this, but she manages a tiny little *fuck you* smile as she turns away, grabbing a few cups of salsa and making her way over to the exit. She pushes the door open with her ass, and places the salsa on a table just outside. The words *Worthy Opponent* flash in my head before she turns and comes back inside to wait for her food.

When she looks up at me, her full mouth curls in a smile. I study her blond hair, freckles, and the whole length of her: forever-long legs in her tiny shorts, breasts somehow contained by the triangles of her bikini top. My attention returns to her face and I catch a glimpse of her open, unguarded expression—some vulnerability or curiosity about what I'm thinking—before she slips her defense back into place.

Her number is called and she picks up an enormous plate piled with some unidentifiable food. Holding it up to her nose, she inhales deeply. "I come here for the carne asada fries." With another little smile, she says, "See you later!" and heads back out to her table.

This girl, I swear.

I hadn't planned on taking my food to go, and with only four tiny tables it's a little awkward to sit in the same small restaurant but not together. My number is called, and after a pause, I grab my plate and follow her outside.

"Incidentally," I tell her, "I come here for the soyriza nachos."

London looks up as I set my food down in front of her. "What are you doing?"

I get it. This is a little weird, and as much as I might like her, I respect that the other night was a one-time thing. But I'm not going to eat soggy nachos in my car out of a Styrofoam container to avoid this.

"Hopefully eating," I say.

She laughs, waving her hands palms down over the table. "No. No. Nope. We don't have dinner together."

I slow my movements, but continue to sit anyway. "Is that the same thing as 'can't have dinner together'? Because I might have missed that in the rulebook."

Her blue eyes narrow playfully as she watches me unroll my fork and knife from the paper napkin. "Please don't make me regret sleeping with you."

"Technically, we didn't sleep. Remember that time we had sex on my couch, though?" I ask, pulling a large tortilla chip free of the pile. "That was pretty awesome."

"Yes," she agrees, pointing an accusing finger at me. "We did have sex on your couch, but—"

"And the floor."

"And the floor," she concedes with an eye roll. "But would—"

"And then back on the couch again."

She sighs, eyebrows raised as if she's making sure I'm done interrupting. I give her a tiny nod.

"Wouldn't it just be a lot easier if we avoided each other from here on out?" she asks.

I nod as I swallow, unfamiliar with being on the receiving end of this particular conversation. "Probably."

She stares me down. I stare back. Her eyes slowly—meaningfully—drop to my plate and then slide to the empty table next to us.

"Does this mean I shouldn't expect any naked selfies later?" I ask. "Or even selfies of you in that bikini?"

"I think you get plenty of selfie texts as it is."

As if to prove her point, my phone buzzes near my water bottle and London smiles, dimples flashing victoriously.

Planting my elbows on the table, I lean in, giving her my most earnest smile. "Look, Fresno—"

"*Fresno. Amsterdam.* You're hilarious."

"—*I'm* not going to make it weird. But all this worry about it being weird is going to make it weird. We're in the same tiny restaurant. We're grown-ups. It's just *food*." I pull a chip free and pop it in my mouth, chewing thoughtfully before saying, "Well, technically it's *just food* with a guy who saw you naked a couple nights ago. But if you really want me to move, I will."

She blinks away, and I can see a tiny flash of guilt cross her features. I've seen London interact with other people—she's bubbly, she cracks jokes and wears a constant smile—so I know this shell she's built around herself is really about guys and romance, not because she's an asshole.

At least, not really.

Looking back at me, she narrows her eyes a little as she studies me, and then bursts out laughing. "You have a giant black bean stuck to your front tooth."

Now that she's pointed it out, I can feel it. I grin wider, all teeth. "I have to do something to reduce my attractiveness to the ladies. It can't be full steam all the time."

London giggles at this as she takes a bite of her fries. "You're insane."

I lean in, and she laughs harder. "Can you believe this is the face of a man who, two nights ago, happily gave you four orgasms?"

She looks up at me, mouth straightening as the memory of our night together causes her cheeks to flush. "Three."

I pull the bean off my tooth and lean back in my chair,

staring at her. Waiting. I remember each of her orgasms *distinctly*—the sharp cry one, the gasping one, the *oh-fuck-oh-my-fucking-God* one, and the sweaty, unintelligible begging one—so I know she is full of shit.

"Okay, maybe four," she says with a little wave of her hand. And then she looks back up at me, brows drawn. "What's your point?"

I shake my head. "I don't have a point. I—"

"I mean, seriously." She's flustered now, blushing hotly. "What is your *point*? What is the point of"—she gestures up and down my body—"of all *this*? The fancy suit and shiny shoes and the fucking hair."

"I just got off work!" I bite back a laugh. "Wait, what is the point of my *hair*?"

"And that smile? You're . . . just . . ." She digs around for the right word, finally coming up with "*absurd*." And I don't know what it is about that word, but it thrills me. Seeing her pretend to be disgusted with me makes me oddly giddy.

"I don't think I know what you mean by 'absurd,'" I goad her.

"You're banging different women every night—"

"Not *every* night."

And here we go. Composed London is unraveling. "Did you always *want* to be the stereotype?"

"The straight-A, water polo player turned pre-law? Yeah, rough path. Scare me straight already."

She leans to the side, scanning the parking lot. "Do you drive a Hummer?"

"I drove you home in my *Prius*," I remind her.

She snorts. "You had a condom in your *pocket*."

"I wouldn't judge you if you had a condom in *your* pocket," I volley back.

Her eyes narrow. I have a point and she knows it.

"And I would have been happy to play video games all night," I add.

She aggressively shoves a fry into her mouth. "You had nothing but Sriracha in your fridge," she says around it.

"There was also celery and string cheese. And I made you come *four times*. Four. Do you even bother to do that with your box of toys beneath your bed?"

London chews on her straw, and then says, "What makes you think I have a box of toys under my bed?"

And I swear to God, she's blushing even more hotly now.

"You deny it?" I ask quietly.

She completely leaps over my question. "You banged someone else last night."

"Technically, I didn't."

She laughs. "So *technically* Aubrey *did* give you car head."

She didn't—she sucked on my neck and reached for my dick until I gently pried her hand away and walked her to her doorstep. But London's already got her mind made up, so why bother?

"You didn't even care that I called you by the wrong name all night!" I fire back. "Why does it matter to you whether I did or didn't get car head?"

Her eyes go wide. "It doesn't *matter* to me whether you

got car head. It matters to me that you won't just let what we did be a fun night, and you insist on"—she makes circular gestures at the table and then in the air—"*food*."

I cough out an incredulous sound. "I didn't follow you here. I'm just trying to be polite. You would prefer that I say a simple hello and take my nachos back to my place? Who's the manwhore here? It isn't me."

She looks to the side, which gives me an opportunity to admire the definition of her jawline, the smooth line of her throat. Her hair is sun-bleached and I can see a few grains of sand clinging to the nape of her neck. What is going on in that head of hers? I can't even begin to guess.

"You make me insane," she says quietly, more to herself than to me, as she stabs a fry into some salsa.

It hits me in an instant. "I think you don't like how much you like me," I say, unable to keep from smiling. "You can't fit me into your Barfly Box of Shame. You want to dismiss me as a dickhead player, but then you think I'm hot and fun and you like watching me eat nachos."

London turns her face back up to me, smirking. "Nailed it."

"Apt phrase." I pause, tossing another chip into my mouth before saying, "You sort of want to kiss me right now."

She leans in, studying my face. "You're thinking too much on this."

It's true. I am thinking way, *way* too much on this. But I also know I'm right. I bend, eating in silence for a minute, but I can feel her eyes on me the entire time.

"What?" I ask, pushing my plate away before wiping my mouth on my napkin.

"I need to head home and shower before work."

There's something there. Some . . . invitation? I feel my eyes go wide, wondering if I should gamble here.

"I live about three blocks away," I remind her.

London stands, carrying her plate to the trash can before turning to me. "*Fine*. But you still don't get to kiss my lady-bird."

LONDON'S COOL IS back in place when she pulls up at the curb behind my car. I watch her climb out and look around my yard as she walks up to meet me on my porch.

"I guess I didn't give much thought to the fact that you live alone in a house in La Jolla."

Tilting my head, I ask her, "Where do you live?"

"A loft downtown," she says. "My grandmother left it to me."

"Well, that's something we have in common then," I tell her, turning to the front door. "This house is Grams's." I slide the key in. "She lives in Del Mar now in a fancy retirement community. My sister, Margot, used to live here with me, but now she lives closer to campus with a roommate."

"Isn't UCSD, like, four miles from here?"

"Probably less, but she's in grad school. Biology. She hates to drive and needs to be close to the lab." I nod to indicate she lead us inside. "Come on in."

It's clear London isn't here for idle conversation. She turns and heads straight down the hall, looking over her shoulder at me when she asks, "Is it okay if I shower in the bathroom down here?"

"Yeah," I tell her, following. "You want company, or you want to rinse off alone?"

She's put on a T-shirt for the drive here and turns to me fully, pulling it up and over her head, unties her bikini, and drops it at the threshold to the bathroom. "If I wanted to shower alone, I would have just gone home."

My brows rise as I stare at her naked chest. "Fair enough."

This whole thing is weird, and abrupt, but I can get on board with it if it means showering with a wet, slippery London.

She climbs in, turning on the water and watching through the glass door as I undress. I follow her in, suddenly aware of the way my cock grows tight, poking her hip when she turns to kiss my neck.

"I can't really figure you out," I admit, closing my eyes when she drags her teeth along my jaw.

"I can't really figure me out, either, if that's any consolation."

It is, actually. She smiles up at me sweetly before turning and picking up the shampoo and putting it in my hand.

"But you're right: despite my instincts, I sort of like you," she says, kissing me once and then turning her back to me. "And I bet you give good shower."

"I like to think so." I work the shampoo into her hair, piling it on top and massaging her scalp. London leans back into me, and the hot water pounds against my chest. "This sort of reminds me of washing Margot's dolls' hair."

London goes still and then very slowly lifts her head and looks at me over her shoulder. *"What."*

I burst out laughing, pressing my face into the warm skin of her neck. "Yeah . . . I can see now that, without context, that was totally creepy. But we used to play doll salon. Being the younger and much-abused brother, I ended up as the shampoo girl. I would bring them to her for blow-dry and style. She would yell at me if I didn't properly condition."

"Margot sounds pretty awesome."

I nod, guiding her head a little to the side so I can massage her neck. "She is. And to this day Sephora is her church."

"It both thrills and vexes me that you're a dude who knows about Sephora."

"And Chico's," I tell her, enjoying how easy this all is— even when we're talking like this in the shower. "Also a place not often frequented by men, but Chico's is my Grams's jam. Come to think of it, Mom is a huge fan of Coldwater Creek." I pause, sudsy fingers deep in her hair. "Jesus, my weekends are dominated by chauffeuring the women in my life."

"A nice counterbalance to the weeknights dominated by chauffeuring the women in your phone."

I feel the way we both go still under the water. Just when I think it's easy between us, just when we're both unwinding, she goes there.

"Did I say that out loud?" she asks, turning her head but

eyes squeezed shut against the slow drip of suds down her forehead.

"You did."

"And are you glaring at me?"

"No." But I won't lie to myself and pretend her impression of me doesn't sting a little. I put my hands on her shoulders, guiding her around to face me. I wipe the soap from her brows, murmuring, "Rinse."

I can see in my peripheral vision that she's watching my face while I coax the water through her hair, rinsing away the suds, but instead of meeting her eyes, I focus on my hands.

"Logan?"

She smiles. "Yeah?"

"Why did you come over here again?" I ask her quietly.

She reaches for the soap and I shiver when her hands press to my stomach and slide up over my chest. "I'm not sure." She meets my eyes and gives me a sweet, tiny grin. "Sorry I was rude."

"You were taking your self-loathing out on me, I think. But then, you didn't have to come over here."

Her grin turns into a wide, dimpled smile. "You're not going to goad me into becoming one of the girls in your phone who insist they never do this kind of thing."

"I'm not trying to *goad* you. It's just that in your case, it seems to be true. Even if you hadn't told me our first night together, I would bet you never do this kind of thing. Not that there would be anything wrong if you did."

She nods, and watches her hands as she lathers up my

chest, my shoulders. I can barely hear her answer over the pounding water: "The sex was good. And I figured you were the kind of guy who can keep it just about sex, which is all I want right now."

"I can."

I think.

I mean, it's never been a problem before, but I'm troubled by how much I want her to like me. "I'm going to be honest, though. You sort of suck at it." Her mouth drops open when I say this, and I quickly add, "Not the sex part—you're very good at that part, if memory serves—but the part where it's just about having *fun* sex together."

Her blue eyes flash up to mine. "What do you mean? I'm not getting emotional on you."

I laugh at her quick defense, tickling her sides. "I mean, you're sort of a jerk to me."

She giggles. "I'm sorry! I swear I'm not a jerk. I just . . . I don't want to date, and the kind of guy I *would* date anyway is nothing like you, but here I am . . . for sex. So yeah, maybe some self-loathing . . . which makes me into a jerk."

I'm trying to ignore the insult in there. "What kind of guy do you date?"

She looks up at me quizzically. "I don't."

I sigh in exasperation, squeezing conditioner into my palm while she washes my arms. I slide my fingers into her hair, saying, "I mean, you're saying I'm not your type. What *is* your type?"

"Bearded. Laid-back. Tattoos."

"Mustard yellow cord-wearing craft brewer?" I ask, and she laughs. "The kind of man who is heavily invested in his mustache wax, so he can get the upturned points just right?"

"Something like that." Her hands move back to my chest, down my stomach again. With her eyes on my face, she reaches lower, sliding a soapy hand down my cock.

Her cheeks flush and I shiver, eyes rolling closed as I jump in her palm. I want to tell her it feels good, I want to kiss her, but I'm immediately so consumed by the feel of her touching me that I'm stuck in place, water running down my face.

She lets out a little moan when her hand slides over the head of my cock.

"Not your type at all," I tease.

Her mouth presses to my collarbone. "Nope, not even a little."

She works her hand over me, slowly squeezing, and then stretches to kiss up my neck.

I cup her face, tilting her to look up at me. "We don't have to do this."

London stares at me, breathing in, breathing out. "We don't?"

What? "Of *course* not."

But she's teasing me. With a little smile, her lips part as she presses her mouth to mine, tongue sliding inside, warm and slick. Everything in me unravels. I find her breasts with my hands, press her to the tile and deepen the kiss, groaning into her mouth as I make tiny circles over her nipples with my thumbs. When I reach between her legs with one hand, finding her already silky with need, she pulls back from my mouth, letting her head fall back against the tile. I watch her—eyes closed, mouth soft and open, pulse thrumming in her throat—as my fingers move around, around, down, around. Fuck, she's sexy, and it's easy to figure out how to make her feel good: she likes being touched on the outside, quick and hard. I bend, sucking the water from her chin, her lips.

Her body slides against mine and I chase her mouth when she pulls back, giving me a tiny brow raise before whispering, "Condom?"

I lean out of the shower, fumbling in a cabinet drawer for one, and somehow manage to stand back up and hand it over without slipping.

She curls it in her fist and reaches for me with her free hand, stroking me, stretching on her toes for a kiss. My mind goes warm and shapeless when I return my fingers to her, and hear her relieved little gasp.

London tears the packet open with her teeth while my fingers stroke and stroke and stroke. I can feel how close she is in the tension in her thighs, so I don't need her to tell me "I'm close," but hearing it anyway pushes an electric charge into my blood.

It goes off like a bomb inside my chest when she adds: "I want to come with you inside."

London looks up into my eyes, smiling almost apologetically for asking for that sort of physical connection with me. "Is that okay?"

I nod, unable to reply aloud because

something

is breaking

wide-open in me.

I rub her bottom lip with the pad of my thumb, nodding again and again.

We're no longer headed toward a fun fuck, the rutting, confident sex I've been enjoying for years. I suddenly can't muster the out-of-focus tenderness I give so easily. This isn't even like the other night with her—two people experiencing something completely different, together.

Here, I'm peeled bare.

I want to make love to this sweet, distrustful girl.

It's confusing to need the reassurance of her mouth on mine, but I bend, taking her lips, sucking and pulling and opening her so I can taste her tongue and draw out those tight, hungry sounds.

She pulls away to focus, and I can feel her breath on my neck and the weight of her attention where her hands work the condom down my cock. Sounds seem to fall away one by one; even with the pounding of the water we're in a silent room, breathing in, breathing out. She reaches lower, cupping me, and at the sharp grate of my grunt I feel her eyes turn up to my face, taking stock of every detail of my reaction.

You're so hard. I don't hear her say this, but I see her mouth form the words, and stare at the water running down her face, tripping from her top lip.

I imagine what she sees: the tightness in my brow, my jaw. I swallow before trying—and failing—to form words. I don't even know what I would say right now, and everything rising up in me feels too intense to voice anyway. Her blond hair is plastered to her cheeks and down her neck. Her eyes are these enormous circles of turquoise lined with dark blue, lashes clumped together. Impossibly red, her lips are swollen from me. But it's the way that the caution has melted from her expression that makes something inside me ache.

She's making me want something I haven't considered in so long. Connection, stability, something familiar and just ours.

"I like this," she says quietly, and the way her eyes linger on mine, I know she's saying more. She's admitting she likes *me*.

I groan, knowing there's no filter remaining in my eyes, nothing hiding the way I'm impatient and needy, breathing so hard I'm panting. I reach for her thighs, pulling her legs up and around my waist and it's so easy to slide into her, wet like this, soft for me. I could slam deep with one push, fuck us both to satisfaction in a few sharp jabs, but it's an inch at a time that I want.

I want to feel that slide, the slow easing in.

I want to watch the relief take over every feature one by one.

I want her to see me.

A tiny flash of pain crosses over her face—a twitch of her forehead, a tight gasp—and I bend to kiss her, whispering, "Okay?"

"Yeah," she says, nodding. Her fingers move up my neck into my hair as a sly smile takes over her lips. "I just *never* do this sort of thing."

I laugh at this, but it melts into a groan as she turns into my neck, sucking, biting. When I'm deep in her I stay there and just push deeper, deeper, deeper, rubbing all over her until she's scratching at my back, pushing against me, slicing these tight, sharp noises straight into my ear.

I knew she was close but I didn't realize how fast it would be.

I pull back to look at her right when she breaks: her mouth falls open, her pussy goes tight, and shards of sound tear from her throat.

With my face pressed to her neck, something in me falls apart and I'm gripping her, fucking her, sucking at her skin and taking as much as I can get. Her orgasm goes on and on until she comes down, gasping for air and just watching me.

Watching me climb, watching me give in, watching me topple over and come with a rumbling groan.

Fuck, I can barely breathe. My arms are shaking and she's so slippery I have to adjust my grip so that I don't drop her. But her hands cup my face, her mouth searches for mine, and then we're kissing.

We're kissing and it's better than anything and I'm still inside her.

Everything is soft, drenched in water and these unwound, relieved touches are making it hard for me to imagine ever turning off the shower. It's such a simple thing—kissing after sex—but it's not. If it were simple it would be routine. I wouldn't roll off right after, take care of the condom before taking care of anything else. I wouldn't be thinking how long until we can get up, or whether she wants to stay over or whether I should offer her something to eat.

But London isn't done with me yet and I don't want to pull out. Not yet. Not quite. I like the feel of her, all pliable in my arms. I like the way it feels to come down in her.

I like the way it feels like we just did something rare together.

She tilts my face in her hands, kissing my jaw, sucking water from my bottom lip. Her blue eyes are bright and glassy, so close to mine. "You okay?"

I nod, whispering, "I think you're going to wreck me," before going back in for more of her mouth, but she ducks to the side.

"You're going to run out of hot water soon." She stretches, shifting her hips back, and I slide out of her before carefully setting her back on her feet.

It's been years since I felt the odd sense of ownership over a body, and the awareness jerks through me like a reflex. I run my hands down her sides to her hips. I smooth my palms over her ass when she bends to turn off the water. I let my hands slide back up her sides and to her breasts when she straightens with her back to me. Bending, I suck at her shoulder, biting, wanting to leave a mark that lets everyone else know that I was here. I like the way she fits against me, front or back, it doesn't matter. We fit.

"Where are your towels?" London looks at me over her shoulder, and she tries to hide a shiver.

"Shit, sorry, hang on." I climb out, wrapping the only towel on the rack around my hips before jogging to the linen closet to get her a fresh one.

She's climbing out when I return and hand it to her. I

watch her dry off from her feet up her body to her hair. I'm reeling from the sensation that she was my *girlfriend* only ten seconds ago.

"Believe it or not," she says, "that was the first time I've showered with someone."

I bring the towel up to my hair, rubbing it dry. "Really?"

She looks up and freezes before coughing out a laugh. "Oh my God, your *face*. You look so proud."

"It's not a huge mystery that guys like to be the first. Discovering America. Inventing shit. Showering with London."

"That's pretty sexist. Women also like—"

I interrupt her gently with one hand up. "Yeah, yeah. But maybe not in the pathological way guys do." I stare at her until she meets my eyes. "Settle down, I'm just happy to be the first. I'm not planting a flag or anything."

Finally, she gives me a smile. Her eyes soften, take in my whole face before she looks into my eyes again. Fuck me, her expression is so sweet, so . . . *happy,* and I take a step forward—

She blinks, gaze cooling, and there it is: she remembers that we're naked under our towels and she's not supposed to like a guy like me. "Can I borrow some clothes? I need to drive home and change for work but don't want to put my sandy stuff back on."

"Didn't plan very well, did you?"

Her eyes narrow and she tries to look annoyed but totally fails. "I *planned* on showering at home."

She follows me to the bedroom, watching as I pull a pair of basketball shorts and a T-shirt out of a drawer.

"Do you want . . . ?" I trail off, holding up a pair of boxers in the other hand.

"Nah." Taking the shorts, she drops the towel and sits at the edge of my bed. Naked. And now I'm left thinking about how she'll be wearing my shorts with nothing between her—

"You're staring."

I blink out of my trance and say the first thing that comes to mind: "You really never showered with a boyfriend? That just seems so . . . obvious."

London shrugs, pulling the string at the waist tight. "I've only really had one boyfriend," she says, and looks up as if she expects me to find this weird. For obvious reasons, I do not. I lift my brows to tell her she should finish answering the question. "We were together a really long time, but no . . . we didn't shower together."

"What a loser, then."

"You have no idea." She laughs, and disappears as she pulls the shirt over her head.

And, *ah,* I get it. "He cheated, didn't he?"

When she reemerges from the shirt, she eyes me warily. "How did you know?"

"You have that All Men Are Assholes vibe."

"It's been my experience that most men are cheaters at some point."

I feel my head jerk back slightly. "'Most men'? That seems a little harsh."

She shrugs. "I'm not really in a business where I meet a lot of sincere gentlemen."

"Why do you work at a *bar*, then?" I pause when she doesn't answer and then wince. "There's no good way to say this, so here goes: You have a degree. You don't need to sling drinks for a living."

"It's not as easy to find a job as you may be thinking, lawyer boy. Also, I like mixing drinks. The schedule is good. I surf during the day and do some freelance stuff in my free time. Bartending makes good money. Freelancing . . . does not. Not yet."

"Freelance graphic design?"

"Yeah. Some drawing. Logos. Videos. Websites." She grows tight; shoulder pulled in, palms pressed together, hands captured between her knees where she sits on my bed. Her body screams, *Can I go now?*

I recognize the posture. I've *worn* that posture. For some reason, it rankles me after what we just did, and makes me want to keep her here longer. Why is my instinct with her always to push, just a little?

"Well, there's never any danger of meeting someone if you work from home, or at a bar where you're sure to never meet anyone you like."

She looks up at me, and her blue eyes seem to glow in the darkening room. "What about you? When was the last time you had someone you'd consider a girlfriend?"

"Freshman year."

She gives me an incredulous look. "That's four *years* ago."

"I know. But we were together for a while before then." I sit at the edge of my bed next to her and bend, resting my elbows on my thighs. I'm still only in my towel.

"Luke?"

I can feel her eyes on my face, and turn to look over at her. Just by her expression I know she's putting two and two together. "Yeah?"

"How *exactly* do you know Mia?"

I smile but I don't feel it move past the twist of my lips. "She's my ex."

"Oh." Her eyes fall closed. "*Oh*. I've heard mention in passing of the boyfriend before Ansel. You *were* together for a long time."

"Our first kiss was when we were twelve."

"And your last?" she asks.

My heart hurts with a phantom limb pain, the way it always does when I remember: we both knew it was the last kiss. "Nineteen."

London stands, opening her eyes, wiping her hands down her sides, and looking around as if searching for something. "I feel a little weird about this all of a sudden."

I follow her when she walks into the bathroom, picking up her pile of discarded clothes. "God, why?" I ask. "*Mia* certainly doesn't care."

"She doesn't know about *this*," she says, motioning between us. "I mean, Mia and I aren't, like, best friends or anything, but we are friends and apparently I've been banging her ex."

"We haven't really 'been banging.' You've banged me twice and actually, I've done most of the work. You can claim thirteen percent responsibility and then you can shirk that, if you want, since you didn't know I was her ex."

She doesn't even crack a smile at this as she walks out of the bedroom to the kitchen, slipping on her flip-flops. "Still. *Ugh.*"

I've hit pause on the growing interest inside me, shut off any real reaction to this. I like London but she's got some weird chick force field around her I'm not even going to pretend to understand, and this Mia thing seems to make it stronger.

"Well, regardless, today was nice," I tell her quietly.

She nods but won't look at me. "It was."

I know she won't use it but I can't help giving her my number. Tearing the back off an envelope on the counter, I write it down and slide it across to her. "In case you ever want another complimentary shampoo."

She stares at it before taking the pen from me, tearing off another piece, and writing something down. With a dry laugh, she slides it to me, grabs her keys, and heads to the front door.

In case of emergency.
Logan: 619-555-0127

After I hear her car pull away from the curb, I dial the number and laugh in spite of myself when a deep male voice answers the call: "Fred's Bar, Fred speaking."

Chapter FIVE

*T*HE STAIRS LEADING down the front of Luke's little La Jolla house seem a lot longer than they did going up. It's like I can't move fast enough and end up taking them two at a time, skipping the last one entirely and landing a little too hard on the pavement at the bottom.

Like last time, my legs are less than steady as I cross the yard, my muscles shaky and the words *What the hell am I doing?* playing on a loop inside my head.

How on earth does someone like Luke hook up with me, get car head the next night, and then show up at my favorite Mexican place looking completely gorgeous and being totally funny and *interesting* and charm his way right into my pants?

Again?

My car is parked at the curb and I look around at the other houses as I unlock the door and climb inside, suddenly conscious of the fact that I'm wearing different clothes than when I went in—*Luke's* clothes—that my hair is still damp and drying in a tangled mess. That I just left a booty call.

I said I wasn't going to do this again, and yet here I am, doing the walk of shame like it's my job, after having sex so good I doubt I could walk without a limp if I tried. No wonder his phone is always blowing up.

I check my mirrors and pull out into traffic, and try not to replay exactly *how* good it was. I try not to dwell on the fact that he drives his sister and grandmother around on the weekends, that he can name the stores they shop in, and that every time I've been around him, he's actually really nice. I'm definitely not thinking about the way I left him standing in his kitchen with only a blue towel tucked low on his hips, or that I can still smell his soap on my skin.

"Complimentary shampoo," I mumble, checking my mirror again before switching lanes. "What a jerk."

And the closer I get to home, the more the thing with Mia starts to bother me. I knew she'd had a boyfriend for a long time, but we *never* talk about him. It's not an omission for a reason; it's just not part of her day-to-day reality anymore. I'm not sure I'd ever heard his name. If I had, it was really forgettable, apparently.

At the bar he'd said they grew up together, not that they were together for *seven fucking years*. It's not really common for people our age to have someone they were with for seven years—it's *huge*. He knew Mia and I are acquaintances, at least, and didn't even think to mention it?

But to be fair . . . I haven't exactly been forthcoming during the get-to-know-you game, so he'd have zero way of knowing it would even be a thing, or that he should talk to me about any of his past relationships. I certainly haven't. We hooked up, that's it.

Still. I asked, and he deflected with an outright lie. And I *am* friends with Mia. Not best friends or as close as I was with Ruby before she moved to England, or even Lola and Harlow, but friends nonetheless. There are a few cardinal rules every girl should live by: always tell another girl when she has something in her teeth or her nose, or when her dress is tucked into her panty hose. Always provide tampons to a fellow female in need and, by extension, alert them of Shark Week accidents. If another female is drunk and needs a friend, help her.

And never, ever go after a friend's ex.

Basic Girl Code.

I know Mia is happy and she and Ansel are the picture of wedded bliss, but I need to call her. Today. Before I lose my nerve.

Lola's on her way out when I step into the loft, and I feel a shiver of guilt make its way up my spine.

"Hey, you," she says, checking her wallet before dropping it in her purse.

"Hey." I slide the door closed behind me, drop my keys on the table, and lean against the wall. "How was L.A.—wait, are you leaving again?"

"I have this . . . thing," she says, "back up there. Oliver's driving with me because I will cry the entire drive if I have to do it alone again."

At the sound of his name, Oliver rounds the corner, smiling when he sees me.

"London Bridge," he says, and bumps my shoulder as he passes. "I gave out one of your cards today. A regular who runs a couple breweries asked who did my site, and I told him about you."

"Thanks, Olls," I say.

As a general rule I don't do commissions for family and friends—things have a tendency to get weird whenever money is involved, and so I try to steer clear—but to this day, Oliver's site is one of the best things I've ever done. And it paid well, too. A few more jobs like that and I'd be well on my way to a kickass portfolio.

Lola closes her bag and does a quick inspection of what I'm wearing. "If I had to guess, I'd say those aren't your clothes."

Crap.

"How do you know I don't wear men's basketball shorts and T-shirts when you're not around?" I deflect, going into the fridge and grabbing the last Red Bull. I have a long night ahead of me. "I have a very eclectic style."

She takes a step toward me and pushes my hair behind my shoulder, so she can read whatever's written across my chest.

"I don't. But I do know that you aren't now, nor have you ever been, a member of the UCSD Water Polo Team."

Double crap.

I turn, waving her off, and put down my drink so I can pretend to sort through the mail. "Borrowed it from one of the guys at the beach," I say.

"Uh-huh. I'd question that, but since you've sworn off men, and I'm in a hurry, I'll take you at your word. For *now*," she adds meaningfully, and loops her purse over her shoulder.

With this little dig I'm reminded that Luke basically called me a man hater, and made some little crack about my "Barfly Box of Shame."

Luke's wrong, *of course*. I don't think all men are assholes. Finn, Ansel, and Oliver are pretty great. My dad can be fun—when he's not cheating on my mom—and I'm quickly beginning to adore Fred. But now I'm irritated all over again and *still* have to talk to Mia.

Lola and Oliver leave and I shower again, knowing the conversation might be a little easier to get through without the scent of Luke's shampoo clinging to my hair.

I'm suddenly starving and eat a tuna fish sandwich while standing at the counter.

I decide to rearrange and fix a hinge that's been squeaking, and check my bank balance on my phone. Basically, I stall.

With the loft paid for and only a few small student loans looming, I'm pretty good for money in the short term. Can I afford to surf all day and work at Fred's at night and get by? Sure. Is there any left for much else? Not really. I wasn't completely joking about the car fund because I actually do need to replace my car, and there's a new graphics program I'd like to get my hands on—one that will let me do bigger sites with more complicated plugins—but there's no way it'll happen if I'm just working at the bar.

Luke has a way of finding all my buttons, and pushing them while wearing that goddamn infuriating smile. Asking why I'm still tending bar is definitely one of them. He's right,

I don't need to, but people don't like to pay for design work from someone without a ton of experience. My portfolio is shaping up, but it's not enough. Not yet. Unfortunately, Fred doesn't have any more hours to give me and I'd rather shave off my eyebrows than ask my parents for money. A second job would definitely help and I make a mental note to ask some of my bartender friends about extra shifts at one of the local clubs.

That could be a good thing. I've gone home with Luke twice now; I definitely have too much free time on my hands.

Which brings me back to what I'm supposed to be doing: calling Mia.

I decide to woman up, and scroll through my contacts, stopping on Mia's name. I don't normally call Mia out of the blue—I might call to track down one of the other girls, or to clarify plans—so she doesn't even have a contact photo next to her name.

She picks up on the second ring and after a moment of frozen, startled silence, I realize I have no idea exactly how to have this conversation.

"Hello?" she says a second time, and I snap back to my senses.

"Hey," I say, pacing the floor of my living room and thankful beyond reason that Lola isn't here to see me. "This is—"

"London! Hey, how are you?"

"I'm really good," I say, and twist a piece of hair around my finger. "How are you guys?"

"We're great!" she says, and she really does sound great, happy, so much so that I have an image of the word actually bursting out of her. "Ansel is all settled in at UCSD, and my dance classes are so fun. The kids are adorable."

"And the house?"

"The house is awesome. We started talking about what we're doing for the holidays this year and it hit me all of a sudden that we are grown-ups who are married and own a home together. Will this ever stop feeling like someone else's life I'm living?" she asks rhetorically. "What about you, what have you been doing? I saw you the other night but you were gone before I could come say hi."

How am I? I finally figured out how to turn on the TV, the sound system, *and* the cable box, all with the same remote. I mainlined the entire first two seasons of *Veronica Mars* in a single day and thus didn't leave the house once that weekend. Oh, and I haven't had to use my vibrator in a week because I've been having sex with the boy you lost your virginity to.

Gah.

I drop down into a chair and scrub my hand over my face. "That's actually what I wanted to talk to you about," I say. "Who I've been doing"—I freeze and my eyes go wide in horror—"*What* I've been doing."

Mia's adorable laugh bursts forth. "Okay?"

"So, listen, I didn't realize it at the time, but I started—" I stop because I started what? Going out with? No, that's definitely not what Luke and I have been doing. "I started hanging out with this guy," I say—and yeah, that's better, not *too* subtle and technically not a lie. "The thing is that when I started . . . seeing him—this guy—I had no idea you two had dated."

"Who *I* dated?" She goes quiet, and then her voice comes back a little smaller. "Wait, are we talking about Luke?"

I briefly consider lying or just hanging up all together, but I know this is something I have to do. "Yeah. I saw you two talking the other night, but didn't really make the connection until today."

I don't know what I expected, but I know what I'd hoped for: a laugh, an immediate reassurance. Something to let me know this isn't as big a deal as it feels.

Instead I get a stunned: "Oh my God. You're seeing *Luke*?"

"I'm not really seeing him," I clarify. "It just felt weird when I found out about your history, with us being friends and all."

"I mean," she starts, and then laughs once, breathily. "Sorry, this just surprised me. It's fine—we've been over a long time, London—it's just a surprise," she says again. "I think my brain needs a second to catch up."

"Mia, just so you know, it's really not a thing between us at all." I'm not sure if this helps my case because now I've basically admitted we're only fucking. "It was this thing that sort of happened; he didn't even have my name right at first."

Oof. *Stop talking, London.*

Her laugh is stronger this time, more convincing. "No, no. I mean, you don't have to explain how Luke is. He's been with girls I know before, it's just . . ." She falls silent, and I can tell we're both struggling to find the best thing to say.

"Weird to hear about it, I'm sure," I finish for her.

"Yeah, a little."

I think of Luke's phone constantly going off, of watching him leave with the brunette. I imagine what it must be like for Mia to see that over and over. And now I feel worse.

"Look, I know you don't know all the details but I'm actually okay now," she continues. I've heard stories of what a mess Mia was, both physically and mentally, in the years following her accident. But that Mia bears no resemblance to the one I met when she returned from France late last summer. The one who was so in love with her husband I have a hard time believing she'd ever been with anyone else at all. Mia sighs through the line. "We just—me and Luke, I mean—we went about things so differently afterward, you know?"

"Yeah," I say. Mia went on to marry the love of her life, and Luke is bringing home random girls every other weekend.

Luke might be all smiles and seem like he's moved on, but a part of me wonders whether he truly has.

"I want him to be happy," she says. "He's a great guy and deserves to find someone a bit more . . . settled. And honestly, London, if he ended up with someone like you and *was* happy . . ."

I feel my eyes widen and I stand from the couch. "Whoa, whoa, whoa," I say. "Luke and I . . . we're not a *thing*. We hung out a few times but that's as far as it went. As far as it's going to go."

She laughs. "I'm just saying, I don't want you to stop seeing him because of me. You haven't broken some kind of Girl

Code. Ansel is my husband, and my whole world. I do appreciate you calling, though."

I nod, even though I know she can't see me. I'm not sure I really feel any better. "Well, like I said, I wanted to be up front with you. Luke seems to keep popping up at Fred's and I wanted to avoid any awkward."

"I have noticed him hanging around a bit more," she says, teasing now. "Wonder why that is . . ."

"I see what you're doing," I say, smiling uncomfortably and sensing my exit from this awkward phone call. "And on that note I'll let you go. I should get to work."

———

THANKFULLY, I DON'T see Luke for a few days, and by the next weekend—just like I hoped—I've managed to land a second job at a club downtown. It's a bigger place, with celebrity DJs and the occasional pop star. It's a lot sexier and younger than Fred's, which means I'm expected to wear something on the skimpier side; there are more students and more young guys, and probably the need for another dimple jar.

It's also a lot bigger, so there are four of us behind the bar at all times, and at least half that many barbacks running around. The girls get hit on—the guys, too—but it's easy enough to put up with because the hours are exactly what I need, the tips are great, and if I can manage both jobs for a couple of months, I'll have the money I need for a car and better software before I know it.

Drunk people who are about to get laid are great tippers.

If Lola thought I was gone all the time before, it has nothing on the first week I'm juggling both jobs. I work almost every day while I learn the ropes, and by the time my only night off comes, I'm nearly comatose on the couch, surfing through channels for what has to be the third time. A forgotten Lean Cuisine congeals on the coffee table next to my laptop; if I had a cat on either side of me this Single Gal picture would be pretty much complete.

My phone rings at my side, and I wince when I see my mom's face flash on the screen. I consider ignoring it—I have never finished a call with my parents and felt anything other than disappointed in myself—but know that that's only prolonging the inevitable. If she doesn't talk to me tonight, she'll call tomorrow, and the day after that. It's probably better to get it over with while I'm in close proximity to the kitchen and that brand-new tub of mint chocolate chip ice cream.

"Hi, Mom," I say.

"London, honey. How are you?"

"I'm good. How are things at home?"

"I'm fine. Busy helping Aunt Cath plan the wedding. Your father's out of town, so it's nice to have something to do."

"Right. Out of town," I say, feeling my face heat. If my dad's out of town, then he's probably with his secretary—a woman he's been cheating on my mom with for years—and it's a subject I've learned isn't worth touching.

"You're not working tonight?" she asks.

"Nope, it's my night off."

"I called to see if you were absolutely positive you can't come out for Andrea's wedding. But if you're busy I can call back tomorrow."

"I'm just hanging out at home. And no, Mom, I just got a second job. There's no way I can make it."

She hums, disapprovingly, and I expect her to push but instead she asks, "Why are you at home on a Friday night? You're still not seeing anyone?"

I take a deep breath and count to ten in my head. "Nope, not seeing anyone."

"I worry about you out there all by yourself. London, you know you'll never meet anyone sitting at home every night. I wanted you to come out so I could introduce you to Paige Halloway's son. He's a few years older than you but—"

"Mom."

She sighs again. A long, drawn-out *why-do-you-always-make-this-so-difficult* sigh. "I'm sure you've heard that Justin is getting married."

The words fall like a sheet of ice across my skin. "He is?"

"He is, honey, and I just don't understand why it isn't you." When she says this, I feel something in me crack wide-open and spill every drop of hope for this conversation, and a hundred others like it. I want to give her a chance, always. And always, I realize too late why I shouldn't.

I put my fist in my mouth so I don't end up yelling. I keep it there because I know what is coming next, her quietly disappointed: "Why you broke up with that boy, I'll never understand."

No, you won't, I think as soon as the words are out of her mouth. *I'll never tell you because it's so much easier to let you think he's the good guy than to let you know how long he cheated on me, and risk hearing you tell me it was my fault.*

"I know, Mom," I say as gently as I can. "It's just all really complicated. But look. I've got to go."

I hang up, and make a beeline for the ice cream.

————

AS FAR AS nights off go—with the obvious exception of the phone call with Mom and the news of *Justin's impending wedding*—there's not much I would change. I needed to sack out and do nothing. It's why Lola didn't argue when I declined the invitation to join her and Oliver for dinner.

But now, with the apartment empty, I'm bored. Bored and strangely restless. And if I'm honest, I've been like this all week whenever I have a second to breathe. I thought talking to Mia would ease my mind, but if anything, it's made things feel more complicated. At the end she seemed almost encouraging about me and Luke, but she was assuming something different about our relationship, I think. And I just don't know if I can handle him—or handle *myself,* with him.

With a look at the clock, I groan and sink farther into the couch, realizing it's only seven. I consider going to bed for a little quality time with Old Blue, but even that doesn't seem as appealing as it used to. I want to simultaneously strangle and congratulate Luke, because it's a sad day when my favorite vibrator is no longer man enough to do the job.

On a whim, I pick up my phone and scroll through my contacts. Ruby's still in London and with the time difference it's only three in the morning there. Harlow is with Finn, and if I text Lola she'll insist I put on actual clothes and meet up with them. I could meet up with Not-Joe, but we usually only hang out solo at the beach, and if we're doing real talk here, he's not the guy I want to talk to anyway.

Luke's number isn't in here, but I remember seeing it on a scrap of paper tucked into my purse. It takes another five minutes of inner monologue and rationalizing before I'm dropping back onto the couch, looking at a new text box.

I'm not actually sure what to do here. Even if I don't have sex with Luke again—which I'm definitely not—I *like* him. He's funny. He knows how to laugh at himself. He takes his grandmother shopping.

There's nothing wrong with friends texting friends on a boring night alone, right?

Why did the snowman have on a happy face? I press send before tossing my phone to the side like it might actually burn me. I have definitely lost my mind.

It takes less than a minute for his reply, Is this my favorite dimpled bartender?

I roll my eyes as I type out, You're supposed to say, "Why, Logan?" You're not very good at this game.

I'm sorry, I couldn't hear you over the sound of me saving your cell into my contacts. Why, Logan?

I'm already laughing at my terrible joke. Because he heard the snow blower was coming.

A short pause. Wow. That was really terrible. I might have to delete your number now.

It was not, I insist. That joke was pure genius.

Ok. It did make me laugh, he types. Per usual.

Usual, I scoff. We've seen each other four times.

Want to make it five?

No.

Ok. What are you doing?

Well, that wasn't the response I was expecting.

Cleaning my guns and researching vasectomies, I type.

My dad had a vasectomy because it made sex a lot more spontaneous, he tells me. My sister told me that on my 21st birthday because I backed into her car.

I blink down at my phone. I feel like I really get your sister, on a spiritual level, I reply.

Luke is an idiot. He is not my type. *Why am I still smiling?*

I know, I'm actually a little afraid of you two meeting.

So what are you doing tonight? I ask.

Same thing I did last night and the night before that, googling Titanfall cheat codes so I can kick your ass. When is my rematch?

That actually . . . sort of . . . sounds fun. I don't answer for a few minutes. I walk to the kitchen and throw away my dinner. I rinse out a few dishes and tidy up again. And then I walk back to the couch and without thinking type, 20 minutes. Prepare for annihilation.

———————

AS I CLIMB the stairs to Luke's house, I'm overcome with a sense of déjà vu. I'm not here for sex—as I keep reminding myself—but I'd be lying if I said I hadn't been thinking about it since the last time I was here. I've never really had a regular booty call . . . is this how it happens?

Not that that's what this is.

Luke's street is quiet and lined with small, tidy ramblers, the windows all lit from within. I look around again as I knock on the door. There's a large pot of daisies near the rug at my feet, and I don't know which idea I like more—that his sister or mom put them there or that Luke did it himself.

A dog barks off in the distance and I can hear the hum of Luke's TV through the open window. I know he's probably in the kitchen from the sound of his steps as they move from tile to carpet and then tile again, and remember that the lock sticks the tiniest bit when you turn it. I have no idea when I noticed any of these things.

The porch fills with light and then Luke is there, smiling down at me. I feel the eye contact in my belly, like the low hum of electrical feedback. Adrenaline seeps into my veins and I consider turning and racing all the way down the stairs. *Friends* aren't supposed to make you feel like this.

"Hey, you," he says, still smiling, and it's enough to send goose bumps along my skin. Taking a step back, he motions for me to come inside.

He's wearing a pair of jeans and a faded T-shirt, and has a kitchen towel slung over his shoulder. The house smells faintly of bread and tomato sauce and my stomach quietly growls. I'm ambivalent about Luke being a better grown-up than me, cooking an actual dinner and cleaning it up while I could barely manage to peel the plastic wrap all the way off of my Lean Cuisine.

"I'm just finishing cleaning up," he says, tilting his head for me to follow him.

His kitchen is bigger than one would expect given the size of the house, and it's clear he was loading dishes when I interrupted him. I sit on a stool and he turns to me, a plastic-wrapped bowl in his hand. "Can I get you something to drink?" he asks. He opens the fridge and sets the dish inside. "I have beer, juice, milk, water, and—"

"Beer's good," I tell him. His laptop is open and on the counter and sure enough, a tab filled with Titanfall tips fills the screen.

He reaches for two bottles and sets them on the counter. "You hungry?"

"Not really," I say, but reach for a leftover piece of garlic bread on a cutting board anyway. I smell it before tearing off a corner and popping it into my mouth. It's fucking amazing. "Who taught you to cook?"

He smiles. "One: I know how to use a cookbook and I have access to the Food Network. Two: my mom and my Grams. They would kill me if I ordered pizza every night."

"Pretty impressive, considering you had a fridge with nothing but Sriracha and celery before," I tease.

He bends to close the dishwasher door and my eyes drag

across his body. No, definitely doesn't look like he's eating pizza every night.

"There was string cheese," he says with a smile. "And in my defense, I'd been crazy busy and hadn't had time to shop. Strangely enough, I've had loads of free time this week."

I don't miss the subtle dig that I've been avoiding him, and wonder if *free time* means he's actually been *sans companion*. Thankfully my mouth is full of garlic bread and I'm saved from asking.

"Titanfall or TV?" he asks casually, removing the tension from the moment. "I think there's a *Buffy* marathon on Syfy tonight."

I'm so grateful for his easy manner right now that I nearly want to launch myself over the counter. And the fact that he likes *Buffy*, too. Honestly: fuck him.

"TV," I say instead.

I follow him into the living room and sit on the couch. The TV is on some sports channel and he takes the seat next to me and hands me my beer. "Can you grab me that remote?" he says, and I do, watching as he takes a drink from his bottle before setting it on the coffee table in front of us. Now that I'm here, I'm not really sure how much TV we'll be watching, but I appreciate the gesture.

Luke settles into the couch and begins flipping through the channels, offering up commentary or asking a question about the various shows. He rests his arm on the back of the couch, behind me. This feels decidedly coupley—next to each other on the couch this way—but there's something nice about sitting here tucked into Luke's side, about his smell and the warmth coming off his skin, so I don't comment or move away.

He begins to ask me something, but I cut him off, turning to face him slightly. "Can I ask you a completely random question?"

His eyes move over my face before settling on my mouth. "Of course."

"Who planted the flowers on your porch?"

He furrows his brow for a moment until he registers what I mean. "Oh. Me?" he says. "Is that weird?"

"I have no idea," I tell him.

He braces a hand on the side of my neck and tilts my face back so I have no choice but to look at him. "Friends busy tonight?" he says, thumb pressing at the underside of my jaw. It's strangely relaxing.

"What makes you think that?"

"I don't know. Guess I can't really imagine you texting me if you had other options available."

"They were busy," I admit. I almost tell him that I don't actually have a *lot* of friends here, and that I tend to separate myself a little from people anyway, so this thing between us is pretty new for me. A little scary.

I almost tell him all of this, but I don't. It's not what you say in this situation I'm trying to maintain.

"Nothing on TV at home?" he asks, smiling as he smooths my hair with the backs of his fingers. I find myself leaning into his touch, my shoulders loosening, my body sagging in his direction. Being near him is a little like slipping into a warm bath.

I shrug and Luke leans in, stopping just long enough to check in with me. I nod slowly and he closes the distance, brushing his lips over mine. "I'm glad you didn't have anything else to do," he says against my mouth. "I'm really glad I have your number now instead of Fred's. I don't want to kiss him nearly as much as I want to kiss you."

And he finally does, making me feel that kiss from the place where our lips meet to the tips of my curling toes. I push him back, lifting my leg on the other side of his hip so I'm straddling his lap.

"Can I put my mouth on you?" he says, hand slipping between my legs, to rub me over my shorts.

I shake my head.

"Why again?"

It feels like my brain is short-circuiting and he's only touching me over my clothes, back and forth and then small circles right where I need it. "We don't do that."

"Right," he says, voice flat, expression guarded. "We fuck."

"Yeah."

"It's not that I'm complaining, mind you," he says, moving to undo the first button of my shorts and slowly sliding the zipper down. "But what about over your panties? I could put my mouth there, suck a little. Maybe hum the alphabet."

"The alphabet?"

"Literacy is very important to me."

"You are so persistent," I say, and try to ignore the way his fingers are ghosting back and forth just below my navel.

"I'm persistent when I want something," he clarifies. "And I *really* want that." He takes my hand and holds it over his cock, and rocks into my palm as if to further illustrate his point. "See?"

I can see the shape of him beneath the denim of his jeans, long and pressed against his stomach.

A wave of heat flashes beneath my skin and I lift his shirt up and over his head in a rush, pulling his mouth to mine.

"Hey, hey," Luke whispers, dragging his teeth over my bottom lip. "Slow down, Albuquerque. We have all night."

"I'm not spending the night with you," I tell him, pulling my own shirt off. I'm not wearing a bra and I suck in a breath when my nipples brush against the smooth skin of his chest. "I'm leaving when we're finished."

"We gonna fuck right here on my couch again?"

"I *like* this couch."

His fingers slide inside my panties and down to where I'm already wet.

I can tell by his open mouth that there was a smart comment on the tip of his tongue, but he seems to have forgotten it. Instead, he pushes the tip of his finger inside me and drags his eyes along my collarbones and down to my breasts, before licking his lips. "Then we'll fuck," he says, closing his eyes for a moment before he grips me by the back of the neck and pulls me to his mouth. "Fuck *slow* this time."

My fingers find his belt and undo the buckle, slipping the leather from his pants and tossing it behind me.

"Yeah," he says, watching me pop open the buttons of his jeans and reach in, wrapping my hand around him. His cock is a living, pulsing heat in my grip. "Oh, God."

He slumps against the back of the couch and watches, eyes dragging from where I'm touching him to where he's touching me, and up to my breasts again. His cock is perfect, just like the rest of him.

"Pants off," I tell him, lifting up while he shoves them down his thighs.

"You, too," he says, and I stand.

I'm so wet the air feels cold as soon as he pulls down my shorts and underwear.

"Fuck, Logan, look at you."

Everything in me bottoms out when his fingers slide up the inside of my thigh and he sucks in a breath—I'm wet to my thighs—and looks at me like I'm a meal and he's deciding what to bite first.

Luke makes a guttural sound, and it vibrates down into my bones when his eyes meet mine. Brown sugar. *Burnt* sugar. Caramel.

"I can't wait until you let me kiss you here." His fingers slide over me, dipping inside, mimicking the movement his tongue would make against me. His other hand smooths up the back of my legs and he kisses my stomach, my ribs, just below my belly button.

"Condom?" I ask, and after a tiny pause, Luke nods

against my skin, reaching down to find one in the pocket of his discarded jeans. I watch while he tears open the foil package and unrolls the condom over his length.

"Come back here," he says, holding the base of his cock in one hand and guiding me over his lap with the other.

He leans in and sucks on my breast, teasing my nipple with his teeth and moaning around it. I sink down slowly and he pulls off with an audible pop, sitting back against the cushions to watch where he's disappearing inside me.

"London."

"Shhhh."

"God. You're so hot."

I move over him, slowly. "Shhhh."

"What?" he says, running his hands down my ribs and stopping at my stomach. "You expect me to be quiet right now?"

"You talk too much," I say, laughing into his mouth.

It's like he has some sort of superpower and already knows exactly how I like to be kissed. Open mouth, soft at first with just a hint of tongue. Biting kisses that move from teasing to frantic in the span of a few seconds. He pulls away for a breath just when I want him to, sometimes blinking up to catch my eyes or even just to look at my mouth. He kisses me like he still can't believe he's doing it.

I adjust the position of my knees and we both gasp as I bottom out, my ass coming to rest on his thighs. He's so deep like this. "Oh my God," I say, and press my forehead to his shoulder while I catch my breath.

His palms smooth down to my waist and he presses his

thumbs into my hip bones. "I want you in my bed," he says through a grunt, moving me, rocking me faster and then slow again. There's a thin sheen of sweat on his forehead and down his chest and I can feel the tips of each individual finger where he grips me. "I want to see you better, spread you out under me. I like the way you look. I like the way you smell. And fuck, Logan, I *love* the way you feel."

"Such a poet."

"You want poetry? I could write a fucking sonnet about the way your tits are bouncing right now. I want to burn the way they look into my brain."

He leans in to bite me, and I can't help laughing again. "You are such a boy."

"Because I like the way you look naked?"

"Among other things," I tell him, kissing his lips. "Shh. You're distracting me."

"I'm trying to have a moment here."

"With my breasts?"

"Your breasts." He sits up, nips at my neck before sucking gently. "Your neck, your mouth, your whole body." His lips trail closer to mine, brushing across. *"You."*

We kiss for long minutes and my movements narrow into small rocks forward and back, just feeling him inside me. I try to keep it together, try not to moan into his mouth or cry out when he reaches down and his thumb starts moving in practiced circles over my clit. I'm trying to keep this about sex, but the way he's looking at me, the way he feels—it's no longer that simple.

I dig my hands into all that thick hair, steering his mouth

back to my breast and watching as he captures my nipple with his tongue. He bares his teeth, sliding them over the sensitive skin and I cry out, feeling him twitch inside me

"You like that." It isn't a question, it sounds like a revelation, like *relief*.

I nod, breath trapped in my throat and eyes locked on his expression of hope, like he wants to please me. Like it means everything to him right now.

"Can you feel it all the way down to your clit when I suck you here?"

I nod again, gasping at the tightening in my belly when he licks and sucks harder, growling around my skin.

His cheeks are pink and he's flushed all the way down his neck. He's watching me, watching *us,* the way we move together and the place where our bodies connect. I follow his gaze and look down between us, the way the muscles of his flat stomach clench, where the beads of sweat have collected in the hollow of his collarbones. I circle my hips and he groans, tightening his grip where he holds me.

"Jesus Christ. Do that again," he says, and I do, moving over him and using the back of the couch for leverage. I could get drunk on his sounds, the moans and whimpers when he thinks he might be getting close, the shaky breaths when he holds off to wait for me.

Luke smacks a hand against the cushion before he throws his head back. "I'm so . . . I'm . . ." he says between short lungfuls of air. His fingers return to my clit with renewed enthusiasm, and he looks up at me. "Like this?"

I can only nod, eyes closed as I try and chase down this feeling, like a cord has been wrapped around my spine, connected to my nipples and where he fits inside me. It tightens with each rock of my hips, each thrust of his.

Tighter.

Tighter.

"Oh, God," I say, the feeling spreading outward.

Tighter.

Luke pulls me down so our foreheads meet and it's so intimate, I'm not sure whether I want to wrap my arms around him, or push away.

He changes the tempo of our movements and I want to scream but he's suddenly so deep and I'm so close . . .

"Fuck, I can feel it. I *feel* it," he says, eyes suddenly wide. "Yes. London."

It's like my muscles stop working as my orgasm twists through me. My skin is too hot but covered in goose bumps, my nipples hard and just shy of sore. I can't think. Luke must sense the moment it happens because he takes over, grip tightening to the point of pain. He presses up into me, hard and fast and over and over until he's coming with a long, helpless groan against my shoulder. When the haze finally recedes, I open my eyes to find him stretched out beneath me, arms splayed across the back of the couch, chest rising and falling and his torso slick with sweat.

I feel like I've just been on a run with Harlow, the kind where she makes us keep going and going until I can't feel my legs and even my fingers are numb. My muscles feel wrung-out and my heart is pounding in my chest, echoing in my ears. I can't catch my breath.

He reaches a weak arm up, brushing my hair out of my face. "Stay over."

Nothing sounds better than falling into his cool sheets and not having to move again for another eight hours, but awareness pricks the back of my neck, tripping the heavy pounding of my heart: I *like* Luke.

I hear his phone buzz on the counter in the kitchen, and it's like he's opened a window, let in an icy breeze. I register that it's been buzzing on and off the entire time we've been in here, but it just didn't matter.

I climb off his lap and fall back to the couch, forcing myself to sit and search for my clothes.

"Hey," he says between breaths. "Did you hear what I said? Stay with me." He reaches for my arm and even the touch of his fingers against my skin is too much right now. "I'll even forget those codes and let you kick my ass at Titanfall."

"*Let* me." I grin over at him, but I know it doesn't look genuine. I am a mass of knots inside. I stand, slipping into my underwear. "Sorry. I really need to go."

He pushes himself to sit up, and groans. "Oh my God, my abs. How is it that I was on the bottom and I'm this sore? I'm taking ninety-five percent of the credit on this one."

I stand to face him. "You wish."

He pauses with one hand dug into his hair. "You know, one of these days I'm going to get my feelings hurt with this little Nail and Bail thing you have going here."

"'Nail and Bail'?" I repeat. I reach for my shorts, but Luke stops me, taking my hand.

"I'm serious." He releases my hand but reaches forward to frame my hips, thumbs stroking the sensitive skin there. *"Stay."*

My voice comes out a little shaky when I try to deflect. "I snore. It's bad."

A wry smile twists his lips. "Fine." Then he gives me the *real* smile again, the one that makes his expression the warmest, sweetest one I think I've ever seen, and drops his hands. "I'll let you go this time," he says quietly.

He watches as I step into my shorts, stays quiet while I pull on my shirt. I feel his attention on my fingers as I button it from the bottom to the top.

When I'm done, he wipes a hand across his mouth, asking, "Do you want to get together this weekend?"

Fuck. Slowly, slowly he's chipping away at my shell.

"Let's just play it by ear, okay?"

Luke closes his eyes, exhaling a tiny, frustrated breath, before pushing to stand. He's still naked, sweaty . . . perfect. I lean in when he wraps his arms around me, and inhale the mix of sex and sweat and soap on his skin.

"Sounds good, Dallas." He bends, reaching up to cup my face and kisses me, slow and warm. I can feel his cock stir against me again, already.

But for once, he doesn't press. He takes a step back, bending to pull on his boxers, and then walks me to the door. He doesn't say anything else as I walk out, down the steps, along the sidewalk to my car, but I feel his eyes on me the entire way.

"Still fun," he shouts from behind me. I turn to see him leaning against the doorframe, practically naked. The porch light overhead throws shadows across his body, accentuating the width of his shoulders, the planes of his stomach, the definition of his hips. His boxers hang so low I can see the suggestion of hair, just above his waistband. Lucky neighbors.

"What was?" I ask.

I can see his smile from here when he answers. "You."

Chapter SIX

Luke

I'M ELBOWS-DEEP IN a legal brief I can barely understand when my phone buzzes on the table at my elbow.

Beeeeeeeeeeers, the text from Dylan reads.

I look up at the clock. Shit, how did it get to be six already? Where?

New place, on Island and 10th.

I groan—I fucking *hate* going downtown during the week.

Anticipating this, Dylan adds, Most of the team is coming. Jess broke up with Cody. We're helping him drown.

I blink a few times, staring in shock at my phone. My former water polo teammate, Cody, has been with his girlfriend, Jess, since high school. In the best of moods, Cody will drink until he's crawling. I can't imagine how tonight will go down.

Still, weeknight or not, I can't say no. Cody, Dylan, Andrew, Daniel, and I have been tight since freshman year when the seniors on the team locked the five of us on the pool deck for an entire December weekend in nothing but our Speedos, with a vending machine full of food as our nourishment, though no money. You don't get through something like that, and go on to win two national championships without sticking together.

Be there by eight, I reply, putting down my phone and packing up my desk.

THE GUYS HAVE taken over two tables as close to the dance floor as one can get and reasonably remain seated. Not five feet from where Daniel has done a complete one-eighty in his seat is a group of girls dancing suggestively, pretending they don't notice the six-foot-eight water polo player turned fitness instructor staring at them.

"Sorry I'm late," I say in greeting, pulling out a chair and sitting down. I've never been to this club—it's new but the décor wants to fool you into thinking it's been here since the seventies. Looking to Cody, I ask, "You good?"

He puts his empty beer glass down next to another one. "No. But don't feel sorry for me. I've been a dick to her lately. I think she might be doing this to scare me straight."

I feel my brows lift. "Well, okay then." I can't tell if he's being truly honest with himself, or if he's in complete denial. Even if he's wrong, and Jess is actually done, I wouldn't blame him for wanting to stay in a hopeful place a little longer. He's been with her for nearly six years.

Six years . . . it's such a huge portion of our lives, and still, it's shorter than the decade I spent feeling like I belonged to Mia. We grew up together in nearly every way possible. From eleven to nineteen she was mine.

The first time I was with someone else it felt like a distraction. Two weeks after we'd broken up, and I didn't want to think too much about how I felt. I hadn't needed to dig deep to understand why I was constantly nauseous and wanted to sleep half the time: I was fucking heartbroken.

But then I got drunk, and kissed Ali Stirling. She took off her shirt, then mine. One foot in front of the other: I got hard. That night, I fucked her three times in her aunt's condo in Pacific Beach. Turns out, sex was still fun.

Until the next morning when I visited Mia at her dorm and broke down. We weren't even technically together anymore but there I was, *confessing,* because that's what we did. All of the air left the room the second the words "I slept with Ali last night" came out of my mouth.

Mia had stuttered out a quiet "Wow," and we both felt it end, like the crack of a gunshot. We were sitting on her bed and had gone completely still, like a photo of us ripped in half straight down the middle. We'd agreed to break up, but I knew neither of us had *felt* it yet. Until that moment we didn't really even know what *broken up* looked like. No one had ever touched me besides Mia, and suddenly that wasn't true anymore. I wasn't the guy who had one love. I wasn't the Luke half of the one-word phrase, *Luke-and-Mia.* I was the guy with an ex-girlfriend. I was the guy who had sex with other people now. I moved on from our first love with a hard shove.

I shiver, blinking back into the present, asking, "Remind me why we came all the way downtown for after-work drinks when none of us work downtown?"

"I do," Cody says.

Silence rings out at the table before Andrew finally can't take it anymore. "Cody, you work part-time at Starbucks."

"Yeah," Cody says. "Starbucks *downtown*."

"Actually . . . I work downtown," Dylan says quietly and we all turn to look at him, confused. Dylan has a way of carrying on three lives, two of which remain completely unknown to us. I've known him since we were freshmen, but if you asked me what he does all day, I would guess he reads, surfs, goes for long walks, and gets lost.

"Wait, *what*?" I say. "Since when do you have a job?"

He shrugs. "Since, like, Sept—"

"We came *here* tonight," Andrew begins, interrupting us, "because you, Luke, banged the bartender where I wanted to go, and—"

"Wait, hold up," Daniel says, finally turning back to the table. "Luke banged the bartender at Mighty Brew?"

I groan. "She wasn't the bartender. She was a—"

Dylan cuts me off. "I think Andrew means that you slept with the bartender at *Fred's*," he says, more quietly. I can hear the question embedded there: Did *you fuck London, Luke*?

Andrew shakes his head, confused. "Luke banged the new bartender at *Fred's*? I was talking about the redhead at Stone at Liberty Station."

Dylan gets up with a huff and heads toward the bathroom. Cody groans, saying, "Pretty soon we won't be able to go anywhere without someone crying in the bathroom over Luke."

"Jesus Christ." I rest my head in my hands and Andrew slides a half-finished beer into my line of sight.

"Here. Drink this."

"Can I get you guys anything else?" a voice asks at the far end of the table.

"Two more of these," Andrew says, and then points to me, saying loud enough for our server to hear, "Luke, you're not allowed to bang this waitress. They serve Ruination here and I'll be pissed if we can't come back."

"Okay," I mumble, closing my eyes and keeping my head down. Is this a conversation that would have made me laugh a week ago? Right now it makes me feel faintly sleazy.

"She's hot," Daniel says a few seconds later, "in that single-serving kind of way."

"Dan—" Dylan starts, having returned surprisingly quickly.

I hold up my hand for him to wait, leaning in so I can hear Daniel better, repeating, "That 'single-serving' kind of way?" What the fuck is he talking about?

"You *guys*," Dylan says with more intent.

But Daniel continues, turning and planting his elbows on the table. "That thing you have, a little treat, that fills you up but you forget it pretty quickly. A Twinkie, a bag of chips. An energy drink. Cute girl, nice body . . . single serving."

In spite of myself I laugh at this shit—Daniel can be *such* a dick—finally lifting my head and taking a sip of my beer. But straight across from me stands Dylan, hunched over the table, wearing a *shut the fuck up* expression. He looks at my face and then widens his eyes when he looks over my shoulder, meaningfully.

I turn, and see that the waitress is right behind me, her back to us as she writes something down on her pad. Her wheat-colored ponytail brushes her shoulder when she straightens, takes a deep breath, and sticks her pen behind her ear. When she turns to us, smile plastered on her face, my heart immediately bottoms out.

"Two Ruinations. Anything else?" she asks, her dimple poking into her cheek as she swallows.

The table falls silent, but my heart is now somewhere under my chair.

London.

London is our waitress.

Her eyes meet mine, and I can't tell. I just can't tell at all if she heard, and if so, how much. Did she hear the part about my apparent penchant for female bartenders? Did she hear what Daniel said? And, oh shit, did she hear me *laugh*?

"We're good," Daniel croaks.

With a little nod and smile, London turns and walks back to the bar.

Daniel bursts out laughing and makes a wry face. "Oops!"

"Dude," Dylan hisses, shaking his head at me. "If she heard you assholes I'm going to be pissed. London is a nice person, and you guys are *dicks*."

"Fuck," I whisper. *"Fuuuck."*

Dylan nods at me, disappointment making his normally

happy face more somber before he turns and heads toward the bathroom in earnest this time. I feel like a complete ass.

Andrew shrugs and immediately moves on, saying something about the U.S. Men's Water Polo team, the Olympics, whether we're all going together to Tokyo to watch them, but I can't do much more than stare into my beer.

We came here tonight because you, Luke, banged the bartender where I wanted to go.

Luke banged the new bartender at Fred's? I was talking about the redhead at Stone at Liberty Station.

She's hot, in that single-serving kind of way.

Pretty soon we won't be able to go anywhere without someone crying in the bathroom over Luke.

In the movies this type of moment-of-clarity turns into a montage of all the moments leading up to it. Maybe the music swells above the dialogue. And it's true that the sound of voices falls away and my heart seems to have returned to my body and is pounding directly against my eardrum. But it's the anxiety I didn't expect. The panic that she may have heard, that I may have hurt her feelings. The fear that I just confirmed everything she suspected about me.

The problem is, it's all true.

Dylan returns to his seat, and looks up at the bar behind me—presumably watching London—his brows pulled down in concerned frustration. Right as he seems to decide to go talk to her, pushing back again from the table, I bolt up, gesturing to him that I'll take care of it and wiping my palms on my thighs as I walk toward the bar.

It's a Tuesday and still pretty early; except for the five of us and a few groups standing over near the DJ stand, the club is mostly dead. London seems lost in thought as she opens two beers and sets them on a tray for another waitress, and so she doesn't notice my approach until I'm right in front of her, rapping my knuckles against the wood.

Startled, she looks up. "Hey."

"Hey." I slide one hand in my pocket, trying to seem less like I'm coming over here to defend my indefensible actions and more like I just wanted to say hi. "Having a good night?"

London lifts one shoulder as she dries off a glass. "Sure. You?"

"Pretty good." I smile but she's not watching, and the words vanish from my head. It's awkward, and she knows it's awkward, and in perfect London fashion, she's not coming to my rescue. "I didn't know you worked here."

She nods as she sets the glass down and lifts another. "Just started."

"Ah."

I'm just going to say it: girls are hard to read. Is she pissed? Preoccupied? Does she want to kiss me so bad she can't even look at me?

"Did you quit Fred's?"

"No, just wanted some more hours." London turns, setting a tray of glasses down on the other side of the bar, and begins putting them away on a small shelf.

"So, London—"

"Did you want a drink?" she asks me over her shoulder.

"No, I . . ."

I what?

I have no idea what comes next.

She turns back around and looks at me, waiting patiently. Do I ask her if she heard? Do I tell her that I didn't really think what Daniel said was funny? The problem is that I didn't think it was funny but I also didn't think it was that big a deal, either . . . until I realized he was talking about London, and—worse—that she'd heard. Would I be here talking to her if she had been across the bar, out of hearing range when he'd said it?

This is the kind of thing she would ask me, and this is what I would be unable to answer.

"I just wanted to say hi," I say, smiling.

Her eyes flicker to my mouth and then she looks evenly back up. "Hi."

"Do you want to come over later?" It comes out so bare; there's no buildup, no easing in. My voice even cracks on the last word.

London's eyes go tight before she slumps a little, giving me a tiny smile. It's a genuine one: sweet, all-American, dimpled. "Your boys seem to prefer when you don't bang the waitress, remember?"

Fuck. "London—"

"Luke," she cuts in gently, as if wanting to be careful with my feelings still, after all of it. "I think I'm not doing that anymore."

KEYS IN HAND, I'm halfway across the dimly lit parking lot when I hear Dylan call my name.

"You're leaving," he says, jogging to catch up. "You just got here."

Scratching my neck, I look past him into the cone of light directly over my car. "I have some things I need to take care of before work tomorrow."

"Look," he says, leaning to the side so I'll look over at him. His shoulders slump a little as he repeats, "Look, man. I don't know how well you know her, but London isn't like that." He looks straight into my eyes. "She's really cool."

London isn't like that, meaning: she's not a girl you can just bang without looking back. I should tell him I figured that out almost immediately, but already this is too much drama for me.

"It's cool, Dyl, I just talked to her."

"I hope she turned you down," he says, and his smile tells me that he means it, but feels bad for saying it.

"She did." I look back toward the club. "How do you know her, anyway?"

"She's a friend of a friend." This is exactly the kind of information Dylan gives. Usually I drop it without thought, but tonight it takes Herculean effort for me to not ask more questions.

"All right," I say. "I'll see you later."

"Later."

I don't feel like going home, to the dark empty house, the bright empty fridge. I climb in my car, turn up the music, and drive without thinking back on any of this to my sister's apartment, letting myself in with my key.

It's almost ten, so I know Margot is either asleep or in the lab, and her roommate is most likely staying over at her girlfriend's house. The apartment is blessedly silent, the fridge is blessedly full.

I'm almost done making an epic turkey sandwich when I hear footsteps pad down the hall.

"Pa," Margot stage-whispers behind me. "There's a bear getting into our food box."

I dig in the pantry for some chips. "You have better snacks than I do."

My sister comes around the counter, and leans back against it. "Because I don't wait until tumbleweeds are rolling across the barren shelves of my refrigerator before I hit the grocery store."

I let out a grunt and turn with an armful of food toward the living room.

She follows me out of the kitchen. I can feel her right on my heels and know that if I wanted to give up conscious thought in favor of food and television, this is the last place I should have gone. I can't help but spill my guts to my sister; it's like a reflex.

"What are you doing here, though?" she asks. "Did you have a bad day at work?"

I settle on the couch and flip on the TV. "It was fine."

"Did something happen with the team? I heard about Cody and Jess."

"Yeah, but he seems to think they'll be okay."

She sits and pulls her leg up on the couch so she can face me. I feel the pinpricks of her stare on the side of my face. "Then what has you stress-eating junk food?"

"Hunger."

"Luke."

I sigh, taking a bite of sandwich and chewing it slowly while I think. Swallowing, I tell her, "I think I fucked up with a girl I like."

Margot jerks upright, shaking her head quickly. "Sorry, what?" She laughs awkwardly. "Funniest thing, it sounded like you said something about *liking* a *girl.*"

I rip open the bag of chips and reach for the remote. "Never mind."

"Are you serious right now?" she asks, sitting next to me. "A girl has you eating chips by the fistful?"

"I'm just hungry, Margot. Lay off."

I turn to Jimmy Fallon and Margot does, in fact, lay off. She digs her hands into the bag of chips, joining me in my late-night emotional munchies. But I can almost hear the interest build in her until she's sitting upright again, hands clenched in fists at her side, just waiting for the commercial break.

When it comes, she releases a tight breath. "Tell me about her."

There's no avoiding this, there really isn't. And maybe I came over because I actually wanted to talk. Who the fuck knows, but I'm here now, so I may as well let it all out. "Her name is London."

"I don't know a London. Is she from here?"

"She went to UCSD, studied art. I didn't meet her there, though." I scratch the back of my neck. "She works at Fred's."

"Sexy cocktail waitress?"

I throw her a wary glance. "Sexy bartender." I ignore her amused snort. "Anyway, our entire first night together I called her *Logan* and she didn't bother to correct me. I don't know if she ever would have. Dylan said her name when we saw her next and I was horrified, but she didn't *care*." For some reason, this detail feels important. It says so much about her, and about the "us" that has existed for the measly two weeks.

Margot snorts. "I like this girl."

"Yeah, well, she likes you, too." When I look at her, I see her eyebrows raised in a silent question, so I add, "I told her about your abusive role as my supervisor in Doll Salon."

My sister smiles proudly.

"We hooked up a few times, and—"

"In one night, I assume?"

"No, asshole. Over a few different days."

"Wow." She rolls her eyes. "Long-term then."

I take a sip of my water and set it back down on the table. "You wonder why I don't like talking to you."

"Oh, please. I'm the *only* one you like talking to because I don't stroke your enormous ego." Punching my shoulder, she urges, "Go on."

"She's wary of guys. Her long-term boyfriend cheated, and I get the feeling there's been a long line of assholes in her life. The thing is, there's attraction there, but I'm not sure she actually likes me. Said I was a cliché, a manwhore, douchebag, whatever."

"I mean, I *really* like this girl," Margot says, digging in the bag and taking another handful of chips.

"But she's smart and funny and pretty and . . ." I'm so out of practice talking about girls and feelings in the same conversation that I flounder a little, settling on "there was something there. Between us, I mean." But then I tell Margot about what Daniel said tonight, and about the guys teasing me about sleeping with every hot female bartender in town.

It's a few seconds before Margot says anything, but when she does, she puts her hand on mine first, to soften the blow. "They're not wrong."

"Margot," I say, turning to face her. "That's not helping."

She can tell in my voice that not only am I not in the mood but I really am feeling like complete shit.

"Sorry. I just want to be honest."

"I know you do," I tell her. "It's just that, for the first time in a really long time I feel sort of weird about how I've been with girls. I always justified it like they were only after one thing, too, and maybe some of them were. But I know that wasn't always true. And Cody made some crack about not being able to go anywhere where a woman wouldn't be crying over Luke and . . . Jesus. Am I that bad?"

"You're asking your sister if you're as bad a player as your guy friends who are actually out at bars with you say you are?"

"I mean, does it *seem* like I'm that bad?"

She adjusts how she's sitting on the couch so that her knee rests on my thigh. "Honestly?"

"Honestly."

"Kind of. I mean, sometimes we'll be out for drinks and your phone will be buzzing *constantly*. You don't even notice it anymore. Or, we'll be having a nice dinner and some girl will walk up and start talking to you and I can see you struggling to remember her name. It's . . . I mean, I'm used to it now but, yeah. It's sort of shady."

I lean my head back against the couch, disengaging from the conversation and tuning back into the TV and whatever game Fallon is playing with David Beckham.

"I didn't mean to make you feel bad," she whispers. I know this conversation is making her anxious. Margot has a constant struggle with frankness and guilt when it comes to busting my balls.

"You didn't."

"It's just . . ." she starts, fidgeting with her pajama top, "you went from Mia—and only Mia—to *everyone*. There was no in-between."

"I haven't wanted anyone the way I wanted Mia," I argue.

"But someday you will," she says. "Maybe it will be London. And you said she's wary of guys, and then she sees you tonight at the bar? No wonder she keeps you at arm's length. Would you trust you?"

A sour weight settles in my stomach. "I know."

"Look, I'm not saying you need to go through the AA of

players or anything, but maybe look at what you're doing and who you are. Your life is this perfect combination of luck and ambition, but you treat women like gym equipment."

I choke on a sip of water. "Margot. That's *horrible*."

She raises her eyebrows as if to say, *Well?*

"Just learn to treat a girl the way you want to be treated," she says. "And I don't mean by playing with their private parts."

I snort. *"'Private parts.'"*

Rolling her eyes, she says, "You were a really good boyfriend to Mia."

This rattles me somehow. It's easier to remember the end, when I was lonely and she was broken and we didn't ever seem to get each other right. I turn to look over at her. "Yeah?"

Smiling, she says, "Yeah. You were. You were perfect. Everyone envied her."

"Well," I say, turning back to the television, "obviously I wasn't *perfect* or she wouldn't have stopped needing me."

Margot goes still before she reaches for the remote control on my lap and mutes the show. "'*Needing*' you?" Her voice is sharp. "She shouldn't ever have *needed* you. Wanted you, sure. Enjoyed being with you, sure. Desired you—*gross*—sure."

Groaning, I make a grab for the remote but she holds it out of my reach.

"You know what I mean," I say.

"I don't think I do. Mia lost every one of her dreams

in a single, horrible afternoon. It changed her, and that affected your relationship. That doesn't mean that *you* fucked up somehow."

"At the end of the day," I say, sliding my plate onto the coffee table, "what we had wasn't strong enough to weather what she was going through. End of story."

Margot gives me a one-shouldered shrug. "True."

I growl at this, wishing she had argued with me. This is why I hate talking about Mia. It just sucked. The whole thing sucked, there was no rhyme or reason to any of it—her accident, her distance, my heartbreak, our breakup—so it still feels like a raw wound. I hate uncovering it. But it was just a breakup. They happen every day.

"Luke, you were nineteen!" Margot says, raising her voice. "Sure, you said some shitty things to her because you were hurt, and she was terrible at talking about her feelings, but you guys grew apart."

"I know. I just never saw it coming," I tell her, leaning across her lap to reach for the remote.

"Do we ever see the big things coming, though? A predictable life never changed anyone."

I turn on the sound, and turn up the volume to let her know we're done talking, about Mia, about London, about me.

Chapter SEVEN

I DROP MY KEYS in the bowl by the door, kicking off my shoes. They thump loudly onto the wood floor in the otherwise-silent loft. Lola and Oliver are either at his place or asleep, but for once I'd really love someone else to be here to distract me from my foul mood.

I don't exactly feel like playing Titanfall.

I feel sort of queasy after what happened tonight with Luke and his friends. I'm not exactly upset by his behavior the way I was when I found Justin banging someone in his bed. And I'm not disappointed to see—yet again—that Luke is exactly the guy I thought he was.

But damn, I realize I wanted to be wrong about him. That feeling—the highly unwelcome desire for him to have been *relationship material*—makes my stomach feel twisty and gross.

I inhale a couple of bowls of Lucky Charms and crawl into bed, sleeping like a stone and silencing my alarm when it tells me it's time to hit the surf.

Instead, I wake up much later—at *ten*, in fact—to laughter trailing down the hall from the living room, and the deep, over-lapping sounds of male voices. Without bothering to put on actual clothes, I shuffle out in my Doctor Who pajamas to greet Lola, Oliver, Ansel, and Finn with a mumbled, "Hey, guys."

They return my greeting as I move robotically to the kitchen. Bless her heart: Lola has made coffee. I pour myself a cup and then join them, curling up on the end of the couch beside Ansel.

"Where are the other two?" I say, meaning Harlow and Mia.

"They're meeting us at Maryjane's in a few," Finn says, and I look around the room, wondering if it's just me or if everyone else has gone oddly still.

I also register with faint curiosity that it's midweek, they all happen to be off work, and no one has asked me to come along.

As if realizing this, too, Lola jerks into motion, standing and walking into the kitchen to refill her coffee. "No surfing today?"

At her question, I remember with a lurch why I didn't feel like getting up—Luke and his unfortunate friends—and shake my head. "Too wiped."

She nods, returning to us with her mug and settling back down on the floor next to Oliver.

I sip my coffee, swallow, and ask, "What are Harlow and Mia up to?"

It seems like a completely normal question. After all, when he's in town, Finn lives with Harlow in La Jolla, and Ansel and Mia just bought a house in Del Mar. Still, I'm met with silence.

Like, *weird* silence. And once again, the group's dynamic seems to elude me.

"They had to pick up some stuff," Oliver says, glancing quickly to Lola. "How's working at Bliss going? Do you like it there?"

Shrugging, I tell him, "It's pretty busy. Good tips, nice bar. I like the other bartenders. Probably not too surprising that the crowd is a bit sleazier than at Fred's, but you know downtown . . ." I trail off, smiling at him over the top of my coffee cup.

"Luke can protect you," Ansel chirps brightly.

I swear I almost *hear* the screeching of brakes rip through the room.

"Luke?" I ask.

Ansel's smile slowly straightens as the awkwardness settles; it happens in perfect tandem with the dropping of my stomach.

His cheeks are a deep pink as he glances helplessly to Lola, then back at me. "I'm sorry. I thought you and Luke were . . ."

And suddenly, I get it. I get why Mia isn't here. I get why they didn't invite me to breakfast.

"We're not," I say quietly, letting my head fall against the back of the couch. God, this is mortifying. "We hung out a few times before I realized he and Mia . . . I mean, that's not the only reason why we aren't a thing; we wouldn't be anyway."

Panic rises in me like steam filling a room. I don't mind the outsider feeling I've had occasionally with Lola's friends—

they're all so well-intentioned and inclusive that I never feel like a seventh wheel—but I definitely, *definitely* do not want to fuck up with them.

Straightening again, I turn my eyes to Lola. "I was going to talk to you—"

"It's okay," she says quickly, speaking over me.

"—but it wasn't serious, I swear. We aren't together."

Lola's calm eyes hold mine. "It's okay, London."

But it's like I can't stop talking. "I honestly didn't know he was Mia's ex, and then I called her—" I look to Ansel, explaining now: "I felt really weird about it, but she seemed totally okay . . ."

Throughout all of this, Ansel shakes his head quickly, murmuring, "No, no, no," and reassuring me, "She's fine."

"She is, I swear," Lola urges, moving over to me to sit on the floor by my legs. "Honey, Mia is fine."

But in the remaining tension, the mental calculation isn't that difficult to make: "*Harlow*'s not fine, though, is she?"

The awkward silence returns, heavier this time, and I glance over at Finn.

He gives a casual wave of his hand. "She'll get over it."

And fuck, I do not want to be the reason a girlfriend of mine has something to *get over*. But at the same time, it rankles me a little that she's white-knighting it for Mia, when, by all accounts—including her own—Mia doesn't need it.

Maybe Lola sees this reaction cross my face, because she puts a hand on my knee. "London. It's just what Harlow does. React first, think later."

Finn snorts.

"We were all so close growing up," she explains. "And when they broke up, it was weird how fast Luke sort of . . . moved on. We all got into the habit of silently disliking anyone who slept with him, like they were the ones changing him, like it wasn't *his* decision."

I look back over at her, giving her a wary smile. "That's insane. These women aren't black widows hunting an innocent guy. Luke is in charge of his game."

"I know," she says, wincing as she nods. "It's just a habit because old Luke was so loyal and committed." When she says this, my heart does a painful little dive. Despite everything else I've seen, that version of Luke isn't very hard to imagine. "But maybe you can see why it's weird for us? I mean, not for *me*," she adds quickly. "Honestly, London, I think it's kind of cool. It just took Mia a beat to feel that way, too, and by then she'd called Harlow—"

"Her first mistake," Finn adds dryly.

"—and Harlow got protective," Lola finishes with an apologetic shrug. "It's her thing."

"I get it," I tell them, and I do. But although I don't want anyone feeling like I've mis-stepped somehow, I also don't want to feel like I have to defend myself for sleeping with a guy I had no way of knowing broke up with my friend over four years ago. And the overlapping way that they're all reassuring me does nothing to quell the outsider vibe I'm getting.

"I really don't want things to be weird," I tell them.

"They're not," Lola says, and then revises: "I mean, if they are, it's just a blip. Seriously, you wouldn't have even known about it if you hadn't come out here before we left this morning, because I swear Harlow will be over it in a couple of hours."

She means this to make me feel better, but it doesn't. I "wouldn't have even known about it" because no one would have bothered to tell me. Like some mess of mine would have been cleaned up, negotiated away during their breakfast UN summit or something.

"Okay, cool," I say, getting up. I move to the kitchen and rinse out my mug. "But seriously, tell me if there's something I need to say to either of them."

Everyone nods with sympathetic enthusiasm at this—they know how scary it can be to be on the receiving end of Harlow's anger—but surely they can't really imagine what it's like to be *me* on the receiving end of Harlow's anger. She doesn't know me the same way. I might just be a temporary part of this group, after all. She might not feel the *need* to get over it.

Once again I curse the bum deal of having a long-term boyfriend suck up all of my social life for years and then cheat on me, leaving me isolated as hell. I have a hundred acquaintances, and few true friends. Is it me? Am I a surface skimmer, relying on a dimpled smile and small talk to make people feel at ease, to trick them into thinking they know me?

The only person I have to call and process this with is Ruby, and she's so far away and knows this group even less well than I do. The one person around here who sometimes seems to understand me best is Not-Joe—*Dylan*—and I didn't even know his actual name until a couple of weeks ago.

But that's not entirely true: *Luke* seems to get me, better than I'd like to let him believe. Unfortunately, he's flaky, has douchey friends, is a womanizer, and—after this morning's drama?—is completely off-limits.

THE LAST RAYS of sunlight cut through the entryway to Fred's as I open the door the next night. I haven't worked here that long, but after a few shifts in a row at Bliss, Fred's feels familiar, comforting. I'm glad to be back.

Fred is behind the bar when I get there, and he looks up, smiling as I near him.

"We missed you around here, kid," he says. "The other bartenders are all scared of me. It's not the same without someone here to give me crap."

I laugh as I tie my apron around my waist. "I'm glad my insubordination tickles you."

"You have fun at your fancy new place?" he asks.

"It's fine," I say with a shrug and a little smile, and Fred already knows me well enough to leave it at that.

I start my usual routine and check my station, jotting down the things I need to bring from the back, what needs to be refreshed. "Been busy today?" I ask.

Fred nods and leans back against the bar. "Some softball tournament is in town, so a lot of new faces. Young, too," he adds with a grin. "Better get your jar ready."

He isn't kidding, and the first half of my shift goes by in a blur. By eight that night Fred has dropped seven dollar bills into the car fund and thus has started suggesting I take another couple of shifts at Bliss.

I'm on my way to the back with a pitcher of margaritas when I see Luke. He's leaning against the pool table, hands tucked into the pocket of his dark jeans while he talks to a guy I don't recognize. His hair is soft tonight like he hasn't put anything in it, and it falls forward, obscuring his eyes. Of course it doesn't block the cut of his jaw, the line of his neck where it disappears into his gray T-shirt, or the way his Adam's apple moves as he swallows.

He's texted me four times since the night we had sex on his couch . . . *again* . . . this last time less than a week ago, but I haven't answered any of them. As a buffer against his presence, I mentally check off the reasons why:

Flaky.

Douchey friends.

Womanizer.

Off. Limits.

So I resent the physical reaction I'm having: my heart is definitely beating a little faster, and there's a distinct flutter of interest between my legs.

When did my body become such a traitor?

He looks up just as I place the tray on the table, and catches my eye. I'm not sure when he got here, but he doesn't look surprised to see me at all.

I ask the table if there's anything else I can get them before heading back to the bar. Fred is talking to one of the regulars when I slip behind the counter. I make two gin and tonics, pour a few beers, and have just started unloading a pack of Red Bull into the cooler when I hear a throat clear behind me.

"You didn't answer any of my texts, Logan," he says.

"A disorienting experience?" I ask with a smile, closing the cooler door and turning. "What can I get you?"

"Just a beer, please," he says, looking up at the TV. "That looks interesting."

I follow his gaze to where a trailer for a horror movie plays during a commercial break. " 'That'?"

He shrugs. "I heard it got pretty good reviews."

"I'm not really a scary movie person," I tell him, bending to drop a dirty rag in a bin beneath the bar.

"What kind of films do you like?"

I blink up to him. "What kind of . . . did you say *films*?"

He spins the beer coaster in front of him. "I did."

"Comedies, I guess?"

Nodding quickly, Luke says, "Yeah, I like those, too."

He's being so odd, and doing that thing where he fidgets when he's uncomfortable. Granted, things are totally weird between us, but I actually miss cocky Luke a little. Maybe he, too, is thinking back to what happened at Bliss. Maybe he's wondering how much I heard.

Maybe the fact that he's trying to make it okay between us should make me feel better, but, given everything, it doesn't.

"Are you going to ask me about the weather next?"

He breaks his attention from the television and looks over at me. "What?"

"Why do you sound like you're reading for the lead in *The 40-Year-Old Virgin*? You're being weird."

"I'm not—"

"Yeah, you are."

He runs a hand through his hair. "I think I'm just a little off today."

"Can I ask you a question?"

"Yeah," he says, nodding. "Sure."

"Do you have any girl *friends* you don't bang?"

His eyes narrow. "Of course I do. Margot—"

I hold up a hand to stop him. "Let me rephrase that. Do you have any female friends you just hang out with, who you are not related to, and who you have never banged, and/or never think of banging?"

He looks mildly offended. "Yes, Logan. Several."

Leaning my elbows on the bar, I lower my voice, telling him, "Really? Because you've dialed down the flirtation tonight, but you're acting like a robot. It's like you have two settings: pickup artist or awkward."

"Like I said, I'm just in a weird mood," he says quietly.

"Luke?"

His shy smile melts me a little. "Logan?"

"You don't need to have your dick out for someone to like you."

The smile is dialed up a few hundred degrees. "Is that right?"

"Would I lie to you?"

This makes him laugh. "You've ignored all of my texts," he says again, as if this proves me wrong.

A waitress drops a ticket on the counter and I reach for it. With an inward wince, I realize how easy it is to fall into flirtation with him—I'm even initiating it.

Flaky.

Douchey friends.

Womanizer.

Off. Limits.

"I worked pretty much nonstop," I tell him.

Luke takes a pull from his beer and then examines the bottle. "You know, one of these days I'm going to turn into a raging alcoholic and it'll be your fault."

"*I* drive you to drink?" I ask.

He tears the corner of the label and begins to slowly peel it away. "No. But I hang out in bars hoping to see you. Eventually all this is going to catch up with me and I'll look like my uncle Steve."

Unease pulls my shoulders up tight. It's not only that Luke bangs *all* the women, it's that now I realize being with him could jeopardize my friendships. "You could always hang out somewhere else, you know."

"I don't really want to, is the thing," he says, and winces a little, as if the admission is as unsettling to him as it is to me.

Someone steps up to the end of the bar, and I motion to Luke that I'll be right back. When I return, he doesn't look any happier than he did. Luke checks his phone and then looks toward the door.

"Expecting someone?" I say.

"Dylan," he tells me. "We're driving up to some bookstore or something. How do you know him, anyway?"

"Friend of a friend," I say with a shrug. "And he surfs, so I see him down at Black's Beach sometimes."

"Maybe we—" he starts to say, when the outside door opens and a couple of his friends from the other night make their way inside.

"Sutter!" one of them shouts, pointing in his direction.

"Your fan club is calling," I tell him with a smile, picking up a towel to dry a load of dishes.

"When will I see you again?"

"I'll be here," I say, but I can tell it wasn't the answer he was looking for. He continues to watch me for a moment before he sighs, and glances back to where his friends have begun circling a group of girls playing pool. Of course they are. He nods to tell them he'll be right there.

"I'm assuming you'd shoot me down if I asked if you wanted to do something later?"

"You would be correct," I tell him. The door opens again, followed by the sound of voices and cheers as another large group of men in softball jerseys files in. Another team, I'm guessing.

Luke stands and pulls out his wallet, laying a few bills out on the counter to pay for his drink. "Then I guess I'll see you, Logan," he says, and smiles before he heads to the back.

Chapter EIGHT

$\mathcal{I}$ STARE UP AT the ceiling, piecing together the last few inter-actions I've had with London. It's odd to have things ended so abruptly and have no say in it. I get why she doesn't want to hook up again. I get why she thinks I'm not her type. The problem is, she's Stonewall London right now, and there's no convincing her that I'm worth her time.

I forgot how much I hate the twisty restlessness of *feelings*.

The partners at the firm are all at Lake Arrowhead for a meeting, and the pre-law legal interns most definitely aren't included. We can barely be trusted to carry a legal brief from one office to the next let alone have input on firm policies and the most critical cases. It means I have a few days off, but the timing is awful. I don't want to be left alone in my own head.

I've filled the day with errands: taking Grams to her physical therapy, helping Andrew move his old fridge out of the garage, swimming some laps. And by the time I need to leave to have lunch with Dad, I can feel the tension in my shoulders, all along my back.

This is normally when I'd be in the mood for a good

fuck, but London, Mia, a blur of limbs and mouths and eyes in between . . . I can't seem to find exactly what it is I want.

The UC San Diego campus nearly vibrates with the impending end to the school year. Students lounge on the open lawns, throw Frisbees over clusters of seated groups, and walk lazily down the path as if there isn't a class to attend.

Ahead of me is a guy who looks really familiar . . . it takes my brain only a second to place him, and when it does, my stomach drops.

Ansel is speaking to a female student. He's tall, and has bent slightly to make eye contact and gestures with his hands while he talks. There's nothing remotely sexual in the way he's so attentive, but even just looking at him I can see how much it matters to him that she understands whatever it is he's saying.

Goddamnit. He's a nice guy.

I glance over my shoulder down the path, back the way I've come. I could avoid him by retracing my steps and walking around the humanities complex, but for some reason I don't move, even when the option occurs to me. With each second that ticks past, I lose my ability to disappear without him noticing.

And then he looks up over her shoulder, and sees me standing there watching. I can see the mental filing he needs to do to place me, can see recognition dawn, and then he swallows and looks back down to the girl.

Within two seconds, she's making her way down the path, and he's making his way toward me.

What would I do in his shoes? Would I just serve up a right hook? Would I keep walking?

He stops a few feet away "Luke."

"Ansel. Hi."

We exchange the briefest, most awkward handshake in the history of time.

Up close, and away from the dim light of the bar, I can tell that he's got a few years on me. It's not just in the set of his brow, but the way he's watching me: even, calm, unintimidated.

"What are you doing here?" he asks.

"My father is a director of the Biocircuits Institute. He works just . . . over there." I point past him and he follows my attention behind him and toward the science buildings. "We're meeting up for lunch."

When he looks back at me, his brow lifts, and he lets out a quiet, "Ah."

"But I saw you there, and wanted to talk to you."

Ansel nods once, a clear *So go ahead and talk* gesture.

"I was a complete dick the other night. I want to apologize."

His dark brows shoot up and his head jerks back slightly, telling me this isn't what he expected me to say.

"I knew Mia was with someone," I tell him, "and I knew that she'd moved on. I mean," I quickly add, "I had, too, of course. But I didn't know she was *married*. It threw me."

He nods, but his expression remains unreadable. "I can understand that."

"Still, I was a little surprised by my own reaction when we met." I smile. "Because it would be crazy to still have baggage over a girl four years later, right?"

He laughs, eyes relaxing somewhat. "Maybe not," he admits. "We *are* talking about Mia here. I might have baggage a century later."

This makes me laugh a little, too. "Fair enough."

His smile straightens. "And we're talking about a very traumatic time for both of you, no? You were together for a very long time, and then she nearly died."

I feel like I'm punched in the stomach anytime I think about that day: the call from Harlow, my frantic drive to the hospital, pacing the waiting room for the entire fourteen hours she was in surgery. And it never really got better. It was the worst thing I could have ever said to her but no matter how much I regret it, it still feels true: *It feels like the girl I loved died under that truck.*

"She needed someone after the accident, and it wasn't me," I tell him, realizing—maybe for the first time—how true it is. "It really is that simple."

He nods, blinking away and over my shoulder. "At any rate, there's nothing you need to fix with me," he says. "I know that those memories cause Mia pain and she feels like she's lost someone in her family because she doesn't know you anymore. I've learned from experience that it's never a good idea to try to move on and pretend nothing ever happened." His easy smile from the other night returns, and I find myself thankful; his professional expression is so much more intense. "You should come over for dinner sometime. We have an amazing new house and Mia is dancing again—she is very happy. She would love to see you there."

With a pat to my shoulder, he moves past me down the path.

———————

BY THAT NIGHT I need to get out of the house. Dylan texts just as I'm leaving to grab some soyriza nachos and when he asks if I want to meet up, I can't think of a single reason to say no. I'm not really in the mood for the whole club scene, but as much as I want to see London, I can't bring myself to go to Fred's, either. There's a fine line between hanging out to flirt with someone who may or may not return your interest, and being pathetic. I feel like I'm dangerously close to that line.

We meet up at Clove—a newer club I've only been to a few times—and unless London has obtained a *third* job, I assume she won't be there to overhear me acting like a total and complete dick.

We find a table near the bar and have a few drinks, and by the time Daniel and Andrew meet up with us I'm feeling pretty good. The music is great, the girls are hot, and if I'm not mistaken, there's a long-legged brunette in the corner who definitely seems to be paying me some attention.

I can feel her watching me, our eyes meeting for just a moment when I glance over Andrew's shoulder. I blink away, hoping it looks like I'm just sweeping my gaze across the room. I'm split entirely down the middle. On the one hand, a good fuck tonight would be amazing for distraction. And also because sex? Is good. But the other half of me still feels a touch of hesitation over the remote possibility of London turning into something good. I wonder if maybe I should have gone to Fred's after all. I want to go back and poke at her, tease her, find that easy rhythm we had. I hate feeling like the only way I can talk to her is if we're going to fool around. I prefer the idea that she was right, that I don't need my dick out for someone to like me.

The brunette works her way through the crowd, and once she's within a few feet of me, we make eye contact again and I know there isn't an easy way to escape this without being a total jerk.

"Hey," she says, and then perches her straw between her glossy pink lips.

"Hi."

"Having a good night?" she asks.

I nod, giving her my easy smile. "Pretty good."

She tilts her head and holds my gaze for several breaths. "I'm glad you're here."

My brows go up. "I'm . . . glad I'm here, too."

I expect her to give me her name, to ask me to dance, to do anything but say what she does: "Do you want to get out of here?"

"Do I—?" *What?*

"Yeah," she says, biting down on her straw. "My place."

I blink, hard. I mean, even for me, that's fast. But adrenaline dumps in my veins and I become someone familiar, someone less complicated, reflexively relaxing at the prospect of bending her over the bed and fucking her until I forget London's name. I nod, putting my beer down on a cocktail table behind me and taking her offered hand.

I feel good.

This is good.

This is easy.

And what the fuck, Margot, really? This is a perfect example of what happens ninety percent of the time: a woman approaches me, in a bar, and clearly wants to get laid. And yet I'm the one who needs to evaluate his actions?

Come to think of it, I feel pretty great after a week of downtime, after the interaction with Ansel. Maybe what I really needed was some closure with the Mia situation, some better way to let that ship sail. Margot is right: it's good to know Mia is happy, to know that she's living a life that she chose, that she's built. After I talk to her directly, I'll feel even better.

The nameless brunette walks me toward her Camry and unlocks the door. She has a great chest, toned legs, and a full, fuckable mouth. "Want to ride along or follow me?"

But there's no sparkle in her eyes, no fire, no quick tongue and teasing smile. No dimples. I close my eyes against the image of London. London was just a trigger, a catalyst, a shove. I need to clear the air with Mia, and in order to do that, I had to feel something first. London made me feel something, however brief; I know that now.

But I also know that if I drive myself, I'll drive myself home.

"I'll ride with you." I open the passenger-side door and look across the top of the car at her, pointing to my chest. "Luke."

She laughs, nodding her head like what I've said is really obvious. "I know, silly."

And then she climbs into the driver's seat.

Okay.

I lower myself in beside her and before I even have my seat belt buckled she cups my junk, leans across the console, and whispers, "I want you to come all over me."

Pulling back, I force a smile as I try to hide my mild revulsion. I mean, it's a hot image and usually I like when girls are honest about what they want, but this one lacks all subtlety. She's jumped from introductions to straight-up porn.

Her hand is all over my thigh as she drives, from my knee to my hip and then over my dick and she rubs and rubs, half-chafing, half-pleasurable. I have to close my eyes every time she touches me so I can feel it.

Otherwise, I'm oddly numb. *Is it her? Is it me?* I feel like I'm watching this happen from the hood of the car, looking through the windshield.

She does a tiny striptease at every red light, and with every button she unfastens, the question pounds in my temples:

What is your name?
What is your name?
What is your name?

It matters. Would it have mattered two weeks ago? It

might have been funny; a story I shared with the team about the-time-I-fucked-a-girl-at-her-place-and-never-got-her-name. But now not having a name only makes me uneasy. London made it matter.

I squeeze my eyes closed again and my stomach lurches as she careens into a parking spot, tires squealing as she stops.

Her building is only about a half mile from my place, and once inside the lobby she presses me against the stairwell, kissing me, smearing lip gloss on my chin and mouth. Each time she pulls away, it feels like a sticker being peeled from my skin until all the lip gloss is gone and it's finally her soft mouth, the feel of real skin on skin. She's making these tiny giggling moans every time I grab her ass, dig my fingers into her waist. I switch it up, hating this sound she makes because there's nothing genuine about it, nothing honest.

Turning, she takes my hand and leads me up one flight of stairs to apartment 2A, and I'm shaken by a wave of déjà vu. She rubs her ass against my crotch as she bends to unlock the door and then turns, pulling me inside by the hem of my shirt. I look behind her into the apartment and concerned awareness warms my neck, my face.

I've been here before.

I look at her face—her lip trapped between her bleached-white teeth, her eyes hooded and seductive—and I suddenly need her to tell me her roommate isn't home, her roommate is asleep. Something.

I'm terrified that I've fucked the roommate, and that

she'll show up and find me here and it'll turn into a complete nightmare.

"Do you live alone?" I finally manage.

She shakes her head. "Melissa's at work." Now her eyes glint. "Why? Do you think she should join in? She'll be home at midnight."

I exhale in relief. That's two hours from now. "I'm good like this."

She gives me a wolfish smile and grabs my belt loop before turning and pulling me down the hall behind her.

In her bedroom, she shoves me against the wall and grabs the collar of my shirt, ripping the buttons off. It's so comical, so over-the-top that I want to laugh. This girl is all Blue Steel Porn Star. I stare in bewilderment as she starts to strip, whipping me across the chest with her shirt, wiggling out of her jeans, dragging her panties down my chest.

I have the most ridiculous thought: if Margot could see this moment, she would be on her ass laughing. It's so funny, so absurd that I want to be laughing with her.

But God, that is not helping get my dick hard.

I close my eyes and let go, give in to the rush of hooking up with a complete stranger. Her hands are determined and rough, scratching down my chest, jerking my jeans down my hips. On her knees she's everything women think men want: all tongue and teeth, big eyes focused on my face, sucking and popping and cooing on my dick.

Condom on. She wants to ride me. I'm hard in a desperate way, like I might lose desire, not like I might go off

in a flash. Her sounds are over-the-top and all for my benefit: gasping, screaming, little growls about how big my dick
is, how she's going to come all over it, how she wants me
to fuck her sore and then something incomprehensible. Her
hands are in her own hair, pulling in the agony of the pleasure of it.

She's a terrible actress, and if anything it's making me lose
steam. I'm a lazy asshole, falling back on easy habits. I squeeze
my eyes closed harder at the mild sting I feel at the thought.

But when I close my eyes, on impulse I think of
London—her warm skin, the weight of her breasts in my
palms, and the sounds that burst out of her, escaping as if
she's losing a battle—but there is nothing reminiscent of sex
with London in this moment, no matter how desperately I dig
for the memories of her.

Suddenly, the idea that I need to think of London in
order to stay hard lights a fuse of panic in my chest. I'm a
fucking *idiot*. I know what I want, and I'm wasting time not
being near her. I've earned my college degree, played water
polo with some of the best athletes in the world, but I'm *exactly* the same person I was over four years ago, the day I
walked into the beach condo and fucked Ali Stirling.

I reach for the overacting beauty riding me, needing it to
be over before I think too much, get too deep into introspec-
tion and freak out right here. I stroke her just right—pressing,
circles, steady—and she surprises herself when she starts to
need more, and faster, and the pleasure turns real. I recognize
the stutter in her hips, the jerking tension in her thighs.

Desperate eyes meet mine. "Slap my tits!" she yells. "Slap my tits!"

Startled, I blink up at her. "Wh-*what*?"

"Slap them. Bounce them. Fuck, just do it!"

I hesitate, and with my blood instantly cooling with dread, reach up, doing as she asks and feeling myself wilt inside her even as she's coming with a scream, nails dug into my chest.

Like it's flipped some switch, I know why she didn't tell me her name.

I know why the apartment felt familiar. I never fucked her roommate.

I've fucked this girl before.

And forgot.

MARGOT CAN BARELY breathe she's laughing so hard.

"You were so wrong to tell me," she gasps when she finally comes up for air. "I am never going to let you forget this night. Not ever."

This has easily been the worst night of my adult life. I am so disgusted with myself and I know there are only two people I can share this with who will hold me accountable: Margot, and Dylan.

"I didn't want to tell you," I growl. "I called Dylan first, but he was too high to engage in a conversation. I had to talk to someone."

"God, I can see why. This is *so bad*. Like how could you not recognize her? Her face? Her boobs? Anything!"

I shake my head against the phone, lying down on my couch with a groan. "I don't know! I think she was blond before? She looked sort of familiar? But Margot—and this is the worst thing I'm ever going to say but too fucking bad, you're stuck with me—she sort of looked like a million other girls. Long brown hair, skinny, big tits, lip gloss."

"So when did you figure it out?"

Slap my tits! Slap my tits!

Shaking my head, I say, "No. No way am I telling you that."

"Oh, God, you're right, I don't want to know."

We both fall silent and I can hear her television in the background. "Will you come sleep here tonight?" I ask.

"Luke, it's late."

"Margooooooot," I whine. "I feel gross and this house is so big and empty."

"Are there even sheets on my bed?"

"I'll put some on."

She huffs out a little breath and I know I've won. "Fine, you big baby. I'll be there in ten."

MY BIG SISTER makes me popcorn and hot chocolate and then lets me have the good throw pillow. Her price: a foot rub while we cue up Jimmy Fallon on the DVR.

"Thanks for coming over," I say, skipping through the first commercial break.

She closes her eyes. "Shut up."

I give her a series of overly dramatic wide-eye blinks. "You're the best big sister ever."

"I know." She stretches, pressing her foot into my hand. "More on the arch. I was standing all day today at the bench."

I wince. "Your feet smell."

Margot snorts. "You went home with a stranger before realizing you'd already boned her before."

Sighing, I admit, "You're right, I'm grosser." I take a deep breath before telling her the other important event of the day. "So, hey. I ran into Ansel on campus today."

She opens one eye. "Ansel?"

"Mia's husband."

Her mouth forms an O several seconds before she lets out a small *"Ohhh."*

"You would have been proud of me. I went up to him and apologized for being a dick to Mia."

She pushes up on one elbow, eyes wide. "And?"

"*And* . . . he's a good guy." I tell her about my conversation with him. "I still need to talk to Mia, but I felt about a million times better about it after."

"Luker, can I ask you something?"

I press my thumb into the ball of her foot. "Sure."

"Do you ever look at Mia and think about—"

I drop her foot, holding up my hand. "No. *No.* Not anymore." At her blank expression, I add, "I don't want to sleep with Mia."

She bites back a laugh. "Okay."

Margot can barely keep from cracking up and dread settles in my gut.

"That's not what you were going to ask me, is it?" I ask her.

"Nope."

I drop my head. "Damnit."

"Luke: you have a problem with sex."

I smack her calf. "Just finish your question."

With an evil grin, she asks, "Do you ever look at Mia and wonder whether she's gone home with someone she'd already banged before, but forgot?"

Reaching for her ribs, I dig a knuckle there, tickling her until she shrieks.

"Fuck you," I yell over her screams, "ask the real question."

"Okay! Okay!" she gasps, swatting at my hands. "Do you ever look at Mia and think it's cool to see her so happy again?"

I let my head fall back against the couch so I can think on how to answer, because the truth is, I feel a lot of things. The simple answer is I *am* happy for Mia, because she's an amazing woman with so much love to give, and deserves it. But it's also complicated. I feel bad I couldn't be what she needed. I feel disappointment in myself for the way I reacted to that part of my life closing, and that I went to such extremes to open another. I hate that I'm still sad sometimes over the way things ended with Mia, and even sadder that it wasn't until I met London that I felt anything at all.

"It is cool, yeah," I tell her, and Margot must see everything behind my eyes because she gives me a small smile, and then kicks me in the stomach.

"Ow! Jesus Christ, I changed my mind, I don't want you to sleep here."

She pulls her feet from my lap. "I just wanted to knock you out of that little funk you're slipping into. You had a shit night, but you'll learn something and move on. You might be an idiot sometimes, Luker, but you're not dumb. Just don't make the same mistake again." She hesitates, adding, "I mean, *again*."

I rub a hand over my ribs and glare at her.

"Now, it's late and I need to get to bed." She leans over and kisses the top of my head. "I love you. Don't stay up too late."

"I won't," I say, impulsively adding, "I think I want to call London."

I expect a certain degree of shit for this but instead I get "I think this is a great idea" before she walks down the hall to her bedroom. Once the door clicks closed, I pull my phone from my pocket. It makes me laugh, a little, that I've missed seventeen texts in the time I've been talking to my sister, and none of them are from the girl I want to talk to.

Even in the time it takes me to work up the nerve to call her, two more come in: one from Dylan, telling me to come join them at Andrew's, and one from a girl I spent one night with and who lives in Seattle.

What the fuck is my life?

Without thinking more, I swipe my screen and find

London's name. She's probably at work and won't check her phone for a few hours. I'm afraid I'll lose my nerve in a few hours. I press her work number.

"Fred's Bar," she answers, and my heart does an irritating clenching thing.

"Logan? It's Luke," I say.

She's quiet a beat too long for my liking before she says, "Hey."

"Hey." I know she's at work and I have to cut to the chase before she's called away. "So I was thinking, maybe we could hang out."

"Hang out?"

"Yeah," I say, smiling. Never before have I felt like such a nervous idiot. "It's a saying the kids use these days when they want to do something together. We could hang out at the beach. Or hang out at dinner. See?"

Laughing, she says, "I don't think that's a great idea."

"I know you don't," I tell her, sitting up straighter. "But I promise I will make it one hundred percent worth it. I'll turn off my phone. I'll pay for dinner. I won't order a single Heineken."

"You're calling me at work to ask me out on a date?"

"I worried you wouldn't answer your cell if you saw it was me calling."

I close my eyes at the sound of her laugh again. It's breathy, and in it I can hear both exasperation and the "no" she's about to give me. "When are you thinking?" she asks.

Hope explodes, warm in my blood. "Tomorrow?"

I can imagine her chewing her fingernail while she thinks. "I work tomorrow night," she says.

"How about during the day? I mean, obviously the law offices are closed."

"During the day?"

"Yeah."

Her hesitation lasts a million years. "I have . . . inventory."

"Inventory?"

"All day," she says quickly. "It's, um, starting at like ten or maybe earlier? I need to look at the calendar, that, um, Fred has in the office. And then it goes until, maybe like right when I start work?" She pauses, adding, "Actually, the next couple weeks are really bad for me overall."

I can't decide if I love or hate that London is the worst liar in the history of time. It feels like the real-life version of watching her gun me down on-screen.

"Oh, yeah, no worries. Well, have a good night at work," I tell her. "And maybe we can find another time."

I end the call and fall back on my couch, swearing up a storm of frustration into a pillow.

Chapter NINE

London

*W*E TURN OFF University and make our way up the tree-lined Park Boulevard into Balboa Park. Lola sits in the driver's seat of her new Prius, singing along quietly next to me, her hair tied back with a green and white scarf. Mia is in the backseat, looking up something dance-business-related on her phone.

I'm trying to be cool, bouncing along to the music. But inside, I'm sort of a mess.

Harlow said she'd meet us at the park.

This is the first time we'll all be together since my phone call with Mia, and since I found out Harlow was upset about me being with Luke. Lola insisted we should take advantage of this shared day off. She insisted what we all needed was girl time. She insisted it wouldn't be weird.

But let's be honest: I'm sort of a novice when it comes to intimate girl friendships, and Harlow's temper is legendary. It's *totally* going to be weird.

It's a perfect day: the sky is blue with only the fluffiest, most innocent clouds overhead. The air is warm in the sun, cool in the shade, and wherever we go it's heavy with the scent of salt water. I want to believe there isn't any further drama to be found here but even I, a staunchly anti-drama advocate, can't imagine we'll all just pretend that nothing happened.

"Everyone's okay, right?" Lola says, breaking the silence.

I can't tell if she's asking me, or Mia.

"I'm good," Mia says from the backseat.

"I'm good, too!" I chirp.

I can feel them both look to me. We pull up to a stop sign and the Prius falls so completely silent, I can practically hear the brightness of my answer echoing through the car.

"We're all best friends, you know," Lola says, but she waves her hand in a circle, clearly including me. "I think that's just why Harlow flipped. She's cool."

"Good," I say, grinning over at her and determined to not apologize again. I appreciate the gesture she's made, of helping me feel as tight in the group as the rest of them, so I try to focus on that instead of pointing out the obvious, that I wasn't around four, three, or even two years ago when Luke and Mia would have been working through anything. Besides, it's moot anyway, and the more we talk about Luke, the more it becomes a *thing*.

It's so not a thing.

When he'd called me last night, I'd been in the middle of an order and had to double-check that it was actually him on the line, and not some random guy who'd managed to get my name off their receipt . . . though admittedly none of them call me Logan.

Was Luke really calling to ask me out? Luke *Right now I'd be terrible at anything more* Sutter? Fred watched me with the most amused expression and I had to turn my back to him, because the look of surprise on my face would have been enough to have him questioning me for the rest of the night.

Luke sounded so sincere that, for a moment, I'd been caught off guard. I *like* Luke—which is actually part of the problem.

So I'd lied, telling him I had to work when I could have simply said I already have plans.

Which I do.

I hate lying.

I'll call him later, I decide. I'll admit that I panicked, that I wasn't prepared for him to call me at work. But I'll make it clear—without being harsh—that the best he and I can ever hope for is friendship.

We pull into the lot and everyone piles out of the car, stretching limbs and turning faces up into the sun. Balboa Park is an enormous park in the center of urban San Diego. The zoo is one of the best in the world, there are more gardens and museums than can be visited in a single day, but we usually come for the giant stretches of lawn beneath the brilliant blue sky.

We find a shady spot under a towering tree, and spread out a blanket. I slip off my shoes and revel in the cool grass slipping through my toes before I plop down, hoping to shut my brain off for a few hours.

Lola opens the picnic basket and tosses us each a bottle of

water before brandishing a small box of cupcakes. "We're eating dessert first."

"I do not need a cupcake," I groan, stretching out on the blanket. "I polished off an entire pint of Ben and Jerry's when I got home from work last night."

"At Fred's?" Mia asks, bending to straighten her side of the blanket. Her dark hair is cut shorter again and skims her jawline as she leans forward. It's a cut most people could never hope to pull off—angular, maybe even a little harsh—but with her delicate features and creamy skin, I'm pretty sure she could be wearing one of those hats with the beer cans on it and still manage to look gorgeous.

Mia is of course lovely, but it's moments like these where I can really see her and Luke as a couple: beautiful, petite, porcelain-doll Mia, and Abercrombie & Fitch Luke who has better cheekbones than any woman I know.

"Yeah, Fred's."

"I can't keep track of your schedule," Lola says, handing me a cupcake anyway.

"Because she works too damn much," Harlow says, startling me as she seems to appear out of nowhere. She sits down next to me. "Hey, everyone."

We all return the greeting . . . and when she looks over at me, yeah, it's weird. Her smile is tight, and mine is probably too wide.

But we're all committed, apparently. Harlow takes an offered cupcake from Lola and crosses her legs in front of her. "Guess who I just ran into in the parking lot?"

I don't even bother guessing. Practically everyone I know in San Diego is sitting on this blanket.

Apparently Lola and Mia draw a similar level of blank, because they ask in unison, "Who?"

"Ethan Crumbley."

It clearly takes both of them a few seconds to place him, because Harlow adds, "The UCLA football dude."

"Ohhhhhh," they coo in unison again, and based on their reactions, I wish I'd run into him, too.

"Sadly," Harlow says, licking a little frosting off her finger, "he has not aged too well."

"Oh, that is sad," Mia says. "But I guess he was sort of a jerk, and it's better to see the ex looking like crap than seeing him with someone super hot!"

Oh fuck.

Mia snaps her mouth shut, throwing Lola a horrified look.

Harlow takes an enormous bite of her cupcake and looks up at the three of us who have gone completely silent. "What?" she asks, mouth full. "Finn is leaving for two weeks and if I'm not getting sex I should at least be getting something with frosting on it."

Okay, clearly Harlow did not pick up on the weirdness there and apparently assumed we were just horrified that she managed to eat half of a cupcake in a single bite. I can see Mia relax a little across from me.

I would do anything for a reassuring smile from *someone* today.

"How's Finn adjusting to the filming?" Lola asks.

"Very few complaints, actually," Harlow says. "Which is surprising because Finn usually complains about everything. Nonverbally, that is: his chosen medium of expression is typically heavy sighs."

"Wow, how few things you two have in common," Mia says, and Harlow throws one of her flip-flops at her.

"Well, I for one am thrilled to be out," Lola says. "If I had to spend one more second looking at the terrible mock-ups of the site I'm having done, I was going to lose my mind."

"You're having a new site built?" Mia asks, and Lola nods.

"Yeah, but so far it's been disastrous. This guy came really highly recommended, but so far he doesn't seem to get the art, if that makes sense?"

"I think it makes perfect sense," I tell her, and everyone looks to me as if they've forgotten that I was here. "I could take a look at it, if you wanted?"

Lola looks like someone just offered her a puppy. "You'd do that?"

"Sure, why not?"

"I know how you feel about doing work for people you know," she says, worrying her bottom lip. "I didn't want to put you in a position where you had to say no."

"You're *you,* Lola. If I don't want to do it I'll just tell you."

Lola lunges forward to hug me before reaching for her phone. "I'll forward you the links to everything right now," she says, giddy.

"So what else have you been up to?" Harlow asks me,

somewhat stiffly, stretching miles of tan legs in front of her. "I don't think I've seen you since we all went out."

I blink, looking up into the tree overhead, at the way the branches crisscross back and forth like a giant jigsaw puzzle. I count off on my fingers, "Skydiving, fighting crime, a little brothel business I've been running on the side."

"Now, a brothel I could get behind because one: Ladies getting paid," she says. "And two: It'd give you at least marginally better hours than you have now. Plus, you know, penises. Peni? What is a lot of penises? A bushel?"

"A bushel of penises, Whorelow? Really?" Lola says as she drops her phone back in her purse. "But otherwise, *preach*. She's even working extra shifts at . . ."

I push up on an elbow, intending to interrupt, but at the same time, Lola moves a little to the right and my breath catches in my throat.

This can't be happening.

I sit, eyes zeroing in on the two figures across the lawn, a fit twentysomething guy I recognize, and a girl. Of course there's a girl.

"London? Are you okay?" Lola snaps her fingers in front of my face and I blink back to the conversation. Judging from her expression, I must look like I swallowed a tennis ball.

"Damnit," I hiss, and hunch down. I'm not sure if I'm trying to hide or find a way to escape, but I'm almost positive that's Luke across the park and that I am absolutely *not* supposed to be here. He's also the last person I want to see when Harlow and Mia are sitting right next to me.

"What is it?" Mia asks before she sees him over Lola's shoulder, too. "Oh. *Oh*."

"I should never lie," I mumble to myself. I look around at the blanket, at the food we were just starting to unpack. Lola looks at me in question, so I add, "I told Luke I was doing inventory today and now he's here."

"Oh," Lola says as well, followed by another "*Ohhhh*," as she gets what I mean.

Harlow—who up until this point hasn't been paying attention—follows my gaze before looking back at me. "Why did you tell him you were doing inventory?"

I look at her incredulously for a beat before deciding now is not the time to point out that she shouldn't be complaining about me making up excuses to not see him since she didn't seem too thrilled with me seeing him in the first place. "He called and asked me out," I tell her, and ignore the slow rise of her eyebrows. "It just . . . it wasn't a good idea, and so I lied."

"There was your first mistake," Lola says. "You couldn't even keep a straight face when I asked if you ate all my Corn Flakes."

"I didn't expect him to be *here*, did I?"

"Well," Harlow says, "whatever your story is, you'd better get it ready." She sits up, plastering a calm, oblivious expression on her face and muttering, "Because if that's Luke, he's headed this way."

I'm almost afraid to look, but when I do peek behind me, I see that Harlow is right; Luke is walking toward us, a tall brunette at his side.

I stand, wiping off the butt of my shorts and attempt to meet him halfway. If I'm going to make a fool of myself, I'd rather it be out of earshot.

Unfortunately, he's faster than I am.

"Logan?" he says, looking at me before leaning to one side to see the girls behind me. He takes in my outfit—cutoffs and a thin white T-shirt, my bare feet—the blanket stretched out on the grass and the basket of food, and it clearly doesn't take him long to piece together that I'm not just here on a break from inventory duties.

"Hey," I say, squinting into the sun. I'm hoping my sunglasses are enough to hide the way my eyes keep trying to skim down his body. He's tan and wearing a yellow T-shirt and loose khaki shorts, and I must have pissed someone off in a previous life because Luke Sutter is possibly the hottest guy I've ever known. "Fancy seeing you here."

He looks confused for a moment before he shakes his head. "I was at the zoo. My sister accosted me and forced me out of the house."

"He was turning into a weirdo," the girl cuts in. She's *really* pretty, and it takes my brain about two seconds to process what he's said, that this is his *sister.* The same one who drags him shopping and makes him buy her tampons, who forced him into child labor in her doll salon and gives him epic amounts of shit. I don't even know Margot and she's already one of my favorite people. "So *you're* Logan."

"London," Luke corrects under his breath and, if anything, her smile grows. She has the same thick dark hair and brown eyes, the same perfect smile that seems to light up her entire face.

"I know, baby brother. Lord knows I've heard you talk about her enough. *London this and London that*. Margot," she says, pointing to her chest. "Big sister, favorite child."

"I've heard a lot about you, too," I say. "It's nice to finally meet you."

With a hand cupping her entire face, Luke pushes his sister behind him and takes a step toward me. I don't have to be a genius to know she's going to pay him back for that later. "You didn't really have to work, did you?" he says, eyes theatrically wide. And oh, shit, he *knew* I brushed him off and is now completely relishing having caught me. "Oh my God, is it possible sweet London *lied* to me about inven—?"

"Why don't you guys come eat with us?" I blurt, and motion to where everyone is sitting behind me, surely listening to every word. I look over my shoulder and of course they're all waving. Even Harlow.

I don't know what I was expecting. Maybe I thought he would smile in that way that makes my legs feel less than steady, and insist he didn't want to impose. Maybe I thought he'd make some sort of scene, having figured out that I lied because I didn't want to hang out with him.

What I'm not expecting is for him to look back at his sister and nod, heart-stopping smile in place, while he motions for her to lead the way.

Margot doesn't have to be told twice, already rushing toward the girls. And of course they already know one another.

Luke takes a step to join them before he pauses, stooping just enough to bring his face level with my own.

"I'm glad *Margot* made me leave the house," he says, and if I didn't feel bad already, that does the trick. I like giving Luke a hard time. But I don't want to be a dick to the dick, either.

"You're too well-groomed to be a hermit, anyway," I tell him, and his smile widens as he follows me over to the blanket.

He approaches Mia first, crouching beside her to say something close to her ear. I have no idea what he's whispering, but I sense Harlow watching them like a hawk, monitoring Mia's reaction. Mia nods, smiling as she listens, and then twists to give him a brief hug.

I hear him murmur a quiet, "I'm really sorry."

"Don't be. I'm just glad you're doing so well," she says, and smiles again when he gives her a chaste kiss on the cheek.

The mood seems to ease a little after this. Even Harlow allows herself a tiny smile at him as everyone shifts over to make room on the blanket, with the enormous picnic lunch in the middle. Luke sits cross-legged beside Lola, and of course it ends up that I take my seat directly between Luke and Margot.

My heart is in my throat. I feel like I'm in a fishbowl, every movement being cataloged and analyzed. Am I sitting too close to him? Acting too familiar? Do I look like I've seen him naked? Like I'm imagining it *now*?

The food is passed around and Margot and the girls jump into easy conversation while Luke and I keep our eyes pinned on the picnic blanket.

When I finally have my nerves under control and look up, Lola catches my eye and smiles a little in reassurance. In her expression, I read the *You two are adorable* look there. And she's right: *he* is fucking adorable. It surprises me how happy I am to see him, but also how much it suddenly sucks that I can't really enjoy it without pissing off someone really important to me. For her part, Harlow doesn't seem to be too worried about it; she's not even looking at us.

"So let me get this straight." Margot blinks from Luke to me as she unwraps a sandwich. "London said she had to work so she didn't have to hang out with you?" She is clearly delighted.

One side of Luke's mouth turns up as he slides his eyes to me. "Apparently."

It is obvious to me that it would never occur to Margot or Luke that this would be at all weird, and it makes me like them both, just a little bit more.

"Okay, okay," Margot says, moving to her knees to pull her phone from her back pocket. "Just let me put this in my calendar." She starts typing. " 'The day . . . the tables were turned . . . on my dear, sweet brother . . . and a girl made up a work story . . . so she didn't have to spend time with him.' " She taps her screen once more as if saving it, and smiles. "There. Noted."

"Don't forget to send a group text," he tells her. "Wouldn't want to leave Mom and Grams out of the loop."

She turns her phone to face him. "Oh, the group window is already open."

Luke shrugs good-naturedly and takes a bite out of his sandwich. "I'm man enough to take this."

I glance over at Mia and see she's grinning ear to ear. "At least this time your shame was not captured on film."

"Oh my God, I forgot about that Homecoming!" Harlow says.

"You think I was *ashamed* of that?" Luke asks, leaning closer to me. So close that our arms touch from shoulder to elbow.

He's including me.

He's making it clear he's here for me.

He's saying something to me, and he's saying something to Mia and all her friends: *that is our history. This is my now.*

My heart trips over itself, but falls down down down inside my chest when I feel Harlow's gaze on my face.

I look over to her, redirecting her stern attention. "Okay, what happened at Homecoming?" I ask.

Mia is already laughing, and the sound diffuses the tiny slip of tension that—thankfully—Luke and Margot have yet to notice. "So it's halftime. Keep in mind, this is our senior year, so the boys give exactly zero shits about good behavior at this point. Everyone's up in the stands waiting for the drill team to come out, and this group of naked guys wearing masks burst out onto the field."

I glance at Luke, and realize I've been unconsciously leaning just a tiny bit into him. He smells clean, and warm. I smell his soap, and remember how different it was on my own skin. He's blushing, high along his cheekbones, visible even beneath his tan. He looks like he's barely keeping himself from laughing, too.

Margot nods. "The local newspaper was there—about two thousand parents with zoom lenses, too—and it was like wagging penis—camera flash—ass—camera flash. Our aunt recognized his butt from the photos Grams sent out to the entire family." She can barely get the last word out before she falls over, giggling.

"Oh my God," I say to him. "What were you thinking?"

"Look," Luke says, gesturing down the length of his body. "Sometimes you just can't keep the beast contained, okay?"

There's a collective groan and now everyone has completely lost it, Lola laughing so hard she looks like she can barely breathe. "He had to do community service at the senior center and spent the summer having his butt pinched by old ladies who'd already seen it in the newspaper."

"I can't believe I forgot about that," Margot says, and reaches up to swipe away a few tears. "Oh my God, I'm crying."

"My sides," Harlow says, leaning forward to catch her breath.

"I do what I can," Luke says. He looks completely unfazed by all of this as he takes a giant bite of his sandwich and I can't help but be impressed. It also occurs to me that I haven't seen him look at his phone once, and I wonder if that has anything to do with his sister being with him.

Finally recovered, Harlow turns her attention to Luke. "So now that that's out of the way," she says, and dabs at the mascara just under her eyes. "What have you been doing with yourself?" I hold my breath, but exhale quietly when she says only, "I heard you were going to law school?"

"Hopefully," he says. Luke explains that he's a law clerk—Margot cuts in to brag that he works for the biggest transactional law firm in San Diego County—and that he barely has time to use the bathroom without taking files into the stall with him. He's hoping to attend law school in the fall. "My mommy and sister made sure I mailed off my applications," he says with a grin aimed at his sister, "so we'll see what happens."

Harlow points her water bottle at him. "That is such a coincidence because you know Mia's husband is an attorney."

"Subtle, Harlow," Lola says, and puts another cupcake in her hand. "Why don't you shove this in your mouth for a while?"

"What?" she says, but takes the second cupcake nonetheless. "It's an interesting bit of trivia, don't you think?"

"I know this," Luke says, "because I ran into him on campus the other day and went up to talk to him. He seems like a great guy."

Everyone goes still, except Luke, who casually takes another bite of his sandwich, and Mia, who seems to already know this story.

"He is," Mia says, smiling at him with such gratitude it makes my throat go tight in relief for both of them.

Lola hands out more cupcakes to everyone and the others continue to catch up, talking about Harlow's mom's recovery from a double mastectomy and chemo, Margot's teaching job, about Finn and Ansel, and, of course, about Luke, when he turns to me, leaning in.

"You owe me, you know," he says, and I feel my brows disappear into my hair.

"I *owe* you?"

"Calm down there, Zurich. I don't mean like that. I mean that you lied to me and just gave my sister enough ammunition to last her through the summer."

"Hey, don't look at me," I say, unable to hold in my smile. "It's not my fault you offer up so much amazing material. You're a comedic gold mine."

"And yet you ignore the fact that you lied." His brows draw down, but even so, he can't remove the smile from his eyes. "That wasn't very nice."

He has a point. "You're right, but in my defense I was just trying to keep your expectations manageable. I didn't want you to think there was anything between us that could lead to—"

He holds up a hand to stop me. "We're not doing that. I know." Surprisingly, he glances at Harlow and then back to me. Maybe he catches more than he's letting on? "And I get it. But even you have to admit that this—hanging out?—doesn't completely suck, right?"

"Way to set the bar high there, superstar."

He laughs. "You *know* what I mean."

I pick at the wrapper of my cupcake. "It doesn't suck," I admit.

"You just said I was right. I'm sort of mortified by how happy that makes me." He leans in again, nodding to Margot. "Don't tell my sister."

"Your secret is safe with me."

Luke reaches for a piece of my cupcake and I let him, watching as he tears off a chunk and pops it into his mouth. A smear of white frosting colors his bottom lip, and he flicks out the tip of his tongue, licking it off. He watches me watching him with a knowing smirk.

I swallow, and can only hope it's not as loud as I imagine. Lola—who by all accounts is totally engaged in the other conversation—covertly squeezes my hand on the blanket behind Luke's back. She is such an enabler.

I clear my throat, and busy myself wiping imaginary crumbs from my shorts. "So what have you been up to?"

"Let's see . . . I texted you"—he says with a teasing smile—"feel free to answer those anytime. Practiced up on my video games, did some laundry, hung out at my mom's house, and jerked off a few times." He pauses and his brows come together. "Absolutely *not* in that order."

I cough out a laugh. "I was going to say . . ."

"Uh, yeah. Let's rebrand that conversation and edit out that last part." He reaches for another piece of cupcake, and I hold it out for him.

"Thanks," he says.

I glance over at his sister, who seems deep in conversation with the girls. "It's really great how much time you spend with your family."

"Did you know my room at home still looks exactly like it did when I was sixteen?"

"Really?"

He nods. "Most of my friends' parents have turned theirs into a den or a sewing room or something, but nothing has changed. My awkward adolescence has been preserved like an archeological dig."

"I can't tell if that's terrifying or intriguing," I tell him.

"My bed is in the same place, the posters on the wall, even the corkboard I made in shop when I was in eighth grade is still there, complete with friendship bracelets, concert tickets, and dance photos. I think there's even the condom wrapper I used when I lost my virginity," he says, narrowing his eyes like he's trying to remember. As if it just occurs to him what that would mean, he glances quickly over to Mia, his cheeks coloring again.

"Wow, that's . . . nostalgic." It's a little weird to hear him talk about this, if I'm being honest. My family life is nothing like his.

He shakes his head. "I'm sure my mom doesn't even know it's there. I didn't even realize until I was looking for a phone number last summer and found it tucked between a Tower of Terror Fastpass from 2009 and a ticket stub from a Tom Petty concert."

"That's sort of amazing," I say, picking at a blade of grass. "I'd been gone less than a month and my mom had my room turned into a craft cave."

"I don't know what I'd do if I couldn't go home," he says quietly. "Like, I go back there and I'm twelve years old again.

I can lie on my bed and look up at the pages I tore out of the 2002 *Sports Illustrated* Swimsuit Edition—Yamila Diaz-Rahi was on the cover, just in case you were wondering—the poster of a Lamborghini I swore I'd own by the time I was eighteen," he says with a roll of his eyes. "And I can just be dumb and pretend like nothing else matters."

"I think I'm jealous of your cool room."

"Let's make a deal," he says, and licks a smear of frosting from his thumb. "I'll let you hang out in my room when real life blows, provided you let me feel you up at least once while you're there. Twelve-year-old me would be really impressed with that."

"And they say chivalry is dead."

"Dear God, you would get along with my Grams. I'm actually a little afraid of what would happen with you, my sister, my mom, and her all in one room. Frankly, I don't think I'm man enough to handle it."

I'm just about to tell Luke that that sounds like a bet I'd be willing to take, when he casually reaches for his phone.

Though it's clearly been on silent, the screen is alive with notifications. I have no idea when he checked it last, but he's been with us a good twenty minutes. There have to be at least a dozen alerts there. I feel myself frown and I'm not even sure why.

"So what are you guys up to after this?" he asks, and I wonder if he even notices how he carries on a conversation while scrolling through the screen, practiced eyes flicking down and then back up again.

"Actually," I say, and push myself to my knees, "I should probably get going."

"You have to go?" he says, and immediately tosses his phone to the blanket. He looks disappointed and I have to knock down my tiny, thrilled reaction.

Harlow meets my eyes and—despite the weirdness between us and the cool distance I still catch in her eyes—I'm reminded again why she's one of my favorite people in the world. It's like a bat signal must have gone off above my head because within seconds she's up, looking at her watch and giving some excuse about why we have to leave.

Mia follows suit, helping Lola load up the basket and fold the blanket.

"So when will we all see each other again?" Margot says to the girls, getting out her own phone to check her calendar. They make plans and Luke pulls me over to the side.

"Are you working tomorrow?" he asks.

I consider lying, but decide there's really no point. I like Luke, I want to be friends with Luke. Harlow can't really have a problem with it, and aside from that, what he does with whoever is on his phone or otherwise is none of my business. "Yeah," I tell him, adding, "at Fred's."

"My liver's had a break, so maybe I'll stop by."

He can be so cute when he wants to, it's really annoying. "I'll be there. Be sure and bring lots of dollar bills. That car isn't going to pay for itself."

"You can always start stripping," he says, and then Margot is there, cutting in front of him.

"It was really great to meet you. Anytime you want to help me drive this guy to drink, just call me." She surprises me by pulling me into a hug and I hug her back, meeting Luke's eyes over her shoulder.

"It's becoming my new favorite pastime," I tell her. "Maybe we can start a club."

Chapter TEN

Luke

"NO THANK YOU," Grams says as Mom carries the serving dish to where she sits. "No asparagus for me, Julie. Those white ones make me feel like I'm eating tiny penises."

Dad chokes on a sip of wine and Margot's eyes shoot up to the ceiling while she struggles to keep from laughing.

Our dining room is bright and expansive, with thick cream wallpaper and a large chandelier hanging over a hand-carved cherry table. The décor is way too nice for the kinds of conversations that go down in here when my grandmother is around.

I smile adoringly at my grandmother. "You're a poet, Grams."

"Mom," Dad says in warning, and then looks at me. "Don't encourage her."

"What?" Her milky blue eyes widen innocently at him across the table. "Have you looked at them, Bill? It's been for-ever since I changed your diaper or wiped your butt, so I'm not suggesting it looks like *your*—"

"Can you pass the bread?" Margot interrupts.

Grams picks up the bread bowl with a shaky hand and

passes it to my sister. "Honestly." She shakes her head. "Penises are the strangest-looking organ. If being a lesbian had been an option in my day, I would have definitely gone that direction." She waves a hand. "Not that I didn't love cleaning up after my feral children and cooking for your father for fifty years."

"Oh boy," Margot mumbles.

"Female bodies are so much more pleasant," Grams muses. "With the breasts and legs and whatnot."

I laugh into my water glass.

"You *should* laugh," Grams says, pointing a delicate, withered finger at me. "You love your penis more than anything in the world."

I raise my brows as if to say, *Well, you're not wrong,* but Mom lets out a tiny squeak. *"Anne,"* she says quietly, "Luke doesn't . . ."

The sentence hangs there and the silence bounces around between us.

"Doesn't what?" Grams asks into the abyss. "Love his penis? Don't be thick. Margot tells me Luke hasn't had a girlfriend in years, but look at that smile." She points at me again. "No boy his age smiles like that without a lot of willing ladies around, if you catch my meaning."

"She has a point," I say.

"Luke Graham Sutter," Mom whisper-hisses. *"Honestly."*

"There may be a change happening," Margot says, and then slides a stalk of asparagus between her teeth, biting down savagely. I wince. Chewing, she says, "Remember that text I sent you the other day? Luke has a crush on a girl."

Time stops. Forks go silent. Jaws drop open and dust settles.

"Jesus Christ," I groan, stabbing a bite of chicken.

"Watch your mouth, son," Dad says under his breath.

I glare at my sister. "You're on a tear lately, Margot. Are you trying to push me out of this state?"

"Well, what do I have to lose?" she asks. "You're running out of willing sexual partners in Southern California. Unless you just cycle through them again and forget their na—"

I cut her off with a low *"Margot."*

"Luker?" Mom asks me, ignoring this. "You have a girl-friend?"

"No," Margot answers for me. "There's a girl who refuses him, but he *loooooves* her."

"Are you twelve?" I ask.

My sister winks at me.

"Bubbles?" Mom addresses me again and the delicate hope in her voice makes something between my ribs grow tight.

"You guys," I say, putting down my fork. "Can we all agree it isn't healthy that you're all so invested in me settling down? I'm twenty-three. I graduated *last summer.*"

"You were just so happy with Mia," Dad explains.

"Of course he was happy!" Grams crows. "He was seventeen and having premarital sex!" She cackles and slaps the table loudly.

"Mom," Dad says more forcefully this time. "This isn't helping."

"Can we just stop talking about my love life for once?" I ask.

"We," Margot says, gesturing around the table, "have literally *never* talked about your love life." When I don't argue, she continues: "At least not with you in the room. I just thought everyone might want to know that you've got your eye on someone. And, given that you've lost your sea legs, so to speak, maybe you could use some advice. After all, Mom and Dad have been married for twenty-seven years. And Grams was married to Papa for fifty."

"Fifty-two," Grams corrects her.

"See?" Margot says, smiling at me victoriously. "Fifty-*two*. I'm sure they would love to give you some pointers."

Mom's hopeful smile is back in place. "You want some advice, Bubbles?"

I smile at my sister through clenched teeth and nod. "Sure, Mom."

Dad pats his napkin against his mouth and sets it down beside his plate before leaning back in his chair and studying me. *Oh boy.*

"Be straightforward," he says, lacing his hands behind his head.

"Straightforward," Mom agrees with a decisive nod.

"My best advice," Dad says, "is don't beat around the bush."

Margot snorts. "I agree. Luke tends to beat around the bush *way* too much."

Dad opens his mouth and then closes it, sliding Margot

a disapproving look. "If you like her," he continues with emphasis, slowly looking back to me, "then ask her out."

"But this isn't the one who he asked out and she lied about working, is it?" Mom asks Margot.

"It isn't really that simple," I say before Margot can answer for me, and for a heartbeat I can't believe I'm actually engaging in this. But as both of my parents lean in, encouraged, I realize it's too late. "We went out a couple of times." I glare at Margot when she lifts a finger to correct the inaccuracy, and she drops it, looking—for once—like she's going to lay off. "But I've been . . . playing the field a bit," I say, delicately. "And I don't think she likes that about me."

"Well, of course she doesn't, honey," Mom tells me sweetly. "Girls want to feel special."

"Take her to a dance," Grams suggests with a wide smile.

I break it to her gently: "We don't really do that anymore, Grams."

"Well, then take her somewhere she likes," she says. "Does this gal like the movies?"

Dragging a hand through my hair, I admit, "I have no idea if she likes the movies. She's a bartender at night and surfs all day."

Mom's hand drifts in for a trembling landing on her throat. "She went to college, though?"

"She graduated with my class at UCSD," I reassure her. Mom visibly relaxes. "I think she's just figuring out what she wants out of life."

"Well, there you go," Dad says with a firm palm to the

table. "*You're* directed and driven. Maybe you can help her find her way in her career, and she can help you get your head on straight about how to get back in the saddle."

This time my sister's snort is so loud I'm worried a sinus broke off.

"I can't believe you actually said 'back in the saddle,' " I tell him.

He nods, wincing apologetically. "I . . ." He reaches for the wine and pours another glass.

I'm practically vibrating inside, needing to escape the scrutiny. As if spring-loaded, my legs push me to stand and I kiss my mom's forehead, kiss Grams's dust-soft cheek, pat Dad's shoulder, and smack Margot on the back of the head. "Thanks for dinner, Mom. The chicken and penises were delicious. Love you guys."

I grab my sweatshirt from the back of the couch on the way out, feeling like my heart is going to punch its way out of my body. I've given Margot more trouble in her lifetime than I can ever hope she'll repay, but I do like London. I like her a lot, and having it all reduced to a joke, or an amusing conversation over the dinner table, is starting to wear on me.

It bothers me that she felt she had to lie about working, but I get it.

It bothers me that I have no clue how to undo her perception of me, because it isn't entirely wrong.

It bothers me to see her so obviously worrying about what Mia, and Harlow, and Lola would think of us together.

It bothers me that she's so clear that nothing else will

happen between us, but if all I can get from her is friendship, I like her enough to want to work for it.

But even though I know she was working last night, I didn't go to Fred's. I felt like I owed her some space.

"Hang on, Luke." Dad catches me on the porch, stopping me with a hand wrapped around my elbow. The sun is setting over the horizon and it's a dizzying mix of oranges and reds framed by long, delicate palms. Some days I feel like I would be insane to leave this town and move somewhere else.

"I wanted to say a few more things to you about . . . your dating life."

And then sometimes I think I can't escape fast enough.

"Dad," I say, rubbing a hand down my face. "I know you guys mean well. It's just . . . so incredibly unhelpful."

It's an odd thing to register that I love my dad's laugh, but I do. It's so unlike the rest of him—delicate and girlish—because he's this tall, brooding dude with a pretty impressive beard. His love for literature combined with his career as a chemist earned from me the nickname Chemingway at an age when I was old enough to make the joke but not yet appreciate how great it was. Several of his colleagues have since claimed to have come up with it, but in my family, we all know the real score.

"I know it's not helpful," he says. "The last thing you need is the four of us butting in on your relationships status. But it's just what family does." Scratching his cheek thoughtfully, he adds, "You can't imagine how much joy your mother, sister, and grandmother derive from interfering in your love life."

"I think I have some idea." I look past him, down the porch, and back to the ocean.

"My family did the same thing to me," he admits. "I hated it, actually."

This makes me laugh, and I nod, looking back to him. "I bet."

"If you think Grams is bad now, imagine her when she was fed up with her four children and Papa, and on a tear."

"Whoa, yeah."

"You see what I mean?" he says, nodding. "So here's what I wanted to tell you: Before I met your mother—"

I hold up a hand and start to turn away. "Nope. I can't."

Dad laughs again, catching my shoulder. "Oh, just listen. Before I met your mother, I . . ." He fidgets, blinks away from me. "I mean, I *dated*."

Oh, Christ, that's Dad's code for *Bedded a lot of ladies.*

He bobs his head, laughing nervously. "Quite a bit, actually," he adds.

I close my eyes, fighting the urge to shudder. "Dad, I get it."

"It was the eighties," he reasons. "Casual sex was fine; encouraged, even. But when I met Julie, I just knew she was it for me. It didn't mean that I didn't enjoy sex anymore—"

I groan.

"—or that I would have married the next girl who came around. It was *her.*" Dad leans in, forcing me to meet his eyes. "So don't let your mother or sister or even grandmother bully you into thinking you need to settle down if you don't feel it." He pauses, adding, "You'll just fuck it up if you don't *mean* it."

I feel my eyes go wide. My dad doesn't swear. I mean, this man is the only one in our family who goes to church every Sunday, says "dang it" instead of "damn," and winces when Margot swears at the television during Chargers games. To say he's polite is an understatement.

"Thanks, Dad."

But he's not done. "In the same vein," he continues, "if you do really like this girl, then tell her. Try to win her. I met your mom when I was your age, and I never looked back. Not for a single second."

I look up at Dad and try to imagine a younger version of him, one from my early childhood when he would get up at dawn and surf for a few hours before work. One who would come up behind Mom while she cooked and whisper something in her ear that made her giggle and swat at him. Even as a kid, I knew my parents had something good. I think of him now, his easy hand on her thigh while he drives, how he'll never go up to bed without her, the way he listens to her talk about her day while she cooks, with absolutely no distraction—no phone, no television, no newspaper. He sits at the breakfast bar and listens with intent while she rambles on about whatever happened that day in the world of oceanography at Scripps.

They're more than two people who had kids together—I honestly can't think of them as lovers, it just makes something curdle in my gut—but they're also best friends.

I want that.

I want someone who makes me laugh, who challenges me, who listens to me. I want that leg within reach while I drive. I want to wait until someone is done futzing around the house before we head to bed. I need to be someone who a woman can respect and trust enough to spill the details of her day.

I blink, shaking my head. *What the fuck is wrong with me?*

"DO YOU LIVE here?" I pull out a stool at the bar and sit down, placing my phone facedown in front of me. I drove here on autopilot, and when I parked, I told myself it was because Fred's is only a mile or so from my place and my parents' place—it's convenient.

It's not that I was hoping she was working again and wanted to see her.

I just want a beer. And I'm not tired. And I didn't feel like going home.

But of course I'm full of shit.

London looks up and gives me a wan smile. "I could ask you the same question."

"Touché." She smirks at this, and I lean in, adding, "That's one of the things I like about you, Dimples." I slide a dollar bill into her jar.

"That I live in a bar?" she asks. Her dimples flash when her smirk turns into her trademark playful smile, and something strange happens inside my chest.

"I like that you never let me get away with shit. And I like that you're never actually mean when you call me out."

This surprises her. I can tell in the way her eyes widen and her dimples vanish.

"Well," she says when she's recovered, "maybe the amount of shit you try to pull is so epic it's easy to pick the low-hanging fruit."

"Again," I say, laughing. "Touché. But remember: I wasn't actually here last night."

London nods as she wipes the bar in front of me and then drops a coaster down. I try to interpret her expression; was she disappointed? "Can I get you a beer?"

"Actually," I say, perusing the bar behind her, "I think I'm turning over a new leaf. I'll have an amaretto sour. Dylan swears you make the best ones on the planet. I'd like to learn to appreciate them."

She gives me a skeptical look. "That's a pretty sweet drink. Are you sure?"

"I'm trying to get in touch with my feminine side."

Laughing, London shakes her head as she turns. "There are so many possible responses to that, I don't even know where to start."

I watch as she pours, shakes, and serves up an orange, frothy glass. I'll admit, it looks amazing, and reminds me of getting Orange Julius with Mia after school our freshman year.

For once, a memory of Mia doesn't make me feel tight and restless.

Taking a sip, I immediately register my mistake. It's so sweet I almost don't want to swallow. "Nope," I manage once I've forced it down. "Still not my drink."

The bar is dead and London leans forward on her elbows, thinking. "Well, what can I make you instead? Do you like gin?"

"Marginally."

"Scotch?"

I sigh, wincing because I actually hate this question. "I feel like I *should*, because it's such a manly drink and I have such an amazing penis"—London snorts—"but sadly, no. I don't like scotch."

She pats my head with a little smile before standing. "I've got you. Hold, please."

It takes every muscle in my body clenching to keep from launching from the bar chair and hurling over the bar to kiss her. It's like I've opened the back door and let the swarm in.

Burst the dam.

Turned on the fire hose.

I'm *completely* into this girl.

But the problem with Dad's advice is that I know London isn't into me the same way, and that asking her out, or even trying to convince her to come home with me, would only send her packing.

The other problem with Dad's advice is that I don't know that I want to date London. No, that isn't exactly right. I don't know that I *should* date her. I feel too close to my nightmare hookup from last week. I don't want my brain to lump

London in with the masses, to fall back onto easy, casual patterns with her. It's claustrophobic to feel the immediacy of all the other girls I've slept with even when I'm sitting just a few feet from a girl I genuinely like.

I'm covered in a film of my poor decisions, and even though I want to blast it off, I'm starting to fear it will be a more gradual process of wearing it down, filing it away. Learning from it.

I watch her work, mixing up one, then two, and then I see five drinks lined up on a tray. She lifts it, turning, and carefully slides it down on the bar in front of me. "We're doing this the scientific way," she says. "Close your eyes."

I close my eyes, and then something occurs to me: "You're not going to dump these over my head, are you?"

Her husky little laugh makes an entire body's worth of blood rush to my dick. "No, Luke, I am not going to dump perfectly good liquor over your head."

"Because I'm having a good hair day, Logan."

"I see that." She places a tumbler in my hand. "Sip."

I lift it, smell it, and immediately shake my head. "I can't do tequila. I did a bazillion body shots junior year and I think I lost my spleen one night in a toilet."

"God, you're a catch," she says dryly, taking the glass from my hand and replacing it with another.

I sip this one. "Jack? Even with the Coke, it's all I can taste. This is a soft pass for me."

"Let me guess: drunk, bad-decision sex followed by an epic hangover?"

For once, I wish that were the case.

"No, just a lot of associations . . ." *Mia,* I don't say. The first night we ever got drunk, it was on Jack and Cokes. When I open my eyes and look at London, smiling apologetically, I can already see that she's read my mind.

"I think your Jack Daniel's is my Jägermeister," she says quietly.

Scrunching my nose, I tell her, "People don't really drink Jäger, do they?"

"You'd be surprised. Okay, close your eyes again." I do what she tells me and feel my skin grow tight when her hand accidentally brushes mine. "You're a tough customer." London places another drink in my hand. "Try this."

7-Up and some kind of orange-flavored booze. Vodka, maybe. I feel my face pucker at the sugar. "*Way* too sweet. Worse than the amaretto sour."

She hands me another and when she speaks, her voice is confident, if a little distracted. "Okay, okay, sorry, that one was a joke. Time to end this. *This* is your drink."

I lift the glass and take a sip. It's smooth as glass on my tongue, heavy and viscous, tart with lime. Fuck, it's good. "What is this?"

"Vodka gimlet."

I open my eyes and look at her. She's already cleared away the other drinks and is watching my mouth with a glazed look on her face. When she realizes my eyes are open, she blinks away.

"Belvedere and lime juice over ice," she adds, swiping a

towel over the bar in front of me again. And then she turns, leaving me with my new drink to go take the order of a couple who just sat down.

It's impossible for me to not watch her while she works. London approaches the couple with a smile—that wide-open one that makes my heart kick at my breastbone—and as she tosses two coasters down, I can see she's already made them laugh. It's oddly hot to watch her pour from bottles without even really looking at what she's doing. Once or twice she glances my way and catches me staring at her, and instinct tells me to pretend I'm reading something behind her, or watching the game on the television just to the right of her shoulder, but I just can't move that fast, be that blasé. I'm fucking fascinated with the way she looks tonight, hair up in a messy bun, red-framed fake glasses matching her red lipstick, black off-the-shoulder shirt, and cutoff short-shorts doing dangerous things to my libido.

Finally, it's like I'm a puppy dog she can't stand to leave outside anymore and she slumps her shoulders playfully, walking back over to me with a teasing, exasperated look on her face.

"Do you need a buddy or what?"

Instead of answering this, I ask her, "How did you know?"

"How did I know you need a buddy? You look totally patheti—"

"No," I interrupt quietly. "I mean, how did you know that the last one would be my drink?"

She shrugs, straightening. "It's my job to figure those things out."

This feels like an evasion—the truth feels more important than this—but I let it slide, taking another sip. "I'm a little tipsy now, though."

Laughing, she leans in and gives me my favorite smile, the one that feels like it's been tailored just for me. "Careful, now. Don't let your true colors show."

I feel my brow pull together. No matter how gentle she puts it, no matter how much her smile tells me she's not trying to be mean, I hate her image of me. Hate its *accuracy*. "You mean my manwhore flag?"

She looks a little guilty when she straightens again, and turns away. Shit. My words came out sharper than I meant them to, and now I seem like a manwhore *and* an asshole. "Shit. Don't go," I say, rubbing my face.

London turns back to me, putting away a few glasses beneath the bar. "I *can't* go far. I work here, goose."

"I just want to be your friend," I say.

She straightens, eyebrows lifting in surprise. "Wow, you *are* drunk. How did you survive college being such a lightweight?"

I catch her hand when she reaches to tidy a stack of cocktail napkins. "I'm serious. I like being around you."

God, I'm realizing how much I suck at this. She was right, there's no in-between for me, nothing in that no-man's-land between sincere and slick.

She tries halfheartedly to pull away and then goes lax in my grip. "Luke—"

"Please." I rub my thumb over the back of her hand. "Let me show you that I'm not the guy you think I am."

"The problem is there's no chance of that," she says softly. "I like you, too. But not for *me*. You're *exactly* the guy I think you are."

I watch my finger move over her skin. Even after surfing in the harsh salt water every day, her hands are so much softer than mine. "I don't want to be," I say, surprising myself a little.

She gnaws her lip, looking away. "What we did was just for fun." Finally, she frees her hand, and lowers her voice. "It wasn't ever going to be something more than that. I'm surprised we did it twice."

"Three times, Logan. Three *separate* times," I add and she fights a smile. I duck, chasing her attention. "But I'm not even talking about that." And, oddly, I'm not. "Just hang out with me."

Finally, she looks back and meets my eyes. "Not dates? No sex?"

I feel my smile all the way to my chest. "Whatever you want."

"No sex," she repeats, and I don't miss the way she wipes her hand on her shorts. "It won't ever be romantic with us."

My heart warps a little at the finality of her tone, but fuck. It really isn't about that, not with her. "No, I mean . . . totally," I stutter. "No worries. I just want to be your friend."

She studies me, eyes flickering back and forth between mine, as if one of them would lie while the other told the truth. "Just hanging out?"

"Yes."

Her nose wrinkles a little, like she might growl at me. "And you promise to be entertaining, not some sad-sack puppy like this?"

Laughing, I tell her, "I promise."

She grabs a bar towel, wipes down the lip of the sink in front of her. "Fine," she says, watching her hands. "Saturday afternoon." With her head down, she lifts her eyes to me, and fuck, it's the most amazing look I've ever seen on a woman. And here she just wants to be friends. "*I* pick what we do."

I blanch when I look up at the devious grin she's wearing.

Oh, fuck. We're going surfing.

Chapter ELEVEN

*T*HE PLAN IS to meet Luke at Tourmaline Surf Park at two. Any other day this would sound like a suicide mission, but knowing it's going to be packed gives me a small measure of comfort: maybe with a crowd of people around I won't do anything stupid.

I've gone so far as to make a list of goals for the day:

1. Don't let Luke drown.

2. Don't ogle Luke in his board shorts.

3. Don't accidentally have sex with Luke.

I'm definitely going to focus on goals one and three.

The only way to get to Tourmaline is by a road that winds down from La Jolla Boulevard and empties into the parking lot. It's almost always crowded and I'm about to give up and park on the street outside, when on my second pass I spot someone leaving. I put on my blinker to thwart off any would-be thieves, and pull in as soon as it's open.

Even with the engine off, my old car still manages the occasional unsettling knock and ping from under the hood, and I sit, fiddling with my phone and looking around. Luke hasn't texted that he's here yet and I briefly wonder if it's too late to call this whole thing off.

Cocky Luke I can handle, but sweet, earnest, tipsy Luke with puppy eyes asking to be friends? Apparently that's my hard limit.

I can't stall forever, and so I check the time before sending him a quick text.

There might not be any parking, so find a spot on the street, I type, before climbing out onto the hot pavement and making my way to the trunk.

My board barely fits in my small car and is wedged between the folded backseats so the hatchback needs an extra little shove to close all the way. It's not an ideal situation and requires more maneuvering than I might like, but it works.

I've just managed to pull it free when I hear a familiar voice over my shoulder.

"Need some help?"

"I got it," I say, leaning the board against the car and reaching for my bag before locking up. "But thanks."

When I turn, I see he's got his own board tucked under his arm and a towel rolled up next to it. He's wearing a thin white T-shirt and blue board shorts that hang low—*really* low—on his hips. It takes my breath away how good he looks. Warning bells are already going off in my head—and possibly somewhere else. This was a bad idea.

I'm suddenly nervous we'll see Not-Joe here, and he'll

mention to Oliver that he saw us. Then Oliver will tell Lola, and Lola will tell Harlow, and Harlow will get up in arms all over again about all the Girl Code breaking I'm doing by ogling Luke so thoroughly.

Just friends.

Friends is fine.

"You all set?" I ask, looking around. I can hear how tight my voice is. Hopefully he reads it as impatient rather than hard-core swooning.

He gives a small shake of his head and laughs when he admits, "Not even a little bit."

"Nice board, though," I tell him, and run my hand along the nose. "Not too long and a good width for your frame. I'm glad you went with a longboard. It'll make it easier to pop up."

"I like that you're giving me credit, like *I* picked it out and not the guy at the shop." He smiles tightly before looking past me, squinting into the sun.

"Just trying to boost your confidence."

God, this is awkward. We're both flailing around this attempt at friendship. I make a final check of everything I need and then nod toward the water. "Let's do this."

The parking lot is perched high above our destination. Tourmaline is surrounded by sea cliffs that tower over the beach, some as tall as seventy-five feet. There's a pretty steep hill we have to navigate to reach the bottom, and I can hear Luke's footsteps as he follows the path behind me. It's only as we near the sand that I realize he's quieter than usual, and didn't even crack a joke when I mentioned the length of his board.

I try to puzzle this out as I look out over the crystal-blue sky, where the ocean stretches until it melts into the horizon. The surf crashes below us and I can taste the salt in the air. It's like Xanax to my nerves. I suppose everyone has a quiet day. I actually kind of like seeing a different side of Luke.

When we get to the beach, I find a spot with enough room to set down my board. Luke leans his against a large rock and turns to me.

"What's all that?" he asks, watching me dump out my small bag.

"Sunscreen, fin screws, fin key." I hold up the bottle, offering.

"I put some on already, thanks, though."

I nod, unsure how to handle Quiet Luke, shaking the bottle to stall before undressing. But I might as well just get this over with; I've never liked wearing wetsuits, even in the icy Pacific Ocean, and instead surf in a swimsuit. Today's selection is pretty modest—a one-piece—but we're going to be wet and practically naked together for the next few hours; there's no point in letting the moment grow heavy now.

I pull my T-shirt over my head and toss it to the sand before unbuttoning my shorts and stepping out of them.

"I like this place," Luke says, hands on his hips as he looks around—pointedly *not* looking at me. "I've been here before but only for a campfire or something."

"Never to surf?" I ask, smoothing sunblock over my arms and shoulders.

"Ha, no. I barely go in the water."

I stop. "You're kidding."

He ruffles the back of his hair and looks a little sheepish. "Afraid not."

"Wait, I mean . . . How could you have lived this close to the ocean for most of your life and not go in the water? You swim. You were on a national championship water polo team."

"Yeah, that's a *pool.* And nothing in there is trying to eat me."

I cough out an incredulous laugh. "Luke, there's something like—I don't know—*eight hundred thousand* things that live in the ocean, and out of that only a microscopic percent of a fraction would want anything to do with you."

He tilts his head and pins me with a serious look. "I've seen *Jaws,* Logan."

"Do you play bridge?" I ask him.

Clearly confused, he says, "Sometimes, with Grams and some of her friends."

"Statistically speaking, more people have died playing bridge in the last century than by shark attacks in the entire states of California, Oregon, and Washington combined."

"You made that up."

I might have made that up.

I toss my sunscreen to the sand and turn to face him. "I don't understand. If you didn't want to go in the water, then why on earth did you agree to come out here?"

"I already told you, I like you. And when you're not handing me my balls, you're a lot of fun." The corner of his mouth tilts up into a smile before the other side joins it. "Even then."

Honest Luke is really throwing me for a loop. "Do you want to do something else?" I say. "We could, I don't know, see a movie?"

He's thinking about it, looking out at the water with a considerable amount of apprehension in his eyes. "No. No, I think I want to do this," he says, and then begins to nod, like it's taking his body a moment to agree with his mouth.

"You're sure," I say, giving him the chance to back out. "I don't want you to do something that makes you uncomfortable. I promise I'm not keeping score here."

"No, I . . . I want to." He reaches behind his neck and tugs his shirt up and over his head. I feel my lungs constrict at the sight of his bare chest in the bright sun, the definition of muscle cutting down his torso and bisected by sharp lines on his abdomen. I blink away.

"Yeah," he says. "Let's go."

"Okay," I say, voice steadier than I feel, and reach for Luke's board. "Basics first."

With a stick I find in a group of rocks, I trace the outline of his board in the sand and prop it back up again.

Luke watches me, confused. "Why don't you just use the board itself?"

"Because boards are expensive and we don't want to ruin it," I say, and toss the stick back into the brush. "This is your board." I grip his forearms and bring him over to stand in the shape I've drawn, and then point to the various parts. "This is the nose, the rails, the tail. This vertical line down the middle is called the stringer, and will keep you centered. Remember that," I say. I point out the Velcro strap lying in the sand. "I'm assuming you already know this, but this is the board leash; never go in the water without this around your ankle, okay?"

"Got it."

"We'll go over paddling and everything when we're actually in the water, but let's start with the easy stuff." I stand next to him, legs spread just wider than shoulder-width apart. "First, your stance. You need to make sure you're in the center of the board, not too far forward or too far back. No, let me . . ." I say when he tries to mimic my stance, and bend, gripping his ankle, physically moving his feet into position. He's so warm, bones strong and solid under my grip. "Don't be too open; put the arch of whatever foot you lead with right there, on the stringer. The other behind it."

"Like this?" he asks, demonstrating.

I straighten. "Perfect. Being in the center of the board means you'll have more control. Always stay in the center."

He nods and tests out the movement. "Okay, I can imagine what you mean."

"Now, arms up—" I reach forward, trailing my hands down along his forearms until my fingers wrap around his wrists. I can feel the steady beat of his pulse under my fingertips, the heat of his skin. It reminds me of when he held my hands down, above my head, and my mouth suddenly feels dry. I've been trying to avoid looking at his torso and his arms ever since he took off his shirt—knowing I'll only be able to remember what they looked like over me—but realize that's only going to work for so long.

Luke's silhouette is the definition of a swimmer's body. His shoulders are broad, lats bulky like all strong swimmers, biceps clearly defined. His torso is long and lean and I count an eight-pack on his flat stomach. It's a body designed for power and hours of cutting through the water with little resistance. It's a body built for endurance.

And Lord, does it endure. He could take me all night and only come at sunrise.

I really didn't need that reminder right now.

"You okay there, Logan?" he says, and I snap my attention back to where my fingers are still wrapped around his wrists.

"This is for balance," I tell him, pushing on as if my every thought isn't written on my blazing-hot face. "Point your leading arm wherever you want to go, rear arm at shoulder height and flexed with the elbow back." I show him and he mimics the action.

"Good, just like that. Let your body move back and forth, wherever the board takes you. Hips loose, like you're doing the hula hoop."

He laughs. "Tell me I look amazing doing this, okay? And not as ridiculous as I'm guessing."

"Very manly." I make a few adjustments to his posture and stand back to see. "So with your arms, people think they need to keep them at their side, parallel with the rails, but that's wrong. Keep them squared with your hips—" I step forward again, bracing a hand on either side of his ribs. Luke curls inward, away from my touch, and giggles.

"Sorry," he says quietly. "Ticklish."

"Uh, sorry," I mumble, and have to mentally count down from ten before I can remember what I was doing. I've had sex with Luke, seen his naked body over and under me, from behind, and somehow this feels . . . more intimate than any of that.

My cheeks are hot as I reach for him again, and I bring my hands

down

down

down—*how long is his torso?*—to rest on his hips.

I never fully appreciated how low boys wear their trunks until this very moment, now that I can feel the bony ridges and hollows of Luke's hip bones under my fingertips. There are so many shadows on his body, so many places where bone and muscle meet, and for a moment I'm back on his couch, watching these same parts of his body move and flex while he fucks me.

When I blink up, I find him watching, mouth open and hair falling gently forward across his forehead. His cheeks are flushed, too, visible even out in the sun, as if he's thinking of exactly the same thing I am.

I clear my throat and blink away, hoping he doesn't realize I'm not quite as unaffected as I'd like to be, and every one of his smiles is another chink in my armor.

"Stay low," I say, voice rough as I try to get my thoughts

back in order. "You want to adapt to the waves and the way the water moves under your feet. You'll never be able to do that if you're all tall and"—I wave in the direction of his body—"stiff."

Luke chuckles and I roll my eyes. "Bend at your knees, not at your waist—this is the heaviest part of your body," I tell him, and pat his chest. "You need it centered. Too far forward and you're over the rail, see? You'll lose your balance." He bends forward as if to test the theory. Unfortunately this brings his face directly in line with my crotch.

He looks up at me from beneath his hair with a cheeky grin. "Like this?"

The top of his head is literally inches away from my lady parts, and I give him a gentle shove, effectively knocking him into the sand. "Just like that," I say, and step over him. "Aren't you glad that didn't happen in the water?"

He jumps up, knocking sand off his shorts before getting back into position. "I might have deserved that," he says.

I adjust his stance, hands sliding over his skin to angle him this way or that, to bring attention to the parts of his body he needs to tighten. There was clearly a flaw in my plan because I failed to anticipate there'd be this much touching in a surfing lesson.

"So a few more things before we get you in the water—"

"Do I *have* to go in the water?" he asks.

"You have to go in the water."

He looks out over the ocean, worry etched in every feature. Turning back to me he says, "Tell me something you hate."

"Like people who take too long in the shower and don't separate their recycling, or—?"

"Something that scares you."

There are a lot of things that scare me—Luke scares me if I'm being honest, the fact that he's nice and funny and he makes my stomach do strange things. The idea of ever reliving what I went through with Justin . . . that definitely scares me.

"I don't like roller coasters," I say.

"Really?" he asks, and I nod. A tiny disbelieving smile pulls up the corner of his mouth. "Roller coasters are designed to give you the *illusion* of danger without any of the actual danger of death. But surfing"—he motions to the water—"out there you might as well be a tasty morsel in an all-you-can-eat buffet."

"Doesn't make the fear any less real, though, does it?"

"No, I guess not." He looks at the water again before turning back to me. "Let's make a deal. I do this and you go to Six Flags and ride Goliath with me."

I actually snort. "Fuck that."

He reaches for my forearm, thumb brushing over my wrist. "I'm trusting you, you trust me."

I could be wrong, but it feels like he's talking about a lot more than roller coasters. I look into his brown eyes and there's nothing but absolute sincerity there.

He bends at the knee to meet my gaze. "Okay?"

I reluctantly nod. "But I don't want to hear about it when I freak out and end up riding the stupid thing in your lap."

Luke grins. "It's cute that you think I would complain

about that." He holds out a hand to shake and I take it, ignoring how much bigger it is than mine, and that I know exactly what it feels like on my body.

"Okay, okay," I say, pulling away from his grip and shaking my fingers where I hope he can't see. "Deal made. Now, let's get back to surfing so I can see you punk out and I never have to step foot inside that godforsaken amusement park."

"You're really hot when you get all worked up," he says, and I punch him in the shoulder.

I have him lie facedown on his board and we go over the basics of paddling out. One look at his broad, tan back, and I realize I've made another mistake.

"You can spot a beginner because they paddle out with their legs open and that drags in the water," I tell him, and tap his ankle with my foot. "Legs together." I point out a group of guys running out into the water, and I show him how to read the waves, how to tell which direction they'll break. "See that guy right there?" I say. "That's how you want to pop up. Do what he's doing."

Luke mimics his position and lies on his board again. "Pretend there's a beach ball under your chin. Yeah, just like that," I say, and move around to the other side and lie down in the sand next to him. "So you'll see the wave . . ." I start, becoming distracted by the way his gaze flickers over my body, down along my curves and back up again, not even remotely subtly.

When he makes the full circuit and meets my eyes, he breaks out in a huge smile. "I was just checking your position," he says.

"Sure you were."

"What? I like to be thorough. This is the only part I'll be good at, okay? Once we get in that water all bets are off; let me keep my manhood for just a little longer."

I grin up at him, finally pulling my bottom lip between my teeth so I don't let it slip how fucking *adorablehotsweet* he's being.

"So I'll feel the wave . . ." he says, and waits for me to continue.

Nodding and getting my shit together, I say, "You'll feel the push, take two extra paddles to make sure you're actually in it, hands here, under your chest. With your head up you'll roll your body and pop up, knee under your chest, feet under you and into your stance, ready to hula-hoop."

He doesn't look overly confident but he tries it a few times.

"Good! And if you did everything correctly, you should be able to do it in reverse, too," I say, and show him, kneeling down, pushing my legs back behind me until I'm lying on my stomach again. "And just do it until you feel comfortable."

"Comfortable?" He looks less than convinced. "I don't think that'll ever happen," he says, bringing his knees to his chest and popping up.

"Yes it will, look how good you're doing already."

"Yeah, on the beach."

"All in good time," I tell him, rubbing my hand over his warm shoulder. He looks down at my hand, *I* stare at my hand, and we fall into a heavy silence before I pull it away completely. "You ready to hit the water?"

Luke shakes his head, eyes playful. "Nope."

I tilt my head and wait.

"Okay, yeah. I've got roller coasters to get you on, and I've lived a good life already anyway," he says, and we head down to shore.

The water is cold and it takes us a few deep breaths to work up the nerve to dive in together, but eventually we do, surfacing with shouts and laughter. We swim out, stopping where the waves lap just at our waist. Luke has his leash strap hooked around his ankle, and hasn't stopped looking in the frothy water, as if a shark might materialize at any moment and take him down.

"Can you get up on your board?" I ask, and he nods, gingerly climbing up, eyes darting at every little ripple next to him. He's terrified, and a part of my chest squeezes with fondness that he trusts me enough to even do this.

"The waves are that way," I tell him, and he looks up from the water. "You can look at my boobs if you need the distraction."

"Don't think I won't hold you to that," he says.

We work on getting him balanced on his stomach on the board. He slides around a little, complaining good-naturedly, and we talk more about spotting a wave. I quiz him on which direction they'll break. I teach him how to duck-dive and punch through the smaller waves on his way out, and though he never actually looks any less tense, he listens and does everything I ask.

"As the wave comes, you want to push the nose of the board down, sinking it. Arms straight, hands on the rails, deep breath before the wave breaks over you—"

"Why do I need to take a deep breath?" he asks, eyes wide and panicked.

"Because you're going to be underwater."

"Under?"

"You'll be fine," I tell him.

"That's easy for you to say."

"Luke."

He has goose bumps up and down his skin and I'm a pervert for even noticing this right now, but I can't look away from his chest, at the drops of water that cling to it and the way his nipples are pert and hard. I want to flick them with my tongue. God, he has great nipples.

"Will you hold my hand on Goliath?" he asks, and I have to blink back to what he's saying.

"What?"

"I think you heard me, Logan." He ducks his head, adding, "My eyes are up here, by the way."

I snap my attention to his face, biting back an embarrassed laugh. "Fine. Yes, I'll hold your hand on Goliath."

"Okay, good. I can do this," he says, and takes one last look into the water. "Show me this duck bill thing."

"Duck-dive."

"Whatever. All I care about is surviving. I'm listening."

I shake my head and reach for the nose of his board. "So your board is under, you take a deep breath, and the wave goes over. You'll pop right back up and be ready to keep paddling. It takes some time to get but it won't take long to feel when you get it right. And you don't have to go deep. Just enough to get under the wave. Deeper isn't always better."

He snorts. "If that's true then you wouldn't have—"

I slide my hand over his mouth to get him to stop talking, and we both look up at the same time, our attention snagged by something to our right.

A huge set comes up, and we watch another surfer paddling out. "See how he's going right through those?" I point to the smaller swells. "When you paddle out you want full steam because that wave is stronger than you and if you're not working to move through it it'll knock you on your ass. Watch how he pops, look at his stance . . ."

As we watch the other surfer, Luke eventually lets out a "Man, he's good," clearly impressed.

"You could be that good," I tell him. "You're definitely strong enough and a great swimmer. It's all technique and practice. You'll have the small waves down in no time."

"And the big waves?"

"I don't think you're ready for a big wave yet, Blue Crush."

"Very funny."

"Okay, I'll do it and then it's your turn. Deal?" I ask.

He nods and I paddle out, watching the wave. Three more strokes and I tilt my board under, letting it roll over me. I pop back up and do it a few more times before I catch the edge of a larger one.

It's short, and I barely have enough time to pop up and ride before the wave falls apart under me. When I break the surface again, I climb back up on my board and paddle over to him.

"See?" I say, squeezing the water from my hair. "You can totally do that."

"Your confidence in me is impressive," he says, looking out over the water.

"I *know* you can do this, Luke. Come on, up you go."

He looks terrified but lies down and starts paddling out. He looks back at me a few times but keeps moving forward. I stay as close as I can, watching as the smaller waves rush over him, one of them knocking him off his board. Protectiveness surges tight in my chest. He pops back up—looking a bit shaken—but doesn't let it stop him and tries over and over again.

A wave forms off in the distance and I see him size it up before paddling toward it. Butterflies form in my stomach as I watch him, already cheering him on. "Keep going . . . Nose down, hips forward, deep breath! Yes!" I shout, even though there's no way he can hear it.

He disappears momentarily under the water. Then, head turning frantically side to side, he breaks the surface again.

When he spots me, he breaks into a huge smile. "Holy shit. I think I did it!"

"You totally did it!" I say, laughing at how excited he is. "Think you can try it again?"

He nods and climbs back on his board, pushing his hair back from his face before looking out at the water.

Watching Luke as he paddles forward, warm from the sun and wet, twitching with exertion . . . I'm sure I'll never forget this sight. He spots a wave in the distance and aims his board forward. I hold my breath as he dives through the smaller waves and breaks the surface again, before finally popping up to his feet on the last one. He doesn't stay up for long before he's knocked off and it certainly wasn't pretty, but he did it, and I feel wildly, fiercely proud. I try not to stare as he comes back over to me, because I know my adoration would show all over my face.

"I TOLD YOU," I tell him for the tenth time as we paddle back to the shore something like an hour later.

Luke is exhausted but he hasn't stopped smiling. "Now I know why you're in such amazing shape," he says, looking appreciatively at my body. "That kicked my ass."

"But you still did it," I say.

We reach the shore and Luke collapses in the sand, chest heaving. "I did." He closes his eyes and stays there, trying to catch his breath. "My dad's going to flip when he hears about this. He tried to get me out there with him when I was little, but I'd never go. My sister will never believe it."

"Want me to call her? I can text if that's easier—"

"No. You're not getting her number, *ever*," he says, tilting his head to look at me. "The two of you together are dangerous."

"I like your sister."

"And she *loves* you," he tells me, still catching his breath. "The idea of you two hanging out on a regular basis scares the hell out of me."

He squeezes his eyes closed, pinching the bridge of his nose, and I wonder if he's recovered yet from a recent roll that got salt water up his nose.

"You okay?" I ask him, reaching out to brush some sand from his back.

He stills before turning his head to look at me. "Yeah. Just stings a little still."

"I hate it, too. It's why I could never imagine snorting anything on purpose."

He laughs. "God, I tried coke exactly one time, in some blur of parties sophomore year. I knew immediately I would want more, so I never—" He does a double take, noticing my shocked expression. *"What?"*

"Nothing," I say. "But that's gross."

Luke laughs. "Why did you bring up snorting things if you were going to be all weird about it?"

I shrug. I realize it's odd in some ways that I'm a bartender and so uptight about harder drugs, but I am. I've seen too many people turn into complete messes when they play around with cocaine. "It just seems like really bad judgment for an athlete."

Luke barks out an amused laugh, saying, "You *think*?"

This makes me laugh, too. "Sorry, yeah, just had a knee-jerk reaction to it." I have such a hard time imagining healthy, together Luke doing something so stupid.

"I mean, let's be real," he says, nudging my shoulder with his. "I'm not really known for impulse control."

I giggle as I pick up a rock and start drawing in the sand.

"Try not to agree with me so gleefully." He leans in, voice

playful but hiding something tighter beneath when he adds, "Are you slut-shaming me, Logan?"

The words burst out before I've realized I've actually had the thought: "Isn't it ever lonely?"

And goddamnit. What have I said? I've opened up this door, and I absolutely, one hundred percent do not want to step through.

My frank question seems to surprise him: "Totally. I'm sick of it, actually."

"So why don't you . . . ?"

"Commit?" he asks.

Shrugging, I say, "Yeah."

"Because the first girl I've really wanted since I was nineteen thinks I'm an impulsive man-slut."

I go still. Blood riots in my ears, hammers through my veins. "I'm serious."

"Me, too," he says, blinking away and staring at the sand. "I like you. But I also *like* you. I would commit to you."

Silence engulfs us, and slowly I relax enough to notice the crashing of the waves, the cry of gulls all around us.

Luke nudges me again. "I made it awkward."

"Totally awkward," I tease, nudging him back. I knew he was attracted to me, but I didn't realize it was a thing.

A committing-to-London thing.

A crush, feelings, something more than just good sex.

My thoughts are tumbling from the storm cloud inside me, pouring down. I like Luke, too. I'm attracted to Luke. I have fun with Luke.

I just don't trust Luke.

And even if I did, I can't have him.

We watch a surfer catch a pretty amazing wave, and turn to smile at each other in unison.

"I have to admit," he says, shaking his head a little, "it *is* pretty cool being out in the water. Learning the rhythm of the waves."

He bends his knees, propping his elbows on top of them, and we're both silent, watching more of them crash against the shore.

"Thanks for bringing me out here," he says. "I know you didn't really want to, and I appreciate it."

"It's not that I didn't want—" I start to say, but he holds up a hand, cutting me off.

"And it's fine, you know?" He picks up a shell near his leg and brushes the sand off with his thumb. "You know I would never refer to you that way, right?"

I tilt my head, confused. "What?"

He swallows. "At Bliss that night. I know you heard what Daniel said."

"Oh," I say, finally understanding. "I did hear, yeah."

"Is that why you stopped wanting to see me?" He says this in a way that tells me he already knows the answer.

"It's one of the reasons."

"Daniel's an asshole—"

"*He's* not the problem. I mean, he is but . . ." I pull in a breath, trying to organize my thoughts. "The single-serving thing was gross. Guys are disgusting sometimes, but the concept, I get. You and I had a casual thing, a couple of nights that were fun and—"

He turns toward me. "They *were* fun."

I give him a play-exasperated eye roll. "My reaction to that comment wasn't because I didn't have fun. I'm not angry that he said it about me, or that you have one-night stands or even that you agreed with Daniel. I mean, it embarrassed me, yeah, but I got over it." He winces apologetically, and I lower my voice so he doesn't feel berated. "I'm annoyed that guys talk about women like they're *snacks*. Like they're disposable or easily replaceable when something more appealing comes along. So yeah, things between us stopped after that, because I don't even want casual sex with someone who has such prehistoric views on women. But I hadn't expected it to turn into more anyway."

Pink colors the apples of Luke's cheeks and he looks down, nodding. "Well, you're not replaceable," he says. "I just want to make sure you know that."

Butterflies invade my chest, and I swallow, struggling to push them down. "I appreciate that, *friend*," I say.

The word elicits a wry, perhaps wistful smile from Luke, but after a second he says, "What were the other reasons?"

I blink, having lost the beginning thread of the conversation.

"The other reasons why you didn't want to see me—romantically," he clarifies.

"I mean, that's the main one," I say, drawing a spiral in the sand with my fingertip. "I'm not sure I want anything right now. I'm sort of distrustful in general, and you're not exactly easy to trust . . ."

He's quiet beside me, picking up another shell and turning it over in his hand, looking at it. Waiting for me to continue.

"Harlow freaked out a little when she found out that we . . ." I trail off.

"I could tell." He drops the shell and brushes the sand off his hands. "She'll get over it."

Looking at him, I ask, "Why does everyone say that?"

"Because it's true." Luke shrugs. "It's just *Harlow*. She burns like paper, not wood. The fire will be out before you know it."

His casual confidence is exponentially more reassuring than a roomful of nervous Lolas, Olivers, Finns, and Ansels. "You sound pretty confident."

He smiles over at me, but it's actually a little sad. "I was *with* Mia, but Harlow and I were really close. Lola, too," he adds, "but my friendship with Harlow was different. Tighter. Lola was a little more reserved emotionally. Harlow"—he laughs—"Harlow not so much. I was more brother than friend to her. I wonder whether part of her feeling prickly about this is because it makes her realize we aren't all that close anymore, and haven't been for a while. It's certainly the way I felt when I found out they'd all gotten *married* and I had no idea."

I'm not entirely sure what to say in response to this, so I just nod, listening.

Luke squints as he looks out across the water. "Anyway, I assume she worries Mia is fragile about anything related to that time. And she probably is, but I bet not as fragile as Harlow suspects. Harlow is a Mama Bear."

"It doesn't bother you?" I ask him. He turns and looks at me. "That Mia knows we slept together?"

His eyes narrow in a way that tells me he thinks I'm being a little silly. "No . . . ?"

"Okay. Good."

He turns and slowly grins at me. "I'm hoping that our deal still stands."

I search my memory before realizing what he means. "You held up your end of the bargain," I say. "I wasn't lying, you did great."

"Thanks," he says, smiling proudly. "And despite everything I said just now, I really do mean it about the 'just friends' thing. I wanted to be up front about where I stood."

"Thanks for telling me." The sun has shifted lower in the sky and I don't need a watch to tell me it's time to go. "I should go, though." I stand and brush the sand from my legs.

"Work?"

"Yeah."

He bends to lift his board. "My sister is seriously going to lose her shit when she finds out I went in the ocean."

"I had fun." I drag my board up the beach and begin to towel off. "You did so much better than I expected."

"I'm taking that as a compliment," he says, and pulls his

T-shirt on. I almost whimper as all those muscles disappear beneath the cotton.

"Sorry, I just meant most first-timers aren't great."

He smirks, letting this opportunity roll. "I'll text you and we can figure out Six Flags."

My shoulders slump and I groan. "There has to be a loophole in there somewhere."

He shakes his head, grinning. "I'm going to be a lawyer; you think I'd have made that deal if there was some way out? No way. But we can go this summer. Let you work up your nerve a little."

I watch as he bends and straightens his flip-flops to step into them. He's so *sweet*.

He's so genuinely good.

"Are you even going to still be here this summer?" I ask. And with that realization, my heart pistons into my throat.

"Oh, right." He shrugs, giving me his sweet, eye-crinkling smile. "I guess we'll see."

Chapter TWELVE

Luke

*I*T'S SAFE TO say the best way to start off a weekend is *not* by getting your dick swabbed. Any other way is better, trust me.

"These tests are very accurate," the nurse assures me, oblivious to my panic as she glances at my chart. "We'll take some blood, and do a quick sample so we can screen for syphilis, gonorrhea and chlamydia, genital herpes, and HIV."

"Sounds good," I croak. The dreaded swab remains wrapped in the sterile packaging on the tray near her elbow.

"Do you have any pain when you urinate?" she asks me.

"No." I shift, trying to keep the man bits covered in the paper bathrobe they gave me; it barely reaches my thighs. I casually rest my hands over where my junk is totally visible, although I don't know why I'm bothering; I've done this once before and know that this nurse and I will be rather intimately, if clinically, acquainted before we're done here.

"No burning, no discharge?"

Instinctively, I cup my groin protectively. *"No."*

"Well, that's good." She smiles at me as she stands, and moves to wash her hands. "I'll do a brief visual exam and then we'll collect some blood, okay?"

"No swab?" I ask.

She winces apologetically as she turns and dries her hands, opening the trash bin with a foot lever. "I'm very good; it will be quick."

The nurse turns, snaps on a pair of gloves, and walks toward me. That snap rings through the room and I hear every one of her footfalls.

In the end—no pun intended—it *is* quick, although I could go an entire lifetime without having a dry cotton swab stuck up my dick or the awkwardness of having a nurse my mother's age turn over and inspect every facet of my junk. But after giving a small vial of blood for testing, I'm off.

I feel lighter as I walk out of the clinic, checking one thing off my turning-over-a-new-leaf checklist. I'm not particularly worried. Even with Mia, I wore condoms.

It's just the vague nausea that accompanies the *possibility* of STDs. I haven't always been having sober sex, and many times the not-sober sex was also relatively acrobatic. What are the chances a condom broke and I have no idea? What are the chances I got head—never with condoms, I'm an idiot, I know—from a girl with herpes?

I grip the steering wheel tightly in one hand as I leave the clinic and turn up the music with the other, trying to drown out the spiral of panicky thoughts. I have an entire, unscheduled day ahead of me. Only a month ago this would have been my ideal situation, and easily solved: head to Andrew's or Daniel's for beers on the patio, some polo scrimmaging in the pool in the afternoon, and the bar later.

But nothing on that list sounds right today. Daniel is, in fact, a complete douche. He has a newborn son with a waitress he banged for a few weeks, and now has to work his ass off to cover child support, yet still manages to spend most of his free evenings at a bar, trolling for sex. Andrew is only marginally better, but he still tends to cycle through girlfriends every few weeks. Cody is enjoying a suddenly-single sex rampage, so I'm assuming he's given up on re-uniting with Jess. Only Dylan is a genuinely good guy, nice to women, deserves someone great . . . I just hope he's not into London.

London. *Fuck.*

As soon as I think of her, my brain careens full bore into the idea of seeing her today. Surfing last weekend was more fun than I've had in recent memory, and after a week of in-sane hours at work, and not seeing her at all at Fred's, I'm like a dog on a scent—unable to get past the thought of spending the day doing all of the best nothings with her.

I hit the Bluetooth button on my steering wheel. "Call London," I say, and take a deep, calming breath while it dials.

———

"WANT SOMETHING TO drink?" I call out over my shoulder as she takes off her shoes and drops her bag near the door. "I've got beer, water . . . juice boxes . . ."

London comes up behind me in the kitchen, looking over my shoulder into the fridge. "You have *juice boxes?*"

I shrug, trying to lean back without her noticing so I can

get closer. She smells like the beach, and coconut oil. I let myself enjoy the five-second fantasy of us sitting on the beach, London sitting between my legs while I rub oil all over her back. Then she relaxes into me and I rub oil all over her ti—

"Luke? Juice boxes?"

I blink, looking back down into the fridge, focusing on the cold air against my front. "I took Grams grocery shopping last night and she always insists on stocking my fridge, too."

"And she got you juice boxes?" she says, voice softer now. "That's *extremely* adorable. I want to meet this woman."

"She'll be at our wedding."

London laughs, stepping away. "Right."

Closing the fridge, I tell her, "She also got me Ritz crackers and string cheese."

"Does she think you run a day care?"

I laugh. "She likes me to have my snacks," I tell her. When she backs up to let me grab some crackers from the pantry, I catch another whiff of her. "Did you go surfing this morning?"

"Yeah. Just went to Black's for a couple hours."

Black's Beach is probably the best surfing in San Diego County. I know this not because I've spent any time swimming there, but because it was one of Dad's favorite spots back in the day—and I try not to think too much about it also being a nude beach back in the day, too.

"It was pretty busy," she adds. "Entitled surfer dudes everywhere."

My body reacts to her as if she's a girlfriend, and I need

to tell my brain to cut that shit out. Grabbing two juice boxes from the fridge and the sleeve of Ritz crackers, I point to the living room. "I believe we have a date with some Titans."

London follows me into the living room. "You sound pretty confident."

"I've been practicing since the night you spanked me."

"Probably a good idea," she says, and bends to grab a controller off the coffee table. "You sucked pretty hard."

"At the game, you mean. The sex was stellar."

She doesn't answer, but her practiced silence tickles me, and I can't help but push, just one more time: "Does being back here, at the start of it all, have you feeling nostalgic?" I ask her over my shoulder before bending to grab the remote.

"No," she says, and then shoves my shoulder so I know even if she means it, she's not trying to be an asshole.

Even if *I* am, just a little.

We sit down next to each other—definitely not touching—waiting for the game to load. The crinkle of her straw wrapper crackles through the silence and when I look at her, she cheekily punctures the top and slides the straw into the side of her mouth, saying "I love fruit punch" around it.

Fucking *fuck*. I am so screwed.

The best and worst part about being near her is that I know she's not *trying* to flirt. She isn't a cocktease. She's just honestly that cute.

I look away from her mouth and back to the television. "I'm usually an apple juice guy, but I thought it was time to mix it up."

We sign in, choosing our Titans, and drop down into the map without more discussion. When I'm not obsessing about kissing her, being with her is surprisingly effortless. We can just hang, talk or not talk—it's easy either way. It's like being with a guy friend I just really want to bang.

Wait, no.

I fumble with the controller, get shot, and the game resets.

London turns and looks at me with her bright smile. "You okay there, Sparky? I thought you had been practicing?"

"Just had a mental tangent that left me momentarily incapacitated."

She shakes her head, looking back at the screen. "I don't think I want to know."

We drop in again, and this time the action continues for ten, twenty, thirty minutes. Our elbows collide as we work the controllers, and London shoves Ritz crackers into her mouth the same way I do—in handfuls, in the few seconds we have between bouts of action. I'm definitely better than the last time we played together, and it makes for a perfect afternoon. The idea of falling in love with a girl who plays video games, eats crackers like Cookie Monster, surfs, and bartends feels in some ways like the perfect male fantasy, but it's also a little shadowed because I know there is more to London than this. This life—games, bars, girls—for me is just a *phase;* I know with some distance that it isn't going to define this entire decade, or even the rest of this year. I'm going to leave for law school in a matter of months, and it will require me to have true responsibility away from my family. But what does London even want out of life?

I'm pulled out of the preposterous train of thought when she does something really stupid—hits the jump control instead of fire—and is killed.

"Damnit!" she yells, smacking the couch cushion. "Mother-trucking truck!"

I turn to her, smiling in delight. "Did I just kick your ass?"

"I think that's an exaggeration." She looks at her watch. "We were playing for—"

I interrupt her, leaning in. "You were totally thinking about my penis just then, weren't you?"

She throws her empty juice box at me and her eyes widen when I catch it before it hits me and chuck it right at her, hitting her squarely in the chest.

London lunges for me, shoving me back on the couch before lifting a pillow and smacking me in the face with it. Her bubbly laughter hits me in an emotional space, somewhere high, where chest meets throat, and I'm unprepared for her assault, cough-laughing through a flurry of her fingers digging down, tickling me roughly.

I buck up beneath her, growing more aware of what we're doing—wrestling—and what it means—*motherfucking foreplay, ma'am*—and I advance toward her on the couch, swatting at her hands, darting my fingers between her arms to tickle her ribs, and, with my other hand, grab a pillow from behind her and use it to hit her right in the face.

She shoves—hard—sending me off the couch and onto the floor, where she dives onto me, pinning me, wrestling in earnest. We're laughing and yelling and one of us knocks the sleeve of Ritz crackers to the floor and it crunches under her shoulder when I roll over to hover above her, getting the upper hand and finding the place on her waist that, when prodded with a long finger, makes her wail in hysterics.

She smacks my hand when my tickles get too close to her boob, and scream-calls me a pervert so I bend down and blow an enormous raspberry right into where her neck meets her shoulder.

London shrieks even louder, and holy fuck, I am *deaf.* I clamp a hand over my ear, working to fight off her relentlessly tickling hands with only my left hand as defense.

We seem to realize at the same time that I'm over her, lying completely on top of her and situated between her legs and, in unison, we both freeze. I'd climb off her if she didn't have two tight fistfuls of my shirt in her hands and if her eyes weren't currently traveling the slow path from my stomach to my face.

It feels like I count to a hundred in the time it takes for either of us to breathe.

Finally, I feel the slide of her legs up my hips. Feel the give of her body beneath mine, and am suddenly, intensely aware of that soft, warm place between her legs. Her eyes have gone wide and I watch as they make their way back down my face, stopping at my mouth.

"Logan?"

She sucks her lower lip into her mouth to keep from smiling.

I press forward, not much but just enough to feel more, the gentle heat of her. Her eyes grow heavy, mouth goes slack, and I watch a pink blush creep up her chest. In the span of one of her tight breaths I go from half hard to desperate for her.

"Luke."

"Fuck," I growl, bending and pressing my mouth to her neck as I start to rock against her.

I nearly come at the sound she makes, that soft, restrained cry, and I'm fucking her through my clothes, through hers, sucking and licking her skin, just *insane* to be with her like this.

My need for her ratchets up, climbing from this heated infatuation to something more, something that traps my lungs, threatens to break me.

"I missed this," I say into her skin. "*Fuck,* I missed this. The feel of you . . ."

Three rough grinds in and her hands are on my chest, sliding down and over my pecs to the hem of my shirt, where she makes fists in the cotton again.

She could pull it up and off me in a single tug.

I can feel her reaching the fork in the road, and then she hesitates, going still under me. "Luke. Wait. *Wait.*"

I stop moving, closing my eyes where my face is pressed into her neck.

No. Please.

She pushes at my hips with her fists still around my shirt,

pushing me away from her. More than the desperate tension in my body, my heart feels like it might tie itself into a knot.

"We can't," she says through a tight exhale. "We shouldn't."

I push up off her, sitting back on my heels and watching her scramble to her feet.

"Sorry," I say. I fucking mean it, too. I know she's not into me that way, and I keep pushing.

"No, *I'm* sorry," she says. "It was me."

Her hand comes out, gesturing for mine, and I wave it away, pushing myself to stand.

"Ugh, this is awkward," I say in a quiet growl.

Laughing, she says, "No . . ." in a way that totally means *yes*.

I don't really know what to do with myself now. I look to the side, feeling her discomfort and drowning in it.

We look back at each other at the same time. "Do you think we should talk about . . . ?" I ask, trailing off.

"Um, *no*," she says, horrified. "I had a moment of weakness, it won't happen again."

A moment of weakness? As in, she sort of wants this? "But what if I *want* to talk?"

"What's there to say?" she says, shrugging helplessly.

"Just . . ." I pull my thoughts together, sitting down on the couch. "Okay, look. Even when we're just friends, the fact that we've slept together is always hanging between us. I feel it in every second we're together, and I'm lying if I say I don't."

"I figured of anyone you'd be good at pretending it didn't happen," she jokes, but it falls flat.

This totally fucking stings, and I let her see it on my face. "Well, I'm not."

Nodding, she says, "Okay. Sorry."

"And I know you think I'm a total player—and maybe I deserve that—but I've only been with one person since you and—"

"That's, like, *one month*, Luke."

I laugh. "I know, but someday maybe I'll tell you about how comically horrible it was." She starts to ask, but I cut her off. "The point is, I'm trying to turn over a new leaf. And it requires reflection, which is sort of new for me . . ." I trail off, feeling like I owe her the chance to make a smart remark, but I'm actually relieved when she doesn't.

She sits down next to me on the couch, listening.

"But here's the thing," I continue, "four years ago, I was *really* in love with Mia. I thought we were going to be together forever, and I know now that I was young, and it was unrealistic, but when it ended it was *hard*. I mean, we had been calling each other boyfriend-girlfriend since middle school. I didn't want to give that kind of energy to just anyone. At first it felt like I'd be"—I look around, searching for words—"I don't know, cheating, or something, to let myself feel things for someone else, even though Mia and I weren't together. And then, being with girls in a more casual way was just such a relief. It meant that endings would be easier. It became how I operated. It was an evolution, okay, and I'm not saying that I hate myself for it, because I would be lying, but I have a little bit of hindsight now, and it isn't how I want to do things anymore."

She nods, listening with her wide, blue eyes trained on my face. "Okay."

"So I just wanted you to know." I lean back, lacing my hands behind my head and staring at the ceiling. "I know your last boyfriend hurt you, and I don't want you to think all guys are like that. I don't want you to think *I'm* like that."

She nods again, faster now, leaning forward and rubbing her palms together between her knees. She seems a little agitated. I'm inclined to tell her she doesn't have to talk to me if she doesn't want to, but the truth is that I don't really want to let her off the hook if we're doing the sharing thing right now. London is one of the sweetest girls I've ever met, but there's a shell there and I don't have the sense that she talks to people very often about what's going on in her head.

The silence feels like it extends for miles, and in a surreal way it seems like the couch elongates between us, making me feel farther away from her the longer she's quiet. I close my eyes, pushing through it. At some point one of us has to speak, and I swear it will not be me.

Finally, she takes a deep breath and lets it out, slowly. "My dad's been cheating on my mom since I was sixteen. It's sort of an unspoken rule in my house that we never talk about it— even though everyone knows."

I'm initially horrified, but then . . . another piece of the London puzzle falls into place, and it feels like a tiny bomb has just gone off inside my chest. I think of my parents, the way they look at each other, and try to imagine how I would deal with it if I thought all of it was a lie. I can't. "That's . . . I'm sorry, Logan."

"I always told myself—and my mom when we'd argue—that I'd never put up with being treated like that." A few beats of silence pass before she lets out a long breath and continues. "I've known Justin my whole life," she says. "His mom and my mom are best friends, and we were always close . . . but we didn't start dating until the summer before our senior year. He moved here with me from Colorado. I went to UCSD and he was at SDSU, even though his first choice was to go to Boulder. But I mean, San Diego has been my second home. I always knew I wanted to go to college out here, and I couldn't wait to leave Denver." She goes quiet for a few seconds, tucks a strand of hair behind her ear. "I think it was sort of like how things were with you and Mia, where you just assumed that you'd be together forever." Looking over at me, she says, "Apparently, he met someone at the beginning of sophomore year and they were all but living together during the week. I found out because I walked in on them." She pauses, then adds quietly, "Senior year. Right after my grandmother's funeral. He said he had to work, but . . ."

My stomach bottoms out and I let out a long exhale. "Holy *fuck*. Your *senior year*?"

"Yeah. Almost *three years* he was cheating . . ." She trails off, shaking her head. I can't even school my expression right now. My mouth is just gaping open. The fucking *nerve* of this prick.

"And apparently they're still together," she says quietly. "Getting married, actually . . . so there's that."

My reaction to all of this is to want to punch something. "What a bag of dicks."

She nods. "It's taken me a really, *really* long time to stop feeling pissed off. Actually, I still feel pissed off about it. I think when I give my heart, I want to give everything. You make that decision, and it's all or nothing, you know?"

She winces when she says this, as if the admission is somehow embarrassing, and my chest is so tight that I'm not even sure how to respond. I *want* her everything. I want to pummel the asshole who made her feel her love was wasted.

When she realizes I'm struggling to reply, she continues, voice brighter, "Anyway, after I came out of the initial miserable fog of humiliation and heartbreak, the only thing I felt I'd gained was a certainty that I'm a terrible judge of character."

"London," I say. "You're *not*."

"Oh, I am." She smiles at me, and it's so sweetly fragile that it cracks something in me. Pulling her hair up into a bun on top of her head, she holds it there in both hands. Fuck, it feels so good to talk to her about this. For as much as I'm enraged on her behalf, I'm elated to have her here, and just . . . *talking* to me in a way I feel she doesn't with very many people, if anyone.

"I mean," she says, "I can pick out the obvious assholes. That's what bartenders learn to do. But the smarter ones just might be better at hiding it. That's what sucks the most, what I'm actually the angriest about: even if I like someone, I will never trust my judgment. Do you know how that feels? To have been so wrong that it feels like your people meter is just *broken*?"

The weight of this entire conversation seems to hit me at once, and I slump back against the couch. "That's significantly depressing," I agree.

She throws her hands in the air. "I know!"

"It explains a lot about why you're such a hot mess," I tell her with a grin, wanting to make her smile again.

"Same," she says, nodding her chin to me.

"Our relationship histories are totally depressing," I say. "Tell me something funny."

She sighs, thinking. Finally, she says, "*Vagina* roughly translates to *sword holder* in Latin."

I turn to look at her. "It was named *for* the penis?"

"This surprises you?" she asks, looking at me in shock. "Hello? Patriarchy."

"But even back in the day?" I say. "They *spoke* Latin. That means everyone *knew* that vagina meant *sword holder*. It wasn't like now where most people don't know that meaning. A woman would have to refer to her parts as her *sword holder*. 'How's the sword holder?' 'Alas, it's pretty empty right now.'"

"Her '*parts*'?" she repeats with an amused grin.

"What?" I ask, smiling back at her. "You called it your *ladybird*."

"True." She lets her head fall back against the couch again, groaning. "Now I'm all gross and sad thinking about Justin. I need sugar."

"Left side of sink, top cabinet." She rolls her head to look at me, and I add, "It's where I keep the treats."

"Bless you." London pushes to stand and I stare at her ass as she walks away and into the kitchen. I hear her banging around in the cabinets, and then she yells, "Oh my God! Are you okay?"

I sit up, worried. "Yeah, why?"

"You have an open Pop-Tart package with a Pop-Tart in it."

I deflate in relief, get off the couch, and wander into the kitchen. "Yeah. I had one this morning."

Her mouth is agape when she turns to me, holding up the package and saying, "Who the hell has *one* Pop-Tart?"

"I sense . . ." I lick my finger, holding it up in the air. "Yes, I sense mocking in your tone."

"I bet you're one of those yokels who buys the Pop-Tart–sized Tupperware."

I narrow my eyes, slowly repeating, " 'Yokels'?"

"Meaning not only do you *not* eat both Pop-Tarts like a real man," she continues, ignoring me, "but you also need an airtight container because you won't eat the other one within an hour."

I lean back against the counter, smiling at her.

"I bet you don't even like *scotch*," she teases. "Do you have a real penis?"

This makes me laugh and I have to curl my hands into fists to keep from pulling her close to me with a finger hooked through her belt loop.

Tilting her head, she asks, "Do you order salads for lunch?"

"You've seen me eat nachos," I remind her.

"Once. And they were *vegetarian*."

I open my mouth to argue but she cuts me off. "I can see it in your face! You usually order salads. With your dressing on the side!"

This part isn't actually true but I'm having too much fun watching her unravel to contradict her.

She shakes the Pop-Tart wrapper. "I would eat this Pop-Tart to help you out, you know, to even up the asymmetry currently poisoning your box, but seeing as how there is only one, it's a snack dilemma."

Nodding in understanding, I say, "You wouldn't be satisfied with only one."

"Exactly." She shoves it back in the box. "It's like eating only half a banana."

I shiver. "Who eats an entire banana?"

London stills, looking at me like I might have damaged my head. "Who *doesn't*?"

"Me," I tell her emphatically. "By the last few bites it's this awful"—I shudder—"*intense* banana flavor. It doesn't matter how big the banana is, I can't handle it."

"You're weird."

I shrug, palms up. "Apparently. But see, I like to take my time with that one Pop-Tart." She groans when she registers where I am going with this. "*You*, on the other hand—"

"*Stop.*"

"—are welcome to have as many Pop-Tarts as you want when you're here."

She pins me with a wary half smile and I watch as she fights it, finally giving in and letting the grin take over her entire mouth. My chest feels hot, pulse too fast. It's like the anticipation before a match but infinitely better. Whatever it is, it makes me drunk on her. Being near her, making her smile makes me feel incredible. She can see it and I let her. I'm fucking *drunk* on this girl.

Finally, exhaling a shaky breath, she smacks my chest. "You're hopeless."

I grab her hand before she can pull it away, resting it on my chest. I know she can feel my heart pounding, and if what I'm watching happen with her pulse in her throat is any indication, her heart is beating just as hard.

I smile, and watch as it softens something in her expression. "I think you're right," I tell her.

Chapter THIRTEEN

London

I ORDER ANOTHER CAPPUCCINO and weave through the small line to get back to my seat. Most of the staff here know me by name and don't mind when I spend hours at my favorite table: the one near the outlet that actually works. They know I like one Sugar in the Raw in my coffee and that I'll say I don't want a blueberry muffin but usually end up ordering one anyway.

I'm a creature of habit and have been coming to this particular shop as long as I can remember. Summers meant weekdays surfing and then relaxing at Nana's house, and Sunday mornings at Pannikin. She'd have her chai latte and let me order a hot chocolate and we would do the Sunday *New York Times* crossword puzzle, which basically meant Nana would do it and I would people-watch.

Even without her I'm unable to break the routine.

It's April and despite it being the standard seventy–two degrees outside, it's freezing in the store. I settle back into my chair and pull the cardigan out of my bag, buttoning it up before turning back to my laptop.

I blow into my coffee and look back to the screen, to the section of Lola's site I've spent the last few hours coding. Her original designer had created a template full of neon colors and lots of animation, but I've dialed it back down to something a bit more subdued, a palette that will really let Lola's art do the talking. Her images are geometric and bold, and practically jump off the screen. It's strange that while I've been living around this art for the past eight months, I don't think I've ever really appreciated how *insanely* talented Lola is until now.

The door opens and the air-conditioning kicks on directly over my head. I slink down into my sweater and pull my cup closer, hoping the warmth will seep into my fingers, when I hear my name.

Well, sort of.

"Logan?"

DANGER, DANGER.

I blink up to see Luke standing near the counter, and a rush of adrenaline shoots through my veins. His hair is messy and he's dressed in a T-shirt and track pants, as if he's just been for a run. Even a little sweaty—maybe *because* he looks a little sweaty?—he looks better than should be humanly possible. He pulls out his wallet to pay and my eyes drop automatically to the way the damp T-shirt clings to his shoulders and dips in at his waist, down to where his hip bones . . .

The chair across from me scrapes against the floor and I snap my head up to meet his eyes: brown and clearly amused to have caught me ogling him. He sits across from me, drink already in front of him, arms resting on the table, and takes his time doing his own—rather blatant—inspection. I clear my throat.

"You know it's April, right?" he says, and motions to my clothes while he takes a sip from his iced drink.

"It's freezing in here," I tell him, tugging my sleeves farther down over my hands. "It's at least seventy outside. Why do they insist on the arctic temperatures in here? So I can model my finest winter fashions?"

Luke shrugs and takes another drink before glancing at his phone and putting it away in his pocket. He stretches his neck side to side and then glances at the scarf around my neck.

I wait for him to make one of his trademark unfiltered come-ons . . . but he doesn't. It takes me a second to place my reaction as disappointment.

But you're *the one who drew the "just friends" line, London.*

"Did you make sure they put skim in your drink?" I ask, recovering. "Wouldn't want them to sneak whole milk in that drink and ruin the salad you had for lunch."

Luke aims his smile at me, ignoring my baiting snark.

Again: disappointment.

"So what are you doing there?" He taps a finger on the top of my laptop. "Googling cheat codes for Titanfall?"

The twinkle in his eyes loosens an anxious knot in my chest.

I take a sip of my own drink and set it back down again. "Working on Lola's website. She was having some trouble with the guy she hired and I told her I'd fix it for her."

Luke stands and leans over the table to get a look at my screen. "*You* did that?"

"Yeah," I tell him, moving over a little so he can see better. "Her art really does most of the work, I just wanted to build something around that. It's just code and—"

"I'm an idiot, and even I know it's a lot harder than 'just code,'" he says. "Logan, that's a great fucking site. The guys in my office just paid someone a shitload of money to build theirs and it doesn't look half as good as this."

I shrug and turn the screen back to me, returning to the dashboard and doing my best to look unaffected. Praise from Luke has done something strange to my insides. My stomach is warm and fluttery. I have to remind myself to keep my head down because I know this response will be written all over my face.

"Logan," he says this time, a bit more forcefully to get my attention.

I blink up at him, hoping I can keep this overwhelming fondness tucked safely out of sight. "People pay a lot of money for work like this."

"Some do."

He looks at me with the most adorably confused smile. "Then why don't you do more of this and serve fewer Heinekens to douchebags at the bar?"

I tilt my head and consider him through narrowed eyes. "I don't know if you really classify as a douchebag, per se . . ." I tell him.

He looks mock-hurt. "Hey—I didn't say *I* was a douchebag."

"Oh, my bad." I look back down at the screen with an evil little smile.

Under the table he stretches his legs out in front of him and brackets each of his feet against each of mine; the sides of our legs touch. "You're avoiding my question."

I shrug, holding my shoulders up tight for a few breaths. "Because people want experience and a big portfolio to pay you big money. I've done Oliver's site, and now Lola's, but I don't have a *ton* of experience outside of school."

He looks down at my laptop and back up again, meaningfully. "I'm no expert but you seem well on your way here," he says. "Lola's going to flip when she sees that."

I bite the insides of my cheek to keep my smile in check. "Hopefully."

"I still can't believe everything that's happening with her. The comic, a *movie*? I still remember her drawing dicks on the outside of all my notebooks."

I snort. "Yeah, you might want to see if you have any of those lying around because they could be worth something one day. I know I'm keeping the little panel she drew and taped to the fridge. It's an angry cat calling me an ass for drinking the orange juice."

"You did all of this just *today*?" he asks.

I nod and take another sip of my drink. "Yeah, surfed this morning but got here around nine."

He looks at his watch and I instinctively check the clock on my computer. Eleven eleven. I want to make a wish, but my breath catches in my throat at my first instinct to wish for something having to do with this guy across the table from me. Instead, I close my eyes and make a tiny wish for my web design business to take off someday soon.

Looking back up at me, Luke says, "So you're saying you've been working for just over two hours doing the thing you went to school for—and which you're actually really good at and could possibly make great money doing—and *still* managed to snag a few hours at the beach . . . interesting."

"Have you been talking to my mom?" I ask him.

"Yeah, she and I talk most days." He waves a casual hand in the air. "Usually just about how you never call, and how you should find a nice boy to bring home."

"That sounds *exactly* like my mom."

Luke's phone makes a soft chime and I have to tamp down the pulse of irritation I still get whenever it goes off. He looks up, pocketing his phone obliviously. "Want to get some dinner later?"

"Actually I have plans," I tell him, closing my laptop and slipping it into my bag.

His expression falls just the tiniest amount, making me wonder if I imagined it as his eyes flicker down to follow the movement of my hands as I wrap up my cord. "Plans?"

"Fred has a date and I promised him I'd watch his granddaughter."

"Babysitting?" he asks. "How old is she?"

"Five going on sixteen. She's the cutest thing. Anyway, before I head over, I need to run home and shower, eat. You know." I stand and loop my bag across my body before pushing in my chair. Luke stands and my heart takes off at the whiff of ocean and the faint clean smell of his sweat.

Dinner with him sounds nice, though.

Damnit.

He reaches forward to untwist my strap on my shoulder. "All right."

We stand there, the question hanging between us. I can tell he's not going to push . . . for once.

"You wouldn't want to babysit with me," I say, looking up at him through my lashes. "I mean, you'd find that totally boring, right?"

I can't believe I just asked him this. What twenty-three-and-a-half-year-old man in his right mind would want to come along to babysit?

But this is Luke: he gives me a little one-shouldered shrug. "I did letter in dolly hair."

Shocked, I look up at him fully now, watching the smooth line of his throat as he swallows. "You *would* want to come?"

He shrugs again and tosses his cup into a recycling bin. "Why not?"

"You wouldn't be bored?"

His smile melts my heart. "Maybe, but wouldn't it be more fun to be bored together?"

"Are you *sure*?" I ask. I sort of love the idea of having Luke along for the night, especially since I miss the flirty side of him and that can only be remedied with just . . . more time with him. "It'll be tea parties and Barbie."

"Logan, if you keep trying to talk me out of the idea, I

might change my mind," he says, laughing. Luke manages to get a few steps ahead of me and holds open the door.

"Thanks," I tell him. "That would be . . . awesome."

He slips on his sunglasses and follows me into the parking lot. We reach my car, and even though his eyes are hidden behind his dark lenses, I can sense the hopeful way he stares down at me. "So . . . what time?"

There are a million reasons why this is a bad idea, but as I lean against my car door, I find myself wanting to hang out with him so much it almost feels urgent. Luke is managing to break down my walls one smile at a time. Being with him feels a little like letting go of the handlebars and racing down a hill. And it also feels like being wrapped up in the warmest blanket.

How can he feel both like an adventure *and* a comfort?

"Six," I tell him. "And fair warning: you have to bring pizza and let her braid your hair if she asks."

"YOU KNOW, IF I do say so myself, this was a great idea. You're a fantastic babysitter." I wiggle my toes, feet propped up on Fred's coffee table. "Don't ever let anyone tell you you're just a pretty face, Blue Crush."

Luke grins at me from across the room where he's sitting with Daisy at a small table, in an even smaller chair, in the midst of what appears to be an elaborate tea party. His usually soft, floppy hair is spiky now, tied up by fluorescent hairbands in about twenty tiny, crazy ponytails.

He leans toward Daisy conspiratorially and hikes his thumb in my direction. "I *told* you she thought I was pretty."

Daisy slides a couple of decorative flowers into the mess of his hair. I laugh under my breath and sit up. "Well, how could I not? I mean, Daisy must have lettered in dolly hair, too, because yours looks amazing like that. Is she friends with your sister?"

"You said there'd be no teasing," he tells me, and politely thanks Daisy when she offers him more tea.

"That doesn't really sound like a thing I would say to you, Luke."

"Fine," he says, giving me a little wink. "Go ahead and joke, but don't think I didn't see you watching while she put in these ponytails. You love my hair." He leans forward and puts a hand over each of her tiny ears before he adds, "And *I* remember how much you love to get your hands in it."

"You had to cover her ears for that?" I ask. "That wasn't even dirty."

"The dirty part was implied," he says, dropping his hands. "Sometimes the dirtiest things are the simplest. Like your swimsuit the other day: it covered more because you had to move and work in the water, but it was still hotter than some skimpy thing that shows sideboob."

I can only look at him and blink. "But you didn't have to cover her ears for that?"

"Oh, shi— crap. Sorry."

I stand and walk over to them, and without even thinking, brush a finger over a piece of his hair that's come loose.

I think about how it felt to have my hands on his hips while I helped him balance at the beach, or how his eyes moving down my body felt hotter than the sun overhead. I quickly take a step back.

I veer us into safer territory: "You definitely get points for being a good sport."

I expect him to make some crack about "points" meaning blow jobs or something, but instead he just says, "I'm having fun."

"Would you like some tea?" Daisy says, lifting the plastic pot toward me.

"I don't think so, honey. It's pretty late and too much tea might keep us up."

"I'm not tired," she says, and turns back to her dolls. "And I want to keep playing with Luke. He's nice. Don't you think he's nice, Logan?"

Luke snickers and I pinch his arm before kneeling at the table to smooth her hair. "He is nice. And silly goose, you know my name is London."

"But Luke calls you Logan," she says.

"Maybe he can come back and play again," I tell her. "I bet we could get him to read you a story?"

"We're gonna watch *Frozen*. He pinky promised."

I look at him. "You *pinky promised*?"

He leans in. "I used my left pinkie. It's the sneaky one, so feel free to veto."

Daisy agrees to pajamas and teeth brushing if it means Luke and part of a movie before bed. I really can't say I blame her.

We settle into the couch, Daisy on Luke's lap and me—at her insistence—next to them. *Right* next to them, which basically translates into the three of us crammed into one corner, with room for at least four more adults in the space left unoccupied.

She allows him to take the bands out of his hair without much fuss, if he promises to wear her Elsa necklace and never take it off. Ever. She's pretty insistent on this point, and it takes everything I have not to smile as he reasons with her, explaining that he works in a big fancy office and her necklace might not look okay with his suit. In the end they both get their way and find a compromise: Luke only has to wear the necklace for a few hours, as long as he holds her hand.

He'll make a brilliant attorney one day, I'm sure.

Luke is solid and warm at my side, and the TV glows in front of us, painting the room in flickering shadow. It takes a few minutes to get her settled, but soon Daisy is snuggled up and rather pleased with herself that she's pretty much gotten her way. Her hand looks positively tiny in his and I keep blinking down to it, marveling at how much bigger he is than her and how absolutely gentle he's being. I try to pay attention to what's happening on the screen—there's a lot of snow and even more singing—but it's hard to follow amid the crisis I'm having over his holding her tiny little hand. I never find that sort of thing sexy. I don't. I swear.

About five minutes later, Luke's voice breaks into my thoughts: "I think she's out."

I look over to meet his eyes, and in this light he's all

cheekbones and sharp jaw. The ends of his eyelashes glow against the screen.

"Is she asleep?" he asks.

I blink several times before I understand what he's talking about. Right, *Daisy*. The child I'm supposed to be babysitting. I lean forward and sure enough, her eyes are closed, her breaths soft and even. "Yeah, out like a light. Good job."

"I make a pretty good bed, but I think two slices of pizza and a movie did most of the work."

"No, really," I whisper. "This whole night—you've been amazing. You waltz in here with dinner and your dreamboat smile, all adorable and charming and made everything easy. Well done, Mr. Sutter."

"You think I'm charming?" he says, and grins. The glow from the TV accentuates the way his face softens when he smiles, and I have to look away.

"Is that all you took out of that whole thing?" I ask.

"I also got *adorable, dreamboat*, and *easy*."

I laugh, rubbing a hand over my face. "Of course you did."

We watch the rest of the movie together in silence, and I check my phone for the time. It's only then that I realize I haven't heard his go off for what has to be a few hours now. It's not on the coffee table, and when I think about it, I can't even remember when I saw it last. "Did you shut your phone off?" I ask, looking around.

He leans forward to take a drink and sits back with an exaggerated sigh. "Daisy made me. She said it was *rude*."

I laugh. "Well, Daisy is the boss."

"Apparently."

"Think of all the texts you're missing."

Luke laughs softly and rearranges Daisy on his lap so that she's more comfortable. "No, it's fine. This was . . . this was fun," he says with a small lift of his shoulder. "Daisy was cute and you know I like hanging out with you."

Blinking back to his face, I admit, "I have no idea why. I'm stubborn and blunt with you. Sometimes I can't believe the things I say." I want to lean into him, cuddle him. "I might as well just get a house full of cats and call it a day."

He's already shaking his head. "You're *honest* with me. I like that you know where your limits are and you stick up for yourself. I like so many things about you, Logan." He laughs and lets his head fall back against the couch. "We might be here a while. I could make you a list if that helps?"

I look down at my lap and Luke follows the movement, moving to catch my eyes. "I like that you're strong and don't take any of my shit. My sister doesn't, either, and she's probably my favorite person in the world."

His expression falls slightly on this, like it's not something he was planning to say and the words have surprised him.

I swallow and try to make sense of what I'm feeling, and to explain it to him.

"I like that you're so unguarded," I tell him. "That you say what you feel and . . . it doesn't scare you."

"It scares me," he says. "But maybe I'm just happy to be feeling something for the first time in a long time. Or maybe I just hide my fear better."

"It doesn't seem like it. It doesn't seem like you're afraid of anything," I tell him. "Except maybe sharks. And jellyfish—"

"There it is," he says, rolling his eyes while I continue to count off.

"Turtles, starfish, seaweed . . ."

"Logan," he says, and digs for my ribs.

"Okay, okay." I squirm away from him. "But even then, I was really impressed. Even scared, you just . . . you did it. You got in the water."

A beat of silence passes between us and he blinks over to the TV. "Maybe sometimes you just have to," he says finally. His eyes shift back over to me again, and I don't think we're talking about surfing anymore. "Don't get me wrong, I almost peed my pants out there, but sometimes we all have to stop thinking about what could hurt us and just . . . jump."

His words hit me like a fist between my ribs because I *am* scared, and I'm most definitely afraid to jump. Sometimes I see Luke as *that guy,* the one I watched out for, the type of guy who walked out of a club with another girl the day after having sex with me, whose phone never stops ringing with one booty call after another.

But then he's jumping into an ocean when it terrifies him and having tea parties, and telling me about this girl he loved so much that he would have done anything for her. He's doing all of this to spend time with *me,* and it terrifies me how much I want him, because I've been there before and I was so, so wrong.

I know I've been quiet too long when Luke clears his throat and shifts next to me.

"Anyway. I was impressed," I tell him. "It takes a lot to be bigger than your fears."

He looks at me and smiles and heat slithers like fingers along my spine. "Thanks."

"And for someone who'd never been on a board, you really kicked some ass." I realize I'm rambling. I realize I'm stalling.

The air between us is crackling with charge and I don't know how to deal.

He leans in a bit more and tilts his head to look up at me. "I had a pretty great teacher," he says.

I shift forward and he's so close, close enough that I can feel each breath and count the tiny freckles across his nose. He blinks down to my mouth and back up and he's asking if this is okay, giving me time to close the distance or pull away.

I *want* to kiss him.

It takes the smallest effort on my part before I feel him, the barest brush of his lips, the slight catch in his breath against my own. He smells like the apple candy he won in a game of Go Fish, and my mouth practically waters, imagining if I'll taste it on his tongue.

Without thinking I close my eyes and open my mouth and—

Daisy makes a small sound in her sleep and says my name.

We both exhale like we've been holding our breath, before he sits back, pushing a hand through his hair. "Am I a terrible person that I would have given her a thousand dollars to sleep for ten more minutes?" he asks.

My heart is pounding in my chest and I laugh, scrubbing a hand over my face. "I probably would have gone in for half."

Luke shifts Daisy into my arms and trades places with me so I can have the arm of the couch before settling back against my side. We don't talk as we turn back to the movie, and after a few minutes, I feel his finger brush absently along my wrist.

He hasn't looked away from the screen, and I realize he's not doing it to get my attention or pull some sort of reaction from me; he's doing it because he needs to touch me. I wonder if his fingers itch like mine do whenever he's around, or if he feels the same tug-of-war inside his chest.

I don't think I'm in control of the nerves that fire and make my hand move, but with my eyes locked straight ahead, I turn my palm over and twist my fingers with his.

He doesn't say anything, but in my peripheral vision I think I see him smile.

He tightens his grip.

I wonder if he gets that this is my wordless admission that maybe I like him. That he doesn't completely suck after all.

Daisy is softly snoring with her head resting on my right shoulder, and after only a few moments of hesitation, I feel Luke do the same thing against my left.

The weight of him next to me—so solid and strong—feels comfortable and safe, and soon my own eyelids droop. I sink farther into the couch and into Luke, and fall asleep to the sound of the credits playing.

IT CAN'T BE long after when the front door opens.

I vaguely hear footsteps and blink several times before I can make out Fred standing in front of me, holding his phone in one outstretched arm.

"What are you—are you taking a *picture*?" I say, voice hoarse and groggy.

"Do you have any idea how cute you two are?" Fred asks, looking at his phone before turning the screen to face me.

"That's super-creepy, Fred."

I feel Luke stir next to me and he sits up with a start.

"Relax, son," Fred says, steadying his shoulder. "I'm not some dad who just caught you making out with the babysitter."

I realize that we're still holding hands and I pull mine away, ignoring the way I can still feel his palm against my own. "Really creepy," I say, handing over a still-sleeping little girl.

"She was good?" he asks, smoothing her hair.

"An angel, like always. She might be engaged to Luke, though. Fair warning."

Fred laughs and motions that he's going to put her to bed, and I tell him I'll talk to him tomorrow at work.

This is the part that usually gets awkward, where Luke walks me out to my car and we stand across from each other, pretending that we didn't just kiss and that we weren't holding hands like high schoolers. But it seems like the potential for awkward has dissolved between us, and right now it just feels quiet, and calm.

The street is dark, and I fumble for the door handle, opening my car to set my bag inside. When I turn, Luke takes my hand, looking down at the way it fits in his. "I had a lot of fun. Thanks for letting me crash your party."

"Are you kidding? That was the easiest night I've ever had with her. Usually I'm the one with braids and a tiara. Thanks for hanging out."

There's a beat of silence and a dog barks in the distance, and in my head I'm chanting, *Don't ask me to come home with you don't ask me to come home with you, don't ask me, don't ask me . . . Because honestly I have no idea how I'd say no.*

But he doesn't, instead leaning in to place a small kiss against my cheek and letting go of my hand. "Text me when you get home?" he asks.

I nod, a little dazed at the turn in the conversation, and I can't tell if it's relief or disappointment gathering in my stomach.

"Yeah," I tell him. "Sure."

On impulse, I cup his face, and stretch to place the lightest kiss on his warm lips. Stunned, he just stands there, watching as I step back and fight an enormous smile.

His eyebrows slowly rise. "Logan, you just kissed me."

"Only a tiny kiss." I smile up at him and notice the way his eyes flicker to my cheek to look at my dimple.

He holds the door while I climb inside and shuts it behind me. I open the window and he leans down, resting his arms on the frame.

"I like you," he says. I know this, but the admission is so bare that if I weren't already sitting, my knees might feel a little weak.

"I like you, too. Weirdo," I add, and see his smile linger as he steps back and watches me drive away.

It's not until I'm several blocks away that I remember: he's my friend's ex. I don't get to have Luke Sutter.

LOLA AND OLIVER are on the couch watching a movie when I get home. I drop my bag on the floor near the door and wave to them before walking into the kitchen to get a glass of water.

My head swims a little with uncertainty. I'm starting to really want to trust Luke. I'm starting to need his company. But the remaining roadblock—Harlow, Mia, the history of this group with Luke—seems to be the one thing that lingers, and I have no idea how to deal with it. On the one hand, I feel like Harlow is being unreasonable by even having an opinion about any of this. On the other hand, I get it. He was with Mia for so long. There are unspoken rules; he should be off-limits.

"Were you working?" Lola asks, pausing the movie.

I swallow, shaking my head. "I was babysitting Daisy."

She stands, smiling, and joins me in the kitchen. "A wild night, then."

"It was fun, actually." I meet her eyes, and hesitate before admitting quietly, "Luke came along with me."

Her eyebrows rise to the ceiling. "Well, you know he's into you if he joins you for *babysitting*."

I try to laugh, I really do, but it comes out a little strangled and quickly turns into a sob.

In my peripheral vision, I can see Oliver get up from the couch, and walk over to join us, but I just keep staring very hard at my hands cupped around the water glass so I don't have to look either of them in the eye.

"London?" Lola asks, stepping closer and putting a warm hand on my arm. "Sweetie, what happened?"

I shake my head, unaccustomed to crying at all, let alone crying in front of someone.

"Do you want me to stay or go?" Oliver asks quietly.

"You can stay," I manage. "I'm being ridiculous. I don't know what's wrong with me."

They both wait for me to explain my meltdown, and after I swallow down a few more inexplicable sobs, I tell them, "I just really like him."

Lola's voice is both gentle and confused. "You should like him. He's an awesome guy."

Finally, I look up at her face. "I mean, I like him. Romantically."

"And I'm saying, you *should*. He's amazing."

"But Harlow."

It's all I can really think to say. And as soon as I do, the two words hang heavily in the air between us. It should be, *But Mia*—except it isn't, because Mia doesn't care. Or, it should be, *But I'm afraid*—except it isn't exactly that, either, because although part of me is afraid, a much bigger part of me wants to give him the benefit of the doubt.

Like the wise person she is, Lola also lets the words hang there. Instead of growing bigger and more meaningful, though, they start to feel small, and silly.

"I don't reckon it's up to Harlow," Oliver says quietly.

Tilting her head, Lola studies me sympathetically. "Honey, have you been worried about her this whole time?"

I give her a bewildered smile. "I mean . . . yes? It seemed like a pretty big deal. You guys didn't invite me to breakfast the other day, the picnic was fun, but strained. Even Luke noticed Harlow was acting weird."

Lola sighs, giving Oliver a knowing look I can't really interpret.

A toilet flushes down the hall and the bathroom door opens.

My stomach drops with realization.

"Harlow Francesca Vega. Join us in the kitchen, please." Lola's angry-calm voice actually sounds terrifying.

"I didn't know she was here," I mumble to Oliver, who gives me a sympathetic wince.

Harlow walks down the hall, brows pulled down in concern. "What?"

"How much did you hear?" Lola asks.

Shaking her head in confusion, Harlow says, "I was peeing a decade's worth in there. I heard nothing."

Lola turns to her, wrapping her arms around my shoulders. "London here is a mess."

"She is?" Harlow moves immediately over to me. "Honey, what's wrong?"

Oh, God, this is awkward.

I give Lola a look that I hope successfully communicates both *help* and *way to put me on the spot, Castle.*

Lola tilts her head to me. "London likes Luke."

"Didn't we know this already?" Harlow asks, stepping back a bit, and her expression is almost entirely unreadable to me. Her top lip is curled up slightly, brows drawn in tight, and it could be confusion, but it could also be irritation.

I feel like I've just stepped off the edge of the pool and I keep drifting deeper. It's weird to have a group of friends influence a dating decision, but also never really speak directly to *me* about it. Is this what it's like to be part of a group? Whether it is or not, it makes me feel even more on the periphery. I have no-drama Ruby, and I used to have no-nonsense Nana. Both of them always let me know where I stood. Harlow is harder: she's up front, but she circles through a world of emotions in a day. I'm terrified of saying the wrong thing here.

"I don't want to jeopardize friendships," I tell them. "But I honestly have no idea what to make of your reaction to me seeing Luke. You guys mean a lot to me, and I don't want it to be weird for Mia—"

"It's not," Lola cuts in quickly.

"—or you two, or *anyone*," I say. "I didn't realize Luke was *Mia's* Luke, and then after I did, it felt like he was someone different. For *me*."

In my periphery I see Oliver turn carefully and make his way out of the kitchen and down the hall to Lola's bedroom.

The three of us wait for him to close the door, and we then look up to each other in our tiny triangle of awkward. Finally, Harlow leans back against the counter, shrugging a little helplessly. "I'm not really sure what to say. Do I have feelings about it? Yeah, sort of."

This actually gets my back up a bit. "Look, ever since we first hooked up, I've been worried about Luke's history with girls, worried about whether I'm willing to deal with romance again, worried about whether even hanging out with him would jeopardize my friendships with you guys. But if Mia is fine, I don't know that it's fair for you to be upset with me over it."

"I agree," she says, surprisingly nodding. "And since you hadn't brought it up with us, I assumed you didn't care what we thought. I respected that, and was getting over it. But if you're asking me, then I'll tell you: yeah, I had a knee-jerk reaction when Mia called and told me. It's one thing for Mia to see Luke banging anything that moves, and it's another for her to imagine him falling in love again. She's completely in love with Ansel, but of course she had feelings about Luke finding someone, even if we all know that reaction is petty, or unfair."

Lola blinks down to the floor at this, and my heart stretches too thin inside my chest. I get it: I would never get back together with Justin, but the idea that he loves the person he's with now—that he's *marrying her*—is irrationally painful.

"Mia called me and knew that she wasn't being totally fair, but it threw her," Harlow continues. "Luke and Mia started 'going steady' in sixth grade, whatever that means. Her accident fucked us all up—a lot—and when they broke up we"— she motions between her and Lola—"had to figure out how to support Mia best. It meant we lost Luke, and that *sucks*. Because he was ours, see? So yeah, I had an initial reaction, and I'm not sure that it's the right one, but it was genuine."

I know there's a lot of history there—there's a lot of history *here,* between all these women, and sometimes it seems easier to keep it surface-level than to really work to get to know them. But with this honesty from Harlow, I know I want friends like this. I *want* friends who'll worry about my emotions, even when those emotions feel petty or small.

"I understand where you're coming from," I tell her. "I do, and I respect it. But this isn't about Mia, or you, or their past. It's about me and Luke *now*. That's complicated enough." I tilt my head, saying softly, "They broke up nearly five years ago. Mia is married. This isn't really about her anymore . . . *at all*."

"I know. I know." Harlow nods, slowly, and opens her mouth to speak before Lola cuts her off.

"Mia's not even *here*," she says, and I'm not sure if she's talking to me, or to Harlow, or just pointing out in general that this conversation is happening without the most important component. But then she looks directly at Harlow and adds, "And if she were, she would tell us all we need to talk about something else."

Harlow steps forward and pulls me into an unexpected hug. "I'm sorry. I want you to be happy. I want Luke to be happy." Bracing her hands on my shoulders, she pulls away, saying quietly, "I mean, this way we all get to keep him, right?"

"Right," I tell her. "But I don't really know yet what that means for me." I smile at her, shrugging. "So it would be awesome if I could figure that out without having to worry about you getting mad at me if I decide I want more, okay?"

"Okay." She nods, pulling me into another hug, squeezing me tighter. "But if he hurts you, I'm beheading him."

"Okay, Crazytown."

But despite my teasing, my laugh ruffles her hair, and I squeeze her tighter, too.

Chapter FOURTEEN

Luke

$\mathcal{N}$EVER DO I feel more like an underling than when lawyers pile their stacks of briefs in my arms at the end of a meeting, and pat my back as they file out for lunch.

"Send upstairs to Records, would you?" Kevin asks, dropping a folder in my hands.

"Five copies," Roger says with a friendly wink as he gives me a heavy file. "Just put them on my desk when you're done."

"Same," Lisa says over her shoulder. "Thanks, Danny."

I go to correct her—there are only two of us interns, and Danny is the short, black one—but she's already halfway down the hall.

Turning, I see London standing near my cubicle, with an amused smile on her face. My stomach tightens and I immediately remember her smile after she kissed me last night.

I texted her this morning after we babysat together, but in typical London fashion, she didn't answer. The strange thing was, it didn't really bother me. I know that London is struggling with her feelings, and how they're tied into her friendships with Lola and Mia and Harlow. I know that what she's going through actually has very little to do with me at all, and that I need to be patient. To be honest, patience has never really been my strong suit and it's killing me a little, but I've already come to terms with the fact that London is important, and I've got far longer than a few weeks of patience in me.

"Need some help, Danny?" she asks.

I laugh, readjusting the load in my arms. My happiness in seeing her partially overrides the humiliation of what she's witnessed. "What are you doing here?"

She is glowing. She's wearing an orange sundress and sandals; her hair is down and soft, hanging long past her shoulders. I don't think I've ever seen it looking like it isn't windblown.

Fuck, I think I love her.

Something grows tight inside my chest, and I reach with a free hand to loosen my tie.

She holds up a recyclable grocery sack. "I brought us some lunch. I thought you might be hungry."

With this, she has just completely made my day. "You're probably the most amazing person alive right now, do you know that?" She shrugs, jokingly waving her hand forward for me to continue. "And the prettiest. And the best surfing teacher. And, if I may get personal, your rack—"

"Shhh!" she cuts in, stepping toward me, her hand coming up to cover my mouth. We're essentially alone in the hallway, but she does a quick glance around anyway.

I lift the pile in my arms, smiling in apology. "Do you want to go grab a picnic table outside and I'll meet you in five?"

With a little blushing smile, she nods and walks back to-ward the front of the offices.

Never in my life have I made photocopies so fast.

Never at this job have I sprinted up the stairs to the Records office to drop off a set of files.

And never did I ever expect London to show up and want to have lunch with me.

IT'S SEVENTY-FIVE DEGREES out, the air smells like the ocean, I can hear seagulls calling just across the street near the beach, and there is not a visible cloud in the sky. In fact, it's so beautiful outside I know I won't want to go back in after lunch. It's one of the reasons I tend to eat at my desk; the job is a painful slog, the paralegals and lawyers seem to love treating me like the village idiot, and our offices are across the street from the Pacific Ocean. I keep reminding myself being a legal intern is a rite of passage and will be over soon enough, but looking up and seeing London out here in the sunshine, unpacking a big bag of food, makes the prospect of returning to my cubicle feel impossible.

"Hey, Logan," I call.

She looks up and smiles, but her eyes go wide and her mouth drops open just as a voice comes from behind me: "Hey, Sutter."

I turn around, and the woman standing in front of me is so out of context here that it takes my brain at least two full seconds to place her.

"*Harlow?* What th—?"

"Surprise!" She throws her arms out. "Happy to see me?"

I glance over my shoulder to London, confused. "Um, is this an ambush of some form?"

"I asked London to lunch," Harlow says. "And . . . then I suggested we have lunch with you."

I wait, brows lifted in expectation, before I slide my gaze over to London, hoping for some form of silent communication.

Is this cool?

London gives me a tiny smile, a barely perceptible nod.

I can only assume that there's been a conversation I haven't been privy to, and that maybe this is Harlow's way of reaching out, letting London know that this is okay. I walk over, still confused and also totally thrilled—I spent nearly every weekend from the age of eleven to nineteen with this woman—and give her a hug. Harlow squeezes me tight, and I get a face full of her auburn hair.

"Holy shit, you're still using that herby shampoo," I say, filled with an unexpected wave of nostalgia.

When she steps back, Harlow purses her lips at me. "It's Aveda, you plebeian."

"You smell like a commune."

She shrugs, unfazed. "My husband likes it."

"Or he's just too terrified of you to say anything."

A delighted giggle escapes her lips. "You clearly haven't met Finn."

With a lingering smile, Harlow turns, walking over to the

picnic table where London is now waiting and has spread out a crazy amount of food: sandwiches, a few deli salads, olives, chips, and sparkling waters.

I look up at her, quietly telling her, "This looks amazing."

She blushes again—*sweet Lord, what is up with that?*—and then meets my eyes. "Good. This was sort of Harlow's idea—"

"*I* wanted to bring you peanut butter and jelly, but London insisted we stop and pick up something nicer. She might be too good for you," Harlow says, and I have to restrain myself from hugging her again.

I look back and forth between the two of them. "So what brought this on? Are you buttering me up for a Harlow tongue-lashing?"

"Keep up, Luke. If I wanted to rip you a new one I'd have done it already," Harlow says, picking up a sandwich and examining it.

"Right," I say, and pick up a sandwich of my own.

"We had a nice long talk yesterday and London mentioned it was *possible* that I was a little out of line. I thought about it and decided she was right. Case closed. Now, whether you're actually *worthy* of Miss All-American over here," she says, nodding toward London. "That remains to be seen."

I look over at London, who seems to be doing everything she can to avoid eye contact with me. Confident that Harlow isn't here to neuter me, I say, "Harlow, you saw me with Mia every day for years. You already *know* whether or not I'm worthy."

She nods, popping an olive into her mouth. "I'm trying to do the grand gesture here, Luke. I don't remember you being this slow on the uptake."

I want to volley back with something similarly playful, but I'm so grateful to Harlow in this moment that I can't seem to conjure up more than a grin aimed in her direction.

"In case you've forgotten, Harlow is a bit of a bulldozer," London explains, smiling down at the table. She pulls the top off a container of salad, and sticks a fork in it. "Sorry. Already has the dressing on," she jokes under her breath.

"I'll persevere," I answer, intentionally touching her hand when she slides it over to me. She went head-to-head with *Harlow* over this. For *me*. I may need a few minutes to process that.

As if on instinct, London looks up, widening her eyes in a *Be cool* gesture before returning to unwrapping her sandwich.

Harlow watches the exchange with interest. "I miss you, Luker. We all do."

"Yeah, well . . ." I trail off. I mean, honestly, there's so much. We were all so close. Mia, Harlow, and Lola were like family to me, and although we all tried to keep up appearances after Mia's accident, our relationships just *crumbled*. For a couple of years, it was hard not to feel resentful that the friendships with her girlfriends never suffered from whatever it was she was going through. But years later, I know no one is to blame. "I missed you, too."

"Seems like you managed okay," she says, and I can't exactly read her tone. Is she referring to my lack of monogamy?

Is she being genuine and telling me I look good? Does she mean London? With Harlow, I always assume there is a layer of shit being given; the question is always how deep I need to look to see it.

"So what's up with everyone getting married all of a sudden?" I ask her. "You guys have a few days out of college and freak out that you're going to be spinsters, or what?"

She shrugs. "Guess we just found the one."

When I glance to her again, London begins intensively studying her Pellegrino label. She's being *oddly* quiet.

"I hear you're headed to law school," Harlow says, drawing my attention back to her.

"That's right."

"Personally I think it would be amazing if you ended up at UCSD, and—"

"And Ansel was my professor?" I finish for her, smiling. "Yeah, you're not alone there. Margot prays for it daily."

"It would be the *most* awkward."

"I actually don't think it would be that bad." She raises her eyebrows at this. "Ansel seems like a pretty great guy."

Harlow goes quiet, so I know I've surprised her by reiterating this, even when Mia isn't here and I'd otherwise be free to let loose the honest opinion.

"Unfortunately I don't think it's going to happen," I tell her.

"Oh, come on, Luke," Harlow says. "You know you'll get into UCSD."

"I already have," I say, glancing briefly at London. I haven't mentioned any of this yet. I haven't wanted to bring it up because it just seems so . . . serious. "What I meant is that I probably won't accept the offer from UCSD. I got into Boalt. I'm still waiting to hear from Yale, but most likely I'm headed to Berkeley."

London's head shoots up. *"What?"*

Guilt cools my bloodstream. "Yeah, I heard back from a few places last week."

"Holy shit, that's ama—" Harlow's phone rings in her purse and she digs for it, squealing when she looks at the screen and excusing herself to answer the call.

"Hey, weirdo," I whisper-hiss to London. When she looks up, I continue: "Are you going to tell me what's going on? Why are you so quiet today?"

"I had sort of a mini-meltdown when I got home last night. Harlow was there, we had a little talk, and here we are."

I frown and I reach for her hand. "I'm glad—thrilled, actually—but that's not what I meant. Are you okay *today?*"

"I'm just thinking."

"Thinking about wha—"

"Would it be okay if I came over tonight?" she asks, finally holding my gaze.

"Tonigh—?"

"I'd invite you to my place," she quickly cuts in, "but Lola left this morning so I'm having the paint redone and the entire loft reeks."

I can't figure out if she wants to come over to escape her

place, or because she wants to be with me, but in either case, I'm all for it. "Of course. Sure."

She smiles her thanks and ducks to keep eating. I can't really look away. Out in the sun it's obvious that London put some effort into how she looks today: she's wearing a little makeup. Her hair is brushed and smooth. She even painted her nails.

"London?" I ask.

She looks up and I realize I have no idea how to ask her what I want to ask her. *Why are you so dressed up?* sounds kind of douchey and may imply I think she usually looks less than perfect, which is totally false.

"What?" she asks when I've been silently staring at her for too long.

"You look really pretty today."

She scoffs, smiling into her sandwich. "Shut up."

"No, you really do. You're not going to meet some guy after this, are you?" I ask, trying to give her a winning smile.

Laughing, she says, "No."

"A girl, then? I'm cool with switch hitters, but when you look like this, I want you all for myself."

Her smile is enormous, but it's gone in a flash. I watch her tuck her hair behind her ear and pretend to scowl down at her lunch when she whispers, "You're an idiot."

Harlow returns, dropping her phone into her purse. "Never marry a fisherman," she tells me.

I laugh. "Noted."

"They're too sexy for their own good and you'll end up spending your entire paycheck on a last-minute ticket."

I look back and forth between London and Harlow before saying, "I'm confused. You have to fly to see your husband?"

"When he's filming," she says, and then takes an enormous bite of sandwich. It feels like it takes her three years to finish chewing and swallow before she explains, "He's one of the Fisher Men."

I slap the table. "Shut up. I can't wait for that show. Even the promotion is making me feel manly. Wait." I pause. "You're *married* to one of them?" London is shooting me a warning look but I'm too dense to pick up on it right away. "They're all single."

"No, they *aren't*," Harlow says with an edge, and when I look up at London, she quickly tucks away a smile.

Harlow and I catch up on the past few years and then begin stumbling down memory lane. London listens, smiling and laughing at the stories—she didn't grow up with us so she couldn't possibly understand the insanity that was Harlow, Lola, and Mia together since elementary school.

"Luke," Harlow sings, shaking her head, "what would we have done without you back then?"

"Luke was your go-to?" London asks. She's a little skeptical, but mostly fascinated, and *fuck*, I could kiss Harlow right now. How did she know this was exactly what London needed?

"Oh," Harlow says, holding up a hand. "You have no idea. This poor guy. Before we would call our parents we would call Luke. He drove before any of us, and took us everywhere. He rescued the three of us more times than I can remember."

I laugh, because it's true. The girls got locked out of buildings naked I think more than any other humans on the planet, punctured two tires on Mia's piece-of-shit Geo Tracker when they decided to try offroading in the San Bernardinos—hours away from home—and needed me to come get them in Big Bear one night when they'd tried to go camping and had forgotten the tent, had no money for a motel, and Harlow got food poisoning.

They were put in charge of the prom committee senior year—and it's a miracle the entire school didn't end up getting arrested for public indecency, but when the cops came, I made sure they knew it wasn't Harlow who had spiked the punch.

I knew the best way to sneak Mia in and out of her house—not just for fooling around, but to drive her down to the beach and watch her dance at sunrise.

I drove Lola to her evening art class every Tuesday and Thursday night after I got my license.

I would have done anything for those girls, and I did.

I still would.

Harlow and I go from fuming together over something horribly condescending Mia's dad said to her about dancing, to wheezing in laughter, remembering Lola's three-legged Humper Dog that would literally have sex with any vertical limb in close proximity. The girls once playfully held me down to see what would happen if we let him go—trust me, at fifteen I was fine being pinned to the couch by three girls—and the dog eventually just peed on my leg.

All through it, though, London stays pretty quiet, and I'm inclined to not push her about it. I mean, I'm not an idiot; the way she's looking intently at me every few seconds makes me think she's probably mulling over what's happening between us, and her being here—with lunch, all dressed up—has to be a good sign.

But inside, I feel tense, wanting to be alone with her to talk it out—to talk about us and make sure she's really okay, to discuss the prospect of me moving in a few months—but knowing there is no way I can push the conversation yet again. For the first time in our . . . relationship . . . I have to wait for her to come to me.

———

LONDON IS ON my porch when I get home, clutching her bag. Before I even reach the top step, she's speaking.

"I just got here. I haven't been waiting—"

"I wish you would lie to me sometimes," I grumble, teasing. "I like the idea of you hanging out, anxiously pining for me."

Her hand lightly slaps my shoulder as I bend to unlock the front door.

"Want something to drink?" I ask her over my shoulder, dropping my keys, wallet, and phone on the counter.

"A beer?"

I can feel her behind me, looking around before following

me into the kitchen. She's quiet as I open the fridge, reach for a bottle, and pop it open for her.

Turning with her drink in my hand, I immediately run into her. She's there—*right* there—chest now pressed to my arm.

I smile, but it feels badly shaped, wobbly. "Hey."

Her tongue slips out, wetting her lips. "Hey."

She stares at me, studying, and in an instant I realize she's working up the nerve to start something. But I'm still wary enough to never want to make that bet. Maybe she changed her mind and doesn't want a beer. Maybe she wants to add a snack to her order. Maybe—

Her hand comes up from her side, moving up my chest and around to cup the back of my neck.

"London?"

She pulls, stretching at the same time, covering my mouth with hers.

Fuck.

Fuck.

The relief, the soft feel of her, the slide, the sweetness. Her full lips move over mine, sucking at the bottom, coaxing me open, and my pulse explodes. Her tongue licks my lip, my top teeth. I *feel* when she moans before I hear it.

My heart is a fucking monster in my chest, claws thrashing.

I pull back, on that razor-sharp edge of ecstasy and heartbreak, needing to know which way I'll slide. "Are you . . . ?" I don't even know how to end the sentence. I don't want this to be a rash impulse of hers.

I'm *settled* here, in love with her; I couldn't weather a drive-by.

"Just kiss me?" she whispers.

Her fingers tangle in the hair at the back of my head and she stretches, trailing kisses up my chin. Soft, hesitant kisses to convince me, to coax me some more. Once I force my eyes open, I see that she's watching me nervously. As if I might say no. The vulnerability there . . . I am fucking *done*.

The beer bottle shatters near our feet but I need both hands to hold her face. With a groan I take her mouth, tilting her head, sliding my tongue inside and nearly roaring at the stroke of hers, the clench of her hands in my hair. I step forward, moving my hands down her neck, over her shoulders and down her sides, pulling her legs up and around my hips.

My thoughts are nothing but relief and need and need and love and *fuck*, I'm walking in circles, groaning rhythmically into her mouth.

I don't know where to take her. I want her in my bed. In my room. I want her here against the wall.

"Your room," she says, lips moving over my jaw. "Can we go to your room?"

I turn, stumbling down the hall while she kisses and sucks at my neck, her hands digging in my hair, hips grinding into me.

My feet move us to the bed and I lower her there, covering her body with mine and rocking into her, sliding my tongue over hers in the same, slow rhythm.

London scoots up my bed, pulling me up with her, and then rolls us so that she's over me, her pussy pressed right over my cock as she stares down.

"I like your bedroom," she says, breaking eye contact to briefly look around.

I follow the path her eyes take: over the bed, the dresser, to the window. It's a basic room—nice, but unremarkable—and it doesn't take long for our eyes to meet again. Is she thinking about how many other women have been in here? Is she wondering whether my sheets are clean?

I want to tell her everything, as if confessing—I've probably only had sex with two or three girls here, my sheets are clean, I've never slept with someone all night in this bed—but there's no easy way to unload all of this, and what if she's decided she doesn't care anyway?

London reaches for the hem of her dress, now bunched at her hips, and lifts the soft cotton up and over her head. Her bra is white and plain, and she reaches back, unhooking it and letting it fall down her arms.

I watch, helpless, as she reaches for me, unbuttoning my dress shirt, helping me shrug out of it. I toss it aside and wrap my arms around her waist, looking up at her.

"I like you," she whispers.

I exhale, hungry for her and leaning forward to kiss her neck.

The most fucked-up thought hijacks my brain: I don't want to have sex right now. I want to kiss her. Just kiss. Just feel. I want to focus on the way she touches me, the sounds she makes when I touch her. We've charged through everything so far, and I want to go back and feel all the *Firsts* with her.

I glide my tongue across her collarbone, kissing over the rise of her breast and circling around her nipple. Flicking, sucking—she has a perfect body, perfect skin.

In my hair, her fingers grow tight and restless. Her back arches, pushing her chest closer to my face, hips circling, legs seeking a way to wrap around me.

"I'm sensitive," she gasps. "I like that."

I turn my eyes to her, using them to smile as I pull her nipple into my mouth. She watches it come out wet from my tongue, eyes heavy.

"I can tell," I say.

She was so controlled before, even in the shower when I felt at the time like I got all of her. Here, she's exposed and defenseless, looking at me with eager eyes and—

"Luke."

Her voice breaks on the single syllable and she just lets it hang there as she closes her eyes. I don't really need her to say any more because the fear is written all over her face.

Don't hurt me.

A spike of pain wedges between my ribs, and I sit up straighter, kissing her slow, and deep. "Hey," I whisper, repeating it again when she doesn't open her eyes. *"Hey."*

Finally, she looks down at me.

"There isn't anyone else."

Her eyes flicker back and forth between mine before she

nods, cupping my face and kissing me—so sweet, not deep, just a slide of her mouth over mine.

"Here's where you tell me you're not seeing anyone else, either," I mumble against her lips, and she giggles.

But her eyes are serious when she pulls back. "I'm not seeing anyone else."

"Good."

"You realize how this sounds?" she asks, looking back and forth between my eyes again. "You're saying that you want to be in a relationship with me?"

"I believe I've made that abundantly clear."

London stretches over me, catlike, and kisses me once before asking, "Where do you keep your condoms?"

Running my thumb across her lips, I say, "Bedside table." I tilt my head to show her which side I mean, adding, "But I don't want to do that yet."

She thinks I'm kidding, and goes to lightly smack my chest, but I catch her hand. "No, I'm serious."

"We've had sex before, you nerd."

"It was different." I reconsider. "*This* is different."

Nodding slowly, London tries to hide her confusion, and fails, finally admitting, "I want you. I mean, *you*."

"I do, too," I assure her. "God. *Trust* me." I close my eyes, swallow, and steady my thoughts before I look at her again. "But I'm also pretty sure I *love* you," I say, and she stops breathing. "And I really, *really* don't want to fuck this up."

Her mouth moves for a couple of beats before any sound comes out. "You *love* me?"

I shrug, going all in. "Yeah."

As if she only now seems to realize it, she whispers, "You're shaking."

I smile, kissing the corner of her mouth. "Because I'm nervous."

Tilting her head, she lets out a quietly skeptical, "You're not *nervous*."

"I've only ever loved one other person." I reach up, sliding her hair behind her shoulders and cupping her face. Fuck, the way she's watching me . . . "And doing this feels *really* different, okay?"

London nods, and slides off my lap to lie back on my bed, wide blue eyes trained expectantly on my face. "What should we do?"

I smile and lose my breath a little at the way her expression softens. She's never said it, but I can tell London loves my smile.

"I could touch you?" I ask, leaning over her to suck her neck.

I watch her pull her lower lip between her teeth, thinking this over before she whispers, "Okay. I could touch you, too?"

"Me first." I smile into a kiss to her neck, and inch my fingers under the waistband of her underwear. My hand moves slowly over her pubic bone, farther down . . . and she hisses when I spread her, sliding over her clit and lower and—

"*Fuck*," I gasp, pressing my forehead to hers. "Fuck, you are—"

"I know. I know." She slides her hand around the back

of my neck, pulling me down, closing her eyes, working her mouth over mine, working my mouth open. But I want to see her while I do this. Want to witness everything. I give her one kiss and then move back, watching her face as I pull the slickness up and over her clit, circling,

around

around

around

and her eyes fall half closed, jaw goes slack, hips arch into my hand.

"Is that nice?"

She exhales a quiet, "Yeah."

I pull my hand out of her underwear. Her eyes shoot open and she reaches blindly for my arm. "Don't. Don't—"

"Shh." I kiss her. "Trust me." Showing her my intentions, I slide her underwear down her hips and off her legs.

Relief coats her expression, and she laughs a little, stretching to kiss me.

I run my hand over her stomach. Her knees are bent, legs parted slightly. Just enough for my hand, but not for my full attention.

"Spread your legs."

She hesitates, and I kiss her, saying again, "Spread your legs. Wide. Please. I want to be able to see."

With a blush, she lowers her knees to the sides, focusing on my face as I reach forward, touching her.

Something in my chest seems to drop, pulled by a weight in my stomach that makes me feel wild and breathless as I look at her, so open for me. I tease her, slow at first, exploring, telling her I'm patient in every way she needs me to be, but when she reaches for me, running her hands over my bare chest and down, I know she needs more. Faster.

Steady, steady friction.

She whimpers, tugging at the back of my neck, wanting my mouth on hers but I shake my head, telling her I need to watch, I want her to just feel my hand. In truth, I *want* her wild and a little unhinged, I like the way she finally seems to be all in, *needing* my weight over her and my kiss on her mouth. I want her begging for my tongue and my cock and my fingers.

She growls a little in frustration but the way she holds her breath when I speed up, her tight gasp when I slide two fingers into her—it's *everything*. The entire time, she watches my face; I can only feel it, because I'm watching my hand on her, reeling over the way my fingers come out soaked, the way her skin flushes, the way her legs shake as she gets close, hips arching from the bed and into my hand as she starts to tighten, coming with a long, sharp cry of relief.

She shivers under my touch when I pull my fingers out, and run them up and down the soft, wet skin.

Her eyes are closed, arms bent beside her head and fingers curled in her hair.

"You alive, Logan?"

"No." She giggles and I bend, drawing the tip of my tongue over her dimple. I've wanted to do that forever.

My mouth moves over hers and she opens to me, soft and

warm, taking my tongue, my sounds. I want to claw my way out of my skin and into hers somehow, in love, in desperation for more of this. I still don't want to fuck again yet, but my body screams at my brain.

Her eyes come open and she smiles when she realizes I've been watching her as she kisses me.

"Can I . . . ?" she asks, lightly skirting her hand down my stomach. To my belt. I watch as she unfastens it, pushes it aside.

I let out a shaking "Yeah," adding a very breathless "Yeah, okay."

London laughs at my oddly desperate restraint, and I can't blame her. But I mean, *fuck.* I don't want to say no. I can't say no. Not with her naked next to me. Not with the feel of her clenching still echoing down my fingers. If she doesn't touch me, I'm just going to lock myself in the bathroom and jerk off.

She works the zipper down, watching her own hands coax the fabric of my dress pants open. It kills me, it really does. She pushes my pants down and I kick them off before returning to her. Her shoulder lifts and then pushes down as she digs into my boxers, finally looking up at my face. "Come here."

She means the part of me she's taking into her hand, the part she's remembering with her fingertips. And fuck, I don't know why it's so hot that she's said that, that she didn't mean for *me* to come closer, to kiss her, but it is. It's sweet, and re-assuring, and sexy, and I want to let the words burst free—I fucking *love* you—because it's exactly what I feel watching her do this, but it seems like the worst time to say it again.

It's ironic, but I'm stubbornly monogamous, I realize this now. When I commit, I go deep, unable to even imagine letting someone do to me what London is doing now. She's just touching my dick, but it's hers. Every cell in my body belongs to her. Even the tiny image of Mia in my thoughts as I test out this impulse—the nanosecond flash of being with her instead of London right now—is wrong enough for me to want to drown it with the feel of London's mouth on mine, the pleasure of soft, deep kisses as her hand moves up and down— at first reacquainting and then with intent: firmer, faster, her focus just where I need it. I moan into her mouth and she pulls back.

"That's not fair!" she protests, laughing. "You don't get to kiss—"

I cut her off with my mouth over hers again, lips fitting between, coaxing her open so I can lick at her, go deeper, feel like I'm inside her in every way I can be right now.

Because now I know why she wanted my mouth on hers when I touched her. There's an ache in my chest, clawing its way up and out of me, needing to feel her deeper, to thank her or—fuck, I don't know—*show* her what it feels like that she's touching me like this, giving me this kind of pleasure. I rock into her hand, giving in and finally rolling on my side to face her, pulling her by the hip to face me and fucking her fist, reaching between us to lift her leg, pull it over my hip so I can touch her, too.

So wet.

I push a finger into her, stroking her, sucking and swallowing her noises and falling into the feel of her hand on my dick, her slick skin covering my hand.

It's sex, but it's not.

It's sex, but it's *more*.

There are so many ways to love this girl; good God, let me find each and every one of them.

London shifts against me, rocking, rubbing, getting there and she's close—she's holding her breath—and when I look at her I see her eyes on me, looking back and forth between my face and where her hand grips and I fuck into it and it's almost like I can see her thoughts, see it telegraphed, how watching me come undone like this is going to send her falling along with me.

"Come on me?" she whispers.

It doesn't take effort to get there. Fuck, I've been holding it back since the beginning of time—at least that's what my body is screaming. I cut the control, letting it overtake me, fucking hard and fast three, four, five more times into her fist and then everything is warm, shooting down my back, out of me, onto her. On her stomach, her hand. Over her breasts, on her arm. She stares, eyes wide, mouth opening slowly more and more until she's crying out, riding my hand, head falling back as she comes with a staccato of sharp, relieved cries.

She goes quiet, breaths heaving as she lets her head rock forward and rest against my shoulder.

"We're really good at that," she whispers, and then laughs before kissing the center of my chest.

I know we've just finished a round, but I can't imagine *ever* being done with her.

My hand moves carefully back and forth between her legs and she whimpers a little, rocking into my palm.

"Are you sore?" I ask.

I feel her hair brush against my ribs when she shakes her head no.

"London?"

"Hmm?" she hums.

I stroke my middle finger across her clit. "I *really* want to kiss you here."

She arches into me, holding me closer and sliding her hands up and around my neck so she can kiss me.

So she can keep me from crawling down her body and putting my mouth on her.

"You don't like it?" I ask against her lips.

"I like it too much," she whispers. "I'd like it the most of anything I think you could do to me."

I pull back, the question *then why won't you let me?* perched on my tongue.

But she speaks first, whispering, "I can't give my heart away all at once. I want to. But I can't."

I kiss her, and hold there while something tight works its way past my throat. "Okay."

Her blue eyes are trained on my face. "To me, that's the most intimate thing anyone can do."

Nodding, I tell her, "I agree, actually." Moving my hand up her body, I circle my wet finger around her nipple and then bend to suck her into my mouth.

It's a mistake.

I can taste her, and already, only minutes after I've come on her skin, I want her again.

She feels me stir, rolling to face me and reaching for me. "But we've already had *sex* . . ." Looking up at my face, she says, "I don't know why we aren't doing that right now."

I groan, watching her stroke me, feeling emotion tighten my breaths. "I just need to know it's different."

"You seem to feel different," she whispers. "At least that's what you said."

"I mean . . . I need it to be different for *you*."

London kisses me then, a slow, exploring kiss that makes my brain unravel.

She doesn't move to climb on me, or pull me onto her, and this silent admission that she's heard me and won't push it is both a comfort and torture.

————————

I FEEL DRUGGED, pulled up from somewhere low and heavy.

Her hands are on me, frantic and insistent. Pulling me over her, scratching down my back. I feel her, wet against me. The warmth of thighs around my hips. The suction of kisses on my neck.

The slick heat of her.

She gasps.

Yes.

Luke, yes.

I'm dreaming—at least I think I am until the sharp sting of her teeth on my shoulder jolts me fully awake and I realize I'm starting to push inside.

Beneath me she's gasping tightly, asking me to move into her, to be deeper.

I'm so groggy. Her hands are on my face, pulling me close.

"Please. Luke."

"Holy shit." It's all I can say, all I can think as my vision clears and I sink in. "Did you wake me up?"

London giggles and the sound is hoarse from sleep. She runs her hands down my back to my ass. "I don't know." Between breaths she adds, "I woke up." She sucks in a breath, and her thighs come around my hips. "I kissed you." London arches her neck, moaning when I pull out and slowly push back in. "And you were warm and smelled so good."

I groan, rocking into her.

"And then you were . . ." she says, gasping, "you were so *hard*, and you rolled on top of me. I thought *you* were awake."

She's soft and warm, wet all around me, her limbs slow with sleep. I'm groggy, aware of how smooth my sheets are, how desperate she seems when she slides her teeth down my neck. I'm aware of her sleepy, sucking kisses, the wet slide of her all along my cock. London rocks up when I push in and we're moving together in this easy, grinding tandem, so good,

so fucking perfect.

I groan, kissing her through all of it, deep, licking kisses, sucking on her lips, her chin. And fuck, we're noisy together, talking through it all.

It's good, she says.

So fucking good, I agree.

She asks me why on earth I wanted to wait.

And I bite her gently, admitting in a murmur that I wanted to savor her. Admitting I wanted to treat it like something special.

But she tells me it's already special; says it like it's obvious.

And *don't stop, Luke*.

Don't stop.

I'm fucking *smiling*, pressing my face into her neck, and I can't stop the relieved laugh that escapes. I forgot how it feels, how insanely different it is to make love, not just hook up or get off. It isn't two bodies coming into contact for pleasure alone. It's the weird sense of getting *inside* that person, turning sex into a fucking revelation.

But pulling back and looking into her eyes, I know I've never had *this* before, this sort of unspoken understanding of what's happening. Her whispered words are only an inch from my lips. I feel so bare while she watches my face as I move in her. I was too young with Mia to experience this, and too detached after.

It's so good

Luke

It's so good

Oh my God, Luke

she keeps saying over and over, looking right into my eyes, and she could say it a hundred times and the sound of it would never get old. It's hoarse, her voice. Hoarse and pleading, and yes it's good but it could be better and I know it can be. I know it *will* be over time, and *holy fuck,* I can feel it when she starts to come, the way her skin gets hot and her muscles tense, the way she goes still, holds her breath and then it's like a cascade of tiny explosions go off inside her and she's arching, crying out, scratching her short nails down my back.

I bend and fall into my quiet mind and my frantic body, feeling the perfect heat of her tongue, sliding over and around mine. Feeling her pleasure through the vibrating moans. Feeling my body get warmer, tighter, until that relief is building low in my back and taking over every thought. Just the relief of it, the fucking *joy* of being with her like this.

I come with a groan, so deep in her, arching away and I can feel her eyes on me, sleepy and proud. Her hands slide over my chest and back down over my abs until her arms wrap around my waist, holding me over her.

Keeping me inside her.

The thought tickles in the back of my mind: *I came inside her.*

"London, I'm not wearing anything."

She turns her face into my neck, kissing. "I'm on the pill."

It's a relief, but I'm still uneasy with the need to reassure her. "I was just tested—"

"Shh," she says, nuzzling her face into my skin. "You wouldn't have done that with me if you weren't safe."

She's right, but I still feel a little off-balance as the connection I felt with her evaporates slowly as she falls asleep, when she won't talk to me more about what we just did. It feels monumental to me—I'm reeling from the emotion of it—and I'm still inside her. I want to press her, ask her if there is an Us now, if she really trusts me as much as this means she does. But her breaths even out, and she goes still beneath me.

I PULL OUT several minutes later, only when I'm pretty sure it won't wake her. Kneeling between her legs, I stare down at her body. Her hair is a mess, lips pressed lightly together. Her pulse is a rhythmic beating shadow in her neck; her chest rises and falls with her steady breaths. I look lower, to her spread thighs, her skin naked and smooth and flawless.

I'm in love with her body, in love with her mind.

I can't give my heart away all at once.

I want to. But I can't.

And then we had sex without any other words of reciprocation on her part. No admission that she wants more with me, no real reassurance that she's giving me *any* of her heart, let alone all of it . . . and it stings. I realize that it was spontaneous middle-of-the-night sex, and we were more animal instinct than conscious thought, but it still makes me uneasy.

Climbing out of bed, I pull on boxers, shuffle down the hall and into the kitchen, and run straight into my sister.

She looks haggard, in pajamas, with a face that tells me she hasn't been sleeping.

And then the two pieces connect and I realize *why* she hasn't been sleeping. My stomach drops out and I nearly vomit. "Oh, *God*."

Margot nods. "Yeah."

Suddenly very aware of my mostly naked body, I'm relieved that at least I put on underwear. "I didn't know you were staying here tonight."

She slumps against the counter. "The roommate—enjoy the humor here—had the girlfriend over and they were being very loud."

I scrub my face with a hand. "Fuck. I'm sorry."

Margot shakes her head. "Part of me wants to congratulate whoever is in there because that certainly sounded great."

"*Margot*. Gross."

She straightens, pushing past me and opening the cupboard for a glass. "I thought you weren't hooking up with random girls anymore?"

"Not that it's your business," I say, stealing the glass from her and filling it with water. "But London's in there."

Her eyes go wide and she considers this for a few seconds in silence before shaking her head and shivering. "I'd be happy for you if I wasn't still traumatized." She looks me over. "I mean, gross, Luke. You're still sweaty."

"And now we're both traumatized." I gulp down the water. "Seriously, though. You don't even live here anymore."

Pushing herself up to sit on the counter, she's now

close to eye level with me, and studies me closely. "You look stressed considering . . ."

I don't really know what to say. If you'd asked me earlier in the day how I wanted today to end, I would have said, "London in my bed" without hesitation. But now I'm just not sure what it *means* that she's in my bed.

I want it to mean something.

"It's nothing," I say, and when Margot makes an annoyed face, I add, "I worry she's not really taking this as seriously as I am."

My sister looks toward the heavens. "Let me enjoy the irony of this for a second." She inhales deeply, and then exhales. "Man, that's great."

Anger rises inside me. "Margot, are you shitting me right now?"

She looks genuinely confused. "Yes? I think so?"

"If I gave you crap for hooking up with however many women you want, you would tear me a new one. If you slept with a different one every night, you would expect me to pat you on the back and tell you I think your commitment to your sexuality is admirable."

"I wouldn't expect you to have opinions on my sexuality," she deadpans.

"Fine, but you'd expect me to accept it, and not judge you."

She allows this with a tiny nod.

"So why is it different for me?" I ask. "Why can't I have had some wild oats, and then fall in love without it being *ironic* when I worry she doesn't have the same feelings for me?"

"*Love?*" she repeats, eyes wide.

"Yeah," I say finally.

Dropping her head, she stares at the floor for several breaths before mumbling, "Wow. Sorry, you're right. I *am* happy for you. I'm just tired and grossed out."

I lean forward and kiss the top of her head. "We're sleeping now. We'll be quiet."

Turning, I walk back down the hall to my bedroom. London is sitting in the middle of the bed, covers pulled over her lap.

I climb under the sheets and try to coax her down beside me but she resists.

"Was there a girl here?" she asks.

Fuck. She heard our voices. Of course she would be suspicious. And *fuck*. So much for trusting me.

"It's just Margot," I assure her. "I didn't know she was staying here tonight."

London exhales, nodding, and then lies back down, curling into me.

I know I should be reassured by how easily she melts into my side, by the tiny, sleepy kisses she trails up my neck to my mouth—and I am. But none of this is as easy as I expected it to be when she finally came around. I still have so much trust to build, and London still has so much trust to give me.

Chapter FIFTEEN

I WAKE WITH A blanket over my head and a naked chest pressed to my back, bare hips and thighs curled all along mine. My stomach and legs protest at the slightest movement, and I have to stifle a groan as I sit up, carefully extracting myself from the tangle of sheets that seem to barely cling to the bed.

I feel gross: sweaty from exertion and spending the night wrapped around another human being, and sticky from . . . other things.

It's too early to be up but I need a shower. Luke has barely moved and I tiptoe across the floor and out of his room, down the hall toward the bathroom.

The door closes with a soft click behind me and it feels like I can finally breathe again. Though even that hurts a little, too. I remind myself to congratulate Luke on a job well done . . . later.

The bathroom is large for such a small house—definitely remodeled—and I'm so anxious to clean myself up that I ignore the chilly morning air and jump beneath the spray before it's even had a chance to heat up.

"Shit," I squeak, bracing myself against the tile and then

melting as the water starts to warm. The last time I was here Luke washed my hair. I think about that as I reach for the same bottle, the scent of his shampoo mixing with steam to fill the shower.

I realize now that that day is when my plan first derailed. I'd tucked Luke into a nice little box, labeled him and written him off as a good time, and thought that was it. He was fun, a way to scratch an itch, but nothing more.

I hadn't counted on stories about doll salons and shopping with his mother. I hadn't expected him to be so attentive and charming. I hadn't expected the sex to be so good in part because he was so genuinely into me. And I never, not in a million years, expected him to say he loved me.

That last one takes me by surprise all over again and I'm momentarily frozen, blinking away the water as it runs down my face. I'm not sure what to do with something like that. Luke is twenty-three and used to fucking whoever he wants. It's hard to silence the voice telling me he's simply infatuated. That he's forgotten how infatuation can feel a lot like love.

I ignore the way the admission twists my stomach and shut off the water, reaching for a towel before climbing out.

The air is cold on my damp skin, and it reminds me of a morning I'd gone to visit Justin our junior year. He'd been up late studying the night before and was asleep when I got there after closing out the late shift at work. I took a shower and wrapped myself in a towel, realizing I'd forgotten my toothbrush. I opened the drawer, thinking I'd just use his. There was a purple toothbrush there, right beside his familiar blue one. I hadn't thought much of it at the time, but much later I realized of course it was Ashley's, the girl he'd been sleeping with for almost two years by then.

That memory circles around in my head as I stand at Luke's bathroom counter, looking up at my reflection and telling myself for the thousandth time that not every guy is Justin. *Luke* is not Justin. Not every guy cheats.

It's just so hard to break the instinct to keep my arms locked over my chest, guarding my heart.

There's no way I'm looking for Luke's toothbrush. Instead, I do my best to make some order of my hair and brush my teeth with my finger and a tube of toothpaste on the counter.

With a towel wrapped securely around my body, I open the door, intent on finding my clothes and getting home, maybe even trying to slip out before he wakes up.

But walking down the hall toward the bathroom door is his sister.

"Margot. Hi."

Margot, the one he was talking to last night. The sister who more than likely spent the night listening to us having sex.

She stops, meeting my eyes. "London. Hey, I didn't know you were up." She looks like she got only marginally more sleep than I did.

I adjust my towel. "Just needed a shower. You're up early."

A slow, teasing smile spreads across her face. "Actually, I never really went to sleep."

I groan a little.

She laughs. "Sorry, I couldn't resist. Want some coffee?"

I look back toward Luke's room, where the door is still pulled shut, and nod. "Sure."

"Sweet. Let me use the bathroom, and I'll meet you in there."

She steps around me and closes the door, and I walk down the hall to the kitchen.

The sun is just starting to come up, the sky beginning to brighten on the other side of the window. I've been here enough times to know where Luke keeps his dishes and I pull two mugs down from the cupboard, opening doors until I find the coffee. I hear the toilet flush and the water run in the sink and then Margot is there, her taller form hovering beside me as she reaches for the filters.

She looks so much like Luke that it's a little unnerving. They share the same thick dark hair, the same full brows and perfect cheekbones. But it's the intensity of their gaze that's the most pronounced. If I thought Luke was intimidating before he smiles, he has nothing on his sister.

We stand in silence while the coffeemaker gurgles and hisses in the background, and I search my mind for things to say, an icebreaker that doesn't begin with *I'm sorry I kept you up because I was so loudly banging your brother.*

The scent of fresh coffee fills the air and when the machine chimes to signal it's done, it spurs me into action. "So you live closer to campus?" I ask.

She nods, holding out her mug for me to fill. "I still come

over to hassle him when I need to. Maybe do some laundry or steal his towels to take to the beach." She pulls back her full mug with a quiet "Thanks," eyes dropping down to my body briefly. "That's a nice one, by the way. One of my favorites."

I follow her gaze and realize I'm still wearing Luke's Stone Brewery towel. "Oh, boy," I say with an embarrassed smile. "I'm practically naked. In your brother's kitchen."

She waves me off. "Are you kidding? That's the tamest thing I've seen here first thing in the morning." Margot looks momentarily horrified with what she's just said, but I smile, trying to hide the way my heart and lungs take a nosedive into my belly.

"Yeah, well," I say, floundering. "I was just going to get dressed and head home when I ran into you."

"Ahh." She slips a piece of bread into the toaster and adds, "Were you going to leave without telling him?"

There's a hint of protective big sister in her tone, and while I get it, I'm not really sure how to balance that against the scores of possibly naked shenanigans she's just alluded to.

I really like Margot: we share the same hobby in teasing Luke, and my friends absolutely adore her, but after talking to Harlow and Lola two days ago, I'm more and more convinced that I don't have to explain myself, or what's happening between her brother and me to anyone, even her.

"I hadn't really decided yet," I admit, holding my mug up to my nose to inhale the pungent, nutty odor. "Is this the part where you tell me what a great guy he is?"

Margot doesn't get defensive on his behalf. Instead, she

snorts, laughing to herself as she rips off a paper towel and sets it on the counter. "No way."

"Really?"

"My brother *is* a great guy," she says with a shrug. "He's honest when it counts, undeniably loyal, and has a huge heart. But I know he's been a player. It's not really my place to convince you of anything." The toast pops up and Margot reaches into the fridge for the butter dish. "That's *his* job. You're a smart girl, and it's obvious he has feelings for you. But you know what you need more than I do."

The knife spreads butter across the toast with a quiet scratching sound, and Margot smiles at me over her shoulder. That smile melts away any worry I had that she was trying to make me feel unwelcome. In fact, it makes me think she's glad I'm here.

"I really like you, London," she says. "You'll figure it all out."

⸻

THE SOUND OF Margot's car pulling out of the driveway drifts through Luke's open window. He's still in the same place I left him, stretched out on his side, sheet barely covering his hips. I can see a dark trail of hair low on his navel. His bicep peeks out, full and firm, where his arm wraps around his pillow.

I'm still not sure whether I should go, and pace back and forth a few times, glancing over my shoulder at him. His hair is a mess and standing straight up from whatever he had in it the night before, and I laugh a little as I walk over and smooth it back down. One minute turns into two and my fingers slip through the strands, over the side of his face, past his ear and down, tracing his spine.

Luke has a great back. His shoulders are broad, lats flaring along the edges, long torso tapering in at his waist. He's nothing but miles of smooth, tan skin and a map of dips and edges. He's also warm and somehow manages to still smell good after all of the hand jobs and cuddling and sex-without-a-condom and sleeping intertwined.

I really don't want to leave.

With the conversation with Margot still ringing in my ears, I drop the towel and climb back into bed.

I loop my arm around his waist and he stirs almost immediately.

"London?" he mumbles. He finds my fingers where they rest on his stomach and rolls to face me, sleepy eyes blinking open and then squinting at me in the bright room. "Hi."

His hair is standing up and he has pillow creases across his cheek. "What is happening with your hair?" I say, reaching out to smooth it again.

"I was asleep," he says, just before he smiles. "With you."

I look at the mess around us and laugh. "It looks like a storm passed through here. Don't you have to get to work?"

"I'm going to take my first personal day in a year," he says. In a rush of movement he pushes me to my back to hover over me. His eyes make a sleepy circuit of my face and I just honestly can't process the emotion there.

It looks so real.

"Did you shower?" he asks.

"I hope that's okay. I felt sticky."

I could be wrong, but he looks a little proud of himself.

"You can do anything you want here," he says, and tucks his face into my neck and groans. "Fuck, you smell good."

"I hope so," I say, giggling as his stubble tickles my neck. "It's your soap."

He sucks at my throat and then pauses, lifting his eyes to mine. "Was Margot still here?"

"She just left. Is it a matter of genetics that she only made one piece of toast?"

Luke laughs at this as he moves to press more small kisses to my throat.

"Who eats one piece of toast?" I ask. "Do you Sutters have something against eating bread products in pairs?"

Groaning, he says, "*Logan.* I don't really want to talk about my sister right now."

He shifts, lowering his body so he's pressed against me, hips already moving in experimental circles.

We're both naked and the sensation is so startling at first—the gentle drag of skin on skin—that I suck in a breath. This isn't our first time being naked together—not by a long shot—but it's still new enough that it's a shock to the system: so much of his bare skin connecting with so much of mine.

The room is cool; it's near the back of the house and shaded by a couple of large eucalyptus trees that grow just outside the window. Even so, streaks of sunlight still manage to break through, and they catch the dust motes in the corner, warming the foot of the bed. They make Luke's skin look golden, like he's lit from within.

He seems to note this, too, as he looks down our bodies, at how we fit together, the color of his skin against mine. My breasts are so much lighter than the rest of me, the traces of at least three different swimsuits outlined by the sun. Maybe he's used to girls who spray-tan or stay out of the sun altogether, but he seems to marvel at it, how the stark cream of my breasts contrasts with the rest of me.

He places a palm over my nipple and circles lightly, the friction just enough for it to tighten under his touch, have my toes curling against sheets. I've always liked my nipples played with—something he seems to have figured out already—loved the direct connection they seemed to have to between my legs. Each touch or pinch is like a jolt of electricity straight to my clit, and I can feel how wet I am already, that part of me slick and aching for more.

Seeing my reaction, Luke moans and says my name again, biting along my collarbones and back down to my breasts. He's relentless, sucking on one while pinching the other, and it's enough to have me opening my legs to make more room for him, pushing my knees up around his sides.

He moves up to kiss me, tasting my top lip and then my bottom, pulling away just hard enough for it to sting. My lips tingle, and as he moves down along my throat and between my breasts to my ribs, I reach up to feel them, how warm and slightly swollen they are.

"I swear I'm progressive and not a caveman and, thanks

to the women in my family, I'm probably the biggest feminist around, but *fuck,* I like the way my soap smells on your skin."

I laugh and run my fingers through his hair as he kisses down my stomach, whispering how good I taste, smell, feel. When he reaches my hip bone the instinct to stop him bubbles up in my chest but I can't seem to say anything.

Luke hesitates, too, lingering there, sucking at the soft skin of my navel. I *want* this, and every particle in my body pushes against my skin in an attempt to move him lower. Lower.

Luke circles his tongue around my belly button and I rock my hips up, using my grip in his hair to guide him, to show him what I want.

His eyes fly to mine, wide and slightly unfocused. "Logan?" he asks.

I think about Luke trusting me enough to get on that surfboard and how sometimes we have to jump. I think about how he said he loves me.

I want to jump.

I nod and there's a moment of understanding between us before he smiles. "I've thought about this more than is probably healthy."

I feel my face heat. "I probably have, too."

He shakes his head like he can't believe what's happening. "Will you do me a favor?"

"Sure."

"Will you make a lot of noise, Dimples?"

"That's a dollar," I tell him, pinching his shoulder.

"My wallet is in my pants, take whatever you want."

He doesn't wait for anything else and my head falls back against the pillow, spine arched in anticipation as he moves down between my legs. His first touch is tentative: lips pressed against my pubic bone in several small kisses, and then lower, mouth soft and partially open, directly over my clit.

The air leaves my lungs and I cry out.

"Like that?" he says against me, after taking me into his mouth and sucking gently.

"Yeah," I say, nodding. "Again."

He does it again, using his fingers to gently hold me open and suck on my clit, a little harder this time. It's on the edge of being too much and not enough and I can barely breathe, can barely think of why I waited so long to let him do this.

He alternates between kisses and little licks, broad stripes of his tongue that have my hips lifting from the mattress, rocking up to meet him.

"God, yes," I whimper. "I can't . . . please . . ." I don't even know what I'm asking but words bubble up in my throat. "Fuck, right there."

I realize I'm tugging on his hair but when I try to ease up, he shakes his head, meeting my eyes a moment before sitting up on his knees.

"Don't," he says, panting. His cheeks are pink, neck flushed right down to his chest. His mouth is red and *wet,* and as my gaze flickers down his body, I see he's touching himself. He gives his cock a few long, slow tugs as he looks at me, tongue flicking out to taste. "Don't think. Don't censor. You want more?"

I'm already nodding, lifting my lower legs to pull him back down.

He kisses my hip bones and then each knee before sliding my legs over his shoulders. "I *want* you to pull my hair," he says. "I want you to scratch my back and fuck my face and do whatever you want to me."

"Okay," I gasp, unable to process his words or look away as he leans in again, tongue swirling around my clit.

I have to remind myself to breathe as he pushes one finger inside me, in and out, before adding another. I squeeze my eyes closed and focus on the way it feels; on the sounds he's making and the way they vibrate against me.

"I want to do everything to you," he says, pulling his middle finger out and letting it trail lower, until it's pushing against me, pressing gently.

I buck my hips, unable to articulate a thought beyond his name and how good this feels, how I don't ever want him to stop. I've never done anything like this before and now it's all I can think about, letting Luke have this part of me I've never shared with anyone else. He doesn't move any further, just a constant pressure that leaves my thoughts in a tangle of static.

I move one of my hands from his hair and bring it to his face, down along his cheek to his mouth and where it's moving against me. My skin is slick, slippery, and he moans as my fingers slide over it, back and forth alongside his tongue. I've never felt anything like it, so many sensations that I'm unable to tell where one starts and the others begin.

Luke whimpers against me and I catch sight of his shoulder moving, his arm flexing beneath him. The idea that he's as worked up over this as I am, so far gone that he *has* to touch himself, sets tiny fireworks off along my skin. Heat travels up my spine and I'm not sure if he's crying out or if it's me but my orgasm is there, ripping through me red-hot and endless, arching my hips off the bed until I'm shaking, rocking against his mouth.

With enormous effort, I lift my head to see him kneeling over me, hand working over his gorgeous cock.

"Let me," I tell him, and he blinks up, lips turned down as he tries to work out what I mean. "Come up here."

It's only now I realize how out of practice I am, and how long it's been since I've actually done this. I tap his hip and guide him toward me, a leg on either side of my ribs. He reaches for another pillow and sets it behind my head and then he just waits, eyes wide and chest heaving. There's so much skin and muscle, abs clenched tight like he's holding his breath. His cock is perfect like the rest of him and so hard, already wet at the tip.

"Come here," I say again, and open my mouth, watching the way his hand shakes as he holds the head against my lips. I reach out with my tongue to taste him and he whimpers. A feeling of power surges up in me and any trepidation I had seems to fall away.

Luke pushes into my mouth, so gently at first. I curl my hands around his hips and look up at him in a way I hope conveys what I want him to do. I don't want him to think or censor himself, either.

"You want me to—" he starts to ask, and I moan around him. He starts to give himself over to it, spurred on by my sounds and the way I grip him tighter, encouraging him to use me.

His cock slips over my tongue, grazes occasionally against my teeth. Those moments seem to make it even better for him and he swears, fingers pressed against my jaw and my skull as he pushes himself in and out of my mouth.

"London, yes—oh, God, perfect," he says, words stuttered out between shaky breaths. He braces one hand on the headboard just over my head and looks down at me as he moves. "Fuck, I'm not going to last." His ass flexes beneath my hands and he's shaking his head, like he's sad it's going to be over soon. "No. Fuck. Coming," he gasps, and tries to pull away. "London, move. I don't—"

I make a sound of protest and tighten my hold as he starts to come against my tongue. Up to this point he's been so careful not to go too far but I hear him smack the wall overhead, grunting and swearing as I swallow around him.

He's shaking when he finally falls to my side, hands greedy as he pulls me to him and kissing my chin, my mouth, and my nose. I look up to see that his eyes are closed, lashes curled against flushed cheeks. My jaw aches and my heart is pounding so hard he has to be able to feel it.

I want him to tell me he loves me again, but am also terrified of hearing it and being unable to believe him. I hold my breath as he shifts, leaning into my neck and exhaling a shaky breath. I already know it's coming, though, and my heart seems to swell in my chest.

His voice is scratchy: "I really do love you."

I anticipate the sensation of overflowing, of relief . . . but it doesn't come, and I don't know what to say.

So I tease Luke about practically collapsing after he comes, and he kisses me with sleepy lips and arms that seem to barely hold him up. He's happy, and boneless, and falls back asleep within minutes.

I'M IN THE middle of a pretty big order when I hear someone yell his name. It's only around eight o'clock, and a handful of his friends have been playing pool in the back for the last hour, but it's like some group alarm has been tripped as soon as he steps into the bar and comes into view, and a bunch of them look up, shouting at him. There are a few girls I recognize now, a couple of guys I'm sure I've seen him with before, but only Not-Joe who I really know.

Luke waves in their direction but doesn't stop, looping an arm around Not-Joe's shoulder as he bypasses his friends completely and makes his way to the bar.

I put two beers on coasters as they take a seat, and line up a few wineglasses for another order. Luke looks happy and rested.

"Did you sleep all day?" I ask. Teasing him seems to be my default, and it calms the butterflies and nervous energy that have erupted since his arrival, brings me back to my baseline. His adorable, sheepish smile doesn't hurt, either.

Not-Joe doesn't really seem to get our inside joke, but he laughs just the same, happy to take part in any *Operation Give Luke Shit* he can find.

"I'm going to assume you tease me for the same reason Dylan here used to snap girls' bras in gym class," Luke says.

Not-Joe gives him a puzzled look. "Because she wants to see your boobs?"

Luke brings his beer to his lips and looks at me over the top of the bottle. "Something like that."

I shake my head, feeling the resurgence of butterflies as I uncork a bottle of wine and fill the glasses. With a nod toward a waiting table, I pick up the tray and deliver the drinks, actually happy for a bit of breathing room away from his flirty smile and meaningful glances.

I don't get much of a reprieve, however, because on my way out of Fred's office with a spool of receipt tape only a few minutes later, I find Luke standing in the dark little hallway, waiting for me.

"What are you doing?" I ask, even as he's moving closer, crowding me into the corner.

"Am I allowed to do this?" he says, leaning in, mouth hovering just over mine.

My stomach does a somersault as I look up at him. "You're asking?" I breathe, brain scrambled by his proximity.

"I'm not sure what the rules are," he says, and pulls aside my shirt so he can bend and taste my collarbone. "Whether this is something I can do out there." He motions back over his shoulder, but I know he means outside his bedroom, out in the real world. "Because I can think of only two things that would make me happier."

"Two things? What are they?"

"One is falling asleep together in *your* bed, and the other is what we did this morning."

Oh. He crowds into my space a little more and the words hang heavy and meaningful between us. I squeeze my thighs together, hoping to take the edge off the little ache I feel just thinking about *what we did this morning,* but it doesn't help.

I know what he means but I want to keep him talking, keep him close to me. "You mean like if Fred is aroun—" I start to say, but he's already shaking his head.

"I don't mean Fred, I mean what do *you* want? Am I allowed to tell you you look pretty tonight? Am I allowed to kiss you hello? I really want to."

I want him to, too, and so I nod with a shaky breath, thankful he's pressed up against me or I'd probably be on the ground at his feet: a London puddle.

Luke smiles and brushes the end of his nose against mine. "Hi, Logan," he says.

"Hi."

His mouth is so close that I can taste his breath. He leans in, closing the space between us. It's absolutely not a kiss that's suitable for my place of business, all soft lips and slick tongue and warm hands moving everywhere. I wonder if I could pull him into the bathroom, lean against the wall, and ask him to fuck me all over again.

I'm about to ask when a door slams nearby and Luke pulls away, panting. "Holy shit."

I can hear the phone ringing at the bar, the sound of customers talking, and calls from a football game playing on one of the overhead screens. I don't care about any of it.

He takes a deep breath and lets it out. "You need to get back, and I'm going into the men's room to rub one out."

I laugh. "Okay," I say. "But you're staying?"

He nods, kissing me once more, a tiny, soft peck. "I'm staying."

It starts to pick up again and Fred stays at the bar to help. Luke's been back and forth between his group and up here with me, but when someone shouts his name, he points in their direction. "Think I'll hang out and watch the game since you're busy. What time are you off tonight?"

I fill up a shaker with ice and look up at him. "Same as always. We close at one."

"Do you want to come back over? Shorter drive for you . . ."

"In need of another nap?"

He leans an elbow on the bar and looks up at me with wide, brown eyes. "With you? Always," he says. "What time will you actually be able to cut out of here?"

Goose bumps rise along my skin at the idea of another morning waking up in his bed. "It might be later," I say. "It depends on the cleanup."

"Just let me know." He looks around the bar and leans in a little closer. "I'd like to hear you make those sounds again," he says, and my arm freezes, the bottle I'm pouring held in midair. "If I leave, you can text me when you head over. I'll still be up. Okay?"

My brain has basically deserted me and I nod, watching as he smiles and then walks away.

The group Luke is with has grown, practically doubling in size and volume. Fred has handled them for the most part, leaving me to cover the bar and run the register. Luke is standing next to Dylan, hassling him over how he's going to shoot the seven ball into a corner pocket, when I see a girl slide into the space next to him.

Old habits are hard to break, and I can't seem to look away, watching every move he makes and comparing it to what I think it means. Old habits are obviously hard for him to break, too, because more than once I see him looking down at his phone, or pulling it out of his pocket to read a text.

It pokes at a bruise inside my chest, some *thing* that's still there, lurking under the surface.

I've been in sort of a spiral, pretending not to watch Luke, pretending not to care how often he still looks at his damn phone, imagining what's going on inside it and wondering if it's even possible for that girl to get any closer without actually sitting on his lap, when Fred tosses a towel on the bar in front of me.

"Why don't you head out early?" he says. "Luke's still

here and I can handle the rest. Take your boy home and show Miss Tube Top back there that he's taken."

I feel irritation flare somewhere deep in my gut. I look back in his direction and see he has his phone out again, reading through a message before he puts it away again. Does Luke ever contact the women he's with after he sees them? What's even the point of giving his number anyway? Is it just a douchey sort of ego boost? I remember Justin's phone going off on occasion and he'd answer it, slipping out to the garage or backyard to talk, and now I feel vulnerable and gross. Will there ever be a time when that sort of thing doesn't set me off?

"He's not taken," I say.

Fred looks at me, surprised. "Funny, he sure looked taken when he was sitting up here. He follows you around like he's a puppy and you've got his favorite treat in your pocket."

I ignore him, bending to pull a couple of Coronas out of the beer cooler.

Fred gives me his *I'm picking my battles* sigh, and then moves to help someone else.

I keep myself busy, restocking the cooler and deciding that staying behind the bar and staying busy is an excellent idea.

At some point I get a message from Luke, Had to rescue Margot. Don't forget to text when you're leaving.

I pocket my phone and go back to work, watching as the bar slowly empties.

At one, Fred turns off the outside lights, and I text Luke a quick, Leaving in about ten. You still up?

I check five minutes later. No answer.

When the last glass is washed and the bar lights are turned out, there's nothing left to do but make my way to my car. Luke still hasn't answered, and I know that I'm stalling because if I text him again and am met with nothing but silence, I'll think too much about what it means. I wave to Fred and wait another five minutes before typing, Headed home. Exhausted. Let's talk tomorrow.

Chapter SIXTEEN

Luke

I WAKE WITH A start, still in last night's jeans and with the remote resting on my stomach. The room is bright, the other side of the bed is untouched, and there's no sign of London anywhere. The clock shows it's almost eight and I sit up, fumbling for my phone and squinting at the screen, wondering why London isn't here and why she didn't text when she got off like she said she would. I do a quick scroll through my messages but don't see the name I'm looking for, and it occurs to me that something could have happened to her, like maybe she didn't make it out of Fred's or even to her car.

I've never called someone so fast in my life.

It rings three times before London answers, the sound of wind whipping through the line.

"Are you okay?" I practically shout.

"What? Yeah, I'm fine. I'm up at Black's." She pauses for a moment before adding, "Are *you* okay?"

I fall back against my pillow and press my hand to my chest, only now realizing how fast my heart is pounding. "Yeah, I just—you said you'd text when you left and I must have fallen asleep. I woke up and . . ."

London is silent for a moment and I can hear the sound of seagulls overhead. "I *did* text you—twice, actually—but you didn't answer," she says. "You didn't get them?"

I roll to my side and close my eyes. "Yeah, I didn't see anything."

"Did you actually *read* your messages, Luke?"

"I started to," I say, putting her on speaker so I can take a closer look. There's . . . well, there's a few.

Michelle: Wanna hang out?

Dylan: Did you know that polar bears aren't actually white?

Call me if ur bored. 619-555-3344? I have no idea who this person even is.

Tonya: Did I leave my bra at your place on Valentine's? The one with the LED lights?

Leiah: I'm in town next weekend . . .

Scroll . . .

Scroll . . .

CALL ME. Who is *Brunette With Great Rack*?—And did I really put that as a contact in my phone?

"Still reading?" London asks, and I can hear the hard smile in her voice. "Must have been a busy night."

"Quiet, you," I tell her, but *wow*, she's sort of right. I get a lot of texts on a normal day, but I don't think I ever realized how many of them were quite so . . . suggestive. I rarely reply to any, and when I do it's only the girls I might have somehow managed to become friendly with over time, or hook up with again . . . on occasion.

But this is . . . eye-opening.

I'm about to call it quits and give London the big *I told you so,* when I see her name in the middle of a few others.

Leaving in about ten. You still up? And then about twenty minutes later: Headed home. Exhausted. Let's talk tomorrow.

"Oh."

"I guess you found it?" she asks, voice a little tighter now.

I frown. I don't like that London was right about this, and I don't like the way I feel right now. I don't feel proud or like a big swinging dick with girls texting me like this. I feel sort of sleazy.

"Yeah, I didn't see it, I guess," I mumble. "Sorry."

London laughs, but still, it's a little off. Has this always bothered her? "You're a popular guy."

I opt for a subject change. "Well, anyway, I missed you last night."

There's a moment of silence before London answers. "I missed you, too."

I am so fucking crazy for this girl that such a simple admission and my chest is filled with helium. "What are you doing today?"

"I'll probably finish Lola's site, maybe run some errands. Right now I'm just hanging out, thinking."

"Just thinking?"

She pauses. "Yeah . . ."

I don't like the way all of this makes me feel. "Need some help?"

"Some help thinking?" she says, and I close my eyes,

imagining the way her dimples are probably denting her cheeks when she says this.

"Don't you need to get to work today? Or are you taking another personal day?"

"I'm meeting one of the partners down at the courthouse later this afternoon. I have some time this morning."

"You want to meet at Black's? We could work on your pop-up," she says.

"At *Black's*?" I clarify, brows raised.

"Sure, why not?"

"I know next to nothing about surfing, and even I know Black's does not have a bunny hill, Logan."

"There's a section of nude beach here. Maybe I just want to get you naked."

I press my hand to my dick and close my eyes with a groan. "I'll be there in twenty."

***

TAKING THE WOODEN stairs that lead down the cliffside, I spot London's bright orange bikini top almost immediately. She's amazing, just a neon speck in this massive blue ocean, and surrounded by guys who look almost twice her size. I stop and watch her for a minute, noting how patient she is as she waits for just the right wave, how determined she becomes when she finally finds one. It's hard not to want to run out and save her when she gets knocked into the surf, but I realized a long time ago, London doesn't need me to save her from anything.

I continue down to the beach and take a look around.

London's right: for someone who's lived most of his life near the beach, I've spent shockingly little of that time at any of them—this one included. From the sand, Black's is nothing but ocean and giant cliffs all around, and it's easy to forget there's a city just beyond it.

London sees me from the water and I watch as she paddles in, all long arms, strong shoulders, and tan skin. I find a place for my board in the sand—carefully, just like she showed me—and sit down to wait for her. She makes it to the shore and tucks her own board under her arm, crossing the beach and stopping close enough for water droplets to land on my feet.

"Hey," she says, smiling down at me.

I can't help but let my eyes skim the curves and lines of her body, before meeting her smile with one of my own. "Hey, yourself."

She wrings out her hair and then, after a moment of hesitation, straddles my lap.

I let out an intensely feminine high-pitched squeak. "Cold!"

"Oops, sorry."

I fight halfheartedly against her attempts to press her wet, cold chest against my dry, warm one. "You don't look very sorry."

"Because I'm not. I like you in your swim trunks, though," she says, fingers teasing down my sides to tug at the waist of my shorts. "I didn't get to tell you that last time."

With my hands bracketing her ribs, I brush my thumbs

along the skin just below her breasts . . . because this is a thing I can do now. I think.

"You mean when you tried to feed me to the sharks?" I ask. She nods and I lean in, kissing her chin. "I liked your suit, too. It took superhuman strength not to get hard every time you touched me."

"I could barely concentrate; I'm surprised you didn't drown."

I laugh against her skin, running my nose along the column of her throat. She smells like the ocean and sunblock, and I wonder idly how much convincing it would take to get her to blow off whatever it is she's thinking about and come home with me.

I tug a little on the string tying her top together and brush her wet hair over her shoulder. "I want to apologize again for not seeing your texts. I really would have liked to have seen you last night."

"It's fine. Your phone is crazy, I totally get how you missed it," she says, and I feel the vibration of her voice against my lips. She scratches my scalp and tugs on my hair and I moan, almost missing it when she says, "Are you a good monster, or a bad monster, Luke Sutter?"

I close my eyes and lean into her touch. "Can't I be both?"

She runs her finger from my hair to my forehead, down my nose, and over my top lip. Opening my mouth, I take her fingertip between my teeth, and bite it.

"You make me sort of crazy," she says, eyes a little unfocused, mouth slightly open.

"Crazy is good."

"You're like junk food."

I suck a little, and then smile, speaking around her finger. *"Junk food?"*

"Yeah," she says, tongue peeking out to lick her lips. "Pizza. Chips."

Her words scrape up my spine and my heart falls several inches in my chest. I tilt my head to see her face. "I wasn't confused about the term 'junk food,' Logan. Rather, the choice of *metaphor.*"

She pulls her finger free, and touches the tip of my chin. "Like I want to shove you in my face but I worry I'll feel awful afterward." London scrunches up her nose in adorable frustration but then sighs, leaning into me.

So she means pretty much exactly what I thought. I close my eyes again, jaw tight, trying to ignore the visceral pull I feel when she's this close, and instead let the anger and hurt boil up and out.

She wants me but will feel *awful* afterward.

I'm not only unhealthy, I'm regrettable.

"London?"

"Hmm?"

I move her off my lap and stand, looking down at her. "That comparison makes me feel like shit."

She seems to realize exactly what she's said, and her face falls. "No. Luke—"

"I haven't been with anyone else. I want to be with you all the fucking time. I told you I love you, and you call me junk food? How is this any different than Daniel referring to girls as snacks?"

She stares up at me, surprise melting into regret. "You're right, it's not," she says. "I'm sorry, I shouldn't have said that."

"But you think it."

"Luke."

She can say my name as many times as she wants but *fuck this.* I stand and brush the sand from my shorts, grabbing my board before I start to walk away. A hand wrapped around my forearm stops me, pulls me around to face her.

"I already don't trust my judgment and now I'm falling for the most terrifying person possible," she says. "You know why you missed my texts last night? Because they were buried in there with twenty other messages. You think I don't realize that? How many women texted you last night, Luke? Forty? *More?* You used to bang anything with a pussy."

She jolts, like her using such words surprised her, too. Which only makes me wonder how long they've been simmering just below the surface.

I hesitate, scowling at her even though I know *exactly* how right she is. I want to tell her she's a pain in the ass, has no idea what the fuck is going on here or what I'm doing with who, but the first words out of my mouth are the most trivial: "Not *anything.*"

"Fucking hell, Luke." She runs her hands through her tangled hair and stares up at me, exasperated. "Really?"

Maybe I should have gone with my first instinct—to tell her she's right, but that isn't me anymore. "London—"

"Have you considered that the reason you want me is because I'm resisting?" she asks. "Is it the cliché of the challenge? I mean, if we do this, and we're together—"

"I know how to commit," I growl. "I *know* what it looks like."

"Fine," she says, low and flat. "But before, Mia was all you knew. Now you're used to that thrill of discovery, the *chase*. What if sex between us grows familiar? What if we're together five years and you get bored? The thought of being with you, and you taking home some other—"

"Stop."

I turn away. I can't listen. It reminds me of the betrayal I felt when I slept with Ali. The idea of being with someone else when I could have London, of her being with another guy, actually shoves a spike into my head.

She grabs my arm again. "Stop walking away from me. All I'm saying is it's hard, okay? I shouldn't have said what I did back there, but I'm scared." She takes a step closer, voice quiet when she says, "I'm trying not to be, but I'm *terrified* of what it could be like with you."

"God—" I start, squeezing my eyes closed and digging both hands into my hair. I want to focus on what she's telling me, but my fuse has officially run out. "Don't you think this is scary for me, too?"

"Luke—"

A wave crashes, and the edge of the surf touches the very tips of our toes. The tide is coming in, and in a dramatic rush I want to see it crash over me. "Don't you think I'm *already* in too deep?" I tell her. "If you decide now that we aren't doing this, it's going to *hurt*. But that was true a while ago and I decided to roll with it. I decided you're worth it. That's the difference. Fuck, I think I finally figured it out: falling in love isn't about who makes you feel the best, but who could make you the most miserable if they leave."

I HEAR A key in the lock about ten minutes after I get home from work and close my eyes, letting my head fall back against the couch. "No," I say, and my sister's response is immediate.

"Yes."

"I'm not in the mood for this, Margot."

I hear her drop a bag near the door before she flops on the couch next to me. "What makes you think I'm here to give you shit for something?"

"One, because you've been giving me shit for one thing or another my entire life. And two, I had a fight with London and I can only assume that through some form of female telepathy, you've found out and are over here to hand me my ass."

"Wow," she says.

I tilt my head to look at her. "So I'm wrong?"

"Well . . . no."

I nod my head and take another pull from my beer.

"But I did run into Lola earlier, and she mentioned that London came home upset."

I *know* London is upset. I'm the reason *why* she's upset,

and yet hearing it is like a punch to my gut. The thing is, I'm upset, too.

"Right," I say.

"She didn't tell me why—I'm not actually sure that Lola knows why, because London isn't apparently the most forthcoming when it comes to emotions—just that you two had an argument." I don't say anything and she continues. "Do you want to talk about it?"

"Nope."

"Luke."

I sigh, knowing I'll never get out of this. "Sometimes . . . I wish I'd never brought her home."

Margot stays silent, staring forward at the TV.

"I wish I'd never brought her home and then I'd never know how great she is. I'd never realize that I want someone ballsy and self-sufficient. If I never brought London home that night, I'd never realize that I had it all wrong and Mia was never the girl for me. Ignorance is bliss, right?"

Beside me, my sister sighs. "So let me guess, London is still having some trust issues with Luke the manwhore."

I press my fists into my eyes until I see nothing but stars. "So even if that's not me anymore? If I'm not with anyone but London, if I still only want *her*, I'll still be branded that forever?"

She tilts her head. "Well, no. Not exactly. But . . . like, how does she know that?"

"Because I told her, that's why."

"Okay, but—maybe that's not actually enough. Doing

something is a lot harder than just saying it. She has no idea what you're doing when you're gone, or who's texting you God knows what. *I* don't even know, and I'm rude enough to ask." She stands from the couch and walks over to the front door, where she's dropped a heavy bag. "And I didn't actually come over here to lecture you. I came over here to use your washing machine. Playing bossy big sister was just a bonus, I guess."

I'm silent and she steps up behind me, dropping a kiss to the top of my head.

"I love you," she says, "but straighten your shit out."

I have nothing to do but think, and Margot's words play on a loop in my head. London's worry that I'm only interested because I think she's some sort of thing I have to conquer makes me crazy. The thing is, I know myself. I've fucked scores of women, but only loved two. When I love, I do it to the center of the earth. To the part that's liquid, soft, terrifying. I understand why she's scared, because so am I. Losing Mia was like losing a limb. I had to relearn how to do things without a part of me that had always been there. But I worry that losing London would be like losing something vital, some beating, *living* part of me.

I can hear Margot crashing around in the laundry room, singing some emo song at the top of her lungs, and as if on cue, my phone vibrates on the coffee table in front of me. With a sigh, I reach for it, unsurprised when the screen lights up immediately, a handful of messages already waiting. There's one from Dylan asking if I want to go to Comic-Con this summer, but there are a few from girls, too. Some girls I remember, and some I don't.

I never thought much of all the texts and propositions for booty calls—it was always funny, a bit of a game and easy to ignore—but London was clearly frustrated that I didn't see her text last night in the sea of notifications, and she's never even read some of these. What would she think if she saw them? How would she feel? How would *I* feel? It doesn't take a genius to know how I'd react if it were London's phone full of messages from guys—so full that she would miss a message from me in all of the noise—and it's enough to pull my spine straight and zap any last bit of humor from this whole thing.

This was exactly what Margot meant when she said it wasn't enough. It's not enough to tell London I've changed. I have to actually show her.

Chapter SEVENTEEN

London

OLA'S PHONE IS ringing—Lola's phone is *always* ringing—and I grab it from the counter, carrying it down the hall. I can hear the familiar scratch of charcoal against paper as I near her open door, and find her hunched over her desk, finishing a sketch she was working on before she ran out for her deadline pick-me-up coffee.

I knock on the wall just outside her door before stepping in and setting her phone down in front of her. "You left this in the kitchen."

She looks up from her drawing to squint down at the screen and then, deciding to ignore it, looks up at me. Doing a slight double take, Lola pulls off her glasses, whispering a quiet "You okay?"

I nod.

Lola knows that's not true—I came home from the beach with red eyes, slipped immediately into my pajamas, and have barely said a word since—but she's rarely one to outright push.

Back in the kitchen, I pour a bowl of cereal and return to my laptop, clicking through each page of Lola's new website.

It feels a little like someone is sitting on my chest, and

my eyes sting, but I'm not letting myself think about my fight with Luke.

I don't want to deal with it right now.

My fingers seem to move on their own, entering code while my brain races ahead, imagining how this newest illustration will look as a thumbnail next to the others.

Although the film studio has a landing page for the movie adaptation of *Razor Fish,* the placeholder I set up specifically for Lola's site with only her name, a short bio, and a registration link has racked up tens of thousands of hits since they started filming. Adding these last details—along with the idea of making the page *live*—is both thrilling and the slightest bit terrifying.

I absently stir my cereal as I scan the pages again, searching for anything I might have forgotten. After a deep breath of bravery, I call over my shoulder. "Hey, Lola?"

"Yeah?"

"Can you come out here when you're done? I want to show you something."

I hear her chair scrape back from the desk, the sound of her feet against the hardwood, and then she's there, wrapping her arms around my shoulders.

"Hey, sweetie." She starts to say something more when her gaze flickers up to the screen—I'm still working in the site dashboard so I know it doesn't look very interesting at the moment, but she sucks in a breath. "Oh my God. Is this the site?"

I've shown her various graphics over the last few weeks,

had her give me feedback on the layout, and discussed what she wants where, but she hasn't actually seen anything yet, not all together like this.

"Yeah," I tell her. "Are you ready?"

She nods quickly and takes the seat at my side.

"I think it's good but if there's anything you aren't sure about, or want changed, just let me know." I'm babbling nervously, but this moment feels so huge to me. "They're all pretty easy fixes at this point."

She squeals and claps, holding her breath as I click the home page, and she watches it load for the first time. Lola gasps as a simple Flash image—my initial idea for her site—fills the screen.

"Is that—?" she starts to say, angling my laptop toward her to get a closer look.

It's one of Lola's first drawings—from when she was only thirteen or so—of the character who would ultimately become the lead protagonist in her first comic series, *Razor Fish*. The sketch is simple, almost rudimentary, but as we watch, the penciled black-and-white image slowly morphs into a more complicated one. I hear Lola's breath catch again as she registers what she's seeing. Early drafts of her penciled art turn into ink versions, and then various colored images. More and more of her brainstorming panels are revealed, gathering detail as the Flash image accelerates and finally we're staring at the vivid image the rest of the world has come to know: the current incarnation of Razor, the odd creature she created and who practically explodes from the movie poster.

"Do you like it?" I ask, glancing nervously back at her. My emotions are all over the place right now; I'm not sure what I'd do if she hated it. But I don't have to worry. Lola's eyes shine with tears and she leans over, wrapping her arms around my shoulders in a tight hug.

"Are you kidding me?" She's shaking a little and releases me so she can stare at it all over again. "I *love* it. Where on earth did you get all these? These early ones were all hand-drawn. I didn't even know I still had them."

"Your dad kept nearly everything you ever drew, and Oliver managed to dig up a lot of your early digital work," I tell her. "Seriously, they're your biggest fanboys. You'd be amazed to see everything they were able to find. I thought it might be cool to see the evolution, I mean Razor's of course, but also yours as an artist."

"This is the coolest thing I've ever seen," she says, swiping at her cheeks. "Is it done? I mean, can I show Oliver?"

I stand, and gesture for Lola to move into my chair, laptop in front of her. My hands are shaking from her reaction; it was even better than I'd hoped. "Almost. Go ahead and click through all the pages, make sure everything is where you want it," I tell her, "and we can tweak anything that isn't perfect. Then all that's left is migrating it over to the new server and boom, LolaCastle-dot-com is live."

Lola clicks around for a moment and shakes her head. "I can't believe you did all this." She turns and looks up at me. "I'm just . . ." she says, genuinely choked up. "You're amazing."

"It was nothing really," I tell her. And I'm surprised to find—despite my nerves, despite everything that's going on—that it's *true*: working on her site wasn't just fun, it was satisfying. It gave me an outlet for my feelings I've only ever found on a surfboard. "I loved doing it."

"Which is exactly why you should be doing it for a *living*," she says. "I know you love working at Fred's, and I can't believe I'm agreeing with your mom here, but God, you're so fucking talented."

I sigh. "Remember that guy Oliver gave my info to a while back? The one who asked him about his logo?" I ask, and she nods. "He owns a brewery and they're opening a new location. I woke up to an email from him with a proposal to build his site, the retail page, and design all the promo materials. It'd be the biggest job I've ever done—*huge*—and I'd probably have to do it full-time to meet his deadline, at least for a while."

"No more Fred's?" she asks.

I shrug, wincing. "I'm going to quit Bliss first, but even so, I can't imagine how I'd make it work." The idea of not working with Fred makes my heart droop, but the idea of doing *this* full-time? I can't even imagine how great that could be.

"Sounds like it could be amazing."

"Sounds like being a grown-up," I counter.

She puts her arm around my shoulder again and squeezes. "Imagine all the time that could leave for . . . other things."

I reach for the laptop and tap a few keys. "I don't think I'm going to have to worry about *other things* for a while."

"Do you want to tell me what happened yet?"

I feel my shoulders sag with the weight of all that's happened today, and slide back down to the chair at her side. I tell her everything; about how scared I've been to let Luke in, his saying he loved me, about the texts he didn't see and how I blew up at him this morning. I mean to keep everything matter-of-fact, but my voice comes out thin and wobbly.

Lola makes a tiny sympathetic noise and I look up at her. "Honey," she says, reaching for my hand, "I think you're a badass."

I laugh and wipe my eyes with the sleeve of my shirt. "What? *Why?*"

"You put yourself out there. And so did he. You know, Luke was the perfect boyfriend. He was attentive and loyal— then the accident happened and it's like he and Mia were such different people afterward."

I nod. I've heard some variation of this from almost everyone who knew him back then.

Lola frowns, drawing her finger across a pattern in the tabletop as she continues. "Mia stopped talking and Luke slept with one girl after another, but in a way . . . it's like they did the same thing. They were both doing what they thought they had to to protect themselves. Something huge changed inside Luke after the accident: he put this wall around himself and wouldn't let anyone in," she says, and her thoughtful expression shifts into a smile. "Sound familiar?"

"A little," I say, bumping her shoulder lightly. "He said falling in love isn't about who makes you feel the best, but who could make you the most miserable if they leave." I swipe the side of my hand across my wet cheek. "Which is basically what I told myself every day before I met him."

"Is that still how you feel?" Lola asks.

I shake my head. "I don't think he really believes it, either."

Lola toys with a tiny sapphire pendant around her neck that I'm pretty sure was a recent gift from Oliver. "So tell him."

"It's so scary," I say.

"Sometimes scary can be good. He said he *loves* you. He's *yours* now, don't you get that? You're the one person who can be with Luke anytime you want."

An explosion of fireworks goes off in my chest at the revelation.

He's mine now.

I'm the one person—the *only* person—who can see him every hour, of every day.

If he'll forgive me.

Lola continues, oblivious to the thunder going off inside me. "Or pull a Harlow and show up on his doorstep wearing nothing but a trench coat. Simple, but effective."

"As hilarious as I suspect his reaction would be, I don't think I'm ready for that yet."

"I'm just watching you freak out on about a hundred different levels right now, aren't I?"

Laughing now, I sniffle and say, "Yes."

"If this helps you sort through what's going on up here,"

she says, motioning to the laptop before tapping my forehead, "then finish up. Email the brewery guy—because that's for London, and London only—and then call Luke."

————————

I WORK ON the final touches to Lola's site while I work up the nerve to talk to Luke. It takes a while . . . I'm not used to having to reach out, apologize, and ask for something like this.

Finally, I close my laptop when there isn't any other work to be done. His number is at the top of my recent calls list, and I take a breath before pressing his name.

His phone doesn't ring, and instead goes straight to voicemail.

With a hollow ache in my stomach, I make a few more calls, leaving a message for Jason, the guy who owns the brewery. But with nothing else to distract me from my moping, Lola suggests I run to the grocery store. We're out of milk and bread and Lola's favorite yogurt—all things we could go at least a few more days without—but when I open the bathroom cupboard and notice we're down to the last roll of toilet paper, I admit defeat, grabbing my keys and heading out the door.

Lola and I used to do the grocery shopping together, but with work and deadlines sucking up most of our free time, we've started dividing it up. This time Lola's made me a list, knowing that in my current frame of mind I'll probably roam the aisles and end up at home with a trunk full of Lean Cuisines and wine.

I'm halfway through the list when my phone rings with an unfamiliar number. I frown down at it, before realizing it could be Jason, returning my call.

"Hello?" I answer.

"Hey, Logan."

I pull the phone away and blink down at the number again. "Luke?"

"Yeah, it's me. I . . . I wondered if you could talk for a few minutes."

"Um . . ." I look around me, still confused about where he's calling from. "Sure."

"First, I wanted to tell you that I'm sorry and—"

I stop in the middle of the produce aisle, interrupting. "I don't want you to apologize, I shouldn't have said that. It was terrible. I wasn't thinking."

"It's fine," he says quietly. "I understand where it came from. I know we have some things to talk over, and I was wondering if we could do that? If you'd be willing to do that."

"I'd like to talk," I tell him, my heart beating so hard I can barely form a response. "But what I—" I'm interrupted by a voice screeching through the intercom overhead. I wince at the sound, and then again when it seems to reverberate back to me, through the line.

"Wait, where are you—?"

"Are you—?" we both say, before a throat clears behind me.

It's him. My pulse is a hammer in my neck.

I look down at my phone and then back up again, before finally ending the call and slipping it back into my bag.

"I'm so confused," I finally admit, laughing.

"I came downtown to talk to you," he says. "Figured I'd grab a few things while I worked out what I wanted to say."

"Oh." I wonder if this is part of the change Lola was talking about: that Luke—who barely answered texts before, let alone phone calls—would rather have an actual conversation with me than the impersonal blips of text messages.

"I'm sorry," I say again.

Luke takes a step closer and loops his arm around my waist, lifting me off the ground as he pulls me into a hug. He smells like soap and shampoo and I'm incapable of doing anything but cling to him. When he presses his face into my neck and groans, I feel the sound all the way down my body and between my legs.

"So am I." He sets me down gently, and places a kiss on my forehead. "Hand me your phone."

"Why?" I ask, but I'm already handing it over.

Luke puts his arm around my shoulder, pulling me close before snapping a selfie of us with his lips pressed to my cheek. He looks adorable: content, eyes closed, smiling into the kiss. By contrast, I look confused and mildly disheveled.

Releasing me, he says, "Because I need to program in my new phone number."

I watch as he goes to my call log and assigns his name to the number. And only then does it occur to me: Luke called me from a new phone number.

"You got a new phone?" I ask.

He's still typing his name and address and email information into the contact, but spares a glance in my direction. "Yeah."

"Why?"

Handing my phone back, he says, "Too many distractions with the old one."

I swallow and feel the weight of what he's said wash over me. "Oh."

"I don't really want that many women to have my number anymore," he adds quietly. "It's not really fair to them, because I have a girlfriend now."

"Oh." I seem unable to say anything else. Finally, I manage, "That makes sense."

"And more important, it's not really fair to *you*, since I know I wouldn't want to have to put up with that." He tilts his head, catching my eye. "Still okay?" he asks.

I'm pretty sure I've never been more okay in my life. I take two steps forward to close the distance between us, and kiss him. My hands slide over the flat planes of his stomach, his ribs, the wide expanse of his chest. My fingers ghost over a nipple and his lips curve up into a smile.

"I'm trying to keep this grocery-store-appropriate," he growls, reminding me of the last time we were in his bed, with the weight of him moving over me, sweaty and intense. "You're not making it very easy."

"Sorry," I mumble, even as I push up onto my toes to get closer.

He bends to meet me halfway, lips moving with mine, familiar and warm, sucking at the bottom and then letting me have a turn sucking his. He gives me the tip of his tongue in tiny licks, through smiling kisses and quiet sounds as his hands move down my back and over my ass, pulling me into him. I want him in my bedroom, walking backward while I push forward to the bed, climbing over him, feeling his sun-kissed, smooth skin sliding over mine, heating with friction. There are too many clothes and too much space between us, and it's only when someone bumps into us as they reach around for the baby carrots that I remember where we are.

We register this in unison, and Luke takes a step back before clearing his throat.

"So." I smooth my hair, willing my body to back down and relax. "Groceries."

"Right. Groceries." He takes a deep breath to compose himself before his eyes go wide and he points to my cart. "Wow, that is a lot of produce."

"Lola's a healthy gal." With shaky hands, I pick up a carton of strawberries, check the date, and add it to the pile.

We take a few steps and I glance down at Lola's list. I'm oddly distracted and can't seem to focus on anything but the fact that Luke is at my side. "Yogurt," Luke says, grinning as he guides us down the next aisle.

"Right."

"So what have you done today?" he asks, and I laugh.

"I finished Lola's site and did some adult thinking."

Although I'm bending down to read some labels, I can sense that he's turned fully to face me. "More 'adult thinking'? I did a little of my own today."

It feels like my heart has just calmed down after kissing him in the produce section, and it takes off all over again as I quietly explain. "Besides the obvious," I say, "I was thinking about a new job."

He tries to play it cool by pretending to join me in reading the nutritional information on a yogurt container. "Really?"

I hum in agreement. "This guy Oliver knows contacted me about doing some work."

"A site?" he asks, unable to keep up the act, pulling my arm so I turn and look at him. I can feel the tension of the conversation growing between us, the question about what happens when he moves to Berkeley.

"A site, yeah, and designing all of his promotional items. It's a pretty big offer."

I watch him swallow as he nods a few times. "Like . . . how big?"

"It would pay me more than I make all year bartending." Luke goes completely still when he hears this. "So after I tried to call you"—Luke startles at this—"I called and quit Bliss. But I might also have to quit Fred's. That's the part that's holding me back. It's good, but . . . I don't know . . ." I flounder, repeating the word again: *"Big."*

"Big can be good," he says.

He tilts his head for us to keep walking, and we move side by side down the aisle. Luke senses my need to change the subject and tells me more about how his sister ran into Lola and they ended up talking about us for a half hour. We decide they're all a bunch of busybodies but we love them anyway, and have made it halfway around the store before I realize that at some point Luke has abandoned his basket entirely, and his groceries are lined up in the cart right next to mine.

And it's not even weird.

In the cereal aisle I reach for a box of Rice Krispies while he picks out Corn Flakes, and we move on.

A row of Pop-Tarts catches my eye and I stop, picking up a box of blueberry and putting them in with the rest of my things.

"Those are my favorite," he says.

I wink at him. "I know."

He looks at me, confused. "How did you know?"

"There was an empty box in your recycling and another in the cupboard. You've probably gone through it by now, even just eating one at a time. Still weird, by the way."

He gives me the strangest expression but doesn't comment as we finish up Lola's list and grab a few more things for him. We turn in unison near the cash registers, getting in line to check out.

"You know," he says, "we're really good at this."

I tilt my head to look up at him, waiting for him to elaborate.

"This domestic stuff. Look how good our apples look next to each other. My shampoo next to your tampons? It's like they were made to be together in this cart. We haven't argued over what kind of tuna fish to buy and we agree that Ruffles are better than Lay's. It's just—it's nice to know."

I smile up at him. " 'To know'? To know what?"

He bends, kissing my cheek. "To know we aren't just

amazing in bed together, or at a bar together, but actually *together* together."

"It is." I turn into his kiss, letting our lips simply press together as we look into each other's eyes. I can feel his mouth turn into his smile, and watch as his eyes curve into my favorite, playful expression.

"I love you," he whispers when he pulls back only a couple of inches, and then kisses me one more time. My throat tightens with the need to say it back.

But not here. I can feel the person behind us watching, can feel how we must stand out in the bright, impersonal light of a grocery store. I can't look away, though: Luke Sutter is a motherfucking wonder right now, and Lola's words ring through my thoughts. She's right: *He's mine now.*

The cashier begins scanning things from our cart, and the moment quiets, sweetly. I pay for my groceries and he pays for his, and then together we push the cart out to my car.

"Would you need to go to an office for this new job?" he asks, bending to push a bag toward the back of my trunk. I pull another bag out of the cart and he reaches for it, quietly telling me, "Let me."

"No," I answer. "All the programs I need are on my laptop, so I can work from home. Maybe at a coffee shop once or twice a week for a change of scenery."

"What you're saying is, you could live anywhere?" he asks, and the question is full of hope.

"I could." A storm of birds is flapping around in my chest. With the last bag unloaded, he looks down at me for a moment before leaning in, kissing me softly. It's the faintest, slowest, most featherlight kiss I've ever had, and I want to ask him for about a hundred more.

Can I ovulate from a kiss?

"That's good to know," he says, and then points the cart in the direction of his car. "See you at Fred's tonight, Logan."

FRED IS BEHIND the bar when I get to work, and I feel the first real pang of sadness at the possibility of leaving, even to do something I love. I don't have a particularly close relationship with my own father, so getting to hang out with Fred most nights has become something I really look forward to.

Nana would have loved Fred.

Most only-children bear the burden of being their parents' entire focus, carrying the weight of their collective hopes and dreams on their shoulders. My parents—particularly my mom—discovered early on that I wasn't the perfect little Mini-Me she'd always wanted, and opted for disapproval rather than trying to relate to me. I wasn't outright rebellious, but I wasn't a people-pleaser, either, and I spent most of my teen years being reprimanded for one thing or another.

My grandmother, on the other hand, just *got* me, and even though I'm sure there were more times than not where my headstrong personality made her want to sell me to the nearest traveling circus, she knew that the traits that made me a challenging teenager would make me a confident, independent woman.

I do a lot of thinking as I start my shift, about what I should do with my life and where, about how many changes could be on the horizon. I keep going back to my conversation with Luke at the store, and it feels heavier, more important with every passing hour. Luke seems to have settled on moving to Berkeley, but we haven't really talked about it yet. Something in my chest curls in on itself at the idea of being away from him, even now. San Diego has always been my home—even when I was only here visiting during the summer it felt that way. Could I leave it now?

There's a big game on tonight and the place is packed. I see a lot of regulars, and even more new faces. It's a good mix: some younger, some older, and a few in between. I keep track of the drinks of the people sitting at the bar, and carefully monitor a particularly rowdy group of sorority-type girls in a booth near the jukebox.

Luke comes in around ten, slipping up to the bar while I'm covering for one of the waitresses. He's laughing with Fred when I join them, and he reaches out, snags one of my belt loops, and smiles, so fucking wide.

My entire body is full of tiny bombs that detonate when he gives me that smile.

"Hey," he says.

He's changed into a pair of dark jeans and a blue T-shirt that stretches tight across his biceps and across his lats. I run my hands up his sides, feeling him. His hair is soft and falling over his forehead and his smile straightens into hunger when I say, "There you are."

"Can I drive you home?"

"My car is here," I remind him. "Don't you have work in

the morning?" I put a coaster in front of him, reaching into the cooler to grab a cold pint glass, and begin filling it with a new IPA I'm sure he'll love.

He catches my hand for a second as I place the glass in front of him, just long enough for his fingers to ghost over my wrist. "You're the one who closes here and gets up with the sun to go surfing. I want to come home with you. I haven't been in your bed yet."

He says it without a hint of trepidation, and suddenly it's all I can think about.

Luke in my bed.

Luke naked in my sheets.

Luke with his head thrown back against my pillow when he comes.

My voice is noticeably shaky when I tell him, "Okay," and nod to someone trying to get my attention at the other end of the bar. "Go play with your friends so I can work."

"Yes, ma'am," he says, picking up his beer and standing. "And Logan?"

"Yeah?" I ask.

"You look beautiful tonight."

———

IT DOESN'T ESCAPE my notice—or Fred's, for that matter—that I track where Luke is all night. He talks animatedly with his friends and even joins them in a game of pool, but keeps checking his watch, meeting my eyes when he looks up to find me watching him, too.

My breath catches every time. I'm nearly drunk with the giddy feeling that rises like carbonation in my chest and the words that seem intent on making their way up my throat.

I love you.

I blink away and back down to the credit card I'm supposed to be using to start a tab, and have to clear out the sale and start over.

About an hour later I watch one of the sorority girls leave her group and wander into the back room. Luke's not really paying attention—his eyes seem fixed on the screen above the pool table as he appears to argue with Not-Joe about the game—so he doesn't immediately react when she slips into the chair next to him. She leans in, saying something in his ear, and loops her arm through his.

I didn't even know I was holding my breath until he looks over at her, shifting just enough to put some space between them and removing his arm from her grip. Luke shakes his head and, without any more attention given to the moment, turns back to the television. He clearly didn't do it for my benefit—he doesn't even look to see if I've been watching.

My hands tremble as I wipe down the counter and glance at the clock, counting down the hours until I can take him home, and kiss another set of words into his skin: *I trust you.*

IN THE END, I do leave my car at the bar and let Luke drive me all the way back downtown. I don't really want to be away from him; things between us feel settled but not. When is he moving? What will I do?

He holds my hand as he drives, we listen to quiet music, and an easy sleepiness takes over the space between us.

Upstairs, we brush our teeth side by side. Luke brought a toothbrush with him, and when I see him pull it from a small duffel bag, I tell him the story of finding Ashley's at Justin's house. His reply is to spit, rinse and wipe his mouth, and press a wordless, lingering kiss to my temple.

"What a bag of dicks," he says when he's pulled away.

"I'm going to rinse off really quick," I say. And I do mean *quick.* I get in the shower before it's all that warm, soap and shampoo at the speed of light, and practically sprint to my room in a towel.

And Lord. Nothing looks better than Luke naked in my bed.

He's between the sheets already, his clothes in a neat pile on my desk chair. With unblinking eyes, he watches me drop my towel and tie my damp hair into a bun on top of my head. His eyes move down my neck, stalling on my breasts.

"Do you sleep naked?" he asks.

"With you I do."

He nods, rapt, and I pull back the sheets, climbing over him.

He's mine now.

I sit up over him, and feel like we're swimming in a tiny pool of light from the small lamp on the bedside table. His face is just barely in the shadow, but my entire torso is illuminated, and he reaches up, hands cupping my breasts. Between my spread legs, I feel him start to harden more.

"Logan?" he says quietly.

"Yeah?"

His thumbs slide slowly toward my nipples. "*Are* you my girlfriend?"

I nod, and he catches his lower lip between his teeth as he watches his thumbs draw slowly expanding circles around the tight peaks. Warmth floods my body, longing, and I bend down, kissing him once.

"Did you miss having a girlfriend?"

His brows pull down as he considers my question and he cups my breasts again, gently squeezing. "Not in the way you mean. I like being in a relationship, but I wouldn't have wanted to be with anyone before you."

The question seems to come out of nowhere: "Do you ever miss Mia?"

He looks momentarily confused.

"I mean, do you ever—"

His eyes clear in understanding and he interrupts me: "Do you miss Justin?"

I laugh. "It isn't the same. He cheated."

"People get over each other for different reasons," he says patiently. "Just because Mia didn't cheat on me doesn't mean I still love her the way I love you."

I watch my fingers run over the smooth skin of his chest. "I know."

And I do. But it helps to hear him say it.

"I'll fuck up sometimes, I know I will," he says with a tiny, flirty smile. "I'll forget important dates and buy the wrong brand of tampons when you send me to the store and eat the wrong number of Pop-Tarts and most likely say unintentionally sexist things you'll need to point out, but I won't—I promise—ever be unfaithful." His hands slide up my hips to my waist. "I'm not built that way."

I kiss him for that, straightening over him again and running my hand down his bare chest. And then I feel my brain hitting the brakes, slowing further as I watch my fingers follow the map of muscle on his body. My fingertips explore the dips and swells, the long lines of his ribs wrapping around his sides.

He's mine now.

No one else will touch this bare chest.

No one else will enjoy this transition from chest to stomach, from stomach to hips.

No one else will feel the soft trail of hair just here.

He twitches in my hand as I grip him, whispering my name, sitting up beneath me and sucking at my neck.

No one else will touch his cock.

No one else will make him come.

No one else will hear him say *I love you.*

Luke's lips move up my neck to my jaw and he lets out a helpless sound as I stroke up, and down, bending to nibble on his bottom lip.

A quiet groan rumbles down his chest. "What are you thinking about? You're being so quiet all of a sudden."

"I'm thinking that you're mine," I whisper.

He pulls back, looks between our bodies, at my hand fisted around him. "Fucking *all* yours."

We watch what I'm doing for a few more beats of silence.

"What are you going to do with me?" he asks, looking back up at my face.

"What do you *want* me to do?"

"Touch me, kiss me." He lies back down and shrugs a little against the pillow. "I don't know. I want to do it all."

My stomach tightens from the way he watches with wide, intense eyes.

I shift closer, feeling his cock slide over me and he hums, smiling. "This works. You could get yourself off like this and let me watch you come." His grin widens. "I sure do like to watch you come, Miss London."

I smile down at him, tracing the line of his collarbone with my fingertip. "You're my favorite."

His eyes widen playfully. "Your favorite of anyone?"

Something fills my chest, climbs up my throat. I nod, unable to agree out loud because it's true. He *is* my favorite person in the world. "You're so sweet to me."

"Well, I would hope so. I *love* you." He smiles again when he says it, and the way his eyes turn down a little at the corners just as his mouth turns up makes my heart trip over itself.

"I know you do. I feel it." I bend, kissing him. My heart peeks over the ledge and sees nothing but wide-open air. "I love you, too."

He stops breathing, his thighs tense beneath me. "You don't have—"

I cut him off. "I'm not just saying it because you did. You know I wouldn't say that if I didn't mean it."

It hurts and it soothes just watching Luke struggle with this much emotion. His eyes are tight; he swallows a few times.

"Yeah?" he manages, finally, but his voice still comes out a little strangled.

I nod. "I love you."

I know without a doubt I never felt this sort of bone-deep comfort with Justin, and even his widest smile never made me melt the way a single, flirty glance from Luke can.

His eyes search mine for a few, jagged breaths. "London?"

"Yeah?"

"Will you move to Berkeley with me?"

My blood turns to smoke, muscles dissolve. I knew this was coming, at least the inevitable choice of moving together or navigating the distance.

He's watching my mouth, not for my answer but because I'm smiling. I can tell he doesn't know what it means, though, and his eyes grow anxious.

I lean in, kissing him.

"No, babe, stop." He holds me back with one hand curled around my shoulder and my heart trips. He called me *babe*. Not the intentional teasing of Logan or Dimples, but something instinctive, something that rolled reflexively off his tongue.

"Be real with me right now," he continues. "The idea of being up there if you're down here . . . I can still choose UCSD."

I meet his eyes and they're not smiling, but they're clear.

I see for the first time that his left eye is a little lighter than his right, and it occurs to me that I will never forget this detail about him. Every time we are together, we are collecting these things that make up this amazing *Us*, and this one makes my throat grow tight with suppressed tears.

He called me babe.

His eyes are two different colors.

He wants me to move with him to Berkeley.

"I'll move."

His eyes flash wide. *"What?"*

"I'll move to Berkeley with you," I tell him. "I want you to go to your first choice. I don't want to be apart."

"You'll live with me?"

My chest flips at this enormous detail. "Yeah. I mean, assuming that's the situation you meant. We can get separate places instead."

"No," he blurts, quickly shaking his head. "That's what I meant. Living together." His head jerks back in sudden skepticism. "Wait. Seriously? You're serious?"

I bite back a giddy laugh. "Yes, I'm serious."

"You love me and you're *moving* with me?"

I can barely handle his adorable mania. Bending, I slide my lips over his. "I love you and I'm moving with you."

Speaking against my mouth, he mumbles, "Holy fuck. Now we're going to have sex for the first time in this bed. How am I going to last long enough to make sure you come first?"

I laugh harder, and he shakes his head, rolling on top of

me, settling between my legs. "I'm serious. I've never been so excited," he babbles. His cock presses against my clit and I can barely focus on what he's saying; he's so warm, so rigid. "My heart is about to explode. I'm inarticulate. And my penis is too happy to adequately satisfy you right now. I get live-in London. I get shared-bed London. I get to—"

I stretch to cover his mouth with mine, arching my hips, and his cock is there, just *there,* and when I shift, the tip moves inside. His surprised inhale is jagged as he slides into me so easily, and without any more negotiation he's moving, curling his hips over me, demanding and greedy. I feel him there—I feel him *everywhere*—and the intensity of our decision, the idea of having a bed that is ours, a routine that is ours, a *love* that is ours makes my body hypersensitive, my skin feel tight and too hot. I push up into him, working my body on his, wanting him deeper and faster, harder, too. Last night was all about slow: he kissed me everywhere, made love to me in nearly every position I could imagine, but tonight we are fast, immediately sealing the deal we've just made.

He rises up over me, cupping my bent knees and spreading my legs wider, opening me completely to him. Nothing is more intimate than how he watches, how he stares at where he disappears inside me over and over and over. I reach down, touching him, touching myself, feeling it all: wet and heat, hard driving into soft.

I raise my eyes to his face and realize he's looking right at me, gauging my reaction to all of this, and I know now what's more intimate than the way he watched himself moving in me, it's *this:* Luke studying my face while he makes love to me. His eyes are glued to mine as the pleasure starts small and then grows, and grows, until I feel it hooking me, dragging me to that point of no return and I'm unable to look away, and nothing—*nothing*—is more exposed than staring right into his eyes as I let myself fall to pieces. Luke's lips part in awe and he nods in encouragement as pleasure takes over my senses and I beg him quietly, senselessly—

I'm

Luke, it's

it's so

close oh, fuck, I'm close

—his eyes narrowed nearly in pain as he concentrates on getting me there. But my orgasm fully crashes into me and each of my sharp sounds of relief causes a tiny bit of his brow to relax until he's smiling, grinning so wide, nearly laughing at how I clutch at him, at how wild I am. A million tiny explosions pulse between my legs, up my back, in my throat as I'm crying out, a garbled mess of words.

I stare up at him, going limp, and his mouth opens wider, like he wants to say something, but instead he just bends, kissing me—messy and bobbing as he moves with renewed intent—and that elated smile straightens into focus.

Hands tightening on my knees, he spreads my legs even wider, hips pumping. I lift from the bed, squeezing him, wanting to wring every bit of this out of him. He's so hard, fucking me so wild, I feel it somewhere deep and tender every time he stabs forward but if I could get him deeper inside me,

I would. I reach for his hips, urging him into me, and Luke throws his head back as he comes, calling out a disbelieving, "Holy—holy fu—oh, holy *fuck*," and then he stills, jerking above me.

He stops, chest heaving as he looks down at me in wonder. Slowly, he releases his hold on my knees and plants his hands on the mattress on either side of my waist. I feel the silence crash down, realizing how vocal we'd both been, how completely lost in the act.

My legs are sore from being spread so wide, and I carefully wrap them around him, using them to pull him down against me. His forehead rests on mine, eyes closed as we catch our breath.

"Holy shit," he says on a gasping exhale. "*Goddamn, woman.*"

"Luke?"

Eyes still closed, he smiles a little. "Logan?"

My hands come up his neck, cupping his jaw. "In case I didn't make it clear earlier, I'm crazy in love with you."

His eyes open, meet mine, and his smile grows. "*Finally.*"

Epilogue

*T*HREE THINGS FEEL fucking *amazing* about this moment.

One, I'm drinking a really great beer.

Two, my entire family is together—with London—and Mom is making my favorite baked ziti for our going-away dinner.

Because three: last week, London and I signed a lease on a house up in Berkeley.

I glance across the room to where London stands at the kitchen sink, wearing one of Mom's aprons over a jersey dress that shows off her perfect ass. She's talking to Grams, rinsing a colander full of strawberries, looking like she's been in this house a million times before.

I want to roar. Three months into our relationship and I am so fucking gone for this girl, I can barely shut up about it.

I propose nearly every day and she just laughs at me, and then distracts me with sex.

Grams's high, shaky voice jerks me out of my moment: "When Luke was a boy he used to wake up in the morning and say his penis was *strong*."

I choke on a sip of beer, gaping across the room at her. Everyone else has stopped moving, too.

Margot barks out a laugh. "I've been waiting for this moment."

Grams smiles proudly. "He was talking about having an erection, of course."

London blinks, looking over her shoulder at Grams and then me, coughing quietly. "I'm sorry?"

I rub my hand over my face. *"Grams."*

Grams shoos me away with a hand. "I've been waiting twenty years to share that one—don't you dare ruin this moment for me. Do you know how long I've held on to these gems?"

I wave my hand, giving her the all-clear.

"He had a favorite blankie he would shove down his pants while he watched *Barney,*" Margot adds helpfully.

"Margot," Mom chides quietly from the stove, but she's laughing, too.

I take another sip of my beer. "Please, do your best. I make a fool of myself for this woman daily. There's nothing you can say to quell her adoration of me."

I can see every member of my family straighten with this challenge, and then they watch London put the colander down on the counter and walk over, sliding her arm around my waist. "He called me by the wrong name about fifty times the first night we were together."

Silence surrounds us for a single heartbeat and then my family bursts into laughter. With this, London has just joined their ranks and endeared herself to them forever.

I stare down at her, giving her a playfully reprimanding look while she rests her chin on my chest and her blue eyes twinkle with mischief. "I love you," she mouths.

"You're lucky I love you, too."

Her eyes widen as if she's just remembering. "We're *moving* tomorrow."

I lift my hand and gently sweep her bangs to the side. "First stop, Six Flags," I whisper.

"Then surfing in Santa Barbara."

"Then more roller coasters at Great America."

"Then . . . our new place," she says, smile slowly straightening. "And no more bartending." I know she's scared. I know this is huge for her. But she has jobs lined up for months, and her work really is brilliant.

"And then I start school." I bend, kissing her nose.

London searches my eyes, seeking that reassurance I know she won't ask for aloud anymore.

We will be okay.

I am yours.

You are mine.

We're doing this together.

"And then you marry me?" I say.

I expect her to laugh. I expect her hand to cup my cheek and for her to kiss me in her gentle refusal but instead she blinks slowly up to my face. "They have a roller coaster in Las Vegas, you know."

Acknowledgments

THE FUNNIEST THING about this book was our sense at the end that we could have stayed a lot longer with Luke and London. This book came so easily, and their story was so fun and fluffy for us, that by the end we were both surprised that it was over. And that we loved it just the way it was.

Of course, it's pretty nice that, after having to rewrite *Dark Wild Night*, the subsequent book was an easier process, but it just shows us time and again that sometimes it's smooth, and sometimes it's rocky, but it's always worth putting in the effort. So, there's a little bit of advice to you aspiring writers out there: we still struggle, and it's always kind of a shock when it's easy. So get that story down on the page no matter how much it feels like you're trying to get blood out of a rock. It's worth it.

Thank you to every single person out there who reads our books or tweets at us, and who blogs about, reviews, or shares our stuff with their friends. Without you, we have no books. We are eternally grateful!

We love working with our editor, Adam Wilson, so much—not only because he's just really fabulous with punctuation, grammar, and pasting the perfect YouTube clips in our margin notes, but also because he is able to see outside his own life and experiences so well that he can make each character of ours stronger through his basic human intuition. To be able to find the pieces of a character that work and the ones that don't and help guide us in the right direction is pretty amazing. We love writing these books with you, dude.

Holly Root is a rare, encyclopedic human. We have a question—she has an answer. We have an idea—she has some history and context to help guide us. Thank you for every single thing you do—from the tiny email to the long phone calls. You're better than the mathematical equivalent of (cupcakes x unicorns)^4.

Our Simon and Schuster Gallery family is as wonderful as ever: Louise Burke, Jen Bergstrom, Carolyn Reidy, the ever-magical Kristin Dwyer, Theresa Dooley, Melissa Bendixen, Jen Robinson, Liz Psaltis, Diana Velasquez, John Vairo, Lisa Litwack, Jean Anne Rose, Steph DeLuca, Ed Schlesinger, and Abby Zidle. Working with each of you makes us feel like we've just consumed about seven liters of bubbly stardust. Now we can fly!

Team CLo wouldn't be what it is without the beta reading, pep talks, patient ear, and editorial hand of Erin Service, the prereader eyes of Tonya Irving, the social media power-housing of Lauren Suero, and the graphics of Heather Carrier. Please don't leave us because we are really terrible at all of these things and you women are very, very good at them.

We always forget to thank the Google for the help with bartending information or fishing details or places to have public sex in New York, so a retroactive thanks to the Google for the past fourteen books and all the behind-the-scenes help. High fives!

Our families know the drill now and can recognize Deadline Face with barely a glance in our direction. We can't decide whether that's a good thing or a bad thing, but thanks to each of them anyway for learning how to manage a creative personality in the house. We love you guys so, so much.

To the author community, thank you. You know what it means to have this sort of group for support, and we are just incredibly grateful for your friendship, and proud of each of your successes.

And, lastly, to each other: because it's a daily kind of love, there's nothing here that we can't say better on the phone, or in person, or on text, or via email, or over chat, but to imagine doing this with anyone else feels impossible. Left and right, forever.

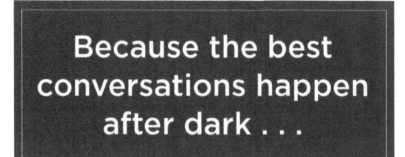